The Counterfeit Attachment

THE BATH SCHOOLMATES

BOOK TWO

HOLLI JO MONROE

First published by Brillig Press 2023

This novel is entirely a work of fiction. The names, characters and incidents portrayed in it are the work of the author's imagination.

First edition

To my mother, the strongest, the kindest, and the best

Contents

London
Russell Square
The Regent's Park
Soho Square
Glenhaven House
Hatchards
Bullocks Museum
Piccadilly
Exeter Exchange
Somerset House
Hyde Park
Strand
Buckingham Palace
London Botanical Garden

One

April 1819

DEAR CHARITY,

Please indulge your old teacher and accept this guide book to London. May it aid you in discovering the most worthwhile places to visit. Alas, there is no ready guide to intelligent bachelors of London, so you must use your best judgment in evaluating any prospects. If you must marry, I can think of no worse fate for you than to be tied to an empty-headed dullard.

With this book, you will be equipped to suggest to your suitors something more interesting than a ride in the park. What better way to test if a suitor's intellect is a match for yours than visiting an exhibit or attending a lecture? Of course with your inheritance, there is no real need to be saddled with a man.

Do not feel obligated to pick one if you would rather not! Whatever the opinion and wishes of your parents you must also consult your own inclinations. Now I will leave off my lecture. Enjoy the book. Write to me. But not of suitors or parties; only of your intellectual pursuits.

Until then I remain, your friend
Honoria Piper

Miss Charity Radforde removed the short note from its place inside her slim red copy of *The Picture of London,* looked at the page she had marked and sighed. She had been in London a full week, but all she had seen were shops and warehouses.

Mother was not interested in museums or exhibits and she dictated their schedule. Today they were to find hats or gloves or some such vital accessory and Charity was resigned to trail after Mother and Penelope as they shopped.

Listlessly, Charity glanced around the empty drawing room—as usual, she was the first of their party to be ready. It was well-apportioned with fashionable furnishings and tall windows that faced Russell Square.

The greenery she could see beckoned her. The square, with its interesting plants, was the only thing she had found enjoyable about London. If only she could spend the afternoon there instead.

As if sensing her thoughts, Mother appeared in the doorway and swept into the room. "Ah, Charity dear, there you are."

Charity snapped her book closed and tried to cover it with her reticule.

Though in her mid-forties, Mother had retained much of the beauty that had captivated Father. Charity shared her auburn hair and rounded face but had inherited Father's strong nose and tall stature.

"Is that what you are wearing?" Mother asked, then shook her head. "Why do I buy new dresses when you refuse to wear them?"

Charity did not reply. Experience had taught her that trying to defend her decision only prolonged the conversation and did nothing to change its outcome.

Mother sighed. "Well, it is no matter, no one shall see you."

Trying not to smile, Charity tipped her head. "Oh? Are we not going out?"

"You are not. I have an important appointment that will likely take most of the afternoon. It is nonsensical for me to return home afterward, so I will just buy what you need."

"An excellent plan, Mother," Charity said eagerly.

Mother eyed her. "I don't want you to spend the afternoon drawing flowers or reading. It is not proper for a lady."

Charity's hands flexed on the guidebook her mother had clearly noticed. She had no interest in being the kind of lady Mother deemed "proper."

"I have told Penelope that you must practice your conversation."

"Mother, I know how to speak in company."

"We are dining with the Grants tonight," Mother spoke as if Charity had said nothing. "I can't have you spouting nonsense about scientific classification systems. Not a single eligible man wants to hear your ideas on such things."

Fearing that she was about to start one of her lectures, Charity nodded. "Yes, Mother. I understand."

Mother paused and her attention momentarily diverted to the window.

"Ah, the carriage is ready. When I return, we will discuss your dress and hair for the evening and which men will be in attendance." Without waiting for a reply, she turned and left the room.

Alone once more, Charity let out something between a sigh and a groan. Would the entire time in Town be like this? Having left home for school when she was eight, Charity had had little experience in living with her mother. She had no experience living with her mother while being expected to find a husband.

Though already two and twenty, she had not yet had a season in London. The deaths of relatives she barely knew had put them in mourning during previous seasons. Charity had been all too happy to prolong her time in Bath by boarding at Mrs. Piper's Seminary for Young Ladies.

But all good things came to an end and she had traded her relative independence in Bath for a tightly controlled life in London. Mrs. Piper had recommended she spend her time visiting museums or attending lectures, but her future was full of house visits, dinners, garden parties, and balls.

She expected it would all be horribly dull, especially when Mother refused to let her talk about anything interesting. Of course Mother wasn't there now and since Penelope had not yet appeared, Charity defiantly opened her book and began reading.

She was halfway through learning about the animals on display at the Exeter Exchange menagerie when she heard footsteps. Charity glanced up just as Penelope entered the drawing room. It was still strange to see her once fashionable friend wearing plain gowns and lace caps.

"Reading? Really, Charity, what ever shall we do with you?" Penelope said severely.

Unsure if her friend was in jest, Charity closed the book.

Penelope frowned. "Don't stop. I am your companion, not your mother." She moved to sit in the opposite chair.

Thanks to attending the same school in Bath, Charity and Penelope had become friends despite their almost opposite personalities. In many ways Charity considered Penelope, Elaine, Mary, and Rosamund her sisters. She certainly knew them better than she knew her younger brother. But the last few years had exacted a heavy toll on Penelope, and Charity was often unsure of her friend.

Of course eloping, being disowned, and then abandoned by her fortune-hunting husband was bound to leave a mark on Penelope's spirit, even if her reputation was still intact.

Only their small group of friends, Mrs. Piper, and Penelope's parents knew the truth. The rest of Society thought her another young war widow. Mother would not have allowed Penelope to be Charity's companion if she knew her full history.

Penelope sank elegantly into the chair. Charity had always envied her grace and figure. Penelope was all soft, elegant curves, while Charity was all sharp, rough angles.

"Of course you can't read all day," Penelope said.

"I know. Mother said we must practice my conversation."

"Yes, she told me as much before she departed. Perhaps we could speak while we walk about the square?" Penelope's warm brown eyes sparkled. "It might take a very long time to accomplish the task. Indeed, the entire afternoon might be needed."

Charity broke into a smile. "Yes, I require a lot of instruction on conversing."

"In truth, there is little I can teach you about real conversation. You are the most intelligent and interesting woman I know."

Feeling warm at the compliment, Charity hugged the book to her chest. "I believe that is the problem. Mother believes my future husband will not want an intelligent wife."

Penelope scoffed as she picked up her work basket. "You can't exactly change that now. Better to find a man who values you."

"Better to not marry at all," Charity murmured.

"What?" Penelope looked up from the basket.

"Nothing."

Charity wasn't quite ready to share her private thoughts about marriage. Perhaps Penelope would understand now. But growing up, she had always schemed for suitors and talked longingly of being a wife and mother. Such a life had never appealed to Charity.

The Radforde's marriage was not a happy one. They rarely occupied the same home at the same time. It seemed that Father's captivation with Mother had only lasted long enough to get an heir.

By the time Charity was ten, she knew she did not want a marriage like her parents. Nor did she long for love like Penelope and Elaine. Even at sixteen she had not sighed over suitors. Charity longed for independence, the ability to do as she pleased and study what she wished. If only she could have stayed in Bath. If only Mother was not so insistent she marry this season. If only she could find a way to live as an independent spinster like Mrs. Piper.

"What were you reading about?" Penelope asked as she pulled out a shirt to mend.

With a smile, Charity opened her book. "The Exeter Exchange, or just Change. It says that the variety and number of animals exceeds that of the Tower menagerie."

"Oh?" Penelope sounded genuinely interested.

Charity leaned forward, ready to read the entire entry to her friend. A knock echoed through the quiet house and they both shared a look. They had not yet distributed their cards about London, so the visitor could only be a close friend.

They remained silent as they both strained to listen as the footman spoke. But instead of a conversation, they heard quick steps on the stairs.

Charity closed her book. She would know those steps anywhere and judging by Penelope's smile, she also recognized them. Miss Mary Gilbert never did anything slow and sedate.

"I think she came alone," Charity said with relief when she didn't hear another set of steps.

"The Hunters neglect her."

Charity wished her mother would be that kind of neglectful. At present, Mary lived with Mrs. Hunter, the sister of her betrothed, Mr. Blosset. Mr. Blosset worked for the British government and had not lived in England for years but was currently on a ship returning to claim his bride.

Mary had been betrothed to the much older Blosset as a child but had only met him once. Though Mary had never complained about her arranged marriage, Charity had always pitied her. However, in the last week she had grown envious of Mary's freedom. The Hunters often left her to her own devices.

Their friend rushed through the doorway and immediately began speaking. "I am so pleased you are still here! I feared you would be long gone and I would never get the chance to accompany you."

Charity had barely risen to her feet when Mary swept her into a brief hug, her bonnet tickling Charity's chin. Mary didn't stop talking as she embraced Penelope.

"Now you can advise me on the ribbons for my new bonnet. Not that I can't buy them on my own, mind, but you always know just the right trimming." Mary crossed to the settee and sank into it. "Even that ugly cap looks lovely on you."

Penelope touched the lace that covered her jet black hair and shook her head. "Don't be ridiculous."

"I'm not. Doesn't she make that cap look lovely?" Mary turned to Charity for affirmation.

"Yes." Charity was rarely asked for her opinion on fashion and was ill-equipped to elaborate.

"See, you are the perfect person," Mary said. "Is your mother almost ready?"

"We are no longer going shopping," Penelope replied.

"Mother had some appointment."

"I declare that is strange, is it not? To plan a shopping expedition only to cancel it is not the done thing." Mary's brows drew low over her blue-green eyes.

Charity shrugged. She had not thought beyond her relief at staying home.

"Well, we shan't let Mrs. Radforde stop us." Mary stood. "I have the Hunter's second carriage and a fiercesome coachman at my disposal. With Mrs. Penelope Aston as our chaperone, we might go anywhere we wish."

"Anywhere?" Charity sat up straighter.

"Now you've done it," Penelope warned even as she was putting her mending back into her basket.

"Really?" Charity could hardly believe that Penelope would consent to the scheme. Perhaps her mischievous friend wasn't completely gone.

"As long as we return before your mother, I see no reason why we shouldn't. But I am guessing you don't want to go shopping."

Charity ran her hand over the soft red leather of her guide book. "I have a few other ideas."

A short while later they were all happily ensconced in the carriage, bouncing along the noisy streets of London while they discussed their destination. Charity tried not to think how this free afternoon might be her only opportunity to visit a place in the book.

"The guide says that the Change contains a full grown lion and lioness, elegant leopard, laughing hyena, porcupines, and an enormous elephant."

"And they have a royal Bengal tiger," Mary added.

"Didn't you have a pet tiger growing up? I understand that all Indian princesses own tigers."

Mary's lips quirked. "I am afraid you've been misinformed. Indeed, tiger's appetites are a strain on a household. My family preferred to keep cobras and monkeys. Of course, unlike you English, they were not pets."

"Not pets?" Penelope said, easily playing along. "Why ever did you keep them?"

"To eat, of course."

Charity giggled and Penelope smiled. Mary's wit was always particularly sharp when it came to misapprehensions about her homeland and childhood in India. Since her dark coloring announced her heritage, she had ample opportunity to practice her rejoinders.

Much of what she said was fanciful. Like all of their friends, Mary had spent most of her life in Bath at Mrs. Piper's Seminary. Charity wasn't sure how much Mary even remembered about her time in India.

"Do you prefer your cobra as a filet or in a soup?" Charity asked with mock seriousness. They discussed the merits of such delicacies until none could keep a straight face.

As they grinned and giggled, she realized how rare such moments had become. Once all five of them might have spent the day laughing together. But they were no longer schoolgirls. Rosamund was a governess out in the country, Elaine was happily married, Penelope had transformed into the staid Mrs. Aston, and when Mary's betrothed arrived in London, she would return to India. They would never all be together again.

The carriage rocked to a halt and their conversation ceased as they prepared to exit. The footman opened the door and the muffled sounds of London became loud and bright. Charity smiled as she stepped onto the street.

The Strand teemed with traffic; carriages, wagons, and men on horseback mingled with pedestrians in a dizzying stew of energy. Mary linked arms with Charity and Penelope. Together they looked up at the tall Corinthian columns and large posters displaying the various animals found inside the Change. It was hardly credible that so many could be housed in even that large building.

A dull roar came from above and the carriage horse shied as if it knew a predator was nearby. She glanced into the street and noticed one rider had lost control of their skittish horse. The animal clattered swiftly away, racing away from the sound.

A thrill raced just as swiftly down Charity's spine, and she turned back to the entrance. If this was her only chance to see a famed sight of London, she was going to enjoy every moment. For one afternoon she could forget her mother and not worry about being a proper lady.

Two

Mr. Edmund Glenhaven drummed his fingers on his thigh as he stared out the morning room window at the London street below. A few vendors with their carts full of wares passed slowly by and a distinguished gentleman on a black horse weaved around them. There was no sign of the Glenhaven carriage.

Mama had said she would return before noon, but it was now ten minutes after. What was keeping her?

Edmund sighed and ran a hand through his light brown hair. Normally he didn't care about his mother's movements or the availability of the carriage. Unlike his father, Lord Glenhaven, Edmund did not have an endless array of important engagements and meetings. How annoying that the one time he had an appointment the carriage was unavailable.

After one more long look at the street, he started to doubt her return. A different method of transportation might be required. As he began to sift through his options, he turned from the window.

He startled, surprised to find his sister standing in the middle of the room.

"Sophy! How long have you been here?"

"I called your name twice." She smiled and a dimple flashed in her right cheek.

"Sorry, I did not hear you."

"I know. I was waiting to see how long before you noticed me." She moved toward him. "Papa said you once spent an entire evening completely insensible to the rest of the family."

Edmund narrowed his eyes. Their father loved recounting that story, but what he always failed to mention was why Edmund had been so deep in thought that night.

Lord Glenhaven had just issued him an ultimatum and Edmund had been trying to decide the course of his life. Surely such a question would distract any man. Was it any wonder that Edmund, who was prone to becoming lost in his thoughts and barely twelve years of age, had been inattentive?

"What are you looking at?" Sophy asked as she joined him at the window. Her fair head didn't quite reach his shoulder—she had not inherited Father's stature.

"I was looking for the carriage."

"Oh, Mama won't be home for hours yet."

"She said she would return at noon—"

Sophy waved away his words. "Mama never returns when she says. Perhaps if you were always left home while they went on calls and attended dinners you would know that."

"But I need the carriage," Edmund exclaimed, insensible to his sister's bitterness.

"Well then, I am sure she will return soon. She is always punctual when she has a reason."

Edmund held back a groan. He had not actually asked his mother for the carriage, so she had no reason to hurry her errands. If only he had known of her habitual lateness, he would have planned accordingly. But Edmund had not lived at home since he was eleven and had rarely stayed with them in London.

"Why do you need the carriage?" Sophy turned her back on the window.

"I had an appointment."

Edmund was not about to tell his sister his plans. If he failed, he did not want to face Father's disappointed glower or Mama's sympathetic smile.

Sophy cocked her head and examined him closely. Her eyes started at his freshly-cut hair, glanced over his new coat and breeches, and ended on his gleaming boots.

"Would this appointment be with a young lady?"

Edmund shrugged. Sophy's assumption was wrong; young ladies were the furthest thing from his mind, but it made for an easy excuse. He did not dare hint at his real purpose.

Sophy's hazel eyes danced. "I knew it! I knew you came to London to find a wife. Mama was unconvinced, but I knew. Papa outright claimed that you were in no position to become a husband."

Father's openly-shared assessment was a slap to the face. As a clergyman with a small living in the country, Edmund was indeed currently unable to support a family in comfort. But what did Father expect when he had refused to help Edmund find a position?

"I told them that you are handsome, clever, and kind and ladies will practically fall at your feet."

"I am pleased I have provided you with such conversational fodder," Edmund said and walked from the window. Even his sister's compliments could not warm his heart.

Sophy ignored his insincerity as she followed him. "I wish I could accompany you. I am an excellent judge of character. I suspect I have a great talent for choosing brides. Kit said I might choose his when he returns."

Edmund held up his hand to stem the tide of her conversation. "Sophy, I must depart. If anyone notices my absence, please only say that I will be home in time for tonight's dinner."

A pleased smile spread over her face. "Oh, I won't tell; it will be our secret." She tapped her nose, their signal for keeping quiet.

Not stopping to consider what sharing such a secret would mean, Edmund nodded and said a hasty goodbye.

At the bottom of the stairs, he glanced down the hall at the closed door of Father's study. For a brief moment Edmund considered marching in there and declaring his plans.

If he announced that he was going to America to conduct a scientific survey, would Father still think him unambitious and unfit to bear his name? But Edmund knew that the great Lord Glenhaven would only ask questions and find flaws in the scheme.

No, it was better to not tell his family until all was settled.

As he strode to the front entrance, he touched his breast pocket to reassure himself that he still had the letter of introduction. The letter might be the key to unlocking his future.

Once on the street, Edmund didn't look for a hack, but settled his hat on his head and began to walk. A good walk always calmed his nerves and eased his mind. With his future about to be decided, the exercise was exactly what he needed.

Though not a resident of London, Edmund was familiar enough with its streets to find his way to Somerset House. Once on his way, he began to think over what he would say to Sir Joseph Banks. It was not the first time he had rehearsed his speech and he struggled to keep his mind on the task.

After reviewing his credentials from Oxford and outlining his subsequent research in the countryside, his mind wandered back to Sophy.

Would she tell their parents that Edmund was looking for a wife? Would he have to keep up the pretext until he was ready to reveal his true purpose? If Sir Joseph rejected his proposal, there would be nothing to reveal. Edmund would never breathe a word about the meeting if it was a failure.

"Sir!"

The cry brought Edmund to a stop. He narrowly avoided crashing into a group of ladies crossing his path to reach a house.

Blinking quickly, he murmured an apology. He really needed to pay better attention. He was no longer in the country and being distracted on the streets of London was inviting trouble. Soon he would be on the busy Strand and would need to keep his wits about him.

The ladies did not scowl but smiled as if he had not practically knocked them over but said something charming.

Edmund didn't return the gesture. He took several steps and then glanced back only to see the ladies watching him, giggling.

It seemed Sophy might have the right of it. Perhaps his lack of income was not a deterrent to some young ladies. If his sister was correct, he would need to be on his guard or a marriage-minded maiden might catch him and ruin everything.

Three

WITH EACH STEP UP the stairs to Exeter Change, the smell and sound of the animals grew stronger. As they gained the top, the walls changed from plain colors to a painted jungle background. At the doors, a man politely requested the two shilling entrance fee.

Charity already had her reticule open and plucked out a crown and shilling to pay for everyone. If Mary paid for herself, Penelope would insist on also paying. It wasn't proper for a lady's companion to pay for such things.

With a wave of her hand, she forestalled their protests. "It was my idea to come." Her friends knew that her allowance was generous. It was one of the few things about being an heiress that she enjoyed.

Before closing her reticule, she pulled out her small notebook and pencil.

"Some things never change," Penelope said.

Charity shrugged. She would hardly miss an opportunity to take notes and sketches of the animals. Whatever was the point if she did not catalogue what she saw?

They gasped as they entered the first room. It was full of iron cages, dozens of them, all holding different animals. Charity immediately recognized the camel, kangaroos, and lion but so many others were unknown to her. Other patrons milled about inspecting the animals with various degrees of interest. She could not settle her eyes; there were too many things to see and she wanted to carefully examine them all.

A scream echoed over the murmur of voices and Charity jumped.

"Look." Mary pointed at the row of cages near the ceiling, each containing several monkeys. One was holding the bars, shaking them as it screamed into the room. "It doesn't look very happy."

"No living thing enjoys being caged," Penelope murmured.

The monkey grew quieter as they slowly stepped into the room, following the stream of people.

Charity took the lead as she moved toward an animal she had read about but had never seen in person. Several feet taller than the biggest horse, its hide looked like a knight's armor, and on its snout was a wicked-looking horn. She paused, taking the animal in before writing down her observations.

"The sign says it is a rhinoceros," Penelope said.

"That is Greek for nose-horned," Charity replied as she began to draw the animal.

"I did learn Greek," Penelope said.

"Yes, but do you remember any of it?" Mary teased as she stepped up to the bars.

Charity held her breath as Mary thrust her hand into the cage and touched the animal's rump. More than one person had been injured by petting animals in menageries. Only a few years earlier, a panther had ripped a woman's arm from her body at the Tower of London.

The rhinoceros didn't turn or even flick its tail. It just continued to chew, docile as a cow. What did such an animal eat?

Encouraged, Charity stepped forward. Before Penelope could protest, she had stuck her hand through the bars.

The hide felt extraordinary, rough and hard, not like skin or fur at all. Charity snatched her hand back and retrieved her pencil from the spine of her notebook. She began to record her sensations before starting a rough sketch of the animal.

Not to be outdone, Penelope also touched the rhinoceros. As she discussed with Mary how it felt, Charity was filled with questions.

Exactly how tough was the skin? Could it fight off a pride of lions? Did it travel in herds or alone?

She wrote these questions into her notebook as they came to her. What would it be like to go to Africa and see such animals in their natural state? Charity envied those intrepid explorers who had first discovered and catalogued the animal.

Penelope tapped her arm, pulling her from her questions. "Come on, we can't stand forever in front of the first interesting thing we see. If we return late, I will be dismissed."

Charity glanced around and realized that Mary had moved on to look at the camels. She took one last look at the rhinoceros before closing her book.

"Sorry. Do you really think Mother would dismiss you so easily?"

Pen shrugged and gently pulled Charity along. "I always thought you would grow out of your scribblings and specimen paintings. You know I am supposed to make sure you are a proper lady. You should be thinking about suitors, not sloths." She gestured to the sign and cage before them. Charity smiled as she observed the furry creature hanging from a branch.

"I find the natural world far more interesting than suitors."

"Quite right. Mere men cannot compare to such beauty." Penelope knocked their shoulders together companionably. "If only I had been of your mind," she added wistfully.

Charity looked down at her notebook and gave a noncommittal hum. Her friend certainly had changed. When they were in school, she had teased Charity for pursuing science instead of a spouse.

She began to sketch the sloth while Penelope wandered back to Mary. Each room brought a fresh wonder and her friends left her to her scribbling while they explored together. More than once they had to circle back and urge her to move faster.

The variety was so vast that Charity could have spent the entire day there. Sketching animals in cages was different from trying to capture them in nature. A linnet might flit away at just the wrong moment, but the hyena had no choice but to stay in place. It was easier for her purposes. Surely if she went to Africa, the rhinoceros would not be so easily touched.

Near the end, they came upon the Bengal tiger. Even laying down, it looked dangerous and fully capable of separating a person's arm from their body. They all stayed far back from the cage. Mary was frowning as she watched the animal.

"Is it very like your memory?" Charity asked.

Mary nodded but her eyes hinted at sadness. "It has been many years, but it seems to me that his coat is very dull. I am sure this climate does not agree with him."

What might it be like to be plucked from your home and forced to live so far away in a cold, strange land? Charity glanced at Mary and realized her friend knew the answer.

"Do you suppose they ever let it out?" Mary asked. "I heard there is an heiress, a Miss Hepburn or some such, that keeps her leopard on a leash and it eats at her table. But then I suppose she must have raised it from a kitten so it would not be quite so dangerous."

"She is a fool," Penelope replied.

"Oh?" Mary seemed unconvinced.

"Such animals are dangerous no matter how they are raised. It is in their nature. I am sure the proprietors keep all the dangerous predators locked up."

"You mean it always sits in that tiny cage?" Charity felt silly for not understanding that fact before. Of course they must stay in their cages. Where in London could they possibly roam?

The wonder of the menagerie dissolved like sugar in tea. It was no longer a beautiful celebration of the animal kingdom, but a sort of prison. The animals were trapped, condemned to a life of unwelcome stares and prodding by strangers. They weren't so different from her. Trapped in London, unable to go where they wished, forced to be on display.

"I wish I could travel and see these animals in their natural habitat," Charity said wistfully.

"It would likely be the last thing you saw." Penelope pointed as the tiger exposed its terrifying teeth and let out a low growl.

Charity was going to say she was willing to take the risk, but a roar filled the room. The sound seemed to penetrate her bones. Her heart accelerated as if she had run up several flights of stairs. Perhaps she didn't want to see the tiger in the wild.

When the roar died away to another growl, Penelope spoke.

"Men are like tigers, dangerous by nature." She turned to her friends. "Which do you think is more dangerous, a tiger or a man?"

"Mrs. Piper would probably say a man," Charity said.

"But a tiger can kill you," Mary argued.

"Can not a man do worse by stealing your independence and condemning you to a half-life?" Charity returned. "And the probability of meeting with an unscrupulous gentleman is greater than encountering a tiger."

"Hear, hear," Penelope said. "Of course, those with a fortune are in greater danger of being hunted by such men."

Charity took her meaning. Mrs. Piper had always warned them to be on their guard against fortune hunters. It was a warning Penelope had not heeded but Charity had always been vigilant.

In Bath, Charity had devised a formula to discover those only interested in her money. If a man complimented her ungraceful figure and smiled at anything she chose to say, then he was most certainly being insincere. Surely the same logic applied to the men of London?

Or was the species of man that inhabited Town more cunning? What might such a subspecies be called? *Homo rakeus*? Charity smiled at her jest.

"Well," Mary said. "It is lucky that Charity has you to protect her."

"Who better than one who knows the dangers," Penelope said. "And in the interest of protecting you, we really must return home."

They rushed through the last room—an aviary filled with stuffed birds—and soon reached the street. In their absence, the carriage had become surrounded by a small crowd, gathered around a massive elephant. The size of two carriages stacked atop each other, the elephant cast a shadow on the gawking spectators.

Perhaps if the elephant had a chance to walk the streets, then some of the other animals enjoyed similar liberties? The thought made Charity smile. But then she noticed its back legs were shackled and an iron collar clamped around its neck. A tall man held a chain connected to the collar giving the impression of a massive dog on a heavy leash. The man spoke brightly to the crowd.

"Yes, ladies and gentlemen, old Chuny is a highly trained Indian elephant and just one of the many magnificent animals you will see inside the Exeter Change."

Charity and her friends joined the outskirts of the crowd. Anxious for a better view, they stepped into the street, joining several others.

"This intelligent beast was featured in plays at Covent Garden and knows an array of tricks." The man made a gesture and a strange noise.

Chuny reached his trunk out and plucked a hat from the head of a watching gentleman. The man spluttered as the audience laughed. Chuny brandished the hat before placing it back on the man's head. The audience applauded.

As Charity clapped, her attention was caught by how the elephant was altering the traffic on the Strand. Horses gave the elephant a wide berth and pedestrians were forced onto the road to skirt around the growing crowd. Like a rock in the middle of a stream, horses and humans flowed around them.

Her gaze snagged on a tall, fair gentleman dressed in buff trousers and blue coat. He did not spare a glance for the spectacle; even as he stepped into the street, his attention seemed far away. His manner reminded Charity of her friend Elaine when she was caught in a daydream. But would even Elaine miss an elephant in the street?

When she turned to point out the gentleman to her friends, she was surprised to discover they were not beside her. Before she could take a step toward them, several things happened at once.

A terrible roar sounded, louder and angrier than any Charity had yet heard. A chorus of frightful whinnies rang out from the horses around them.

Chuny rose up on his hind legs.

The crowd backed away, spilling further into the street and pushing Charity with them.

She caught sight of the man. He paused and looked in confusion at the elephant while behind him a horse reared.

Charity knew he did not see it. With dreadful certainty she knew that the horse would bolt and the man would be trampled.

Without stopping to think, Charity reacted.

"Sir!"

She took two large steps and reached urgently for him. If he didn't move, he might die. His eyes went wide with surprise as she grasped his arm and yanked him out of harm's way. Off balance they stumbled together as the horse rushed past.

His hands came around her waist as he tried to steady himself. They were as close as if they were embracing, close enough for her to see the flecks of brown in his hazel eyes. She could hardly catch her breath. Was it from the excitement or his proximity? She had never been so close to a man. She could feel the warmth of his hands on her waist like sunshine on a summer's day.

"What the devil?" He growled before releasing her and stepping back. His eyes swept over her. "Miss, there are far better ways of catching a husband than literally throwing yourself at them."

Her cheeks burned. "I was saving you!"

His eyebrows rose, disappearing into his hat. "Saving me?"

"There was a horse." She gestured to the street, but the horse and rider were long gone. "It was going to trample you."

He frowned but seemed to consider her statement.

She could not believe the man had been so oblivious to the danger. Did he actually think that some women were so desperate for a husband that they grabbed a stranger on the street?

"You might have died," she insisted.

"Unlikely. Even if there was a horse—"

"So you admit there was a horse?"

"Was there a horse?" He gestured to the street full of the animals.

His condescending tone sparked her anger. Charity had never hit anyone except her brother, but her hands were suddenly clenched into fists. Of course a proper lady would never resort to violence, but then a proper lady didn't try to save hapless men in the street.

This is what came of trusting her instincts and ignoring social conventions. She should have been a proper lady and merely screamed as he was run over.

Four

EDMUND STARED at the woman who had so unceremoniously grabbed him. Her askew bonnet revealed auburn hair and creamy skin. She was taller than most ladies—her angry blue eyes were nearly level with his.

Why she was angry when she had grabbed him? Perhaps she was insane? Edmund did not know exactly what a mad woman looked like. This one didn't appear impoverished nor a thief, but she could not possibly be a lady. No lady seized a stranger on the street. Why, anyone might have seen!

Thankfully, all eyes were on that blasted elephant and their brief embrace had gone unnoticed.

"You should thank me," she said as she adjusted her bonnet.

"Thank you?" He frowned.

"You are welcome."

"I wasn't—"

"Charity!"

Edmund's protest was interrupted by the arrival of a shorter young woman in a plain dress. She looped her arm around Charity's and gave him a dark look.

"Sir, I'll thank you not to accost my charge," she said in an icy tone.

"Your charge? You can't possibly be a lady's companion." She was a mere slip of a girl compared to her taller, broader friend. Surely, she was no protection in the streets of London. This pretty and deranged woman needed protection.

The companion glared at him. Edmund squared his shoulders.

"Your *charge* accosted me."

"I saved you," Charity declared.

"Ignore him, Charity, his type can't be reasoned with," the other woman said in an undertone.

"I beg your pardon." Edmund could not believe this was happening to him. Him, the third son of a baron, having his honor impugned by two strange women in the street.

They ignored him as they turned away and rejoined the crowd. Edmund could do nothing but stare thunderously at their backs.

Charity turned around, met his eyes briefly, and then looked away. Perhaps she felt some shame for her actions? Who was she? Why had she chosen to compromise him? Given that he would never see her again he would never know the answer. He hated unanswered questions.

Edmund clenched his jaw, stopping himself from plunging into the crowd after them. He had been delayed long enough. He spun on his heel and continued his way down the noisy Strand.

As he strode the now short distance to Somerset House, Edmund cursed himself for not stopping earlier and calling a hack. The walk had not calmed him. Walking in chaotic London was not as soothing as walking in a quiet country lane. For instance, there was no chance of being accosted by strange women.

What had the girl been thinking? Had there truly been a bolting horse? Such a thing might explain her actions. But it seemed unlikely a woman's first reaction would be to grab him. Why not just call out?

Edmund shook his head, nearly dislodging his hat. The woman was of no consequence. He needed to focus on what he would say to Sir Joseph Banks. Practice the words that would get the eminent man of science to fund his expedition.

As he adjusted his hat, Edmund's eyes fell upon a church tower before him. He frowned. Somerset House was now behind him. Spinning around, he retraced his steps. As the gate drew closer, his heart began to quicken.

From the Strand, the entrance to Somerset House was three stone arches that barely hinted at the actual size of the structure.

Built to rival the public buildings in the great capitals of Europe, Somerset House contained four wings, a warren of public offices, the headquarters of learned societies, and living quarters. None of this was evident from where he stood, yet the importance of the place before him fell upon him like a heavy coat.

Edmund stepped under the arch and entered the vestibule. He barely marked the Doric columns and vaulted ceiling as he walked the few steps to the door of the Royal Society.

Founded for the purpose of increasing man's knowledge of the world, the Royal Society was where great scientific minds met and discussed their questions and discoveries. Its members had included Newton, Wren, Halley, and many others. Like all thinking men, Edmund was a regular subscriber to their *Philosophical Transactions* publication. Becoming a member of the Royal Society was his dearest wish.

Today he was taking an important step toward that goal.

Edmund paused at the door. Perched above it was a bust of the Society's former president, Sir Isaac Newton. The cold marble eyes seemed to glare down at him, a guardian against the unworthy. He swallowed and inclined his head at the bust, as if asking permission to enter. He squared his shoulders and knocked.

The door swung open and a young porter ushered him inside.

"I have come to see Sir Joseph Banks." Edmund winced at the volume of his voice.

"Is he expecting you?" the porter asked.

"No, but I do have a letter of introduction." He pulled the letter from his breast pocket and presented it.

He did his best not to fidget. He didn't know what his professor from Oxford had put in the letter, but the heavy paper and elaborate seal pressed into the wax certainly looked impressive. He hoped it would be enough to secure an audience with the current president of the Royal Society.

"I know that I don't need a letter to see Sir Joseph as he makes a practice of taking visits from the general public on Thursdays. But of course you know that..." Edmund tried to stop his babbling as the porter took the letter. Could the man hear the pounding of his heart?

The young man eyed the paper carefully.

"I am hoping to become one of Sir Joseph's proteges. Well, perhaps not exactly a protege, but if he would invest in my expedition..."

The corner of the porter's lips turned up slightly. How many eager young men did he see each Thursday?

"If you please, sir. I will show you where you might wait."

He held in a sigh of relief and followed the young man to the antechamber. He had never seen the room so empty. All his previous visits had been for an exhibit or after a lecture when it teemed with people and conversation.

"I will see if Sir Joseph is at liberty to speak with you." The porter brandished the letter.

Edmund nodded. "Thank you. What was your name?"

"Jamison, sir."

"Thank you for your patience, Jamison."

The porter gave a small smile before turning and leaving the room.

Edmund repressed his urge to pace. He glanced at the small knot of men in the far corner before turning his attention to the furnishings of the room. He had never noted the fine plaster ceiling or examined the paintings but now tried to give them his attention. All their elegance was lost on him. He could only think of Sir Joseph, sitting somewhere in the building and deciding his fate.

Many would think him mad for wanting to leave his comfortable and safe life as a country parson for a perilous journey collecting plant and soil samples, but Edmund knew Sir Joseph would understand.

As a young man, Joseph Banks had explored the far reaches of the world with Captain Cook and brought back vast knowledge which had helped him become a baronet. As president of the Royal Society, he had championed countless expeditions of exploration. If anyone in London understood the need to explore and catalogue the world, it was Sir Joseph.

The door opened.

Edmund turned expectantly but Jamison didn't spare him a glance and walked to the group of men. A brief conversation followed and the men were escorted deeper into the building. Were they being taken to Sir Joseph? With the room empty, Edmund gave vent to his nerves and began to pace.

His footsteps echoed a sharp beat that he found strangely soothing. To distract himself, he began to mentally review the taxonomy of the English rose. He started with the kingdom *plantae* and stopped at the genus *rosa*, then attempted to name all the species he could remember. He had gone through thirty when Jamison appeared.

He stopped his pacing and faced the tall, willowy young man.

"Sir Joseph regrets that he cannot meet with you today."

Edmund's heart lurched as he swallowed his disappointment. "Of course, I am sure he is very busy."

He cursed himself for choosing to walk and allowing himself to become distracted by the young woman. If he had arrived earlier, perhaps he would have been allowed entrance before the other men.

"He asks that you attend the lecture tonight where he would be happy to make your acquaintance," Jamison said.

"I regret that I have a previous engagement." Edmund tried to keep the bitterness from his tone. He would do anything to get out of the stuffy dinner his mother had asked him to attend.

"Ah, that is unfortunate," the porter said in measured tones.

Edmund heaved a sigh. "It is no matter. Thank you, Jamison." He pulled a small token of his appreciation from his purse. "I shall just wait until next Thursday." He offered the coin. The young man smiled with slightly crooked teeth and took it.

How old was he? Nineteen? Twenty? How many older and more august gentlemen did Jamison have to turn away each day? How many of them refused to go quietly?

"Sir," Jamison said and then glanced around the empty room. "Have you ever visited our library?"

"The library?" Edmund's forehead furrowed.

"Yes, many of the Society's members enjoy the quiet of the library on a Friday afternoon. Sir Joseph, in particular, indulges in the pastime."

The corner of Edmund's mouth ticked up as he held back a smile. "I do love to read. In fact, I believe that tomorrow I will be seized by a great desire to see the library."

"An excellent plan, sir. I understand that noon is considered the ideal time."

"Thank you, Jamison."

The porter bowed and Edmund left the Royal Society with his hope intact.

Hours later, Edmund's body was in a carriage heading for dinner, but his mind was at Somerset House. He couldn't stop thinking about the opportunity he was missing in order to attend this society dinner.

"Edmund, are you listening to me?"

He turned from the carriage window and blinked as he tried to recall the last thing his mother had said. When nothing immediately came to mind, he dipped his head.

"Apologies, Mama. What were you saying?"

Lady Glenhaven sighed. She was a slight woman with fair hair and green eyes. Her smile would light up a ballroom but at the moment her lips were pursed together.

"Honestly, Edmund, how do you expect to pick the right sort of woman if you don't listen when I tell you who is in attendance?"

"And what do you think is the right sort?" He raised an eyebrow.

"Are you questioning your mother's judgment?" Lord Glenhaven rumbled from his seat opposite Edmund. Father was the very picture of an elder statesman—broad-shouldered, dark hair shot through with grey, stomach growing more expansive each year.

He had little in common with his father. He had no interest in politics, hunting, or estate management, so the only thing they shared was their tall stature. He had inherited his mother's slim build and light coloring.

"Certainly I trust Mama. She found a lovely wife for George. I only desire a description of what she feels would constitute my perfect bride."

Edmund was unclear if Sophy had said something to his parents, but it seemed they were both expecting him to be on the hunt tonight.

"You need a woman who can match your intellect, but is practical and not afraid to disagree with you. A simpering, empty-headed miss will never do," Mama said.

"I agree," Father added.

Edmund nodded. "And are there any other requirements?"

"Oh no, you will not catch me out." Mama smiled. "I will not give you a list so you might point out how a young woman I favor doesn't fit the criteria. I only wish you to be happy and well settled." She reached out and squeezed his hand.

"By which you mean she should have a large dowry."

"A very sensible requirement," Father said.

He clenched his jaw, trapping his thoughts behind his teeth. There was no point in arguing that he did not need to marry a fortune. Father would only insist that Edmund did not understand the world, but it was Father who did not understand.

Father did not understand that being a clergyman gave Edmund the freedom to do the work he loved. He could spend all day studying specimens or reading about the latest discoveries. He didn't understand that Edmund had rejected a job in the government because his ambitions were greater than being an undersecretary of some obscure department. Edmund didn't spend his days writing sermons but planned his expedition instead.

"Let's not quarrel." Lady Glenhaven gave her husband a severe look.

"I just think it would be a fine thing for him to stand on his own two feet," Father said.

"With my wife's money," Edmund muttered into the window, his voice too quiet to be heard over the clatter of hooves.

He would achieve his independence through his own accomplishments, not the parson's noose. Marriage was the last thing he wanted. In the life of a naturalist explorer, there was no place for a wife.

He was tempted to tell his mother that her efforts were in vain. He wouldn't marry any of the women she introduced to him. He wouldn't even court them. If all went as planned, he would be sailing for America in a few months.

"Now," Mama spoke into the uncomfortable silence, "I was trying to speak about the many lovely and accomplished women that will be at the Grants tonight. In particular, I wish you to make the acquaintance of Miss Radforde. Are you listening?"

Edmund pulled his eyes from the window. "Yes, you said Miss Radforde is the richest young woman there."

Lord Glenhaven snickered but Mama sighed.

"I won't deny that Miss Radforde is an heiress, but she is also intelligent and at two and twenty, more mature than others."

"I thought you said this was her first season?" Father's eyebrows pinched together. It seemed his parents had been discussing this Miss Radforde.

"It is her first. She stayed at school until she was nineteen and then there were some unfortunate deaths and illnesses in the family." She waved her hand as if the details were unimportant. "I think her age a point in her favor."

Edmund agreed. He couldn't imagine trying to court a woman that was close in age to his sister. It was comforting to know that Mama would not try and match him with an immature chit. That might make the social functions more bearable.

"Miss Radforde was educated in Bath at Mrs. Piper's Seminary for Young Ladies. It has an unusual reputation. I think she might surprise you with her conversation."

"I look forward to being surprised," Edmund replied.

Unbidden, the image of the woman—Charity—flashed in his mind. He did not think any woman could surprise him as she had. He did not care where Miss Radforde went to school; her conversation was unlikely to be anything unique. He would paste on his civil smile, nod his way through inane topics, and imagine himself at the Royal Society. It would be the first of many such evenings.

The carriage came to a stop in front of an elegant townhouse near Russell Square. Edmund didn't know the exact connection. Father's work in the House of Lords meant he was forever currying favor for one cause or another. This meant the host could be an old gentry family or the newly wealthy owner of a bank. Mama likely mentioned which, but he couldn't recall. In any case, it was clear the family had a good deal of money.

Modern elegance surrounded them as they entered the house and were ushered into the already full drawing room. Edmund guessed they might be the last to arrive. As his parents greeted their hosts, his eyes swept the room with barely concealed boredom. There were several young women present, but before he could wonder which was Miss Radforde, his eyes stopped on the last person he had expected to see.

Shocked into speechlessness for the second time that day, he stared at the woman who had seized him on the street. Charity—it was the only name he had for her—was dressed in a lovely green dress that accentuated her height and favored her coloring.

When she wasn't glowering or babbling ridiculous things, she was an attractive woman. Involuntarily, he recalled the heat of her breath on his cheek and the feel of her waist beneath his hands. When had his mind catalogued those details?

The question fled when he noticed the angry young companion beside Charity. His annoyance rose as he recalled their conversation. Would the young women renew their complaints against him here? Would he be forced to defend himself? Who would believe that Charity had grabbed him? Had this been part of some grand scheme?

As if she felt his gaze, Charity's eyes passed over him. She looked away, only to look back quickly with wide eyes. Her mouth dropped open and he cocked his head in acknowledgment. Color rushed to her cheeks and she turned her back on him.

Such a direct cut might have offended Edmund if he hadn't been relieved. That the young woman was surprised and determined not to know him meant there was no plot to catch him. Perhaps she really had saved him from a horse.

If she wished to ignore the afternoon's encounter, he would certainly oblige her. The party was large; with luck he might avoid even speaking to her.

"I see that despite your protests you have found someone that interests you," Mama said. He had forgotten she was there. He blinked and realized the hosts and Father had left them.

"Whatever do you mean?"

Warning bells began to ring as Mama pulled him further into the room.

"Drop your pretense. I saw the direction of your gaze."

They were making a direct path to Charity and her companion. His heart sped up as his brain acknowledged that he was about to be formally introduced to the women. He swallowed thickly.

Mama patted his hand. "I just knew that you would take to Miss Radforde."

Five

"I CAN'T BELIEVE he is here," Charity lamented to Penelope in a whisper.

How had the ungrateful man from the street found her? Who was he? Would he say anything about that afternoon? Dread settled in her stomach. For Penelope's sake, Charity did not want Mother to know of their trip to the menagerie.

"I won't let him ruin your reputation," Penelope whispered.

Charity's mouth went dry. Why had she not considered her reputation? Perhaps because she had tried not to think about their brief embrace or the interesting color of his eyes.

Penelope was right; the man could damage her. It was possible he had already regaled his friends with stories of a mad woman throwing herself at him on the Strand.

"I wish I had let him get trampled by that horse," she muttered.

Penelope smiled. "It might have made things easier, but don't worry, I am right here."

Charity barely had time to smile back before she heard her name. She turned and was surprised to see he had crossed the room and was now standing before her.

Despite being too skinny for fashion, he looked the perfect gentleman. His cravat was simply tied, light hair well styled. His evening coat was a dark green that complimented his eyes and accentuated his trim stature. Most astonishing was the woman on his arm.

She did not know Lady Glenhaven well. They had only met a few days ago at a garden party and Charity had been more interested in the plants than the people. Unbidden, she recalled Mother's words on their carriage ride home.

"Lord Glenhaven is the third to hold the title. They have two unmarried sons. I daresay one would make for a good conquest, though I can't countenance a marriage. We can aim much higher. But a baron's son will encourage the interest of other suitors."

Charity had not voiced her objection to such a scheme but looked out the window and hoped never to meet either Mr. Glenhaven.

Mother thought Charity's dowry would be enough to capture the "right sort." However, in Charity's experience, men that were interested in her fortune were rarely the sort she wanted to spend her life with.

"Lady Glenhaven." Charity tried to keep her voice even and concentrate on the older woman. If only ignoring the man might make him disappear.

Lady Glenhaven smiled as if they were old friends. "Miss Radforde, Mrs. Aston, what a pleasure to see you both."

"The pleasure is all ours," Penelope replied.

"Please allow me to introduce my son, Mr. Edmund Glenhaven."

There was no denying the introduction. Charity had no choice now but to meet his eyes. They were bright with questions as he bowed and claimed pleasure at making their acquaintance.

She marveled at how easily he lied with his polite voice and neutral phrases. There was no sign that they had ever spoken before. Grateful for all her lessons in deportment, Charity matched him with a demure look and greeting.

"How are you finding London?" Mr. Glenhaven asked politely.

"Very well, thank you," Charity replied. Was he trying to draw her out with his question? Was he waiting for an ideal moment to reveal her impropriety?

"Have you had a chance to explore?" Lady Glenhaven asked. "I recall you had an impressive list of places you wished to see."

"A few." Charity tried not to wince at the insipidness of her answer. Mother had scolded her after the garden party for prattling on about unfashionable places and she was certainly not going to mention the Change. Penelope, who always seemed to know what to say, came to her rescue.

"We still hope to visit many of London's amusements when our schedule permits."

"Then you must allow my son to provide some recommendations. He has spent a good deal of time in London and will know the best places."

His eyebrows rose and Charity suspected some part of Lady Glenhaven's statement was false.

Penelope turned an overly sweet smile on Mr. Glenhaven. "Is there anything you would particularly recommend?"

"I do not think my recommendations would appeal to a young woman. I confess their tastes and actions baffle me."

His glance flicked toward Charity, and she half-expected him to speak of phantom horses.

"I believe most enjoy the theatre or pleasure gardens."

As a fan of the theatre, Penelope readily took up the subject and talked of her expectations.

Charity remained quiet as she tried to work out Mr. Glenhaven. She was happy to keep their previous meeting a secret but took issue with his subtle slight about what young women enjoyed. He already thought her mad; did he also think her frivolous?

Over Mr. Glenhaven's shoulder, Charity saw Mother approaching. The group turned to Mrs. Radforde.

"Lady Glenhaven, how good to see you."

Mother's auburn hair was delicately styled and her fashionable dress complemented her plump figure. She smiled eagerly as Lady Glenhaven introduced her son.

"Your mother speaks very highly of you and I see it was not merely maternal pride."

"I have found my mother to be an accurate judge of character," he returned with his own small smile.

Charity furrowed her brow. There was certainly a double meaning there. Mother nudged her arm and she pasted on a smile. Young heiresses were not meant to think in public.

The conversation stalled. Mother looked at her as if willing her to speak, but she had nothing to say—or rather, she could think of nothing appropriate. She could hardly speak her mind and any interesting topic of conversation would meet with her mother's disapproval.

Filling the silence, Mother launched into a commentary about the kindness of their hosts and managed to sprinkle in a few deft compliments to the Glenhavens. It was expertly done but she felt the falseness of it. Did Mr. Glenhaven sense it too?

As their parents talked, Charity watched him surreptitiously. His eyes flicked to hers and she looked away. She tried to focus only on the conversation—which had turned to the merits of Indian muslin—and avoided meeting his eyes again.

The announcement of dinner was as welcome as a cool breeze on a hot summer day. Charity was ready to escape the Glenhavens. But instead of taking their leave, the baroness and her son shared a brief look.

Mr. Glenhaven offered his arm. "Miss Radforde, please allow me to escort you to dinner."

Charity gave a quick glance at Mother, vainly hoping for some interference, but she looked pleased. Belatedly, she remembered that she was to make a conquest of Mr. Glenhaven. Her hands grew slick at the thought of Mother watching and judging her.

"Thank you," she said and placed her hand lightly on his arm.

Mary had once explained all about snake charmers and their skills at entrancing dangerous cobras in and out of baskets. That seemed easier than getting Mr. Glenhaven to fall in love with her. Penelope could have taught her—she knew just how to capture a man—but Charity hoped her ineptitude would work in her favor. If she failed to attract a suitor, then Mother might give up her marriage schemes and she would be free. But until then, Charity would do her best to draw as little of Mother's ire as possible.

Neither Charity nor Mr. Glenhaven spoke as they walked. An awkward quiet settled between them. As she forced a pleasant smile, she rapidly reviewed topics but could settle on nothing suitable. A sea of conversation surrounded their island of silence.

Mother looked back at them and her slight frown spurred Charity into mindless prattle about the elegance of the furnishings. Glenhaven did not reply. Perhaps he was only polite when his mother was beside him? By the time they reached their seats, she was feeling ridiculous.

As they waited to sit, Mr. Glenhaven leaned in and spoke in a low voice.

"I haven't told anyone about our encounter and I will deny it if you do."

"Oh?" Charity fought the urge to glare at him.

"And let us dispense with idle chatter. Save your breath to cool your soup, I have no intention of marrying."

Heat crept up her cheeks, anger mixed with her embarrassment. How dare he reject her before she could declare her lack of interest! She shouldn't have worried about suitable topics; he clearly did not care. He seemed determined to be inappropriate. Surely Mother would not wish her to charm such a rude creature.

"You rate yourself rather high," Charity murmured without thinking.

Mr. Glenhaven looked at her sharply but was prevented from replying by the arrival of a woman to his right.

Across the table, Charity caught Penelope watching them. She gave her companion a slight reassuring smile and turned to the man on her left. She had only met Mr. Church that evening but she was sure he was the species of man that loved the sound of his own voice.

Mr. Church, a balding man in his early forties, lived up to her initial assessment. As they began the first course, he needed little encouragement to speak at length about his horses and hounds. Charity was only obliged to smile and ask an occasional question. This mode of conversation allowed her to contemplate her next words to Mr. Glenhaven.

At length, she decided to follow her mother's advice and let Glenhaven's conduct guide her own. He had been blunt and rude, so she would do the same. Mother would not fault her once she knew he had no interest in courtship. Mother's injunctions to charm and speak on specific topics simply did not apply to him.

When they changed conversation partners, she turned from Mr. Church eagerly. For the first time, she would be able to speak her mind in company. Though the room was brimming with noise, she pitched her voice lower to avoid being overheard. Without looking at Glenhaven, she launched into her remarks.

"I am sorry, Mr. Glenhaven, that you are laboring under the misapprehension that I would be interested in an alliance. Let me assure you that I would rather be locked in a cage with a tiger than spend time in your company." Charity was proud of the steadiness in her voice.

From the corner of her eye, she caught his fork pausing halfway to his mouth. He raised his eyebrows and returned the utensil to his plate.

"How colorfully you speak. I would apologizefor my assumption were it not well reasoned. I rather thought your mother interested in an alliance." He emphasized the last word as his eyes darted down the table where Mother was no doubt watching them.

Charity smiled as if Mr. Glenhaven had said something witty instead of insulting. The tinge of pink on her ears was hopefully the only indication of her pique.

"I believe you are confused. For it is clearly *your* mother that is seeking a permanent connection. Mine merely wishes me to make an easy conquest. I can reach much higher than a third son with a dull profession."

The words were an echo of what Mother had said and Charity knew immediately she should not have repeated the sentiment. But there was no recalling them.

"You have a strange method for attracting a man. Tell me, are physical altercations and affronts the extent of your repertoire?"

She gripped her fork tightly. "I am not trying to attract you. I have no wish for your good opinion."

"Nor do I want yours."

"At last, something we can agree on."

Charity turned from his smug smile and concentrated on her meal. She found she had no appetite. About the table, everyone was engaged in their own conversations. It seemed her quiet, heated exchange with Mr. Glenhaven had gone unmarked, even by Penelope.

Mother caught her eye; she raised her eyebrows and inclined her head. She could already hear the stream of remonstrances for being silent but for once she did not care. Nothing could get her to speak to the man again.

"We also agree that the church is a dull profession," Glenhaven said as if they had not ceased talking. Charity turned to him in confusion.

"I only settled on the church because it gave me the right opportunities."

"What opportunities?" Charity asked, curious despite herself.

"The opportunity to study extensively at Oxford. The opportunity to earn an income while having the leisure to pursue my interests in botany and geography. I assure you there is nothing dull about exploring the Americas." His eyes were alight as he reached for his glass and took a long drink.

"You've been to the Americas?" Intrigued, Charity leaned toward him. Numerous questions crowded her mind. She had read too many accounts of travels and scientific explorations not to be interested.

He replaced his glass and cleared his throat. "I spoke in haste. I have yet to cross the Atlantic."

"Oh." She was unable to hide her disappointment.

"But I wish to study the distribution of life in the Rocky Mountains."

"As von Humboldt did in South America?" Charity asked.

His eyebrows raised. "What do you know of von Humboldt?"

"I have read everything he has published," she replied, indignant at his doubt.

Her heart beat faster at the admission. If she cared about Mr. Glenhaven's opinion, she never would've admitted her interest in the great naturalist. Mother would be appalled that she had revealed herself a bluestocking.

"If that is true—"

"What reason would I have to lie?"

"To ensnare me," he said with a warm smile.

Charity ignored the flip of her stomach at his look. Her body's reactions were less interesting than learning of his plans.

"I promise I did not read thousands of pages in the hopes of impressing a future suitor."

"That does seem unlikely."

"As unlikely as a country parson exploring the Americas. Are you really going?"

Instead of answering, he chewed slowly and glanced down the table towards a man that, judging by his face and coloring, must be his father. Had Lord Glenhaven instructed his son not to talk about such things with young women?

Glenhaven returned his attention to her.

"I am planning an expedition," he said in a rush. "I am going to catalogue the various physical conditions in the mountains and how they affect the plants and animals."

"Are you wishing to create cross-sections of the mountains like the Chimborazo map?" she asked. Charity had spent many hours poring over the map in her edition of von Humboldt's *Tableau Physique*. She had marveled at the artistry, the precise measurements and observations required to create such a wonder.

His nod was eager. "That is precisely my wish. President Jefferson's Corps of Discovery brought back some excellent observations and samples, but a complete study is needed. One that looks at the entire picture of how things are intertwined."

"The unity of nature," Charity offered, using von Humboldt's own words.

A wide, genuine smile transformed Glenhaven's face. "Miss Radforde, you are full of surprises."

Charity's heart fluttered but she didn't know if it was his smile or his praise she found most affecting. Perhaps it was merely the thrill of being allowed to voice her thoughts without fear of reproach.

As they continued to talk about von Humboldt's travels and theories, she started to wish the dinner might never end. Since leaving school, there were no opportunities for these kinds of conversations. Such things were not discussed in company and Penelope and Mary did not share her interests. Her words rushed out like a dam had broken inside her.

As people began to push their plates back, Mr. Glenhaven abruptly changed the topic.

"I have not yet spoken to my parents of my plans. They think I am in London to find a wife."

In his tone she sensed the same frustrations she felt. How strange the number of opinions and feelings they shared.

"But I have it on good authority that you have no intention of marrying," she couldn't help teasing.

"That was unpardonable of me to say. I should not have assumed you wished to shackle me, but the evidence did support my hypothesis."

"It was a sound hypothesis. But speaking bluntly was wrong. I hope that is not how you plan to repel other young ladies."

"I had planned on being boring and taciturn."

She sighed. "Believe me, being quiet and uninteresting is not enough to fend off suitors."

"Miss Radforde, you are neither quiet nor uninteresting. You might be the most fascinating woman of my acquaintance."

He spoke so matter-of-factly that Charity did not think he had meant to compliment her. Somehow that made his words more precious.

Their hostess rose, ending the conversation. Charity took her cue and stood. Her disappointment at being separated from the men was palpable. How very different the departure was from the arrival. As the ladies walked to the drawing room, Mother came up beside Charity. "Mr. Glenhaven seems very taken with you," she whispered.

Charity held back a smile. If only she knew that Mr. Glenhaven was actually taken with her thoughts on plant distribution.

"Mr. Church did not seem as pleased. You might make more of an effort with him. Though not young or quite so handsome, he is well-established and respected."

"Yes, Mother." Charity knew better than to argue.

"I think we might rely on both calling tomorrow. And when they do, you really must get them to take you driving. It is important people see that you are sought after."

"Of course, Mother."

Since Charity didn't believe either man would call, it was easy to agree. Though if seeing Mr. Glenhaven meant she could talk plainly about things that interested her, she would not object to a visit.

When they reached the well-furnished drawing room, Mother went to speak to their hostess. At her liberty, Charity searched the room for Penelope. Having a friend always about was a great comfort. Penelope seemed thoughtful when Charity joined her near the window.

"I did not think you susceptible to charmers, but I see I was mistaken," she said.

"Whatever do you mean?" Charity frowned.

"Mr. Glenhaven has thoroughly beguiled you."

Charity scoffed. "Don't be ridiculous." The very notion was absurd.

Penelope raised her eyebrows. "Don't deny it. I've never seen you so lively when speaking with a man."

"I assure you I am safe from Mr. Glenhaven," Charity said firmly.

"No man is entirely safe."

In the past, she wouldn't have hesitated to tell her friend, but telling her companion was a different matter. She could not explain the frankness of their conversation without revealing her own impropriety. A genteel lady did not talk of marriage so cavalierly nor insult a man so thoroughly. Once Penelope was the most improper of all the girls at school, but experience had transformed her into a high stickler. Penelope, schoolgirl at Bath, was not Mrs. Aston, companion to an heiress. But Charity still wanted to share some of their discussion.

"I did enjoy his conversation," she admitted. "But only because we talked of von Humboldt's theories on biological diversity."

Penelope looked askance. "I cannot believe it. How could you both be so animated about something so dull?"

"It isn't dull, it's fascinating. Mr. Glenhaven has some very interesting theories about the mountains in America."

"Does he? Well, I see I was mistaken." Penelope smiled and shook her head.

Charity did not think she had convinced her and decided to change the topic. "Mother wants me to stay home for calls tomorrow," Charity said. "I think you might excuse yourself for the morning if you wish."

As a married woman, Penelope didn't have to worry about

impressing suitors or their mothers. While Charity was stuck at home, Penelope could spend her time visiting any of the places in *The Picture of London.*

"That is thoughtful, but as your companion, my place is with you. I am sure Mrs. Radforde expects me to be there."

It seemed Penelope's circumstances kept her as trapped as Charity.

"I am sorry, Pen. If it were my decision I would have us visiting the British Museum."

Penelope shook her head. "And what makes you think I would enjoy that more than morning calls?"

"Or we could go shopping or riding, whatever you would prefer."

"That does sound lovely, but you must learn not to consult my pleasure. I am resigned to my life of trailing after you. We all must play our parts."

"I envy Mary," Charity said.

"Oh? What part of her situation do you envy?"

"She doesn't have to impress would-be suitors or worry about the ladies of London. Being betrothed gives her liberties. If she wanted to spend all day at a museum I daresay Mrs. Hunter wouldn't deny her."

"I suppose their neglect does offer a kind of freedom," Penelope replied after a moment of thought. "But surely you don't think engagement or marriage a way to gain autonomy?"

"No, of course not, I would just be exchanging one master for another. But being betrothed would certainly make life with Mother easier."

Penelope grinned. "Perhaps, but you would have a husband in the bargain."

Charity wrinkled her nose. "A steep price indeed."

"One day you might be willing to pay it. Especially if the man in question has captured your heart."

"That seems unlikely. It would ruin my plan to become a wealthy spinster."

"A capital idea. I would applaud you for accomplishing it."

Penelope was smiling but her approval seemed genuine. Others might scoff and say Charity would be happier as a wife, but Penelope knew the dangers of love and the perils of a bad marriage. Did she dare bring Penelope into her confidence?

When Charity set up her own establishment, she would invite her and Rosamund to live with her. Surely Rosie would prefer living with them to being a governess? They might all be happy and comfortable on very little. And most importantly, they would be free to pursue their own interests.

Rosamund might play the piano all day. Penelope could plan outings and entertain friends. Charity could spend an entire morning talking about biological diversity with other intelligent people.

And there would be no more talk of suitors or marriage.

Six

THE CARRIAGE DOORS had scarcely shut when Lady Glenhaven let out a sigh of satisfaction.

"Well, I call that a very good result." She smiled at Edmund. "I told you Miss Radforde would suit."

"You seemed to be having an engaging conversation," Father added as he stifled a yawn.

"She was most interesting." Edmund did not know what else to say. His interactions with Miss Radforde were so singular, so different than he had expected, that he did not yet know what to make of them.

"Though I must warn you." Mama pursed her lips. "Miss Radforde will have many suitors. I wouldn't be surprised if her mother was hoping for a peer. You would do well to have manners that are generally pleasing."

Edmund held back a frown. It seemed his own mother understood how low the Radfordes rated him. What would she say if he confessed the truth? That the woman thought he was only fit to be a conquest. He felt a little foolish for accusing an intelligent heiress of trying to trap him.

Miss Radforde's statement had wounded his pride and made him attempt to impress her by sharing his plans. The excitement in her eyes had been gratifying while speaking of his dreams had made them feel real.

"It was a shame you could not partner her in cards," Mama continued.

"He doesn't want to appear too eager," Father grumbled. "People will talk even more."

Edmund frowned. How could a simple conversation give rise to speculation? Had he appeared eager for her favor?

"Don't you worry about idle gossip," Mama said. "It is better a man be eager than aloof. Remember that when we go on calls tomorrow. I will introduce you to several excellent young ladies."

"I won't be going on calls tomorrow."

"Why ever not?" Mama asked.

Edmund swallowed. He could not tell her his reason without revealing his future plans.

"Yes, what pressing matters could possibly keep you from accompanying your mother on calls?" Father pressed.

Edmund glanced across the carriage. He would not reveal anything to Father until he had funding and the backing of venerable gentlemen.

"I have a previous engagement."

Father raised his eyebrows and so Edmund continued, hastily creating the only excuse they might accept.

"I am accompanying Miss Radforde to Somerset House."

"Really? Why, that is wonderful!" Mama's surprise was colored with pleasure.

"You invited her to Somerset House? Not a ride in Hyde Park?" Father sounded skeptical.

"She is quite interested in the Royal Society." It wasn't exactly a lie.

"I told you she was unconventional." Mama smiled wide.

He could only hope Miss Radforde was unconventional enough to go along with his ruse. But how was he to ask her to join him?

The next morning, Edmund arose early with no better scheme than to walk about Russell Square and hope he would stumble upon the young women. It was not a completely hare-brained scheme; Miss Radforde had mentioned walking in the square most mornings.

Russell Square was on the north side of Bloomsbury with broad streets intersecting at its corners, surrounded by modern, ornamented houses. A tall railing about his height enclosed the square and a hedge of hornbeam grew up against it, shielding the park from the noise and dust of the street.

Edmund entered the square from the south. He caught the smell of flowers and the laughter of children and immediately understood why the young ladies would take their leisure here. It was a pleasant bit of sculptured wilderness. He followed the walk around the perimeter, the crunch of the gravel under his firm step mingling with the sounds. He passed other walkers—an older couple, a nursemaid with her charge, and two fine gentlemen—but there was no sign of his quarry.

After circling the square, he ventured onto the horseshoe path leading through the center. The lime trees along the broad walk were still young but provided a good amount of shade. Edmund paused to look closer at them. Were they *Tilia cordata* or *Tilia x europaea*?

Inspecting the underside of the heart shaped leaves, he found tufts of white hairs which made the tree *Tilia x europaea*. He supposed using the common linden was the easiest for the landscapers. How strange this species was considered common when it was a hybrid. Did the hybridization aid in its abundance?

He stepped back from the tree and turned over the question as he continued his search.

As he slipped deeper into his thoughts, the path brought him deeper into the square. A movement of white caught his attention and he turned toward a bed of flowers. He blinked in surprise at the young woman who was rising from a crouch. Against the odds, he had found Miss Radforde.

In one hand she held a notebook as the other brushed at her dress, sending bits of dirt and twigs flying to the ground. Had she been sitting on the ground?

He waited for her to notice him as he admired her figure. Her height and shoulders were unusual, like a statue of a Greek goddess. If she were a goddess, then he was her supplicant. He smiled faintly at the fanciful notion. Before sobering, he truly was at her mercy.

He took a deep breath and left the path trying to outpace his nerves. When he was almost upon her, she looked up.

She startled, her gaze sweeping over him, and frowned.

His stomach twisted. It was not the reception he had been hoping for, but it was too late to retreat. Gathering his courage, he swept off his hat and bowed deeply.

"Miss Radforde, what a pleasant surprise."

"Is it?"

His smile faltered but he did not rise to the bait. He needed her to agree to his scheme. She crossed her arms, holding a notebook in front of her like a shield.

"Ah, I see you are a writer." He pointed at the book and hoped she would take the proffered olive branch. Instead, she pulled the notebook behind her.

"When I told you that I walk in the square, it was not an invitation, sir. I should return to my companion."

"Stay." Edmund blanched at his tone. Was she his dog?

Her face darkened and he held up his hands in surrender. "What I mean is, would you accompany me to Somerset House this afternoon?"

"Somerset House? Why would—?" She shook her head. An escaped auburn curl bounced against her cheek. "Mr. Glenhaven, this is most irregular."

He took hope that she had not outright refused him. "Don't you wish to see the Royal Society?"

"I do, very much. It would be an excellent way to spend the morning. But I don't understand why you are asking me here, now. We were in company last night and you never mentioned a wish to further our acquaintance. I can only conclude that your mother—"

"Confound it! I am not trying to court you."

Her shoulders straightened and he realized that was the wrong thing to say.

"That is, you are a very singular—but I had not thought—or rather it would be an honor." Edmund closed his mouth to stop the tide of nonsense.

"How clearly you express yourself," she said dryly. "You will pardon me, Mr. Glenhaven, for wishing to be only with those who truly desire my company. Please tell Lady Glenhaven that your cause is hopeless." She spun on her heel and began to walk toward the path.

Edmund sighed. Why had she not just agreed to the outing? Why must she assume he had other motives? Perhaps she was right to be so cautious; after all, she did not truly know him. He sighed. There was nothing for it. He would have to explain all.

He followed quickly in her wake, careful not to attract attention. The last thing either of them needed was people seeing him chase after her.

When they reached the gravel she turned back to him, fire lighting her blue eyes.

"I promise if you take one more step you will regret it."

"I mean you no offense." He stopped and held his hands up. Had Mrs. Piper's school included training in pugilism? Miss Radforde, with her clenched fist, looked prepared to plant him a facer. "Please let me explain. I promise you will get nothing but the truth."

She eyed him for a long moment. He thought he saw a glimmer of curiosity sparking her gaze. Then, she nodded. "You may explain while we walk. Mrs. Aston will be waiting for me by the statue."

She turned from him and made for the south side of the square. He fell into step beside her and let the words pour out.

"When I encountered you yesterday on the Strand, I was on my way to Somerset House to speak with Sir Joseph Banks about the Royal Society sponsoring my travels. Sadly, he was unavailable and last night's dinner kept me from attending the Royal Society lecture and meeting with him."

"That is unfortunate and explains why you were out of temper, but I fail to—"

"I hope to meet with Sir Joseph today. I have been informed he will be in the library this afternoon. My mother wished me to go on calls with her and I could not explain why I was unavailable because—"

"Because she does not know of your plans. Yes, I see, but what does this have to do with me?"

He sighed, wishing he did not have to admit the next part.

"You were correct, Miss Radforde, my parents wish me to court you. An appointment with you supersedes meeting other eligible young ladies."

"So you told them that we arranged to go to Somerset House?"

"I did."

Having confessed everything, Edmund felt ridiculous. What must she think of him?

They walked for several steps in silence. The statue loomed before them. The bronze Duke of Bedford looked stately in his Roman robes as he leaned on a plough and contemplated the land that had once housed his estate. There was no sign of Mrs. Aston near the granite pedestal.

Miss Radforde stopped and turned towards him. "Your story has the ring of truth. And I agree, a visit to Somerset House would be better than dreary social calls. I will accompany you."

Edmund smiled and would have thanked her, but she held up a hand.

"I wish there to be no confusion. I have no interest in a courtship with you."

Edmund swallowed his pride and his reply. To offend her now would be folly. He had her consent; he did not need her good opinion.

He placed his hand on his heart. "Miss Radforde, I assure you that the sentiment is entirely mutual."

Seven

CHARITY WATCHED Mr. Glenhaven as he strode away with a mixture of frustration and admiration. She respected his commitment to accomplishing his dreams but was annoyed by his blunt manner and awkward explanations.

The crunch of gravel drew her attention and she turned to see Penelope. Her friend was frowning.

"Ah, Penelope, there you are."

"Do not play innocent. What was Mr. Glenhaven doing here? Did you plan an assignation?"

Charity was startled into a laugh.

"This is no laughing matter," Penelope said gravely. "Why was he here?"

"He wants to escort me to Somerset House today." She thought it would be easiest to stick with a version of the truth.

Penelope pursed her lips and firmly laced Charity's arm through her own. Without preamble, she pulled her back toward Radforde House.

"Charity, I did not think I would have to tell you that clandestine meetings with men is foolhardy."

"But I did not..." she paused. Would it upset Penelope more to know that Mr. Glenhaven had found her without invitation? Before

Charity understood the situation, his appearance in the square had been unsettling. Since she could not explain the extenuating circumstances, she decided not to speak.

Penelope continued. "What do we know of this Glenhaven? What are his motives? His family is good, but his pedigree is no guarantee of gentlemanlike behavior. What if you..."

Charity ceased to listen properly; she was in no danger from Mr. Glenhaven. The man was utterly indifferent to her. And their outing was nothing more than a convenient excuse. Someday she could explain it to Penelope, but now she endured the lecture in silence.

Hours later, she sat near the drawing room, unable to concentrate on her reading. *The Picture of London* lay in her hands, the page turned to the description of Somerset House, but she paid more attention to the sounds outside than the words before her.

Each time she heard a carriage, she glanced out the window. On the fourth instance when she turned back to her book, she noticed Penelope watching her.

"I am merely anxious to be off before callers arrive," she explained.

"Of course."

"I have no interest in Mr. Glenhaven," Charity declared for the fourth time that morning. She snapped her book closed, rose from her seat, and crossed the room to prove she did not care.

"And yet you agreed to spend the entire afternoon with him."

After Penelope had finished her lecture, Charity had convinced her to go along with the scheme. It had required repeated declarations of disinterest in Glenhaven, emphasizing the advantage of avoiding calls, and promises not to arrange further assignations but her friend had begrudgingly agreed.

Charity was grateful that she didn't have a different companion. A higher stickler would have forbidden the outing and tattled to Mother. But Penelope had instead obtained permission. It was not lost on Charity that Penelope had more practice in subterfuge. How many lies had she told Mrs. Piper while Mr. Aston was pursuing her?

Before she could reply to Penelope, Mother entered the room. Charity pulled the book behind her back.

"Come, Charity dear, let me take a look at you."

Obediently, she moved to Mother's side and submitted to inspection.

"The pink is very smart, but I think Betsy has done your hair rather too plain."

Charity held her breath. She did not want to go upstairs to have her hair restyled.

Mother tipped her head and pursed her lips. "I suppose nobody of import will likely see you. Why Mr. Glenhaven wishes to take you to Somerset House instead of a nice ride in Hyde Park I do not know."

Mother sighed and then launched into a litany of reminders on how Charity should behave. Knowing them almost by heart, Charity barely listened.

"Dear, do pay attention," Mother said. "Your conduct must be unimpeachable."

This too she had heard before. "Yes, Mother."

A heavy knock interrupted their conversation. Charity looked to the window and saw a stately landau carriage before the house. Mother hastily took her seat and reached for something from her work bag.

"Charity, put that book away," Mother hissed. "We can't have Mr. Glenhaven see you reading."

Penelope smirked but Charity said nothing. Repressing a sigh, she retrieved a sampler from her bag and sat.

Though the design was simple, she had been working on it for more than a month. When she was meant to be sewing, she often hid a book in her lap and read.

She waited until Mother looked down at her work before sliding the guidebook into her reticule. She took up her sampler. No sooner had she set her needle to the fabric was Mr. Glenhaven announced.

He strode into the room, dressed in the same fine blue coat from that morning, and greeted everyone with cordiality. Despite his smiles and compliments, Penelope fixed him with a stern look.

His manner was at such odds with their earlier conversation. When he had an audience, he was adept at the role of a gentleman. When they were alone, he was plain spoken to a fault. Charity wasn't sure how to feel about such a changeable nature.

After the inane pleasantries, they were on their way to the carriage.

The landau was spacious and elegant, providing ample room for all three of them. Charity and Glenhaven took the seats facing forward while Penelope sat opposite. The open top would allow for a breeze and easy view of London as they drove.

As the coachmen set the horses in motion, Mr. Glenhaven smiled at her. It was less studied but more charming than his drawing room smile.

"I hope that you will all find pleasure in this outing," he said. "We should be able to see almost anything you wish."

Penelope turned to her. "What does the book say?"

"The book?" he asked.

Charity lifted her chin. Let him judge her. She pulled the small, red book from her reticule. "*The Picture of London*. My teacher gave it to me."

"An interesting gift."

"Mrs. Piper is a thoughtful and intelligent woman," Penelope said.

Mr. Glenhaven's raised eyebrow was his only reply.

"It has all sorts of details about London and the things to do and see," Charity added.

"Well then, I would love to hear what it has to say about our destination."

Charity couldn't tell if he was sincere, but she flipped to the page on Somerset House and began to read aloud. The entry was longer than others and dwelt particularly on the architecture and statuary.

As she read, Mr. Glenhaven leaned over, his head and shoulder drawing close to hers. His proximity filled her with a strange agitation. What could he mean by drawing close? Was Penelope right and this was all an elaborate trap? When she glanced at him, she saw his eyes moving over the words.

"Is my reading inadequate?" she asked.

When he gave no indication of hearing or moving away, she snapped the book closed.

Mr. Glenhaven startled and pulled back. He frowned. Charity felt that he would have scolded her if they had been alone. Penelope watched them with quick eyes. Realizing how strange her reaction must seem, Charity offered the book to him.

"Here, you may read it."

A faint hint of red appeared on his cheeks. "No. I thank you. I was merely curious. Please continue."

Annoyed, Charity opened the book again. This time as she read, he stayed firmly on his side of the carriage. As she finished the entry, the streets grew louder. She looked up. They were nearing the theaters and would soon arrive.

"I would like to visit the Royal Society first. I hear their library is extensive," Charity said.

Mr. Glenhaven's lips quirked. "An excellent idea."

Penelope wrinkled her nose but made no objection. Her silence reminded Charity that this trip was different. They were no longer just friends exploring the city but an heiress and her chaperone with a suitor. Penelope was to be their shadow.

That would never do.

"Pen, what would you like to see after the Royal Society?" Charity asked.

Penelope smiled. "I thought the view of the Thames from the terrace sounded interesting."

"The book says the terrace is closed to the public," she said apologetically.

"Oh."

"Never fear, Mrs. Aston," Mr. Glenhaven said. "I shall gain us permission."

"Oh please, do not trouble yourself," Penelope replied.

"It will be no trouble." He waved away her concern. "I don't want you to miss the grand view."

The carriage turned onto the Strand. A few pedestrians littered the pavement and even fewer carriages clattered along the street. How different it was from the other afternoon. What made a street busy one day and quiet the next?

A large stone edifice with rusticated arches and Corinthian columns came into view. How strange that she had driven on the Strand several times but had never marked the decoration. As the carriage slowed, she tried to make out the masks on the keystones of the arches, a detail she would not have noticed without the book's description.

As she climbed from the carriage, she had to tilt her head up to catch the statue at the top of the building. It could scarcely be seen from this vantage point. Was there a place in the building to view it? Or perhaps from across the street?

When she looked down, Glenhaven was watching her, hand extended. Penelope was standing on the sidewalk watching them. Charity's ears grew hot as she stepped down and waited for a caustic remark. Surprisingly, he said nothing as he offered his arm and led her the short distance to the archway.

Encouraged by his lack of censure, Charity didn't restrain her curiosity as they stepped under the arch. She gazed up at the vestibule's soaring arches and vaulted ceiling. A few people occupied the space, entering and exiting the door with the bust of Michelangelo that, according to the book, led to the Royal Academy.

When Charity glanced at Mr. Glenhaven, his attention was fixed on the opposite door. His steps slowed and she was obliged to slow with him. Was he nervous about the meeting?

"If Sir Joseph is not there, are we to spend all afternoon waiting in the library?" she whispered.

He tipped his head. "I had not thought... I suppose you could wander with your friend while I wait."

Charity pursed her lips, fighting her annoyance. He had made no pretensions about the visit. It was not about her pleasure, but his plans. Her presence was necessary, not desired.

With a barely contained sigh, Charity nodded. "Let us go then and hope he is there."

At the door they were greeted by a wiry young man that smiled broadly and greeted Glenhaven by name.

"Jamison," Glenhaven returned, "We would like to tour the rooms."

"Of course, sir. You are most welcome to explore. Might I recommend beginning with the Royal Society library?" The cheeky porter practically winked.

"An excellent plan," Glenhaven said a little too loudly.

A real suitor might have asked for her opinion before committing to a plan. Charity was sure Penelope would notice his lack of consideration. Perhaps that would help in convincing her friend that he was not a fortune hunter?

They entered the grand entrance hall and ascended the impressive staircase. Despite herself, Charity forgot her frustration as she examined the paintings and murals.

Mr. Glenhaven stayed beside her, but she felt his mind was far away. It reminded her of when her friend Elaine would get lost in a fancy. When they reached the anteroom, Mr. Glenhaven seemed to remember his role as guide.

"This room is used for receptions. On Thursday evenings both the Royal Society and the Antiquaries meet and afterwards everyone comes here to take refreshment and discuss the proceedings."

Charity was suddenly more interested in the room. The night before it had been filled with the great minds of the nation, the air alive with their discussions of what had been presented. Would that she could attend and take part in such discussions.

He gestured to a door on the far side and they made their way to the Royal Society rooms. With each step, Glenhaven's posture grew more rigid. Charity didn't attempt conversation but glanced at him sideways.

The library almost took her breath away as the wonderful smell of leather and paper swept over her. Tall shelves and long rows of books lined the walls. It was not the sheer number of volumes that excited Charity but their contents. Unlike most libraries, these were not works of fiction but a representation of the Royal Society's knowledge.

She turned to Mr. Glenhaven to share her joy, but he was frowning.

"He is not here," he murmured.

"I am sure he will be soon," she replied.

"Of course. If you will excuse me, I need to speak with Jamison." He turned and then spun back. "Please enjoy the library until I return." He bowed quickly and was gone.

Charity might have been slighted by his abrupt departure if the library did not await her. Penelope took Mr. Glenhaven's place at her side and wove an arm through hers.

"Well, he is certainly an interesting gentleman," she said.

"Does that mean you no longer fear his motives?"

Her companion laughed, which earned them a stern look from a portly man at a nearby shelf.

"Hush," Charity said. "I don't wish to speak of Mr. Glenhaven. What is he to this bounty of books?"

Penelope nudged her shoulder. "Unlike you and Elaine, I am not excited by the mere smell of paper."

Charity pretended shock. "You don't want to read the latest treatise on natural philosophy?"

"You speak as if that is a fault rather than a virtue."

How different they were. Charity looked at the library and felt only excitement but Penelope probably wished to be anywhere else.

At school, Mrs. Piper and Miss Minerva had encouraged each girl's unique interests. It was only as she grew older that Charity realized how strange society found her interests. She was grateful that her friends did not look down on her. Penelope would tease but never ridicule.

"While I look at the books, you might take a turn about the room," Charity said. Penelope always enjoyed being active.

"An excellent suggestion. Though as your companion, I will be ever watchful and shall rush to your side the moment your suitor returns."

"Then for both our sakes, I hope he is long delayed."

Penelope raised her eyebrows but made no further reply before dropping her arm and wandering away.

Once alone, Charity was free to explore.

The sheer quantity of books threatened to overwhelm; there was so much knowledge in the world and she knew so little. She reached out and touched the spines reverently, wishing she could gather an armful to take home. What would Mother say? The realization that she would have to hide the books stole some of the joy but not enough to dampen her spirits.

She began to read the spines and soon stumbled upon a title she couldn't help but pull from the shelf. It was bound in black with gold lettering that proclaimed "Lewis and Clark Journals."

She flipped open to the frontispiece and paused to admire the drawing of Captain Meriweather Lewis. It was a simple portrait showing a man with a receding hairline, Roman nose, and large ears. He was not at all what Charity thought an explorer should look like. She couldn't help but think Mr. Glenhaven, with his high cheekbones, piercing eyes, and tall, slim stature, looked more the part.

She turned to the title page. "History of the Expedition Under the Command of Captains Lewis and Clark." Smiling, she began to flip the pages. There was no time to read the book but surely it would have illustrations. There was something marvelous about such drawings. She longed to see plants or animals that lived halfway around the world, things that were new and undocumented.

With each flip of the page she grew more disappointed. There were no drawings, just paragraph after paragraph of descriptions. Why had the author not included images? So much could be gleaned from careful illustration. Von Humboldt, with all his beautiful language, understood their value. They were her favorite part of any treatise on the natural world.

She returned to the beginning of the book and sank into the words, letting them pull her into their current. The world around her receded, the sounds of the library, the gruff male voices and turning of pages, all fell into the background.

With each flip of a page, she found herself growing jealous of Mr. Glenhaven. Soon he would see all these wonders for himself. He wouldn't be trapped in London, forced to entertain others and constantly bowing to his mother's whims.

If only she could attain such freedom.

Eight

EDMUND RETURNED to the library and found Miss Radforde standing at a shelf with her nose in a book. He paused, unable to resist the opportunity to examine her.

As he watched, Miss Radforde's eyebrows drew together, her full mouth pursed, and she tapped her chin. What had caused such a look? What was she reading? His curiosity eased some of his nerves over the impending meeting with Sir Joseph.

He had spent much of the morning lost in his anxiety and feared he had been ill company. Hopefully, the arrangements he had just made would compensate for his inattention. He began to cross the room.

When he was only a few steps away, the door to Sir Joseph's private chambers opened. Edmund's stomach flipped and he nearly stumbled.

A well-dressed man was wheeled into the library by a swarthy servant. Though Edmund had never met Sir Joseph Banks, he recognized him immediately from his portrait hanging in the nearby meeting room.

His white hair was pulled back from his broad forehead in an older style. Despite the chair he looked robust, with intelligent eyes, broad shoulders, and long legs. Edmund could easily imagine him as a younger man on the prow of a ship, sailing around the world.

As Sir Joseph's keen eyes scanned the library, Edmund squared his shoulders. They were in the same room, now all that remained was an introduction.

He quieted the fluttering in his stomach by reciting the taxonomy of butterflies in his head. *Animalia, anthropoda, insecta, lepidoptera*, his mind stumbled after the order. What family would stomach butterflies belong to?

Sir Joseph's gaze paused not on Edmund but Miss Radforde. The older man's lips pressed into a line and he murmured something to his servant.

Edmund glanced at the oblivious Miss Radforde. Was Sir Joseph displeased with her in some way? Surely if women were not allowed to visit Jamison would have said something? Whatever irritated him was Edmund's fault since he had brought her here. He closed the few steps between them.

"Miss Radforde," he whispered.

She startled. Looking up from her book she blinked rapidly and frowned at him.

"What?"

"Sir Joseph approaches."

He turned his back on her widened eyes and found Sir Joseph upon them.

The baronet gave Edmund a calculating look. Summoning his courage, Edmund addressed the living legend.

"Sir Joseph, I am Mr. Edmund Glenhaven." His voice was steady, but his heart trembled. The butterflies had somehow made their way up to his chest.

Sir Joseph inclined his head thoughtfully.

"I, uh, provided a letter of introduction yesterday but you were unable to see me."

Recognition lighted the older man's eyes. "Ah, yes. Apologies. My Thursdays at the Society are always excessively busy." His voice was deeper than expected. "How fortunate to have you here again, though it seems you brought a guest."

Edmund glanced at Miss Radforde who was watching the exchange.

"Miss Radforde, allow me to introduce Sir Joseph Banks. Sir Joseph, this is Miss Charity Radforde."

"It is a pleasure to meet you, sir."

"The pleasure, I assure you, is all mine. The rooms of the Royal Society are rarely graced with such a fine figure."

Miss Radforde smiled and then looked to Edmund, as if waiting for him to speak. Since when was Miss Radforde at a loss for words?

But of course, before such a great man everyone must be unsure. Edmund, despite all his rehearsing, struggled on what to say next. His practiced speech about his studies felt suddenly boastful and out of place. How to introduce his request in a delicate way?

Sir Joseph filled the silence. "I am only sorry we cannot offer better entertainment. I know our collection holds little to interest a pretty young woman."

"Oh no, sir, I am very pleased with the books here."

Sir Joseph's lips twitched. "There is no need to feign interest in…" He gestured to the book in her hands. "Pray, what are you reading?"

She lifted her chin. "It is an account of Captains Lewis and Clark's expedition into the American interior."

"And you are interested in such things?"

Though Edmund had made a similar mistake the night before, he bristled at Sir Joseph's skeptical tone. When she did not immediately defend herself, he could not stop his own reply.

"Miss Radforde has a great interest in natural philosophy; indeed she has a very keen mind."

"Oh?" Sir Joseph raised his eyebrows.

Miss Radforde glanced down at the book in her hands and bit her lip. When she looked up, Edmund caught a determined glint in her blue eyes.

"At the moment, I am primarily interested in the botany of the Americas. I have read the journal of Mr. Gass, but this newer publication seems to be a more complete account of the expedition. Unfortunately, it is a dry reporting of the journey, not a proper survey of their discoveries. There are no drawings or detailed descriptions like what von Humboldt includes. It seems to me a dedicated scientific expedition is needed. Do not you agree?"

Edmund's heart nearly burst with gratitude. He couldn't hold back his grin. How neatly she had brought up the purpose of their visit. What would he have done without her?

"There is much of the world still left to catalogue," Sir Joseph said. "Is it not the Americans' responsibility to survey their corner of it?"

"Undoubtedly, it is their responsibility," Edmund said. "But do you think them truly interested or capable of such an undertaking? The Corps of Discovery, as they called it, was primarily concerned with mapping and military matters. The descriptions are tantalizing but far from a complete study."

"And you think you are the man for such a study?" Sir Joseph was too perceptive not to understand the purpose of the conversation.

"Indeed, sir, I do. I have a comprehensive plan for such an expedition." Edmund spoke with more confidence than he felt.

There were probably a hundred men more qualified than him. And Sir Joseph, with his vast network of connections, likely knew all of them. He might even know of a man already doing the work Edmund had planned.

The older man considered Edmund with narrowed eyes. It felt like several minutes but was probably only a few seconds before Miss Radford spoke.

"Is not the Royal Society's motto '*nullius in verba*'?" she asked. "Would it not then go against the spirit of the society to trust in the Americans' reports?"

How did she know just what to say? To use the Society's mantra of taking nobody's word to undermine Sir Joseph's objections was inspired.

Sir Joseph's lips twitched but he did not smile. "An excellent point, young lady. But one I am not prepared to argue at this time. We should speak further." He glanced at Edmund. "You may both attend my breakfast on Sunday. I believe, Miss Radforde, that my sister will be interested to make your acquaintance. And, Mr. Glenhaven, we will have ample opportunity to discuss these plans of yours."

Edmund could hardly believe it. To be invited to Sir Joseph's famous Sunday breakfast was beyond his wildest expectations. Miss

Radforde had proven an unlikely champion and the architect of this success.

With minimal fumbling, Edmund expressed his gratitude. Sir Joseph excused himself and signaled to his servant.

As Sir Joseph was wheeled away to a far corner of the library, Edmund turned to Miss Radforde. Her eyes shone with the same excitement that filled him.

"Miss Radforde, you are a wonder."

A light pink suffused her cheeks. "You did not think me pert? Mother says I should keep strong opinions to myself."

"What nonsense. If you had not spoken, we would never have been invited to breakfast."

She smiled. "You think so?"

"Yes, I owe you a great deal." Impulsively, he grabbed her hand and pressed it between his. He could not begin to express the warmth in his heart. "Thank you for accompanying me."

She glanced at their hands and Edmund released her. What had come over him?

He stepped back and glanced away. Mrs. Aston was approaching them. He had almost forgotten the young companion. Had she seen him grasp Miss Radforde's hand? If she had, she would likely appear angry, but her look seemed curious.

Still, if the woman was going to scold him, he preferred not to be in the library. Having gained Sir Joseph's good graces, it seemed best they leave.

"Now that we have accomplished my object, shall we go?" he asked.

Miss Radforde agreed and signaled to her friend. As Mrs. Aston moved to the door, Miss Radforde gave a longing look at the book in her hand. Edmund suspected she could have happily read the book all afternoon. With a small sigh, she placed it back on the shelf and took his offered arm.

"Who was that gentleman in the chair?" Mrs. Aston asked when they entered the outer room.

"Sir Joseph Banks," Miss Radforde replied.

Mrs. Aston looked impressed, but Edmund wasn't sure if it was the title or the man himself she admired.

"He is the president of the Royal Society," Edmund explained. "And thanks to Miss Radforde, he has invited us to his Sunday breakfast."

"It is practically an informal meeting of the Society. Distinguished minds gather to discuss the sciences and debate discoveries," Miss Radforde hurriedly added. "It is a great honor."

"But Charity, you know your mother plans to attend church and then go for a ride in Hyde Park," Mrs. Aston said in mild reproof.

Miss Radforde's face fell. "Oh, yes. I had forgotten."

"Surely, Mrs. Radforde will change her mind when she realizes you have been invited by Sir Joseph Banks? You need only explain the honor."

"No." Miss Radforde shook her head. "Telling her the nature of the breakfast would only set her against it."

Edmund could not believe that to be true. "But—"

"Let us speak no more about it," Mrs. Aston cut over his objection. "We shouldn't be standing about when there is still so much to see."

Edmund was reluctant to drop the topic but saw he had no choice.

"Quite right, Mrs. Aston," he said. "Let us go. As promised, I have arranged access to the terrace."

His words had the desired effect. Their eyes lit up and they eagerly moved to the grand staircase.

"When did you get permission to visit the terrace?" Miss Radforde asked after only a few steps down.

"When I left you in the library."

"Oh."

"Where did you think I went?"

She shrugged. "I assumed to seek out Sir Joseph. That was your sole object in coming here."

Without Miss Radforde he would not even be at Somerset House, let alone in possession of a coveted invite to Sir Joseph's breakfast. How unfair she would not be able to attend. He must ensure she enjoy the rest of the afternoon.

"Yes, apologies for my distraction," he said. "I was nervous and quite sure Sir Joseph would laugh in my face. But now, thanks to you, my business is concluded successfully. So I can devote myself to your entertainment."

"Careful, Mr. Glenhaven, you sound like a suitor."

Her conspiratorial grin sent a rush of warmth through him. It was no wonder Mrs. Radforde thought her daughter could reach higher than him. She was intelligent, attractive, and clever.

As they came to the door, Edmund smiled at Jamison. Thank heavens the porter had taken a liking to him. They exited the North Wing into the vestibule. Edmund looked up and nodded at Sir Isaac Newton's bust.

The vestibule was busier than when they arrived, but the traffic was still concentrated on the Royal Academy. No doubt there were some new paintings on display. They turned their steps to the courtyard.

At the statue of the King, they paused to admire the craftsmanship and discussed the architecture of the building. Edmund was only mildly surprised to learn that both young women had an extensive knowledge of sculpture and architecture. It seemed Mrs. Piper's school was quite comprehensive.

As they approached the terrace, it was easy to see why it was closed to the public. Here the building was not yet finished. Scaffolding lined one of the walls and workers called out from high above them. A young boy stood at the barrier.

"Mr. Glenhaven, sir?" the boy asked.

"Yes."

"Come with me, sir. But we must be quick."

The group kept pace with the boy. They passed an area covered in work dust and filled with a large stack of bricks before emerging onto the terrace. The women caught their breath and even Edmund had to admit the view was well worth the money he had paid Jamison for assistance in accessing it.

Below them, the Thames lapped against the walls of the building. Before them, the river teemed with craft both large and small going under the grand bridges in the distance. Though the river was bustling, it was almost peaceful when compared with the loud clamor of the streets.

To the east lay St. Paul's dome, to the west Westminster Abbey's Gothic spire, and between them a multitude of roofs and church steeples piercing the sky. Across the river in the distance, the green Surrey hills stood out against the blue.

The young ladies exclaimed over the prospect and together they pointed out objects of interest as they walked the length of the terrace. Mrs. Aston moved further away, peering directly down into the water in an attempt to watch a barge sail under the arches below them. According to Miss Radforde's delightful guidebook, Somerset House had its own docks. Miss Radforde stood at the balustrade staring out at London. Edmund moved to stand beside her.

"Does your book have an entry for each sight?" Edmund asked.

Miss Radforde gave him a sad smile. "Yes, and this may be the closest I come to visiting them."

He frowned. "I thought you planned to explore London?"

"My time is not my own. Mother has many engagements and expectations for how I will spend my time here." Her voice was heavy with resignation.

"Do you truly think she will not allow you to go to Sir Joseph's?"

"I know she will not." She sighed and tucked an errant strand of hair back into her bonnet.

It was unfair that a young woman as bright and curious as Miss Radforde was denied such a simple thing. She deserved to enjoy all that London had to offer. Though his reasons had been selfish, Edmund was pleased that he had enabled her to see Somerset House.

"I must say, Miss Radforde, that after today I am in your debt. If I can assist you in visiting any sight in London, please do not hesitate to appeal to me."

She tipped her head at him as if she could not quite believe his offer. "I appreciate the sentiment but there is no debt to be settled. You need not concern yourself with my schedule."

The rejection was like losing his footing at the edge of a stream. One moment he was examining an intriguing flower, and the next he was soaking wet. What had he expected? This flower had thorns.

He stared out at the Surrey hills and cursed himself for his hasty offer. She had been quite plain that she didn't wish for courtship. And though he joined her in that wish, her rejection still stung.

As she left him to join Mrs. Aston, he tried to push away his disappointment. That the young lady thought him unworthy of her company should not matter. He had not come to London to help Miss Radforde sightsee. She probably had dozens of men clamoring to escort her about town.

Edmund told himself to be grateful for her rejection. He did not have time to waste with Miss Radforde. He had to obtain supporters, put together a team, buy his supplies, and leave for America. And all that would start with going to Sir Joseph's breakfast.

In the two days between meeting Sir Joseph and attending his breakfast, Edmund did his best to prepare for the gathering of great minds. But nothing quite prepared him for the wave of doubt that swept over him when he arrived at Sir Joseph's home in Soho Square.

He sat in the hack cab, staring at the fine brick house and a large arched window overlooking the square. It seemed impossible they would allow him inside. What if the servant shut the door in his face? He would be humiliated and Father would be proven right.

That last thought spurred him to action. Edmund reminded himself that he had been invited, took a deep breath, and climbed from the carriage.

A dark-skinned servant dressed in green livery opened the door revealing a large oblong hall. Edmund gave his name and the servant bowed and led him up the twisting stairs. Edmund's heart skittered with each step, the rumble of voices and scent of tobacco reaching him long before he reached the floor.

On the landing open doors beckoned him into a large drawing room, filled with morning sunshine and bursting with people. Men clustered together in small groups—the majority of the visitors were men—holding plates of food or cups and saucers. Edmund surveyed the room but did not recognize a single face.

He swallowed down his discomfort and reminded himself again that he had been invited, he belonged there. These men were the same species as him. With a deep breath he silently repeated the taxonomy of *homo sapiens*.

He got as far as the *mammalia* class before wishing Miss Radforde was beside him. If she had attended, he would not be reduced to standing at the edges muttering to himself. He would have been assured of an interesting conversation partner and the curiosity of the predominately male guests. What might she say of the gathering?

"Welcome, sir."

Edmund blinked and focused on the older lady who had approached him. Her brown silk dress hugged her wide frame. Her beaked nose and eyes strongly resembled Sir Joseph. He began to bow.

"No need to stand on formalities," she said briskly. "If we could find my brother, we could get a proper introduction, but that might take half the morning." She gestured to the press of people. "Much easier to just introduce ourselves. I am Miss Sarah Banks."

Edmund, charmed by her practicality, inclined his head. "Mr. Edmund Glenhaven."

She nodded, her riotous white hair swaying with the movement. "I thought as much. Joseph mentioned you might come. You are planning a scientific survey of the Rocky Mountains, is that correct?"

"Yes, ma'am. That is my hope."

"Your hope? Come, you are either going or not. A hope will not get you across the Atlantic nor propel you halfway across a continent."

"An astute observation, ma'am," he said, not knowing what else was expected.

She shook her head, clearly unsatisfied with his reply. "My brother mentioned you would be bringing an intelligent young woman."

"My acquaintance, Miss Radforde. Unfortunately, she was unable to attend."

"Pity, I was looking forward to meeting her, but I guess you will do." She wrapped her hand around his arm. "Now, who shall I introduce to you?"

For the next hour Edmund was inundated with new acquaintances. Some names he recognized from journal publications, a few had such large reputations that he was awestruck in their presence. It was truly a gathering of mighty minds.

Miss Banks was welcomed by all and affectionately called Miss Sarah. He suspected she often served as a guide for new guests. She mentioned Edmund's planned journey to everyone they met. He fielded several polite questions, but most were more interested in their own conversations or talking to Miss Sarah. He was more accessory than man; she might as well have carried a lap dog.

When they entered the second, smaller drawing room that faced the square, they found Sir Joseph. They joined the circle of conversation without fanfare. The baronet acknowledged him with a nod but did not stop his rapid speech.

After a few moments Edmund understood they were discussing the latest expedition to Africa. He had little interest in discovering the source of the Niger river and so could contribute nothing.

He thought instead of how he might turn the conversation to exploring the Rocky Mountains. Could he mention Lewis and Clark's use of waterways? Before he could work out how that might be done, Sir Joseph addressed him directly.

"Mr. Glenhaven," Sir Joseph said. "The African Society is in great need of talented young men. Have you ever considered changing your focus from America to Africa?"

The eyes of everyone in the circle turned to Edmund like he was some exotic animal. He tried not to squirm.

"I have not, Sir Joseph."

He rubbed his chin. "Well, think on it. You might find it a better course than your present one."

Edmund clenched his fist as he inclined his head. He could do little else without insulting the august gentleman.

No amount of thinking would change his mind. He was simply not interested. The type of exploration he most valued was not scaling mountains or tramping through jungles to fill out blank maps. Understanding why a certain plant grew on the mountainside was far more fascinating.

Sir Joseph did not address him again and Edmund soon excused himself. There was little hope of turning the tide of conversation to a scientific survey in America and he had promised Mama he would not be gone all morning.

Miss Sarah accompanied him to the landing.

"It was a pleasure meeting you, Mr. Glenhaven. I hope you will continue to attend these little salons. I am sure next week you will have more opportunity to converse with my brother. You might oblige me and bring Miss Radforde."

"Perhaps."

The noise of the first floor faded with each step down the stairs. Edmund's feet were heavy. He was no closer to getting the Royal Society's support than before. With Sir Joseph encouraging him toward Africa it felt as if he was even further from his goal.

If Miss Radforde had been beside him, would it have been different? She could have found a way to turn the conversation to the Rocky Mountains. The woman had a seemingly endless supply of surprising conversation. With her beside him, Edmund might have found the courage to be bold.

He exited the house and reached the street. As he began to walk, church bells rang out across the city, marking the hour. Was Miss Radforde beneath one of those bells? Was she still at St. George's lingering in the churchyard? If he walked to Hanover Square, could he talk with her? It would not take long; it could not be above half a mile.

How strange that he wished to talk with a near stranger about his morning. But he wanted her opinion on Sir Joseph. He wanted to see her face when he told her of Miss Sarah's desire to become acquainted with an "intelligent woman."

He pushed the desire away.

Even if she was to be found, she was likely surrounded by suitors, men who were titled or heirs to grand estates. The type of men her mother wished her to marry.

That thought alone had him turning in the opposite direction. Miss Radforde was not his confidant and he did not need to burden her with his thoughts nor seek her opinions. He would take his own counsel and make his own way.

Nine

THE MORNING AT ST. George's Church had proven as tedious as Charity had expected. The building was grand enough and the sermon interesting, but Mother only seemed to care about the other parishioners. She had spent services whispering information about those in attendance in Charity's ear. Afterwards, she had trailed after her as they spoke to those Mother deemed worthy.

Or rather, Mother spoke and Charity made noises of agreement. In Bath, amongst her true friends, Charity was rarely silent. In London, with a mother she didn't truly know, she found silence to be the safest course. Why speak when it only led to disapproval and lectures?

She fought off boredom by classifying Mother's various conversations. For though Mother spoke to many different people, her mode of conversation was entirely dependent on her audience.

With careful observation, Charity had narrowed the field to four distinct types: flattering, gossiping, informative, and dismissive. Some were immediately recognizable, such as Mother's praise of the Glenhavens, but others were more nuanced. The difference between gathering information and trading gossip sometimes escaped her.

She wondered if Mr. Glenhaven would be able to help devise better categories. They had touched briefly on the challenges of classification at their dinner. He might be the only person of her acquaintance who would understand the jest.

For the hundredth time that morning she wished she was in Soho Square. The conversations there must be more varied. Who was in attendance at the breakfast? Had Mr. Glenhaven secured his funding? It was no small thing to be sponsored by the president of the Royal Society. Charity admired Mr. Glenhaven's ambition.

Would that she had half his daring, then she might have asked Mother about attending the breakfast. But she did not see the point in asking when she knew the answer. Such an outing would never be permitted. Even if there were a dozen titled bachelors, Mother wouldn't allow Charity to be labeled a bluestocking.

"Charity?" Mother's voice broke through her thoughts. "Why don't you go and wait for me in the carriage."

"Yes, Mother."

Gratefully, she made her way to their landau where Penelope already waited. She had not been forced into conversations, but then she probably would have enjoyed socializing. At least she would have enjoyed it if she were still an heiress and not the companion of one.

"I am sorry. It seems Mother wishes to speak to everyone," Charity said as she settled in the seat across from her friend. The long stream of carriages had diminished to only a handful.

"It is important for her to maintain the right connections. What better place than on blessed ground?" Penelope replied archly.

She was sure Penelope was right, but she didn't care about the right connections.

"I would rather be in Soho Square," she muttered.

"With Mr. Glenhaven?"

Charity held in her sigh. "As I have said, my interest is in the other guests and conversations, not in Mr. Glenhaven."

"You can honestly say that you have no interest in the man?" Penelope leaned forward.

"I found his conversation entertaining, but I have no designs on..." Charity paused, recalling his offer on the terrace.

"You may not have designs, but he might."

Charity had not told Penelope of Glenhaven's offer to help her visit more places. What would she make of it? In the moment she had been surprised and offended. It seemed a strange thing to propose merely out of gratitude and she did not want to accept help from a practical stranger. But was Penelope right? Did he have some other motive for the offer?

She shook her head. "You don't understand. He is not staying in London long." She stopped short of revealing his secret.

"That does not matter. You might have a short courtship or a long engagement."

Charity scoffed ungracefully. The very notion was ridiculous. She was not Penelope; she would not marry a man she barely knew. Nor would she be like Mary and spend years exchanging letters with a faraway fiancé.

"Pen, please, your concerns are unfounded. Mr. Glenhaven is not my suitor. I doubt he will even call again."

Saying the words aloud, she felt a twinge of disappointment. He was presumptuous, absentminded, and blunt, but he was also a man of information who did not care if she spoke her mind. More than once she had thought of their conversations and the freedom of being herself in his company. Perhaps she should not have rejected his offer so quickly.

"Here is Mother. Speak no more about it."

"What a splendid morning," Mother said as she settled onto the forward-facing bench beside Charity. "Despite your dullness there were many who I think will further our acquaintance." She smiled and settled back into the cushions.

How strange that Charity could say nothing and still be considered a desirable acquaintance. Or was her silence the chief attraction? No, her fortune was undoubtedly what drew them.

The carriage jostled as it began to slowly roll forward.

"Really, my dear, you must try to at least speak. We can't have people thinking you are mute."

"Yes, Mother."

She grit her teeth and looked down at her hands. If she spoke it was wrong, if she stayed silent it was wrong. Was there any way to satisfy

Mother? Perhaps if she studied her modes of conversation further, then she might hit upon precisely the right things to say.

A breeze fluttered the ties of her bonnet as the carriage made its way to Hyde Park. She looked up from her hands and tried to enjoy the unobstructed view of the teeming streets and sights of London.

The landau was one of the few things Charity and Mother both enjoyed. She loved being able to observe the world around her and Mother loved being observed by others.

Their progress soon slowed as the traffic grew thick around them; too many carriages and horses all heading to the same place.

The Picture of London said that fifty thousand people might take the air at Hyde Park and Kensington Gardens at one time. Charity had thought the number an exaggeration, but being surrounded by people streaming toward the entrance gate made her reconsider.

"It is rather crowded," Penelope said.

"Yes dear," Mother replied with an air of superiority. "That is precisely what I hoped. We must be seen, you know, and Charity looks very well today. Do not you agree?"

"Very well," Penelope said.

"I dare say any man will be taken with her."

Charity squirmed in her seat. She knew she was not as pretty as Penelope, no matter her hairstyle or cut of her gown. If a man found her pleasing, it would be because their fine horses and large carriage indicated their wealth.

"Is that the Hunters?" Penelope changed the subject.

Looking at the carriages before them, Charity soon saw Mr. Hunter, his mother, and sister sitting elegantly in their landau.

"Mary is not with them," she said.

"They probably left her at home," Penelope replied.

"That is rather unsociable of her," Mother said.

"Mary doesn't need to be sociable. She is already betrothed." Charity managed to keep the bitterness from her tone.

Mother sniffed. "That is no reason to hide away. She still needs to make alliances amongst good society."

"To what end?" Penelope spoke with some of her old forcefulness.

"When Mr. Blosset returns, they will marry and then sail for India. If she is to live abroad, she doesn't need to make friends in London."

Mother narrowed her eyes but made no reply.

What would it be like to have Mary's freedom? If she was betrothed, Charity might have spent the morning at Soho Square instead. It seemed to her that Mary's engagement was the perfect kind.

With her betrothed far away, she had all of the benefits with none of the drawbacks. There was no man to dictate to her and no expectations to catch a husband. Charity would quite like to be betrothed, as long as she didn't have to actually marry anyone.

"It is a testament to Mr. Hunter's generosity that he allows Miss Mary such freedom. I am sure he would extend similar privileges to his wife. Don't you agree, Charity?"

"Yes, Mother. He would think himself very generous."

Penelope's lips quirked but she didn't reply. Her friend knew Charity's low opinion of the man.

Undeterred, Mother continued to sing Mr. Hunter's praises for several long minutes.

Charity did not care for Mr. Hunter. He was a man with a large estate and small mind. He made no secret that he was not pleased with the arranged marriage between Mary and his uncle. He had told Charity that his uncle should not have a "native wife." Never mind that Mary's father was as English as Mr. Hunter's and her mother as Christian a woman as ever lived. Charity tolerated Mr. Hunter's presence because he was currently Mary's guardian, but she would never consider him as a suitor.

Mother was of a wholly different opinion. She always spoke highly of him and had insisted Charity partner him at a card party last night. It was the longest night of her remembrance. It was fortunate that the Hunter's carriage was too far away for conversation. Charity wished she could always avoid speaking to the man.

Her wishes were not to be fulfilled.

On Tuesday she was forced to dance with Mr. Hunter at a private ball, on Wednesday she suffered through a ride in Hyde Park, and on Thursday she endured a lecture for not being more encouraging to the man. By Friday, Charity told herself she would do anything to avoid another mind-numbing interaction.

In the course of the week she came to regret her rejection of Mr. Glenhaven's offer. What might her days have been like if she had spent them with him? She could have spoken freely. She could have seen London. Most importantly, she could have avoided Mr. Hunter and placated Mother.

That Friday morning Mr. Hunter arrived at Radforde House accompanied by his mother, sister, and Mary. Immediately after the greetings, Charity moved to Mary, linking arms and declaring she wished to take a turn about the room. Penelope joined them with alacrity. Arm in arm, the three of them moved around the perimeter. She would walk over thistles the entire half-hour if it kept her from conversation with the insufferable man.

"Whatever is the matter?" Mary asked lowly as they moved out of the hearing of others. "Oh is there a secret? I do love a secret."

Charity gave a noncommittal hum.

"She is avoiding Mr. Hunter," Penelope whispered.

Mary smiled. "Really? But he has said several times how grateful you must be for his company and how much you enjoy your time together. Surely, his judgment is not so inaccurate?"

"'Tis no laughing matter, Mary. Mother truly wishes me to consider him."

"Then consider him," Mary said. "Consider his pride and his arrogance and the annoying way he sniffs when he thinks you are being difficult. And once you have carefully considered all these amiable qualities, you may reject him."

Resisting a groan, Charity made a face. It was undignified behavior but only her friends could see.

"Save your breath," Penelope said. "I have been trying to get her to speak up all week."

"It is not so simple."

Mary and Penelope thought it was easy, but Charity knew better. All her life, she had struggled against her mother's iron will. Her schooling, her clothes, her hairstyle, Mother always had an opinion and it was always the correct one.

At Mrs. Piper's school, Charity had grown into her own opinions and, with the help of her friends and teachers, learned they were valuable. Each year when she returned home for the holidays she shrunk back into the role of the timid, obedient child. It was easier than arguing for the entire fortnight.

Now, after years of agreeing, she felt incapable of successfully contradicting her mother. Like ivy climbing a young tree, Mother had enveloped her until she was strangled, her life a mere trellis for Mother's wishes.

If she told Mother about Hunter's bad qualities, it would do nothing but earn her a long lecture. She could practically hear Mother saying that she was being too nice in her requirements and that she was too young to know what was best.

Even if Mother agreed with her, Hunter would be replaced by another suitor, perhaps one even worse. Charity was as caged as the animals in the Change. What she needed was a way to satisfy Mother that didn't involve tedious men. But how, when only a suitor would satisfy her?

They had taken one turn about the room before Mother called out.

"Now, Charity, that is enough walking. Come and take some refreshment."

"Yes, Mother," Charity said.

She returned like a dog called to heel.

Ten

THE GLENHAVEN CARRIAGE came to a gentle stop before the Radforde's London townhome. Anticipation swelled inside Edmund as he stepped from the carriage.

"I hope this visit will improve your mood," Lady Glenhaven said as he handed her out of the carriage.

"Is there a reason why it should?" Edmund would not fuel her hopes.

Mama considered him for a long moment but said nothing.

In the last week he had been forced to attend far too many social functions and meet far too many uninteresting young ladies. Though beautiful and well-bred, none had been surprising or scholarly in their conversation. This made it easy for him to discourage their attentions. Lady Glenhaven had decided that his lack of success was due to heart-sickness for a particular young lady.

Mama was wrong about the state of his heart, but she was correct in assuming he wanted to see Miss Radforde again. Quite unintentionally, he had found himself looking for her auburn hair at the many functions Mama had coerced him to attend. Despite his resolution on Sunday, he had often wished to confide in her about Sir Joseph's breakfast and his plans. At present, she was the only person in England to whom he could talk openly.

When they entered the drawing room, Edmund struggled not to frown at its occupants. Mrs. Radforde presided in a large armchair, beside her sat a dowdy lady with grey-streaked blonde hair. Near the window, Mrs. Aston stood beside a young lady with dark hair and a golden brown complexion. On the settee, Miss Radforde sat between a young man and young woman. The two shared eyes and hair color and, though of darker coloring, Edmund assumed they were related to the older lady.

"May I introduce Mrs. Hunter, and her children Mr. Hunter, and Miss Hunter," Mrs. Radforde said, confirming his guess. "And Miss Gilbert." She motioned to the young woman with Mrs. Aston.

Edmund did not know the Hunters but from his conversations with Miss Radforde, he recognized Miss Gilbert as a school fellow. The necessary greetings were made. He caught Miss Gilbert's assessing eye for a brief moment before she returned to speaking with Mrs. Aston.

Edmund escorted Mama to a seat near the other matrons and accepted some refreshment. She immediately fell into conversation with the older ladies, leaving Edmund to turn and join the discussion on the settee. He stood beside the seated group and drank his tea.

Mr. Hunter was speaking earnestly, his attention entirely on Miss Radforde.

"So I wrote to my brother and told him—"

Miss Hunter turned to Edmund. "Our brother is in the army," she said proudly.

"Oh, what regiment?" Edmund asked.

"Do be quiet, Isabella," Mr. Hunter scolded.

"Mr. Hunter is telling us about his business in the East Indies," Miss Radforde explained.

"Not my business." Mr. Hunter seemed affronted. "I assure you, my estate is very profitable. I have no need to enter into commercial interests. My brother, being a second son, is the one who has business there." Hunter turned to Edmund. "As a younger son, I am sure you understand the need to make a living."

"Yes," Edmund replied dryly.

Hunter was baiting him. No doubt he thought them in competition for Miss Radforde's hand and wished to highlight his assets. Mama had said there would be other suitors. Were they all so condescending?

Miss Hunter turned to Edmund.

"Do you have interests in the East Indies?" she asked. "It seems such a marvelous place. I have always wanted to go myself. Jonas, that is, my brother, always has such fascinating stories. And Mary, Miss Gilbert that is, says she prefers India to England. Can you imagine? But I think it a very good thing she does because once she marries my uncle, they will live there. Does it not sound like a wonderful adventure to live in India? But I will miss her terribly. Won't you miss her, Miss Radforde?" Miss Hunter did not wait for Miss Radforde's answer. "I am sure you will miss her. Everyone will miss Mary, for she is so very lively."

Edmund held back a smile at Miss Hunter's breathless speech. She was much like his own little sister. Sophy was forever reading Kit's letters and waxing long about the wonders of sailing the world like her older brother.

Miss Hunter continued. "I have begged Mama to let me go to India and live with Jonas. But she says I shall not."

"Which is most proper." Mr. Hunter cut off his sister's prattling.

She frowned.

"India is no place for you. I am certain no true lady would wish to travel so far from England's shores. Do not you agree, Miss Radforde?"

Edmund bristled at the condescension. Had he intended to insult Miss Gilbert, his future relation and Miss Radforde's dear friend? Was he so unfeeling he thought such a slight would endear him to Miss Radforde? Insufferable man.

Edmund turned to Miss Radforde in expectation of a cutting reply. But instead of defending her friend with a quick set down, she gave a tight smile.

"I, uh," Miss Radforde began. "That is, I think that surely there are both sides to the question."

Edmund could scarce believe his ears. Why did she prevaricate? Did she worry about offending Hunter? Did that mean she wanted his good opinion? The thought turned Edmund's stomach.

"I honor your open mind," Mr. Hunter said. "But when you have more time to consider I am sure you will agree with me."

Edmund's teacup rang against his saucer, drawing everyone's attention.

"I believe Miss Radforde knows her own mind," he said.

Hunter raised his chin and narrowed his eyes. "I believe I know Miss Radforde's mind better than you."

Mrs. Hunter chose that moment to announce their departure. Mr. Hunter's goodbye was all that was gallant. Were they in company often? Was he the reason she had refused his offer? Did she enjoy spending time with him? Of course, it was not his business with whom Miss Charity Radforde associated, but Edmund was disappointed in her judgment. Could not she see the man was arrogant and unfeeling?

With the Hunters and Miss Gilbert gone, Mrs. Radforde encouraged Edmund to sit on the settee. He perched on the edge and allowed himself to be peppered with questions by Mrs. Radforde. Unlike her daughter, her conversation was mundane. They discussed the theater and the weather while Miss Radforde remained silent. He cast surreptitious glances at her, but she did not join the conversation.

"The day is exceptionally lovely," Mrs. Radforde said. "I am sure Charity would enjoy a turn about the square. Isn't that right, dear?"

"Yes, Mother," Miss Radforde replied.

Edmund flattered himself that she sounded eager and not resigned.

Lady Glenhaven raised her eyebrows slightly, but Edmund didn't need her silent signal.

"Allow me to accompany you, Miss Radforde and you, Mrs. Aston," Edmund said.

"A splendid idea," Mrs. Radforde answered for them.

For once Edmund was grateful for a managing mama.

As they made their way to the front of the house and out the door, Edmund could not decode Miss Radforde's feelings. Her face and posture were frustratingly neutral, like a statue of Artemis, rather than a woman of flesh and blood.

When they passed through the break in the hedge and entered the walk, Miss Radforde sighed and a ghost of a smile crossed her lips. Mrs. Aston slipped into step behind them, far enough not to be included in any conversation but close enough to listen to every word.

"Thank you for giving me a break from the drawing room," he said.

"I believe my mother is the one you should thank," Miss Radforde declared.

"Ah, there is the forthright Miss Radforde I expected," Edmund teased.

"I merely stated a fact." She pulled her hands behind her back and widened the gap between them.

"You must admit that you were quite different this last quarter hour."

He found her grimace reassuring. Perhaps she only tolerated the man for the sake of her friend? He wanted to ask but it seemed impertinent. He glanced back at Mrs. Aston and moved a little closer to Miss Radforde.

"Whatever the reason, I am glad to have a private word," he said in a quieter tone.

"Why Mr. Glenhaven, was that an attempt to be charming?"

"Merely a statement of fact."

She shook her head and the corners of her lips rose. Was that charming? He hardly knew how to charm a woman but perhaps he should learn.

"What did you wish to say privately?" she asked.

Hearing it repeated back to him he understood how she might have misinterpreted his words.

"Nothing untoward, I assure you. I wanted to tell you about Sir Joseph's."

Her quick nod and bright eyes were more than enough encouragement. He launched into a brief description of his morning in Soho Square. She listened with eager concentration and he regretted again that she had not been able to attend.

"And that was all Sir Joseph said?" she asked when he had finished.

He nodded. "I attended the Royal Society last night but only managed a brief word. The man is besieged with friends and admirers. I am not even sure he fully remembered who I was. But he mentioned seeing me on Sunday. And so I will attend the breakfast again and aim for a better outcome. But I confess my hopes for his support are dwindling."

"I am sorry. I have heard these great men can be fickle. But he would be a fool not to back you."

Edmund's steps felt lighter, sharing his burden had eased his mind. He should have called on her earlier and saved himself days of worry.

They walked a few moments in silence.

"I think you should look beyond Sir Joseph. He is not the only man of wealth and influence in London. The Linnean Society or the Horticultural Society might also be interested in supporting you."

"Perhaps."

Edmund had considered this, but he didn't just want money. He wanted Sir Joseph's seal of approval. If a man of such stature endorsed him, then Father could not question his merit. He would not be a clergyman with dreams, but a legitimate, respected naturalist.

Instead of admitting his reasons, he decided to change the subject. "This square has an interesting variety of flora."

"It truly does," she replied. "I believe the gardener must be dabbling in some hybridization."

"Oh?"

"The petals of the roses in the center beds are larger than normal. I thought perhaps a combination of *rosa gigantea* with a damask."

"Likely *gallica* or *Phoenicia* since they are already blooming," he offered.

"Precisely."

His mouth ticked up. "It is a rare woman who readily knows the Linnaean classification for flowers."

Her chin lifted and shoulders stiffened. "It is not so uncommon. I am sure several of my schoolmates could do the same."

"Do not mistake me, Miss Radforde, I am impressed by your knowledge and perception. Tell me, how did you come to notice the different sizes of the petals?"

Her posture relaxed. "I make studies. In the mornings, Penelope walks and I sketch."

He recalled how she had seemed guilty when he found her among the flowers. "The notebook," he said. She had stored it away so quickly he had almost forgotten.

"Well remembered."

"And is your interest mainly in flowers?"

"I am interested in many aspects of the natural world, but I am fascinated by plants. At Mrs. Piper's, I received some training in botany and botanic painting. In Bath, I would take notes and make sketches of a specimen while it was before me. Then I would make a full color study on larger paper."

"Do you not continue the practice in London?"

She hesitated for a few steps. A light breeze brought the scent of roses, smoke, and horse manure, reminding Edmund that contrary to the greenery before them they were still in town.

"Since coming here the opportunities to make studies are rare. I do not have the time to translate anything into a larger painting."

"That is a pity."

"I believe you mean that." She paused and looked at him strangely, then turned and continued walking.

Was his genuine interest so hard to accept? He glanced back at a frowning Mrs. Aston. If he moved quickly, she might not be able to hear them. He lengthened his stride and caught up with Miss Radforde.

"You aren't one for false words," she said when he had drawn even with her. "Did you also mean what you said on the terrace? About helping me visit other sights in London?"

"I was in absolute earnest. After the past week I am even more eager for such outings. They would be vastly preferable to the engagements my mother has arranged. You know I spent a half-hour discussing *Fordyce's Sermons* yesterday? I think the lady thought to impress me with her piety."

"A reasonable assumption when speaking to a clergyman. That seems more interesting than feigning interest in the size of a man's estate. Why should I care about the number of fireplaces the house has?"

"Many people do care about such things."

"I do not."

"You do not want to hear about the fireplaces at my parsonage?"

She shook her head but didn't hide her amusement.

"Are you sure?" he asked. "It is a short recitation for there are only two and one of them smokes. However the chimney piece—"

"Please, let us talk of anything but that," she said gleefully.

That she was uninterested in such things spoke volumes about her character. Had Hunter regaled her with such information or another of her suitors? He resisted the impulse to ask.

"What shall we talk of?" he asked. "I am yours to command."

She did not reply immediately. He took his eyes from the path and found her brow furrowed like it had been in the library. The question was a simple one, but it seemed she was piecing together a difficult puzzle. After a few moments she spoke quietly.

"But then people might assume we are courting."

The whispered words brought him up short. He stopped and turned toward her.

"I beg your pardon. You wish me to court you?"

She stopped and faced him. "No! That is exactly what I wish to avoid."

The words should not have hurt. He had never desired her good opinion. But there was only so much candor a man could endure.

"I was merely thinking that if you began escorting me to places about London, people would talk, and our mothers would scheme even more."

"That is very probable," he allowed. Though he did not see how an additional visit to a museum or gallery would cause much fuss.

"Although, perhaps..."

"Perhaps what?"

She shook her head. "It is most improper."

"More improper than embracing a stranger on a public street?"

"The tiger roared and the horse...I saved your life!" She waved her hand. "That is not what we are speaking of."

"What are we speaking of? I confess I am confounded."

"An idea, a hypothesis really." Her words began to tumble out in a rush as if she were in a race against her better judgment. "My mother will not rest until she has found me a match. I need a way to satisfy her without exchanging one jailer for another. Lady Glenhaven seems equally determined for you to marry, though you are more interested in your expedition than a wife. Both of us might benefit if we spent time together. Instead of endless calls and dinners, we would attend museums and lectures, all that London has to offer. The arrangement would satisfy ourselves and our mothers."

She took a deep breath and looked at him expectantly. He had thought her mad when they first met, and now he wondered if that impression had been correct.

Needing movement to think, he began to walk again. She kept pace with him.

"You think that if I court you then our mothers will be placated?"

"But you won't be courting me. We will only be spending time together, just as you offered."

"I did not offer to pretend to an attachment."

"You make it sound sordid."

Edmund growled, frustrated by her rebuke. "I am trying to show you the flaws in your logic. If we spend time together as you suggest, the natural conclusion will be that we are courting, which will lead to an expectation of marriage. When I leave for America without a betrothal, both our standings will suffer."

"That would serve my purpose. Since I do not wish to marry, my standing does not matter."

"What?" His eyebrows rose and he wanted to stop and look her in the eyes.

But she continued to walk, heedless of his surprise.

"We could always say I rejected your offer. That might be more believable."

He frowned. "Because you can reach much higher than a third son?"

She winced. "No! I did not mean that. That is, you have many fine qualities—any woman would be lucky—but not me, of course, because I do not wish—"

Her floundering softened his bitterness. She must have seen the amusement in his eyes for she paused and shook her head.

"You started all this with Somerset House," she declared.

Her remark was well aimed. A week ago he had pled with her in this very square for a large favor. He was still in her debt. But her suggestion was very different from his small lie.

The scheme would require they spend many hours together, but time spent with Miss Radforde would be an improvement to his current situation. For all her faults, she was an interesting and intelligent companion. And he was flattered that she had chosen him.

He might have suspected another woman of nefarious motives, but she had been quite clear she was not interested in courtship or, it seemed, marriage. Perhaps she truly wished to enjoy his company with no expectations. He could repay his debt while keeping her away from men like Mr. Hunter. Surely that was a worthy cause.

Miss Radforde remained quiet while he considered her offer, seemingly content to wait until he had fully examined her plan. Edmund appreciated the space to think. So many people grew annoyed when he became preoccupied with his thoughts. Their steps slowed as they approached the break in the hedge where they entered the square. He had not realized how short their time together had been. Mrs. Aston would soon close the distance between them.

"I believe that we must first test your hypothesis." He raised a hand to quell her reply. "I will agree to a single excursion. After your service at Somerset House, it is the least I can do. After, we shall evaluate and decide if we might be able to tolerate your arrangement."

She smiled broadly and his shoulders lifted. He quite liked making her smile.

"And what are you seeking to prove with your test?"

"That this is not an elaborate ruse to capture me," he teased.

She scoffed. "If I were on the hunt for a husband, I can assure you I would not resort to such a method. And many would say I should be worried about your intentions."

Mrs. Aston was mere steps away, but Edmund couldn't help a last retort.

"Ah, but you propositioned me," he murmured.

She cast him an exasperated look, but the arrival of her companion prevented a response.

Edmund could not stop grinning as they crossed the street. He might not agree with her hypothesis, but he was happy to test it. Despite his reservations, he was looking forward to spending more time with Miss Radforde.

Eleven

As the Glenhavens disappeared through the drawing room door, Charity smiled broadly. Against the odds, she had found a way to avoid her mother's disapproval and do what she wanted. Indeed, Mother had eagerly agreed to Mr. Glenhaven's suggestion of a visit to a museum. How many more places might she agree to if Mr. Glenhaven were Charity's escort?

The possibilities made Charity giddy and she was almost grateful to Mr. Hunter for unknowingly pushing her to find an escape. Of course it was Mr. Glenhaven that truly deserved her gratitude.

A few minutes in his presence made her realize how untenable it was to spend her time with men like Hunter. One conversation about roses helped her see that a change was needed. And his previous invitation to Somerset House had shown her the way to accomplish that change.

She was still surprised by her own temerity at suggesting the idea, but since he had agreed, she did not regret her impropriety.

Turning from the door, she caught Penelope's assessing gaze. What had her friend heard in the square? Charity would need to explain somehow. She could lie to Mother and all of society, but she would not keep her friend in the dark.

Mother waited until the footsteps faded then she spoke. "Well,

Charity, I believe you are well on your way to capturing Mr. Glenhaven. I knew the walk was just the thing to encourage him. Though I do wish he had chosen a more suitable activity for tomorrow. I don't care what Lady Glenhaven says, going to Bullock's museum is not the done thing. You must spend as little time as possible there and ask him to take you for a promenade in Hyde Park afterward."

"Yes, Mother."

Charity had no intention of following the advice. She would not rush visiting the renowned museum, examining the specimens gathered from around the world, or walking into the Pantherion. The room was said to transport one from the streets of London to the center of a tropical forest. Why would she wish to exchange that for a walk about Hyde Park?

That evening after dressing for dinner, Charity picked up her notebook and thumbed through her drawings. She paused on the sketch of the rose. How wonderful it had been to share her observation about the square's plants with someone who understood. She smiled as she thought of the new drawings she would make. If Glenhaven agreed to more outings, she might need to purchase a new notebook.

"That is a very pretty color," Penelope said as she entered the room.

Charity glanced down at her blue silk petticoat. It was new and chosen by Mother, of course. Charity didn't care much for fashion but felt it suited her.

"Thank you, Pen. That dress is always lovely on you," she said. Compared to when they lived in Bath, Penelope had far fewer dresses in much more muted tones, but each made her appear to advantage.

Penelope leaned against Charity's bedpost. The room was well-apportioned, with space for a large bed, sitting area, and desk. Near the window, and its view of the square, an empty canvas sat on an easel. After years of living in a small room at Mrs. Piper's, the space felt too large for comfort.

"I see you are already preparing for tomorrow." Penelope gestured to the notebook. "It seems your Mr. Glenhaven is not as indifferent as you believed."

"He is not *my* Mr. Glenhaven. I beg you, do not assume any affection between us. We have a wary friendship and a shared desire to spend our days doing more than sipping tea and attending garden parties. When we spoke in the square, I—"

"I know you think that," Penelope interrupted Charity's attempt to explain her plan. "But Charity, you do not understand men. I see the way you are together and I do not trust him."

Charity bristled at the patronizing tone. "That is unjust. Not every man wishes to trap a young lady. He is different, he has goals. He has agreed—"

"You don't know him." Penelope cut her off again.

"He is not Aston," Charity snapped in exasperation.

Penelope turned red, her back going straight as a fireplace poker.

"You know nothing of—" Her teeth clenched and her body shuddered with suppressed emotion. She met Charity's eye defiantly. Penelope's temper was fiery, but it had been years since Charity had seen her give into her anger.

"I don't care what you think, Charity. I am your companion and I will do my duty. I will not let him take advantage and if you do not listen, I will tell your mother to bar him from your company."

Charity's mouth fell open. "You wouldn't."

"I will do whatever I must to keep you from ruining yourself."

Penelope spun on her heel and stalked from the room.

Charity stared blankly after her. How had things come to such a point? She had only wished to explain the unique circumstances, but her friend wouldn't listen. Of course, that was no excuse for bringing up Aston. The subject was still tender. But it was true that Penelope's experiences had left her prejudiced. Her friend would believe every man was as dangerous as a tiger.

But Mr. Glenhaven was no tiger. He was different. His interest was centered on his dreams, not on capturing her affection. There would be no impropriety, no elopement because neither of them were interested in marriage. Unlike Penelope, Charity's judgment was not clouded by affection and she would not repeat Penelope's mistakes.

That evening and the next morning, Penelope and Charity maintained an icy silence. If Mr. Glenhaven noticed the tension between them, he had the good sense not to remark upon it.

On the way to Bullock's, Penelope remained quiet while Charity and Glenhaven talked genially about the museum and classification systems. Charity snuck a few glances at Penelope but could not determine what she thought of the conversation.

Frustrated at her need for approval, she decided to forget about Penelope and her opinions. She was going to enjoy the museum. Once inside Bullock's, it was easy to ignore her friend. Charity was swept away by the wonder of everything on display. Only a few steps inside and she was pulling out her notebook. Soon she was completely absorbed in making a study.

She bit her lip as her pencil flew across the page. She glanced up at the glass-enclosed specimen and then back down as she strived to capture what she saw—a scrubby bush with gnarled grey bark on its rugged trunk. The flowers were tiny and yellow, stacked upon each other, forming a spike surrounded by ragged leaves. It was labeled "*Banksia Serrata*, in flower."

Charity had seen drawings of *banksia serrata* and was thrilled to make her own. It was one of the many plants Sir Joseph Banks had catalogued on his trip around the world with Captain Cook.

What a marvelous thing it would be to discover a new plant, to be the first to document it, to have a hand in naming it. Would Mr. Glenhaven have that honor? Perhaps he would discover a new animal or have a land feature named for him. Mount Glenhaven had a certain appeal.

With that thought, she remembered her escort and looked up from her notebook. He hadn't disappeared nor was he waiting impatiently. He stood a few feet away, his gaze on a collection of bows and arrows. His eyes were unfocused, his mind apparently elsewhere. What was he thinking of?

Charity smiled as she lowered her head to put the finishing touches on her sketch.

How delightful it was to have the time to make a study of the specimen before her and not be rushed past the cases—there were an abundance of cases. The claim that there were thirty thousand different articles on display was not an exaggeration.

It was understandable that *The Picture of London* said one could return to Bullock's museum many times. The sheer number and variety of items from around the world astonished her. She suspected even Penelope was impressed.

Charity closed her notebook and looked for her friend. She had expected Penelope to hover nearby, but she was on the other side of the room near the carriage that had carried Napoleon to exile. But instead of examining the vehicle like those around her, Penelope was watching Charity.

Did she think by moving away she might catch them in an impropriety? That Glenhaven would attempt a seduction the moment Penelope was not near? Absurd notion. The man had spoken of nothing but the displays and the methods of classifying plants and animals.

She crossed to Mr. Glenhaven and, when he didn't turn from his absorption, gently touched his arm. He turned to her, blinking quickly.

"Oh, Miss Radforde, I'm sorry, were you saying something?"

She held back her smile. He must have been very engrossed in his thoughts.

"I think we might continue to the next room."

"You have finished your drawing?"

"Yes, thank you for waiting."

He shrugged and offered his arm. Charity realized it was the first time since school that she hadn't been teased or censured for drawing. How wonderful to not feel strange or a burden. They began to stroll past the cases containing pouches and belts from South America, more items from Captain Cook's travels. Charity had little interest in such things.

"Miss Radforde, I gather that you are not often allowed the opportunity to make your studies."

"My mother does not see the point in them."

He furrowed his brow. "The point? Pardon, but having seen a sample of your work, it is clear you have aptitude."

"What empty flattery. You have not even seen my sketches."

"I may have examined your drawing as you worked."

Heat blossomed on her cheeks. He had looked and thought she had aptitude? His praise meant more than all the pretty compliments she had received on her clothes or dancing.

"You should tell your mother you need time to foster your talent," he said.

"Telling my mother would not help my cause. She believes it is an unfit occupation for a young lady of my station."

"Preposterous. Why, the queen and all the princesses are trained in botanic illustration. I understand they take great pride in their skill."

They had reached Penelope and Charity was relieved she didn't need to answer. How could she possibly explain what she did not understand? Sometimes she thought Mother disapproved of things Charity enjoyed simply because she enjoyed them.

"Are we ready to proceed to the Pantherion?" Penelope asked.

Charity glanced about. There was still so much to see; she could spend the entire day looking. But she was already trespassing on Glenhaven's time and no doubt Penelope was bored.

"Yes, let us go," Charity said.

As they proceeded to the entrance of the Pantherion, Charity stared longingly at the cases they passed.

"It is very kind of you to sacrifice your pleasure for your friend," Mr. Glenhaven said.

"She has been more than patient," Charity replied. "As have you."

"I have thoroughly enjoyed our time and continuing our discussion of the Linnaean system of classification."

Charity smiled at the reference to their earlier conversation. She had not held back in stating her opinion or sharing her questions and Mr. Glenhaven had spoken to her as an equal. It was all that she could have hoped. She wanted to ask if he thought their test a success.

The corridor before them was unlike the rest of the rooms. Some artisans had transformed it into a rocky cave. They made noises of appreciation as they entered the dimly lit space and walked towards the light and the tempting scenes awaiting them there. When they finally stepped into the Pantherion, they paused to take in the wonder before them.

Like magic, an exotic forest had appeared in the middle of London.

Greenery draped the room, and animals, frozen in time, were posed as if going about their lives. Thanks to the elaborate paintings on the walls it seemed that the forest continued all around them.

"Oh, look at the snake!" Penelope cried, her excitement breaking her reserve.

They followed her direction and saw a snake wrapped around a deer, its coils squeezing the already lifeless body.

"It's a boa constrictor," Mr. Glenhaven said. "They don't bite like other snakes. It is quite an ingenious method of attack. You see, they coil around their prey—"

"That sounds terrifying," Penelope said.

"Oh, well, I suppose if you are the deer, but the process is actually fascinating," he replied.

Penelope gave him a disgusted look. "I am going to look at the birds."

Mr. Glenhaven frowned as Penelope moved away. "Sorry, I forgot myself. I wouldn't normally talk about such things with ladies."

"I found it interesting," Charity said. "Do go on."

His lips twitched into the half smile she was beginning to favor, and he proceeded to tell her all he knew about constrictors. She was able to return the favor by sharing information about the other animals in the room.

They moved toward a tree filled with baboons and other primates and examined the animals in silence. Glenhaven had a particular way of furrowing his forehead as he studied things.

"According to Linnaeus, these fellows are our cousins," Mr. Glenhaven said.

"I see the family resemblance," she replied.

He chuckled. "You don't think such an assertion blasphemous?"

"As a clergyman, surely you are the best qualified to judge."

"Careful, Miss Radforde. That sounded as if you might respect my opinion."

"Perhaps I do."

When had that happened? She turned from the primates and moved to a now familiar animal, a stuffed rhinoceros.

"A large monster, perhaps related to the unicorn?" Mr. Glenhaven asked playfully.

"If unicorns exist, I imagine they would be less..."

"Ugly?"

She tipped her head. "They have one in Exeter Change. A live one, though it barely moves."

"I gather that you did not care for it?"

How had he known?

"The animal was very confined. It didn't even react when we touched it. In the wild it is probably quite dangerous, but in the cage it seemed forlorn. I pity them in their cages."

"It is horrible to be so restricted."

Charity hummed her agreement.

A companionable silence fell between them. She snuck a glance at Mr. Glenhaven and found he was looking at her as if she were the one on display. Perhaps he might understand how trapped she felt. Words came to her, the need to confess overwhelming. She needed someone to know, to tell her the scheme was not impossible.

"I hope one day to set up my own establishment," she practically whispered.

His eyebrows rose but he did not laugh. Encouraged, she continued.

"Nothing extravagant, but a good home with a large garden where my friends might live if they wish."

"Do you have the means for such a thing?" he asked curiously.

"When I come of age, I will have more than enough."

"So you wish to remain a spinster?"

"Is that so surprising? Many respectable women are unmarried. Mrs. Piper gets on very well without a man and I will have the advantage of wealth. I have no need for a husband."

He frowned.

"You think my plan absurd?"

"No, I was merely considering the idea. It is not so unusual to remain unwed. Many women are forced into such a situation. But to choose to be a spinster is certainly unique and I suppose you can always change your mind."

"I can, but I won't."

"A flawed assumption. Nobody knows how they might feel in the future. If you fell in love..."

She swallowed as he trailed away, seeming to realize, as she did, that the conversation was not entirely proper. Love was not a topic she wished to discuss, certainly not with Mr. Glenhaven. They should have stuck to the animals.

Charity turned to move away but his hand stayed her. The gentle touch on her elbow sent a shiver up her arm. When she turned back, he released her.

"It is admirable that you have such a clear plan for your life."

She wet her lips and nodded, not trusting her voice. If he did not think her dream was impossible, perhaps it was achievable?

With a lighter heart, she paced to a tall green tree. Although good recreations, none of the trees were real. According to her book, the museum claimed they were exact in detail and had used plants or drawings of plants as models.

"It is a banana tree," Glenhaven said.

Charity was happy to change the subject. "If only it were a real tree. We might sample the fruit. I have heard it is very singular," she said.

"There is a banana tree in Kew Gardens. Perhaps we might visit together?"

"That would be wonderful." She turned to him with a hopeful smile. "I would love to see the botanic gardens at Kew."

How did he know the places she would like best?

"But," she said, "does that mean you think the test successful?"

"It means I would like to take you to Kew." He grinned.

It was not a proper answer, but his mischievous look gave her hope. Surely, he could now see that spending time together was a beneficial arrangement?

On her part, she was surprised by how easy it was to be in his company. As long as they avoided further talk about love or marriage, Charity would be perfectly satisfied to pretend to a courtship. She hoped he came to the same conclusion.

Twelve

Outside Bullock's Museum the sun hid behind clouds, but the day was warm. Clusters of pedestrians strolled the sidewalk and horse hooves clattered in the street. Many of the carriages, on their way to Hyde Park, were full of people dressed in high fashion.

Edmund glanced at Miss Radforde wondering if he should offer to drive through the park. Her attention was fixed upward at the Egyptian statues that flanked the window above them. Beside its plain brick neighbors, Bullock's Museum stood out with its elaborate windows and statues. He did not think they had such buildings in America; certainly there were none in the wilds of the frontier.

Miss Radforde's eyebrows pinched together in concentration, a look he was beginning to recognize. If his observations were accurate, any moment she would make a thought-provoking remark.

"According to my book," she said without looking at him, "this facade is meant to imitate the gateway to an Egyptian temple. Is it very like one?"

"I don't know. I have never been to Egypt. But it is an impressive display."

She hummed.

The morning had proven her supposition. Spending time with her was preferable to trailing after his mother. And, contrary to his fears, they had not argued or grown tired of each other. Indeed, he was eager to prolong their time together.

Miss Radforde's opinions on Linnaean classification were original and her observations astute. Her thoughts followed a different path than his and he found their exchanges encouraged him to think deeper. If he agreed to her scheme, he might spend many mornings in such scintillating company.

"Miss Radforde, would you like to ride through Hyde Park?" he asked.

She turned from the building slowly, her eyes settling on him. "Not particularly."

Edmund attempted to hide his disappointment. Clearly, she was eager to be rid of him.

"Might we walk to Hatchard's?" she asked.

Perhaps not.

"Certainly, if Mrs. Aston has no objection." He inclined his head to the young companion.

Mrs. Aston had barely spoken all morning, doing a good imitation of a shadow as they moved through the museum.

"If Miss Radforde wishes to go, then of course we must go."

"I do wish it."

Edmund ignored the undercurrent of animosity between the women.

"Excellent," he said and offered his arm to Miss Radforde.

As they entered the stream of pedestrians there was little opportunity to speak. Many of the faces Edmund vaguely recognized. He had met far too many people with Mama in the last two weeks. He caught sight of a man he did remember, a man he had no interest in acknowledging.

Dressed in the bright colors and tight clothing of a dandy, Mr. Fitzroy was hard not to notice. He moved through the world like he owned it—a skill learned quickly when one was heir to a title and large estate. They had attended the same schools, run in the same circles, but Edmund found him insufferable and did not consider them friends.

He could not avoid a meeting, Fitzroy had seen him and bobbed his head. Begrudgingly, Edmund acknowledged the man and braced himself for the impending conversation.

"I am terribly sorry, but I have just seen an acquaintance," he said to Miss Radforde. "Might I introduce you and Mrs. Aston?"

Miss Radforde glanced back at Mrs. Aston before she agreed. Edmund didn't see what passed between the ladies, but he hoped Mrs. Aston's scowl would serve to deter Fitzroy.

Edmund briefly made the introductions. Fitzroy's eyes lit up in recognition at the name Radforde and he was all politeness to the ladies.

"How strange to see you in London, Glenhaven," Fitzroy said. "I thought you never left your little parish." He smirked at Miss Radforde. "I never knew a more stay-at-home fellow."

"Oh," she replied in a neutral tone.

Edmund was used to Fitzroy's veiled insults, but Miss Radforde's lack of defense was disheartening.

"Yes, my profession does keep me from London. But I rather like having something active to do. I could not bear to spend all my time gadding about."

Fitzroy laughed, giving the impression that they were chums instead of adversaries.

"And yet today you find yourself in our fair metropolis." Fitzroy turned to Miss Radforde. "Did you enjoy your walk in Hyde Park, Miss Radforde?"

"I have enjoyed our outing," she replied. The stiff politeness of her tone and the vagueness of her words were so at odds with her character.

"We have just come from Bullock's Museum," Edmund said.

Fitzroy made a tsking sound. "Bullock's? Why, Miss Radforde must have been bored to tears."

"No, indeed. I—" She paused as if unsure how to continue.

"Say no more," Fitzroy grinned as if he knew a secret.

Why had she become tongue-tied in Fitzroy's presence? Did she care for his title? Could she possibly wish to impress him?

"I enjoyed every minute of our visit," Edmund declared.

"Of course *you* did," Fitzroy replied. "But one can't expect a lady to find such things enjoyable."

Edmund waited for Miss Radforde to reprimand Fitzroy, to tell him how wrong he was but she remained silent, a statue on his arm. He looked back over at Mrs. Aston and was pleased by her scowl but she too did not speak.

"I think it best not to assume what Miss Radforde enjoys," Edmund said. "Now you will excuse us, we really must be going."

Fitzroy smiled and bowed elaborately over Miss Radforde's hand. "I hope we might meet again. And when we do, I promise something more exciting than a museum." He barely acknowledged Mrs. Aston.

Miss Radforde smiled but did not express a wish to meet Fitzroy again.

It baffled Edmund to see her so restrained. But she had acted similarly with Mr. Hunter. Was her behavior dependent on the man? Or was she only different with him? He did not know if it was flattering or insulting that she was so open with him.

They continued to walk; Mrs. Aston trailed silently behind them.

Edmund glanced at Miss Radforde and was surprised to see a small smile on her lips.

"What?" he asked sharply.

"I was merely thinking how amusing Mr. Fitzroy's opinions are."

"Oh?"

"He will be very surprised to learn that such a stay-at-home fellow is making an expedition to America."

"Or to learn that you greatly enjoyed Bullock's."

Her smile grew wider, confirming Edmund's opinion that she had not cared for Fitzroy. Which made her behavior all the more frustrating.

"Why were you so silent?" he asked.

Her forehead crinkled as she frowned. "With Mr. Fitzroy?"

"Yes, you might have said the museum was your idea or that you enjoyed it."

"Mother believes being a bluestocking a character defect. To show enthusiasm for a museum is unseemly."

"Unseemly? That's—" he shook his head. Saying rude things about Mrs. Radforde would never do. He began again. "Showing enthusiasm for a museum is not unseemly and will have the added benefit of helping you quickly discern who is worth talking to."

"You don't like Mr. Fitzroy."

He did not, but that was beside the point.

"I don't like you hiding your true opinions to please those inferior to you in taste and intellect. Good sense is in short supply, and it is a pity to pretend you don't have any."

She colored. "Since you believe I have such good sense, I will thank you not to lecture me. You may not care what others think, but I do not have that luxury." Her words came out in a frustrated rush.

"You care what Fitzroy thinks?"

"No, but I—" she shook her head. "I don't expect you to understand. It is different for you."

Edmund didn't understand but he wanted to. Why would an intelligent heiress who had declared herself uninterested in marriage hide her true self? Was it merely to please her mother? Or was there something else?

If Edmund did not agree to her plan was she doomed to always hiding? He glanced back at their disapproving shadow. He did not think Mrs. Aston could hear him but he leaned closer anyway.

"Miss Radforde, I have decided to agree to your plan."

Her eyebrows rose; her pursed mouth relaxed into a smile. "Truly?" The pure happiness in her voice was undeniable. Edmund felt like he had given her the key to her cage.

They reached the door to Hatchard's and Mrs. Aston joined them as they entered.

Brightly lit, lined with shelves, and containing that unique smell of paper, leather, and glue, the bookseller was an inviting oasis. Instead of focusing on the display with the latest titles, Edmund found himself watching Miss Radforde. There was much that needed to be said before they embarked on their ruse.

As she took in the shop, she smiled sweetly, as if greeting an old friend. Her eyes returned to him.

"I would like to see if they have the latest Curtis Botanical Magazine."

"Of course." Edmund gestured to the corner where the periodicals were kept. Mrs. Aston followed them but with less focus than before.

As they browsed the titles Miss Radforde spoke. "Mrs. Piper had a subscription to Curtis but since leaving school I have not had the opportunity to read one."

"Then I hope they have it," he said.

If she had been reading Curtis regularly that accounted for some of her knowledge. What else did she enjoy reading?

When Miss Radforde found the coveted magazine, her face brightened. She opened it and instantly appeared engrossed. Realizing he could not just look at her, Edmund plucked a copy of Ackerman's Repository and flipped through the pages without really seeing the words.

After several long minutes Mrs. Aston drifted away to examine the stationery and Edmund tried to concentrate on the page before him.

"You cannot tell anyone of our arrangement," Miss Radforde whispered, with her eyes still on the magazine.

Edmund smiled but did not look up. Her bluntness might be his favorite quality.

"I agree."

"Do you have a plan? For how to proceed?"

"To take you to every interesting place in your guidebook." He peeked up at her and was gratified by a swift glance from her gleaming blue eyes.

"Every interesting place is impractical," she teased.

"Then the places that you most wish to see."

"That is very generous of you." She turned the page of her magazine and he did the same though he had not read a word. "When we attend the same ball, you must dance with me, of course."

"I make it a habit not to attend balls. Unless you think it necessary for our ruse?" Edmund thought he wouldn't mind a ball if it meant dancing with Miss Radforde.

There was a brief pause. "If we are seen together during the day that should be sufficient," she reasoned aloud. "I would rather spend our evenings at lectures, though I don't think Mother will permit it."

"If she thinks my intentions sincere, won't she wish to encourage them?"

"Yes, but she might want me to make more conquests," she said bitterly.

"Well, you will just have to tell her that you wish to spend time with me."

Miss Radforde sighed. "Yes, I will."

Edmund could not interpret her sigh or her reluctance. This idea was hers.

"Do you suppose..." She paused long enough that Edmund looked up at her. She was chewing on her lip, her forehead furrowed.

"Suppose what?"

She looked up and met his eyes. "That spending time together is enough for people to believe we are forming an attachment?"

"It takes very little for gossips to matchmake. However, I believe we must appear to enjoy one another's company."

She raised her eyebrows.

"I know, it is a difficult proposition," Edmund teased.

"I do enjoy your company," she said.

He tried to ignore the heat creeping up his neck and tapped his chin as if in thought. "You should be sure to say as much when in the hearing of others. That should help our cause. You might gaze longingly at me on occasion. We might stand a little too close in public."

"Do be serious." She looked down at her magazine, flustered.

"I am quite serious. I have observed several courting couples and a certain obsession with proximity and long looks are *de rigueur*." Edmund's observations were limited to his brother George and a few couples in his parish, but he felt the principle correct.

"Oh."

"If you do not wish it, we do not need—"

"No, your reasoning is very sound and it should not be a hardship." Miss Radforde's voice was steady, but Edmund sensed her agitation.

What was the source of her disquiet? Did she find the idea of being close objectionable or the opposite? An experiment was in order.

He looked about. Mrs. Aston was paying for her stationery and he expected she would soon join them. He set aside his magazine.

"I shall demonstrate."

He closed the space between them until his chest brushed her shoulder. She peeked back at him, her blue eyes wide. He resisted the urge to look in them and looked down at the drawing of a lily instead. As if intent on the page, he leaned forward.

The movement brought their cheeks close. The tickle of her curls made his skin tingle. His neck flamed. The experiment was yielding a different result than he predicted. Her proximity was surprisingly affecting.

He swallowed thickly. "You see, it is simple. To an observer we look quite enamored." His whisper was rough.

"I see, most instructive," she murmured.

"Charity."

They both jumped, putting distance between them.

"Mrs. Aston." Edmund turned to the unwelcome arrival and tried to regain his composure.

"I was showing him the illustration," Miss Radforde stammered like a child caught stealing sweets.

"I do not think it as good as Miss Radforde's drawings," Edmund added, a little too loudly.

Mrs. Aston did not even glance at the magazine. She regarded them with narrow eyes. "We should be going," she said.

"Of course," Edmund replied. "Miss Radforde, let me purchase the magazine for you."

She thanked him as she handed the periodical over. He strode to the counter, grateful for some space from the two women. If Mrs. Aston was any metric, it did not seem there would be any difficulty in convincing society of an attachment. However, there was a real danger of fooling himself.

As he handed over his coins to the clerk, Edmund reminded himself he could not develop feelings for Miss Radforde—no matter how affecting her presence or interesting her conversation.

She had made her opinion of him and marriage quite clear. He was bound for America. She wished to be an independent spinster. Their arrangement was merely a convenient way to escape their mothers' plans. It could never be anything more.

Thirteen

As they left Hatchard's, Charity ignored Penelope and her disapproving looks. She ignored her on the drive back to Russell Square and as they said goodbye to Mr. Glenhaven. She would have continued ignoring her but once the door closed on the street, Penelope turned to her.

Charity raised her hand to forestall the censure.

"I am tired. There will be time enough to harangue me before the ball. Why don't you go and tell my mother about my failings."

Penelope's frown turned to shock. "That is not—Charity, you must know that I am not some spy."

Charity sighed and hugged the periodical Glenhaven had purchased to her chest. It would be pointless to remind Penelope that she had threatened to tell Mother everything. She would deny it, but reporting on Charity was part of her position as companion. Charity was glad she had not told her that the courtship would be a sham.

Penelope sighed. "Let us talk later, after we have rested."

Charity nodded and escaped up the stairs. Once in her room, she leaned against the door and took a deep breath. A slow smile spread over her face. Glenhaven had agreed. She would be spending many mornings exploring London with him. Her mind wandered over the day, all she had seen at Bullock's, their discussions, and their conversation in Hatchard's.

Her smile slipped.

She looked down at the Curtis Botanical Magazine and resisted the urge to turn to the page with the lily. She had not expected such a reaction when Mr. Glenhaven had stepped beside her.

She knew he meant nothing by standing so close and bringing his face near hers, but her body had still heated. His proximity should not have affected her. She had danced with men and walked beside them; she had even been in Mr. Glenhaven's arms, but it had never produced such a fluttering in her stomach.

Thanks to many conversations with her friends, it was easy for Charity to develop a theory. But she fought the logical conclusion. She could not possibly be infatuated with Mr. Glenhaven.

She did not have any of the other signs that she had observed in her friends. She was not preoccupied with him or anxious to see him again or about to wax poetic about his hair. No, there was another explanation.

His demonstration had surprised her. Her physical reaction was nothing but nerves and confusion. The more time they spent together, the more such things would become easier. Wouldn't they? She simply could not be infatuated with him; that would ruin everything.

Charity shook her head. She would not taint her victory with worry. She pushed away from the door and moved to her easel. Mother would be out until the evening and she itched to make a painting of the *banksia serrata*.

A few hours of painting would be a good distraction. As she retrieved her supplies, Charity recalled Mr. Glenhaven's encouragements. He was right; she needed to ask Mother for time to pursue her botanic studies.

What would he think of her paintings? Would he praise or censure? She suspected he would be honest and point out the flaws, regardless of her feelings.

She stopped and frowned. She should not be thinking of his opinions. Putting him from her mind, she applied herself completely to her painting. It took little effort to become engrossed in the project.

When they entered the ballroom that evening, Charity searched the crowd for Glenhaven. Though she had no reason to expect him to be in attendance, she couldn't help looking.

Even with her height, the crush of people made it impossible to survey the entire room. It was an ornate and modern space bright with beeswax candles, filled with fashionable people. She had already forgotten which earl or viscount owned the home.

"Charity, dear, do not gawk so. I daresay anyone worth meeting will make themselves known." Mother's voice bristled with censure. Charity dropped her eyes to her hands.

"Yes, Mother."

Mother led them through the room, searching for a place she thought best suited for observing and being observed. The progress was slow as they stopped to greet friends and acquaintances. Charity could not recall many of their names but soon found herself engaged to dance with a Mr. Simmons and Mr. Dyer.

"I am glad he asked you," Mother said after the Dyers walked away. "But let us hope for some more eligible offers."

Charity nodded.

"Such as that gentleman," Mother gestured toward the windows on the left. "That is Viscount Banham's heir."

Charity followed Mother's direction and was surprised to recognize Mr. Fitzroy. He stood surveying the room lazily. He was not as tall as Glenhaven, but his features were more in fashion. No doubt many thought him handsome. His dress was impeccable, his bearing distinguished, though Charity preferred more muted colors and a less haughty air. He was to be a viscount? Glenhaven had not mentioned that detail.

"He is looking this way. Charity, dear, capture his attention."

Even if Charity had the first notion how she might accomplish that task, she had no desire for Mr. Fitzroy's attention. But it did not matter, for he had recognized her. His lazy smile grew and he inclined his head in acknowledgment. To her horror, he began to move toward them.

"He is moving this way," Mother said with barely contained excitement. "Would that we could arrange an introduction."

"We were introduced to Mr. Fitzroy this morning," Penelope said. "He is a friend of Mr. Glenhaven."

"Well, how very fortunate." Mother smiled like a cat delivering its latest kill. "I knew Mr. Glenhaven would be a useful conquest."

Charity agreed with Mother but introducing her to Mr. Fitzroy was the least useful thing Glenhaven had done. They all turned to greet the soon-to-be viscount as he approached.

"Miss Radforde, what an unlooked for pleasure," Mr. Fitzroy said warmly.

"Mother, may I introduce Mr. Fitzroy?"

They conducted the usual pleasantries and made the obligatory comments about the crowds and the weather. Fitzroy was all that was charming and complimented Charity prettily. She might have been flattered if she cared at all for the man's good opinion. Before they separated, Charity had agreed to a dance.

"Now I call that an excellent result," Mother said when they were alone. "Charity, dear, you must not be so quiet while dancing. A man as refined as Mr. Fitzroy will expect his wife to have wit and vivacity."

"But not intelligence," Charity murmured.

Mother was too in raptures to hear but Penelope barely stifled a giggle. Charity met her eyes and they shared a smile. She hated fighting with her friend, but the middle of a ballroom was not the place for their conversation. There were more people to greet and dance invitations to accept.

All too soon Charity was escorted to the dance floor, leaving Penelope behind with Mother. In Bath, Charity had been the one to stand on the sidelines and watch as Penelope flitted from partner to partner.

Penelope adored dancing and the men adored her. It was unjust that she now had to sit with the old matrons, her head covered in a dull cap, and watch the festivities. But that was the role of a companion and no wishing could change it.

Mr. Simmons was a broad man whose conversation consisted of studied compliments and whispered comments about their fellow dancers. Mr. Dyer proved to be a more interesting conversationalist but a much worse dancer. While in motion, his concentration was entirely on his steps, leaving large silences between them. She could not imagine Mr. Glenhaven being so awkward.

Charity wondered what Mr. Dyer would say if she shared her love of museums. Mr. Glenhaven had said sharing such information would help her discern who was worth associating with.

But what would she do with such knowledge? Mother certainly put no stock in Charity's opinion. But perhaps revealing her true interests would lead to less dance invitations. Mother need never know why the men had changed their minds. But how long before she worked out the reason why, and how long would the lecture be when she discovered it?

After three dull dances, Charity was willing to take the risk. It was Fitzroy that gave her the opportunity to follow Glenhaven's advice.

"Now, Miss Radforde," he said as he escorted her to the line, "isn't this much better than a dusty museum?"

"Bullock's is not dusty," she said tentatively.

"Oh?" Fitzroy quirked an eyebrow.

"Indeed, it is a fascinating place," she added more strongly.

"Come Miss Radforde, Glenhaven is not here, you can tell me how truly dull you found it and him." He winked.

No doubt it was meant to be charming, but Charity thought it condescending.

"I requested we visit the museum. I have a great interest in natural philosophy."

Fitzroy's eyebrows rose comically high, but he quickly mastered his expression. "How singular."

Riding the elation of speaking her mind, she continued. "And Mr. Glenhaven is not dull. His conversation is very engaging."

The dance separated them. Charity's quick heartbeat was due to more than the steps. She was proud of her audacity. What would Glenhaven think when she told him?

When they returned Fitzroy was smiling again. "I am pleased to know that in addition to being a fine dancer, you enjoy the exercise of your mind."

"You are?" Charity could not hide her surprise.

"Yes, so many young women think only of fashion and dancing. It is refreshing to find one with an appreciation for more."

She was too confused to provide an immediate reply. Was Fitzroy sincere or was this another type of flattery? The dance soon made conversation impossible. When they had gone down the line and could speak once more, Fitzroy surprised her again by asking what she enjoyed about Bullock's.

She answered cautiously, speaking only of the wonder of the Pantherion and nothing of the *banksia serrata,* her botanical painting, or her interest in learning about plants from around the world.

Fitzroy appeared to listen intently and asked thoughtful questions. The conversation for the rest of the set was unexpectedly enjoyable and her pleasure must have showed for Mother praised her "fine smiles" when she returned.

"I expect Mr. Fitzroy will be visiting us very soon," Mother said. "It is a pity you are promised to Mr. Glenhaven on Monday. But then if you are unavailable, it might increase Fitzroy's interest. Such men don't want things that are too easily won."

After several similar raptures, Penelope spoke. "Charity, do you wish to go to the retiring room?"

"Yes, indeed."

Mother waved them away with a smile.

Arm in arm, they weaved through the room. The crush of people had only grown in the hours since their arrival. The retiring room was blessedly empty and Charity collapsed into a settee. Penelope gave her a sympathetic smile as she sat beside her.

"Tired?"

"Exhausted. Do you think Mother will let us depart soon?" Charity asked.

Penelope's smile grew. "Aren't you promised for the next dance?"

Charity made a face. "I could pretend to twist an ankle."

"Your mother will see through that."

"True." Charity sighed. "I danced with a viscount's heir. Surely that has earned me a reprieve."

"I think you are the only woman in this ballroom who thinks dancing with a handsome lord a punishment."

"He isn't a lord yet."

Penelope ignored her correction. "And you appeared to be enjoying Mr. Fitzroy's company."

She could not refute the claim. "He was an interesting partner."

"More interesting than Mr. Glenhaven?" Penelope raised her eyebrows.

"Mother certainly thinks so."

Charity bumped her shoulder, good naturedly. It felt lovely to tease with her friend once again.

Penelope turned serious. "She might change her mind once I share what I have learned about him."

"What have you discovered?" Charity sat up and looked at her friend.

"They say Fitzroy is a rake and a fortune hunter. He only pays attention to rich women and is as changeable as the weather."

Charity's stomach sank. She had naively thought Fitzroy might be different. He had only feigned interest in her conversation about the museum because he wanted to ingratiate himself. But like all the rest, he cared only for her money, not her person.

"Who supplied such information?"

Penelope shrugged. "Chaperones have ample opportunity to talk while our charges dance. The others are a wealth of information."

"And did the other chaperones have anything to say about Mr. Glenhaven?"

"Only that his family is well-respected and he is relatively unknown to London." Penelope paused and took a deep breath. "I was perhaps too quick to judge him."

Charity accepted the small olive branch and reached for Penelope's hand. Relief washed over her as her friend entangled their fingers and squeezed. It was soothing to no longer be at odds and know that she was not mistaken about Glenhaven.

"Thank you, Penelope, for watching over me. I know you would rather be dancing than playing spy."

Penelope patted their joined hands. "You must not worry about me. My purpose in London is not to seek my own enjoyment. I have accepted my fate. Don't look at me like that, it is true. I had my carefree youth, now I am committed to ensuring that no young woman is deceived as I was."

"You are a fierce protector," Charity teased.

"I only want what is best for you. If that means marriage to a good man, then I will be happy."

"I have no wish to marry."

"Wishes can change. The heart is not easily governed."

The sentiment was so similar to Mr. Glenhaven's that it gave Charity pause. She had seen love do strange things to people and had always assumed she was immune to such passions. But that was before Mr. Glenhaven had stood so close that she could smell the sandalwood musk of his soap and a swarm of *lepidoptera* had erupted in her stomach.

"Please don't be angry," Penelope said, misinterpreting Charity's long silence. "I only mean that it can be easy to confuse ardor with love. The weakness of the flesh can lead you into great folly. I don't want you to make my mistakes."

Charity swallowed as she added the information to her theory.

So what she felt at Hatchard's was mere weakness, not infatuation? She would need to be careful not to mistake her body's reactions for something else. That they were pretending to an attachment would make the task more difficult. It was fortunate that she and Glenhaven perfectly understood the nature of their arrangement.

"I will be careful," Charity said. "I promise."

"And I promise to keep vigilant watch. But I won't apologize for speaking my mind when I think you are in error."

"I understand."

On impulse, Charity hugged her friend. "Thank you."

Her previous frustrations with Penelope's protectiveness had flown like a swallow in winter. Her friend only wished to help her, to spare her from heartache and poor decisions. With Penelope's and Glenhaven's help, Charity would be able to enjoy her time in London.

Fourteen

AFTER SPENDING Saturday with Miss Radforde, Edmund arrived at Soho Square with more confidence and a different plan for Sir Joseph's breakfast. Miss Radforde had shown him the wisdom of seeking other patrons. The house was bursting with men of learning and wealth; surely he could convince one of them to support his expedition. And perhaps once he secured their support, Sir Joseph would follow.

Within a quarter-hour of his arrival, Edmund was fortunate to be introduced to the Scottish botanist, Robert Brown. Though in his forties, the man's curly hair and robust voice made him seem much younger.

Edmund eagerly asked Mr. Brown about his time as a naturalist aboard the *HMS Navigator* and the two were soon sharing techniques for collecting specimens. Brown's mind for detail was astonishing. As he was explaining his use of microscopes to examine plants, Miss Sarah Banks approached.

"Oh, Mr. Brown," she said. "I am so pleased you have met Mr. Glenhaven. Are you giving him advice on how to catalogue the bounty of a new continent?"

"Ack, what's this you say, Miss Sarah?" Mr. Brown turned inquisitive eyes on Edmund. "Are you going on an expedition?"

"I am putting one together, sir. I wish to explore the interior of North America."

"What? By yourself? A young fellow like you?"

Edmund tried not to let the incredulity discourage him.

"Now, Mr. Brown, do not be so surprised," Miss Sarah chided. "Sir Joseph was only three and twenty when he sailed off to Labrador."

"Yes, but he was with the Royal Navy. Expeditions are much easier when someone else is doing the navigating."

"Well, I am sure that Mr. Glenhaven will hire expert guides once he is in America."

"That is my plan, ma'am."

"Of course he will need guides," Mr. Brown agreed heartily. "But you will also be wanting a gardener to help with collection. An artist is essential as well, one specially trained in botanic illustration would be best. I can ask Bauer if he might recommend someone."

"An excellent idea," Miss Sarah said. "Of course he will need to pay all of them." She smiled at Edmund with a twinkle in her eye. "Have you made any progress in finding supporters for your expedition?"

Mr. Brown burst into boisterous laughter, drawing the attention of others in the room. "Ah, now I see your plan, woman." He clapped Edmund on the back. "Are you in need of funds, son?"

"I am in search of patrons. I had hoped the Royal Society might sponsor me." Edmund could not believe how quickly the conversation had come to this point.

"But my brother has other things on his mind," Miss Sarah said.

"He has much to occupy him," Mr. Brown agreed. "Still, if he sees potential in Mr. Glenhaven, I am sure he will give him an opportunity. Now don't scoff, Miss Sarah. Most of the scientific men in London owe their success to your brother. Still," Mr. Brown pulled at his chin. "I think Sir James might be interested in speaking with you."

"I would be most grateful if you would arrange an introduction." Edmund wanted to ask if he meant Sir James Edward Smith, the president of the Linnean Society, but was afraid of looking foolish.

"Not so fast, young man. Let us discuss your plans and I will determine if they are sound enough to proceed."

"Of course." Edmund bobbed his head enthusiastically.

Mr. Brown smiled as he put an arm around Edmund and led him deeper into the house. The building stretched further back than he expected. They entered a large room, empty of other guests. Each wall was covered in shelves that were a mosaic of red and green. The red leather-bound books were almost overwhelmed by the plants, both living and pressed between glass, that occupied the shelves. Edmund scarcely knew where to look. He couldn't wait to tell Miss Radforde about the room.

Mr. Brown went to a shelf and began to rifle through rolled-up parchment.

"Should we be here?" Edmund asked. The room did not look open to the public.

"Never fear. Among other things, I am Sir Joseph's librarian."

His mind at ease, Edmund wandered to a desk in the center of the room. A large microscope was surrounded by glass slides. It was much finer than the microscope at his parsonage. What plant were they examining? He leaned forward to look in the eyepiece.

"Ah, here we are."

Edmund straightened and turned. Brown waved a large rolled-up paper at him and Edmund hastened to help open it on a nearby table.

"Now, show me where you plan to go."

The paper was a map of the American interior. Though recently made, it contained large blank spaces of undocumented territory. Those blank spaces quickened Edmund's heart. His expedition would add new plants and new understanding to the world.

Brown was one of the few men who knew what that felt like. His surveys of New Holland had opened and documented the southern continent's flora. If the botanist thought Edmund's plan sound, any number of men might be willing to back him.

Hours later, when Edmund finally left the house, his mind was like a beehive swarming with thoughts and hopes. After careful questioning, Brown had agreed to speak with others on his behalf. It was not yet a sponsorship, but it was a giant step in the right direction.

How different the breakfast might have been if he hadn't heeded Miss Radforde's advice? He might have sat at Sir Joseph's heels, hoping for a scrap of attention and come away disappointed. He could not wait to tell her the result of her counsel.

He arrived at his parents' elegant town house in excellent spirits. Sophy greeted him at the door, her dimple flashing as she smiled up at him.

"Oh, I bet I can guess where you have been." The green in her eyes sparkled in mischief as she laced her fingers around his elbow. "Please, tell me all about her."

Edmund frowned. "About who?"

Sophy rolled her eyes and batted at his arm. She was nearly seventeen, more woman than child, but she was still his little sister.

"Don't be coy. You have been out to see Miss Radforde."

"No, I haven't."

"Then where were you all morning? Mama was upset you did not join us at services again until I mentioned that you might have gone to St George's to see Miss Radforde."

Edmund might have shared his good fortune, but Sophy had already proven untrustworthy. He had no doubt that she had told their parents that he was searching for a wife.

"I shan't tell you, yet." Edmund tapped his nose.

Sophy grinned and tapped her nose in return.

They entered the drawing room to find Mama at her correspondence and Father reading the paper. Done up in yellows and greens, the room reminded him of flowering cowslips on a country road.

"Look who has returned," Sophy announced.

Mama and Father glanced up. After a nod, Father returned to his paper.

"Edmund, there you are," Mama said. She waved a card in her hand. "The Burkes have invited us to a garden party on Thursday. Shall I accept for you?"

"Of course I cannot go," Sophy murmured before slumping into a seat.

"I would love to accompany you, Mama, but I am promised to Miss Radforde that morning."

He had not made plans with Miss Radforde for Thursday, but he would think of something.

Mama's eyes lit up. "Oh? Another outing?" The curious excitement in her voice made Edmund feel a little guilty.

"Yes."

Mama raised her eyebrows, clearly hoping for more information.

"He also saw her this morning!" Sophy declared.

Edmund shot her a look but chose not to contradict her. He could hardly tell the truth.

"Truly?"

Mama clearly wished for more information about his morning, but he would not give it. He wasn't lying to them, not really. He was just omitting facts. Just as he was omitting the reason he was in London and his plans for the future. He hoped, with Mr. Brown's help, to soon tell them everything.

"I will send your apologies," Mama eventually said.

"Thank you," he replied.

When the truth came out, Mama would be disappointed. She would worry for his safety just as she did for Kit, though America was much safer than the Navy.

Edmund glanced at Father, but his face was covered by the paper. It did not seem that he was listening at all. Despite telling himself that his father's opinion did not matter, that he had given up that right the day he refused to help Edmund find a living, Edmund still wanted his approval.

He couldn't help wondering if Father would be proud or angry when he learned about the expedition. A part of him wanted to be vindicated, for Father to finally understand why he had chosen the church instead of a government post.

There was no way to know his father's opinion until all was disclosed and then it would be too late for it to truly matter.

The next morning, Edmund bounded from the carriage before it had fully stopped at Radforde House. He was escorting the ladies to the British Museum, and though he had been several times, he was anxious to see it through Miss Radforde's eyes. As he made his greetings to the mother, his gaze kept straying to the daughter.

Her hair appeared particularly red in the light shining from the window and her striking blue eyes met his. The corners of her lips turned up in welcome and he flattered himself to think she was pleased to see him.

He had never known the pleasure that could be conferred by a pretty woman anxious for his company. Impatiently, he waited for the formalities to finish so they might speak privately. Upon exiting the house, Edmund turned to the ladies.

"I thought we might walk the short distance to the museum?"

Miss Radforde looked at Mrs. Aston who smiled and nodded. Was walking the key to Mrs. Aston's good favor?

He offered his arm and Miss Radforde slipped her hand around his forearm. To all the world, they looked like a couple out for a stroll. They had only taken a few steps away from Mrs. Aston when Miss Radforde spoke lowly.

"You are doing it a little too brown, Mr. Glenhaven."

"Pardon?"

"Your enthusiasm this morning was marked. I assure you, Mother and Penelope don't require such a display."

Edmund pinched his eyebrows together. He had not been thinking of their ruse; he had almost forgotten it in his eagerness to see her. But it was clearly in the forefront of her mind. Had her smiles all been for show?

His pleasure soured.

"You mustn't frown like that either," she said.

"Pray tell, what expressions am I allowed?"

Now she frowned. "Are you angry with me?"

Edmund was but he couldn't properly say why. So he shook his head and tried to recapture his previous enthusiasm.

"Let us talk of something else," he said. "Did you enjoy the ball?"

"It was a ball." She shrugged as if no other explanation was needed.

"Did you dance?" Edmund couldn't help being curious. Had she liked any of her partners?

"That is the stated purpose of a ball."

"But not its true purpose."

"Oh? And what is the true purpose of a ball?" she asked archly.

"To see and be seen, to share gossip, to judge ones neighbors, to assess potential marriage partners." Edmund listed them off quickly. He had given a great deal of thought to the role of the ball in modern society.

"I saw and was seen, indulged in some minor gossip, and found no potential partner."

The declaration made his step a little lighter.

"How was your breakfast in Soho Square?" she asked.

"It was a breakfast." He flashed a smile at her. "I took your advice and looked beyond Sir Joseph. I was introduced to Mr. Robert Brown."

"The botanist?" From her tone he knew she understood the significance of the acquaintance. "I have seen the results of his time in New Holland. He will be a great help in your planning. How did you meet? What was he like? Will he help you?"

Edmund loved her eager curiosity. He shared all that had transpired. She listened with what, he was coming to realize, was her characteristic attentiveness and asked several insightful questions. He was explaining the proposed route when she sighed wistfully.

Edmund paused. "What?"

She shrugged. "Nothing. It is just... you are fortunate to have such an adventure before you."

"Fortune favors the bold and your advice made me bold. Without your assistance, I would still be hoping for Sir Joseph to notice me."

Color rose to her cheeks and she ducked her head. Then she looked up and changed the subject.

"Ah, here we are."

She was right; they had reached their destination.

The museum was housed in the old residence of the Duke of Montague and built in the French palace style. A twelve-foot wall separated the grounds from Russell Street and stopped at the large square tower that marked the edge of the courtyard. The entrance was under a pediment and small portico. It was a grand old edifice, but Edmund preferred the modern lines of Somerset House. The multiple chimneys pointing into the sky caught his particular attention.

He nudged her. "Shall we count the fireplaces?"

She tittered. The porter bowed to them as they walked through the gate and into the gardens of the courtyard. The day was mild and several people wandered about the even paths.

"What do you wish to see first?" he asked. "I am sure your book provided you with some direction."

"I thought perhaps the bird collection on the upper floors. Mrs. Aston likes birds and I wanted to see the black swan and the picture of the dodo."

"That sounds capital."

They entered the building and made their way through the hall and to the staircase. Though the stairs were wide, she stayed beside him as they climbed. At the first landing, she paused to take in the painting on the ceiling. Edmund followed her gaze. What a curious mind she possessed and a unique ability to notice what others might ignore.

A half-naked Apollo with laurel leaves in his hair stood next to a youth who was gesturing toward two large white horses.

"It is Phaeton petitioning Apollo to drive his chariot," Miss Radforde said.

"As I recall, it was a disastrous ride," he replied.

"Yes, he froze the earth and then burned it before being killed by Zeus."

"A tale to discourage hubris, I believe," Mrs. Aston added.

"Or to explain what they did not understand," Miss Radforde returned. "Ovid claimed Phaeton made Africa a desert with his poor driving."

The young ladies continued to climb and discuss the meaning of the myth, leaving Edmund to trail behind.

His own circumstances made him sympathize with Phaeton. They both had an absent father and a monumental task. Was a young, ambitious man, eager to prove himself, capable of steering the chariot of knowledge? Would he fail just as spectacularly in his endeavor? Edmund feared he would be struck down and thrown from the halls of learned men for incompetence. But he wasn't driving alone, surely with Mr. Brown's help, he would succeed.

They strode through several rooms, paying little heed to the art, manuscripts, South Pacific curiosities, and collected shells. They paused in the room with the minerals and discussed soil types.

Edmund wished he had a notebook and pencil to record his thoughts. Miss Radforde had given him an idea on how to improve his soil collection method. Since the types of soil in the Rocky Mountains would have a great impact on the types of plants able to thrive there, accurate measurements were crucial to his success.

His mind was still occupied with rocks and minerals when they entered the room full of stuffed birds. Unlike the Pantherion, they were all carefully labeled and prosaically positioned. He paused beside Miss Radforde as she pulled out her notebook and began to sketch. Lost in his thoughts, he wasn't sure how long they remained in companionable silence.

"Mr. Glenhaven, you are frowning again."

Her whisper pulled him back like a diver rising to the water's surface. The world around him clarified.

"Apologies, I was—"

"Lost in thought, I know."

Her lips quirked and it was easy to replace his dour expression with a smile.

"What were you thinking of?" she asked.

"The expedition, soil samples, the skills my fellow travelers will need to make it a success," he replied, trying to recount the paths where his mind had wandered.

"Have you an idea of who you would like to accompany you?" she asked.

"I have been so isolated in the countryside that I know of only a few likely candidates. I imagine my sponsors will tell me who I should take."

She frowned as she closed her notebook.

"You think I should choose my own companions?"

"No. I was just thinking..." She glanced down at her notebook. "You will be discovering entirely new species and seeing new vistas, but I will be here." She gestured vaguely at the room full of static birds.

He understood her wistfulness. He had felt it himself when listening to Kit recount his travels around the world. It was like he was waiting for his life to begin while others were living theirs.

"There is much to be explored here in England. You might make a complete study of some county or other," he suggested.

"I might. Perhaps in a few years when I come of age and gain my independence," she said with a note of defeat.

She ended the conversation by moving to a case with several bird nests.

Edmund watched her with his hands behind his back. She flipped to a new page in her notebook and began to write. It was a terrible shame for a mind like hers to be idle. She simply must find a project worthy of her intellect. Perhaps he could help her find something in London?

Mrs. Aston came up beside him. He offered her a smile, but she did not return it.

"What did you say to make her melancholy?"

"Nothing."

She raised a skeptical brow. Edmund settled for something close to the truth.

"We were discussing her taking on some kind of scientific survey."

Mrs. Aston nodded as if that explained everything. "You should not have dissuaded her. She is more than capable, and she enjoys such work." Her tone was that of a disapproving teacher.

"I said nothing against it. Indeed, I encouraged her. She has a rare eye for detail."

This seemed to catch the companion off guard. She glanced at Miss Radforde, who was staring carefully at the nests, then looked back to him.

"You would want your wife to have such a pastime?"

The question was a bit forward, but he answered. "If she wished, I would buy her all the paint and paper she could use and even arrange the travel."

Mrs. Aston hummed but he could not tell if she was satisfied with his answer. Though the companion made him uncomfortable, Edmund was glad Miss Radforde had such a champion. Would she ask other suitors the same question? What would they say?

The idea that Miss Radforde might marry a man that did not appreciate and encourage her talents was unwelcome. She did not belong presiding over house parties and balls. No doubt she agreed, no doubt that was why she wished to remain unmarried. If she was an independent spinster, she would not need a husband's support or permission.

The strange pressure on Edmund's heart eased as he imagined Miss Radforde in her own establishment surrounded by her friends and spending her days tramping through the countryside drawing its wonders.

When he returned from his journey, they would discuss their findings. Indeed if she was a spinster, they might spend many afternoons together. They might even....

His thoughts stuttered and came to a halt. A realization hit him like a fall from a tree. She was pretty and kind, curious and insightful. He esteemed her above all other women of his acquaintance. Though he did not think he loved her, the evidence led to an obvious conclusion.

She would make him an excellent wife.

What an inconvenient thought!

The lady had no interest in marriage, and he was in no position to take on a wife. He was leaving for America. Trying to court her now would be foolish. All thoughts of marriage must wait until his triumphant return.

When he had gained respect and renown, he might approach her. Then he wouldn't be a mere country parson or an overlooked third son. He might even be a baronet, if he gained a title, as Sir Joseph had from his discoveries. Then she might consider him worthy of more than a pretend courtship.

But when he returned from America, there was no guarantee that Miss Radforde would still be a miss. There were many years of hard work before him. Could a woman so wonderful, so sought after, truly remain single?

Perhaps it would be better to approach the subject before his departure. But any pursuit would be futile, for Mrs. Radforde thought her daughter could reach higher and Miss Radforde did not want a husband.

He must reconcile himself to the truth.

Miss Radforde had asked for his help in eluding suitors. He could not betray her trust by becoming one of them. He had agreed to pretend with her, not pursue her.

Fifteen

Charity looked out on the residences of Mayfair and tried not to frown. The entire point of her arrangement with Mr. Glenhaven was to avoid insipid outings like riding about Hyde Park, so why had he decided to take her there?

If they had been alone in the carriage, Charity would have asked him to explain his reasons. She glanced at Penelope sitting across from her on the seat. Why had Mr. Glenhaven been so keen for her to accompany them?

They were in an open carriage; it was not necessary to bring a chaperone to the park. Mother had broadly hinted that Penelope could be left at home, but Glenhaven had specifically included her.

Something had changed in Penelope's attitude toward Mr. Glenhaven since their visit to the British Museum. Instead of being the stoic shadow, she was smiling and talking with him. He seemed equally engaged by her conversation.

Did he prefer her? All the young men in Bath had always favored her pleasing figure and charming manner. Charity had never minded that she was considered the lesser because it kept her from dull conversations. But conversations with Mr. Glenhaven were not dull.

Although his current conversation with Penelope was not particularly interesting. They were discussing their families, precisely the kind of topic that Charity never engaged in—she cared more about a man's opinion on von Humboldt than the ages of his siblings.

"Is not that exciting, Charity?" Penelope asked.

"Yes, very exciting," she said, hoping to conceal her ignorance of the actual question.

"What in particular excites you about it?" Mr. Glenhaven pressed, a spark in his eye.

Charity lifted her chin and matched his gaze. "Oh, I think all of it is quite thrilling."

His lips quirked and her ears grew hot. It was clear he knew she had stopped paying attention.

"I did not know you enjoyed driving in the park." Charity changed the subject.

"I confess I do not enjoy it, but fortunately a drive is only a small part of today's activities."

"Oh?" Charity sat up straighter and glanced at Penelope. Her companion's smile drooped into a frown.

"Mr. Glenhaven, you told Mrs. Radforde that we were driving in the park," Penelope said primly.

"And so we shall. We will enter at Chesterfield Gate and exit at Hyde Park Corner."

Charity smiled. That route only took in a tiny section of the park.

"Where are we really going?" she asked.

He grinned like a kid about to open a present. "The London Botanic Garden."

"Truly?" She leaned toward him, her entire body alive with excitement at the prospect of exploring the botanic garden.

"Mr. Glenhaven, I must protest," Penelope said. "This was not the agreed destination."

While Charity knew Penelope was right to object to the subterfuge, she hoped she would not insist they do nothing but ride about the park.

"Mrs. Aston, I did not mean to cause alarm, only surprise." He smiled broadly at Charity and it warmed her to her toes. His attention to her pleasure was gratifying.

"Surely there is nothing wrong with visiting a garden in addition to riding in the park," Charity said and turned to her friend with pleading eyes.

Penelope's lips became a thin line and Charity was sure she would deny the detour, but instead she sighed and nodded.

"I suppose there can be no real harm."

Charity barely restrained herself from clapping in excitement, but she was not able to restrain her smile. She looked out on the streets with more pleasure than before.

The short journey to Hyde Park was easily borne and Charity grinned at everyone they passed. Observers likely thought her excessively pleased with her company and their supposition would not be entirely incorrect.

When they exited at Hyde Park Corner, they slowed to let a small column of foot soldiers pass on their way to the barracks. The yeasty smell of ale filled the air and Charity furrowed her brow.

"There is a brewery nearby," Mr. Glenhaven answered her unasked question and pointed to a building on the right.

Immediately after the brewery, they turned down Sloane Street and in a few moments the botanic garden came into view. It was a long garden enclosed by an iron railing that paralleled the road.

As they drove beside it, Charity looked inside at the neatly laid out beds. She nearly bounced in her seat with excitement at the sight of the glass conservatory, hothouses, and cottage forming a square in the center.

Mr. Glenhaven explained that the garden was expressly designed to foster the science of botany and horticulture. There were lectures in the library on Monday and Thursday. On the advice of Mr. Brown, he had become a subscribing member.

When they reached the gate, they only waited a moment before the porter emerged and opened it and waved them through. The carriage came to a stop before the library, a cottage-style building that seemed at home with the abundance of plants.

Charity could hardly wait to be assisted out of the carriage. She beamed down at Mr. Glenhaven as he offered his hand. When she was on the ground beside him, he did not immediately let go.

"You are pleased with the surprise?" he asked.

"Yes."

"And will you countenance another?"

She nodded. What other surprise did he have planned? He turned to assist Penelope from the carriage. Charity, too impatient to wait, took a few steps toward the ornamental shrubs. But before she could draw close enough to examine them, Mr. Glenhaven called to her.

"Miss Radforde, are you ready?"

She turned and crossed the few steps to them. She was reaching for his arm almost before he offered it. They walked in companionable silence. He did not interrupt her observations, allowing her to drink in the plants without commentary.

They came across two older women sitting before a plant, two umbrellas shading them from the climbing sun. The shorter and thinner one was sketching the plant while the plumper one read a book. The reader glanced up and briefly acknowledged them.

Could that be her someday? Quietly spending her morning making a study with a friend beside her? Charity glanced back at Penelope. Would she wish for such an arrangement? It was hard to imagine Penelope sitting and reading a book so contentedly. Perhaps Rosamund might be prevailed upon to sit with her instead. Charity smiled at her thoughts. Like Elaine, she was giving in to fancy.

Their steps brought them further into the garden and to a small pond full of aquatic plants. Under the shade of an awning, three chairs sat before the water, along with an easel and small table of painting supplies. Charity wondered where the owners had gone.

"I thought you might enjoy making a study while we are here," Mr. Glenhaven said.

Eyes wide, she glanced between his smiling face and the empty chairs.

"This is for me?" she asked.

"We can move the chairs to whatever you wish to study. I thought the aquatic plants might interest you."

"They do, thank you."

She settled into the seat, barely able to contain her excitement. She looked at the plants before her—a riot of greens, yellows, purples, and white—and deliberated what to study. The bright yellow of the marsh marigold, with its heart-shaped leaves and complicated flower seemed a good challenge.

Despite the large paper and easel he had provided, she reached into her reticule and pulled out her small notebook. It would be best to make a preliminary sketch.

Mr. Glenhaven and Penelope also sat, but Charity barely paid them any mind as she began her study. The drone of their voices, like the buzzing of a beehive on a summer day, faded into the background. Her earlier worries about Mr. Glenhaven's preference had disappeared in her joy at his thoughtfulness.

Charity had completed her preliminary sketch and was taking off her gloves so she might start to paint, when she felt a tap on her shoulder. She glanced up to see Penelope standing behind her.

"I am going to take a turn about the gardens," she said.

"Of course, whatever you wish," Charity replied.

Penelope looked at Mr. Glenhaven and then back at her with raised eyebrows. Charity looked over and realized he was engrossed in reading a small book.

She wasn't sure of Penelope's meaning. Was she warning her about being alone with him or commenting on his choice of occupation? Though they had made up, Charity had not told Penelope of her arrangement with Mr. Glenhaven, and she wasn't sure she should.

Penelope was her chaperone now, not her confidant. What might she say to Mother about this morning? Would she tell of their stop in the garden? Would she report that they had sat near each other but had seemed more interested in the plants?

As Penelope began to walk away, Charity nudged Mr. Glenhaven's arm.

"Hmmm?" He did not look up from his book.

"I think Penelope suspects something," Charity whispered.

This caused him to look up. "I beg your pardon?"

Charity indicated her friend's retreating back. "I think she might know that this is all a sham."

He furrowed his brow. "How?"

"Well, you aren't exactly acting like a suitor."

"Are you unhappy with—"

"No! This is wonderful! I can't think of a better way to spend the morning. But you must admit, it is not exactly traditional."

He shrugged. "I think your friend knows your interests and will find me catering to them evidence of affection."

Charity realized that she had made that very assumption. Was this all for show then? A way to convince Penelope and others they were courting? Certainly he had given some thought to her pleasure, but kindness was not love.

She bit her lip. "Yes, I am sure you are right."

"May I see your sketches?" he asked.

She looked down at the book in her hands. She hadn't let many people see its contents. She wasn't embarrassed by her work; she just didn't know many people who were interested in it. Wordlessly, she offered it to him.

He shook his head. "No, let us look at them together."

The gravel skittered as he pulled his chair closer to hers. Their shoulders touched and she felt the same heat she had experienced at Hatchard's. She swallowed thickly and turned her attention to her notebook.

His bare hand brushed hers and sent a shiver up her arm. Biting her lip, she told herself such physical reactions should be ignored but her mind was too busy listening to her body. It was like sitting too close to a fire. He leaned closer, his face inches away. His breath made goosebumps rise along her neck.

She inhaled shakily.

"Is this how a suitor would act?" he murmured.

The words took a moment to sink in but when they did, disappointment washed over her and doused the fire. His proximity was all for show. It meant nothing.

She shifted slightly away from him and tried to focus on something, anything else.

"I drew this while at school," she said, ignoring his question.

"It is incredibly detailed," he said, leaning closer to the page. "How did you learn?"

She took a breath, feeling better now that he had shifted away.

"My teacher, Miss Minerva, always encouraged us in our talents."

"I thought Mrs. Piper was your teacher?"

"Mrs. Piper is the proprietress of the school and became our teacher after Miss Minerva married. It was Miss Minerva that showed me *A Curious Herbal* and pointed out that it was made by Mrs. Blackwell."

"Blackwell's Herbal is unmatched for its detail and accuracy, a good model for you. Is that when you first formed your plan to live as a spinster?"

He flipped the page to her next sketch. It was a lime tree, with particular detail paid to the leaves. With his eyes on the page it was easier for her to answer his question.

"I don't know. I was certainly impressed with Mrs. Blackwell's work and wished to embark on a similar project. But the idea has come slowly. As I have considered my future these last couple months, the desire has grown."

He hummed in response and turned the page. This time he asked her about her sketch of a wren, and they passed several long moments discussing small birds. Finally, he turned the page and looked up.

"What do your parents think of your plans?"

The sudden and personal nature of the question caught her off balance. She shrugged.

"I have not told them, but I can guess what my mother will say. I am not sure about my father. We don't communicate often."

"He is not in London?"

"He had business on the Continent. We expect he will return late summer."

He looked back down at the notebook. "And what will you do if they both insist you marry?"

For any other man the question would be impertinent, but with Glenhaven, honesty felt natural.

"I guess if I cannot convince them of my sincerity, I will have to put parental loyalty aside and refuse them."

"And do you think you will be able to do that?"

Charity didn't know. She wasn't even able to tell her mother that she wished to read instead of do needlepoint. Could she really defy her parents over the subject of marriage? But it was precisely because marriage was important that she should defy them. A husband was for life.

"When will you tell your parents about your expedition?" she answered his question with her own.

"Once I have everything arranged," he said gruffly.

"Are you worried they will disapprove?"

"My father's opinion of me can only rise."

Charity frowned. "Surely, that is not true. You are intelligent and ambitious with a respectable profession; he must think highly of you."

"That is kind of you to say." He paused and looked at her notebook. His thumb absently rubbed the paper. "I am a disappointment because I didn't follow the path he chose for me." He looked up and met her gaze, his eyes bright.

"I am sure he will be proud of your explorations," she said.

"Perhaps." He shrugged. "But it will likely disappoint my mother. She wishes me married. Of course, taking on a wife now is impossible. I will be away for many years." He looked at her as if expecting her to argue the point, but there was nothing to argue.

She nodded. "Quite impossible in your situation." Why had such an obvious fact left her feeling cold?

He looked back at the notebook.

"Apologies, I am keeping you from your study." He pushed the notebook into her hands.

Charity didn't wish to end the conversation; she loved to make her studies but enjoyed talking to him more. As she turned to the easel, she spoke.

"Have you made a particular study of any aquatic plants?"

"I have."

He spoke at length on his work and the dynamic interaction between the plants and animals in a pond's ecosystem. As she worked, they discussed von Humboldt's theories and how the unity of nature was on display even in a small pond.

Over an hour passed in pleasant conversation. Penelope occasionally rejoined them but never sat for long. She would rise and circle the area when she grew restless.

Mr. Glenhaven drew close to Charity several times. She was never sure if he was truly admiring her work or using it as an excuse to appear like a suitor. When all she had left was coloring the details of the leaves, he excused himself to go and retrieve a book from the library.

As Charity considered if the yellow was bright enough and worried she had not quite captured the unique heart shape of the leaves, Penelope joined her.

"Did Mr. Glenhaven go to fetch the carriage? We should be departing. Even your mother wouldn't believe we could spend this long at Hyde Park."

Charity knew her friend was right but resented it all the same. If only she were in charge of her own time. With a sigh, she stood up from the easel and stretched.

"It is a very good likeness," Penelope said as she examined the painting. "You have a talent for this work."

"Thank you. It is a shame I can't bring it home. Mother would be quite suspicious of our excursion if I returned with such a thing."

"You could always tell her what we did for the morning."

Charity scoffed and moved away from the easel. Where was Glenhaven? Penelope followed.

"I am sure she will not be upset when she understands that it was all Mr. Glenhaven's idea."

"It is certainly possible that she might understand. But it is just as likely that she will ban Mr. Glenhaven from the house. You forget that Mother thinks him only fit to be a conquest, not a husband."

Penelope tilted her head slightly and furrowed her brows. "But you think him fit to be a husband?"

The question brought Charity up short. It was not something she could consider. He was leaving. He had declared his intention not to marry. Their time together was not a courtship, no matter how it might look from the outside.

"You are right, we should go," Charity gathered her reticule and with a longing glance at the marsh marigold drawing, walked away. Penelope followed a few steps behind. Charity could feel her questioning gaze on her back.

Her curiosity wouldn't allow Charity to ignore Penelope's question. Did she think Mr. Glenhaven would be a good husband?

He was far from perfect. He lapsed into his thoughts and became oblivious to everything else. He had a high opinion of himself and was too blunt and honest.

But he was also handsome, and intelligent, thoughtful and perceptive. When she became lost in her own thoughts, he was patient. She enjoyed his conversations and his silences.

Did that mean he would be a good husband? Charity wasn't sure. She hadn't made a study of what kind of man she would marry because she didn't wish to marry.

It was irrelevant if Glenhaven was the paragon of a perfect husband. Nothing would change the simple fact that he was leaving for America and she was staying a spinster.

Sixteen

EDMUND PAUSED at the entrance of the coffee house and searched for Mr. Brown. Clusters of well-dressed gentlemen gathered together in earnest conversation beside individuals silently reading the provided newspapers. Scattered tables sat in dim corners and before bright windows. He spotted Mr. Brown's curly hair in a quieter corner.

The botanist had approached the leaders of the Linnean Society on his behalf yesterday and Edmund had come to hear his fate. He took a deep breath and touched his breast pocket. He felt the crinkle of paper there and, despite his nerves, it made him smile. Miss Radforde's drawing sat near his chest as a good luck charm.

Weaving through the maze of chairs, he soon reached the Scotsman. Mr. Brown looked up when Edmund was almost upon him and smiled. The look sent relief flooding through Edmund.

"They agreed?" he asked as Mr. Brown stood to greet him.

Brown chuckled. "Aye."

Edmund sat in his chair and pulled it close to the table, leaning forward on his elbows. "What exactly did they say? When will I speak with them? Should we go over what I will say?"

Brown waved his hands. "One question at a time, my boy." He

settled his bulk into a chair and leaned back. "There is still much to be sorted, but the Linnean Society will support your expedition."

"What?" Edmund had only hoped for an audience with the men. He hadn't intended Mr. Brown to secure funding for the expedition without him.

"They, of course, have a few requirements for the company."

"Requirements?"

"They feel the expedition will be greatly enhanced by the addition of more specialized men. A zoologist, geologist, cartographer, and landscape painter would increase the knowledge that can be gathered."

"I see." Edmund understood the wisdom in having more specialist on the expedition but that was a lot of people to lead. His excitement was tempered by the idea.

"And of course they would like some say in who you bring on the survey. They want to ensure the highest quality."

Edmund nodded. Would they give him good men or use the expedition to reward proteges? There was no reason why the men couldn't be both. And Edmund was in no position to argue with their choices. They were funding the expedition and he should be grateful. Why wasn't he happier at this turn of events?

"I am sure whatever the Linnean Society wishes to add will be a great help."

Mr. Brown smiled and leaned forward. "You are an intelligent young man. And don't worry, you will have some flexibility in your companions. I daresay you will like most of those suggested. Some are young men, eager to make a name for themselves, but a few are older, more experienced. It should make for a fine balance. And you can pick your own secretary. A good secretary is invaluable for such trips."

"Yes, I can see how one would be."

Edmund hadn't even thought to bring a secretary. But if he was now head of a large expedition, one might be necessary. It was a lot to take in.

Brown continued, seemingly unaware of Edmund's growing unease. "I do think you should trust my judgment when it comes to gardeners and botanic artists. Their task will be to help ensure what you discover is properly catalogued. You don't want anyone not up to the task. I will make a list with Bauer. He always knows who is available and worth their salt."

On this Edmund was able to wholeheartedly agree and he was grateful for the advice Brown could provide. What would Miss Radforde think of his change in circumstances? Would she be impressed by the honor bestowed? His hand went again to his breast pocket. Mr. Brown cocked his head at the gesture, his bright eyes expectant.

Edmund cleared his throat. Not wanting to explain himself, he latched onto the first thought he had.

"I have a sample here from a botanic artist that is a friend of mine. I thought you might give me your opinion of their skill." He pulled out the folded-up drawing and passed it into Mr. Brown's eager hands.

The man unfolded the paper and flattened it on the table. As he looked over the bright yellow flower, he hummed and leaned closer. The noise in the coffee shop seemed to grow louder as Edmund waited for the illustrious man's opinion.

"This is quite good, a buttercup variety if I am not mistaken."

"It is marsh marigold," Edmund couldn't help saying.

"Ah, I see, they should have included the roots and represented the stamen separately. But the detail is fine, the scallops on the leaves quite precise. With some work they could be a first class illustrator. Are you considering asking him to join your expedition?"

"Perhaps." Miss Radforde accompanying him was impossible, but the idea pleased him.

"Well, if they don't wish to go to America, I can arrange a meeting with Bauer. He is always happy to help a young man starting out in the profession."

"I will ask, thank you."

Miss Radforde would love meeting Mr. Franz Bauer, the head gardener to the royal botanic gardens in Kew. He hoped the fact she was not a young man wouldn't matter. Edmund reached for the drawing and carefully refolded it before returning it to his breast pocket.

Brown turned the conversation to the expedition and they talked long over what needed to be done. By the time Edmund left the coffee house, he felt overwhelmed, like the morning he had stood at the base of Snowdon with the intent to reach the top before evening.

Could he climb this metaphorical mountain? The journey alone had daunted him. How would he lead a large company? Should he insist on less people? But then the Linnean Society might retract their support. No, he needed to abide by their advice. He would tackle the problem just as he had the mountain by being prepared and taking it one step at a time.

With so much to do, Edmund was annoyed that he had promised to attend a dinner with his parents that evening. Instead of working on his plan, he would be forced to engage in small, tedious conversations.

But that evening, when Edmund entered the drawing room, he realized his conversations would be anything but tedious. Miss Radforde was there.

She was dressed in blue—he thought blue suited her particularly well—and standing beside her mother, nodding and smiling politely.

As if she could sense him, her eyes strayed from her companions and found his. Her smile transformed into the wide, genuine one he preferred. Warmth spread to his toes at the reception. How different it was from the first time she had seen him from across a drawing room.

"I said you would be glad you came," Mama murmured from beside him.

He gave her a wry look but did not correct her. Before he could cross the room and speak with Miss Radforde, dinner was announced.

Edmund was disappointed when he was unable to maneuver a seat beside her. She sat between Lord Glenhaven and a smartly-dressed young gentleman. Both men made him uneasy for entirely different reasons.

During the meal, he tried to not let his attention stray to Miss Radforde but found it difficult. He kept noticing things that spurred questions. Who was the young man? What was Father saying to her? Why was she frowning? Why was she smiling?

When the meal ended and the ladies stood to leave, she cast him a conspiratorial look. He hoped he might join her soon and discover the answers to his questions. He accepted his drink but barely touched it as the other men began to talk about Parliament votes and army commissions.

Father was not the host but seemed to be holding court as the other men hung on his every word and asked his advice on delicate matters. Edmund seemed the only man in the room who didn't ask Lord Glenhaven for advice.

The young man that had sat beside Miss Radforde banged his empty glass onto the table. "Gentlemen, may I propose we adjourn to the drawing room?"

Many of the older men chuckled at his brashness but Father looked askance.

"Oh, to be young and on the hunt for a bride," their host said.

The young man acknowledged him with a tip of his head.

Edmund frowned. He did not like the mercenary gleam in the man's eye. He would inflict his company on Miss Radforde all evening if allowed. If this dinner was an example, it was no wonder Miss Radforde had requested his assistance.

Around the table, a few others expressed the desire to adjourn and Edmund readily stood with them. To his surprise, Father also rose to his feet. Usually he lingered longest over drinks, sometimes not coming to the drawing room until it was time to leave.

As they funneled to the door, Father put a hand on Edmund's shoulder.

"A word."

Glancing at the backs of the others, Edmund inclined his head. They slowed their steps until they were alone in the short hallway leading to the drawing room. The flickering golden light brought out the grey in his father's hair.

"Are you entirely sure that Miss Radforde is worth your effort?"

"I beg your pardon?" Edmund straightened his shoulders.

"I do not think she will suit. Your time would be better spent elsewhere."

Edmund tried to keep his emotions in check. He had not asked for Father's opinion in the matter and he normally did not care, but the words were like a spark to tinder.

"Miss Radforde suits me perfectly. Indeed, no woman could be a better match. I cannot think why you are set against her."

"And I cannot understand why you prefer her at all. After her insipid dinner conversation, I am baffled that you have spent so much time in her company. She is certainly rich enough and her father well-connected, but those qualities are not difficult to attain. Your mother and I will find someone more worthy."

Edmund grit his teeth. "I thank you for your concern, but it is unwarranted. I am perfectly capable of managing my own affairs. Now if you will excuse me."

Pushing past Father, he stormed to the drawing room door. He paused outside of it and took a deep breath to calm his nerves.

Father always thought he knew best. After one conversation he had made his decision. He had no notion of Miss Radforde's character, of her intellect and talent. Edmund knew that Miss Radforde endeavored to hide her true nature, but Father should trust Edmund's and Mama's judgment, instead of declaring his own to be the superior.

Upon entering the drawing room, Edmund's mood did not improve. Miss Radforde sat in the corner near the window, the other young man sat beside her smiling and talking animatedly. He curled his fists as she smiled and bobbed her head.

Was she interested in the man? He observed her closely. Her shoulders were rigid and her smile did not reach her eyes. He surmised that she would prefer a change in conversation partners. He could think of only one way to test his hypothesis.

A few strides brought him to her side. Ignoring the other man entirely, he addressed her.

"Miss Radforde, would you like to take a turn about the room?"

Her face brightened at his invitation. "Why Mr. Glenhaven, that sounds refreshing." She turned to the other man. "Please, excuse me."

Edmund couldn't help giving him a smug look. He gaped back briefly before his expression turned hard.

They took several steps before either spoke.

"I should not have done that," she said.

"What?"

She leaned a little closer. "Mother thought him a very good prospect."

"Higher than a baron's third son?" The words did not sound as teasing as he intended.

"Why, Mr. Glenhaven, you sound as if you are jealous."

"Shouldn't a suitor be jealous of a rival?"

"A real suitor might be, but I assure you he is not a rival. I have no interest in the man."

Her words did not alleviate the knot in his chest. They reached the end of the room and turned to pace along the next wall. Several eyes watched their progress. His mother seemed pleased while the other young man watched them narrowly.

"He certainly believes you are interested," Edmund said.

"I cannot help what he believes."

Edmund paused at the next window and pretended to look outside so they might turn their backs on everyone. It was as private as they could be in a crowded room.

"You could be less encouraging."

She swung her head to look at him. "Encouraging? I haven't encouraged him. My dowry is all the encouragement he needs."

The anger in her voice reminded him of their first dinner when she had stunned him with her knowledge and insight.

"You could ask him his opinion on von Humboldt. Then he might realize you are not a simpleton who would be easily manipulated into marriage."

She did not reply. She flushed and her lip caught between her teeth as she struggled not to retort. Her restraint made him ashamed of his own conduct.

"My apologies. I did not mean... That is... I know you have your reasons and your mother... I only meant that such men could be easily put off if you wished." He attempted a teasing tone. "I am only trying to help you in your goal to remain unwed."

She scoffed quietly.

"I am serious. I have given great thought to how you might stay a spinster."

She nudged his shoulder. "Let us not talk of my plans. What of yours? What did Mr. Brown say?"

Edmund had almost forgotten about his meeting. He bounced a little as he began to tell her his news and she tugged him back into motion. They circled the room twice as they talked. Her eyes glowed with excitement as he recounted the conversation. In sharing it with her, it no longer felt like a possibility but a reality. He was really going on his expedition.

"So now you must collect all the participants for the journey?" she asked.

"Participants and supplies and a great deal of planning."

"A daunting prospect."

"Yes, it is overwhelming." Unintentionally, his fear colored his words.

Gently, she touched his forearm. "I am sure you are up to the task. And you have Mr. Brown to guide you."

He covered her hand with his own. It was so small, fitting inside his and yet its touch brought him strength. He hated the thin material that separated their skin. When their hands brushed in the garden, hers had been delicate and soft. At least he could still feel her warmth through the gloves.

After a long moment, he recalled they were in a drawing room in full view of others. He dropped his hand and she released his arm.

He cleared his throat. "Mr. Brown had a suggestion for a botanic illustrator I might take with me."

Her brow furrowed at his change in topic.

"I showed him the marsh marigold you drew."

Her mouth dropped open slightly. "You didn't."

He nodded. "I hope you don't mind that I had it retrieved from the easel. He admired your skill and recommended I ask my friend to come with me to America."

Her cheeks grew a delightful shade of pink. He preferred the color to her bright, angry flush.

"He thought me good enough for your expedition?"

"Of course he did. Your talent and attention to detail make you an excellent choice."

"But he did not know I was a woman. He would not have suggested I go to America if he knew."

Edmund shrugged.

She turned and stared out another window. He paused to admired her profile, the delicate hair brushing her neck and the strong angle of her nose, before turning to the window himself.

Her shoulders rose and fell but her sigh was barely audible.

"I must content myself with the wonders of England," she murmured.

Edmund could only hum in agreement. It was important to him that she was able to live the life she wished. He hoped she could find a project like Mrs. Blackwell and her herbal. Surely that would bring her satisfaction.

He did not want her to be besieged by suitors and forced to sit stiffly and smile politely. While he was in England, he would keep her from dull men and make her smile. And he would do it not because of their arrangement, but because he wanted to see her happy and fulfilled.

Seventeen

Charity enjoyed the next three weeks more than she could have hoped. She still attended the functions her mother chose, but those were bearable because Mr. Glenhaven kept their excursions constant and varied. Contrary to Penelope's complaints, they did not always visit museums or go to lectures.

They enjoyed an afternoon at Saint Paul's Cathedral admiring the architecture of Wren. They spent a morning exploring Westminster Abbey—which Charity did not like as well as Bath Abbey. They saw the Corn Exchange, India House, Adelphi buildings, and more. They even returned to Somerset House to gawk at paintings at the Royal Academy.

Every time she saw Glenhaven, he brought fresh news of his plans. He met frequently with Mr. Brown and other associates to organize and offer positions in the expedition. At first, Charity enjoyed hearing everything, but now her joy was occasionally tempered by jealousy. She grew frustrated that she was to be left behind. This was a small irritation and, on the whole, Charity's happiness exceeded her expectations.

She should have known it wouldn't last.

On Wednesday afternoon, Mr. Glenhaven escorted Charity, Mary, and Penelope to Guy's Hospital to attend a lecture on practical biology.

The lecture hall was simple. Wooden floors and benches faced the speaker and a table full of specimens. As the room slowly filled with people. Glenhaven led them to a bench in the middle. Penelope took the seat nearest the window.

"At least there is something to see this time," she murmured.

Mary and Charity shared a look as they sat beside her. No matter the subject, Penelope had no interest in lectures. In Bath, Charity and Mary had often attended them with Miss Minerva. Occasionally Rosamund or Elaine would join, but Penelope steadfastly refused. She had declared her spirits were depressed by quietly sitting and listening for hours.

In Bath, Penelope could choose not to go, but now she was Charity's vigilant shadow. Though Charity regretted the arrangement, Penelope steadfastly insisted that her pleasure should not be consulted in their outings.

A hush fell over the room as Mr. Salisbury entered and strode to the front. He was a short, unremarkable man, but had a reputation for informative and detailed lectures.

Mr. Glenhaven had originally proposed they attend Mr. Salisbury's evening lecture in the London Botanic Garden, but Charity had rejected the idea. Mother had been making comments about Glenhaven monopolizing her afternoons and Charity did not want to antagonize her by requesting an evening.

Charity reached into her reticule to withdraw her notebook and pencil. Beside her, Mr. Glenhaven shifted, closing the space between them. She looked up. Another man had joined them on the bench, necessitating they all sit closer.

The problem of Mr. Glenhaven's proximity had persisted.

As they were about London, he often found reasons to lean close or whisper in her ear. Though she knew such actions were part of their ruse, Charity could not stop her heart from beating nor her temperature from rising.

Now Mr. Glenhaven was a hair's breadth away and she felt his nearness from shoulder to ankle. She swallowed and considered moving closer to Mary.

Glenhaven shifted. Their knees bumped and his thigh pressed

against hers. How would she ever pay attention to the lecture if her mind was centered on where they touched?

He shifted again. His thigh moved away but now their upper arms brushed. Goosebumps erupted in the wake of the contact. Could he not sit still?

She glared at him and saw he was holding his notebook and patting his coat pocket, wholly unaware of the riot of sensations he was causing. It was unfair that she seemed to be the only one affected.

"My pencil," he murmured by way of explanation.

She cast her eyes to the ceiling before offering her pencil.

Blessedly, he stopped moving.

"Oh," he said, "I cannot leave you without."

She opened her reticule and retrieved a second pencil. She waved it at him with a raised eyebrow. He looked sheepish as he took it. After the first two times he had forgotten a pencil, she had started bringing an extra.

She turned to the front, slid closer to Mary, and did her best to ignore the man beside her. She refused to be distracted.

At first it required great concentration, but soon she was fully immersed in the lecture. She took notes, devoured the knowledge and forgot to be self-conscious of Glenhaven.

When he leaned in to whisper in her ear, her concentration scattered like dandelion seeds in the wind. She bit her lip as a shiver ran down her neck.

What was he asking? Something about collecting something?

When he paused, she could only nod. Would that be enough to satisfy him or would he speak more? He leaned away and disappointment flooded through her. How could she both enjoy and hate her reactions to him?

There were times when she wished he was a real suitor and his whispers and touches were promises of something more. In the last two weeks she had repeatedly risen from a night's sleep filled with dreams of his embrace. She was often telling herself to be sensible and forget such foolishness.

At the conclusion of the lecture, Glenhaven turned to her with a smile that was now familiar but no less charming. With a flourish he returned her pencil.

"However did I manage without you, Miss Radforde?"

"I wonder that myself." She shook her head as she took the pencil.

"When I finally settle on a secretary, I shall bring them to Radforde House so you might train them on my eccentricities."

"I fear I will not have enough time; there is so much to teach."

"Then perhaps I should just make you my secretary?"

Charity knew he meant it as a compliment, but the idea of being his employee did not please her. She wanted something else, something more.

"Should we go speak to Mr. Salisbury?" she asked and stood.

The briefest frown crossed his face before he also stood and led the way into the aisle. Before they could join the small crowd forming at the front, Penelope spoke lowly.

"Charity, we cannot dawdle today. Your mother was very clear on that point."

Mary made a face at the news but did not protest.

Charity cast a longing look at Mr. Salisbury. She had especially wanted to make his acquaintance since they had visited his botanic garden. But Penelope was right; Mother had not been pleased with their plans for the afternoon.

She turned to her escort. "My apologies, Mr. Glenhaven, but I must return home."

He did not object but looked disappointed.

In the carriage, Mr. Glenhaven sat opposite Charity, allowing Mary to sit beside her, and she was able to listen to his thoughts on plant propagation without being distracted. While Penelope seemed more interested in watching the people on the streets, Mary added several of her own insights.

The conversation after a lecture was Charity's favorite part. The give and take of ideas, the decanting of the presentation to its most interesting insights. Mr. Glenhaven always had such fascinating thoughts, at times she felt she could talk with him all day.

As they turned into Russell Square, the conversation shifted to farewells.

"It really was too kind of you to escort us this afternoon, Mr. Glenhaven," Mary said.

"It was my pleasure to be in your company," he replied with a warm smile for Charity.

She held her breath in anticipation of his next words. Though he always asked for another meeting, she had started to grow nervous—he normally did not wait so long.

"A pleasure I would like to repeat. They give concerts in the London Botanic Garden. Are you available to attend tomorrow night? We might speak with Mr. Salisbury then."

"Oh, that would be wonderful," Charity said.

"But you can't go, Charity, for we are going to the theatre," Mary said. "Remember? I believe it is Hamlet? Or Macbeth? Or some such serious thing."

"Unfortunately Miss Radforde is engaged for Thursday evening." Penelope summed up the situation more succinctly.

Charity held back a sigh. She had forgotten about going to the theatre with Mary and the Hunters. The carriage came to a stop, but no one moved to exit.

"I understand," Mr. Glenhaven said. "Then perhaps Friday? We could ride in Hyde Park? Mrs. Radforde would approve of that, I wager."

Charity ignored Penelope's scoff as she readily agreed. "I think a ride in Hyde Park would be lovely."

She hoped it would be just like their last "ride" to Hyde Park. They had not revisited the garden. Charity suspected that Penelope had spoken with him about the subterfuge.

The footman appeared and while Mary and Penelope were assisted out, Mr. Glenhaven took the opportunity to lean forward and whisper.

"Apologies, I should have engaged you for Thursday night sooner.'"

"Aren't you going to the Royal Society?"

He shrugged. Was he willing to forgo the meeting to spend time with her instead?

"I thought I might spare you a dull evening," he said.

"Rest easy; the theatre with Mary will not be dull. And Pen enjoys Covent Garden."

He looked as if he might say more, but the footman was waiting and her friends were watching.

"Until Friday, then."

Her heart did a little flip at his soft voice and tender eyes. Was he merely making a scene for Mary and Penelope's benefit?

She nodded. "Until then."

Once back in the drawing room, Mary and Penelope took up needlework, while Charity sat down to finish a letter to Mrs. Piper. She could hear them whispering over the scratch of her pen but paid no mind. She was too busy describing the week's activities. Thanks to Mr. Glenhaven, she had plenty to share with her old teacher.

"Charity, do you think you might marry before the end of the season?" Mary asked.

Ink splattered onto the paper as Charity abruptly turned. "Excuse me?"

Mary was smiling slyly but Penelope looked expectant.

"Mr. Glenhaven has not...he will not... there is no..." Caught off guard, Charity struggled to explain without sharing any secrets.

"I only ask because I would hate to miss the wedding. With the pace you are moving, Blosset will return, marry me, and take me away before your banns can be read. Though, perhaps he won't return until next summer, in which case I imagine I will be available for the wedding."

"Mary, you don't understand," Charity said.

"No, I don't, you two are clearly an excellent match and—"

Penelope hushed Mary as a footman entered the room.

The man bore a summons from Mother. Charity exchanged a look with her friends. Mother wishing for a private word did not bode well. Charity hoped she did not want to discuss the same topic as her friends, or she would be trading one interrogation for another.

With leaden steps she made her way through the house.

"Charity, dear, come here," Mother said briskly as she entered.

Mother's private sitting room was less fashionable than the drawing room, but the furnishings were still elegant. She sat enthroned upon a large chair, looking severe. Obediently, Charity moved to stand before her.

"We need to talk about Mr. Glenhaven." Mother gestured for her to sit.

Charity swallowed thickly as she sat opposite. Despite her tall frame, the chair seemed to swallow her. She had been dreading this conversation. Over the last seven days, Mother had been increasingly cool toward Mr. Glenhaven.

"You must spend less time with him." Mother got directly to the heart of the matter.

"I can't." The words were out before Charity could stop them. "I mean, I can't refuse his offers," she amended.

"My dear girl, you don't need to refuse, you need only tell him you are otherwise occupied. In time, he will come to understand that his addresses are no longer welcome. Now, don't frown so. It is a perfectly acceptable way to end an association."

"Why must I end it? Isn't he eligible?"

Mother sighed. "I grant you that he cuts a dashing figure, and his connections are good. But Charity, he is a third son and a bookish clergyman with little income and less sense. He simply will not do. He has served his purpose by helping bring you to the notice of others. It is time we looked higher. I think Mr. Fitzroy or Mr. Hunter will do nicely. Don't you?"

Charity gritted her teeth, her cheeks heating. She had underestimated her mother's desire to capture a title or grand estate. Even Penelope's information about Fitzroy had not deterred her. Charity didn't object to Mr. Fitzroy's company—unlike Mr. Hunter, he was interesting to talk with—but she would never marry him.

"Don't look at me like that," Mother scolded. "This is for the best and one day you will thank me for my help."

Charity could not give her customary agreement. An ocean would soon separate her from Glenhaven; she would not sacrifice the weeks they had left.

She swallowed and took a deep breath. "I do not wish to refuse Mr. Glenhaven's invitations."

Mother frowned. "I feared this. Have you fallen in love with him?"

"In love?"

She was not in love with Glenhaven.

She liked him, she enjoyed the time they spent together, and he made her heart flutter, but that was not love. Was it? If she told Mother that she loved him, would she allow them to continue? It was tempting to tell such a monumental lie.

"I... I don't know. I greatly esteem him. I enjoy his company above all others."

"Well." Mother paused and pursed her lips. "I see. I guess this was to be expected. You know so little of the world and have spent too much time in his company. All the more reason to drop the acquaintance. Girls always fancy themselves in love when so much exclusive attention is showered upon them." She sighed. "I know you will not thank me now, but once you have a broader experience you will see. More suitors will open your eyes to his faults; the contrast will provide clarity on your feelings."

Charity stared down at her hands. "Yes, Mother."

There was no point in arguing further. Mother would have her way. On Friday, Charity would talk to Glenhaven, explain her position and hope he would have a clever idea to help her.

Mother continued for some time discussing the merits of new suitors and Charity's responsibility to charm them. She dwelt on suitable conversation topics and activities. It seemed she was worried about Mr. Glenhaven's influence on her. Charity gave the appearance of listening.

With each passing moment, she became convinced that Mother would not give up her plans for a great marriage. Why had Charity thought a pretend courtship would deter her? The past weeks were a mere reprieve from the rest of her life. Even if she rejected Fitzroy and Hunter, Mother would find others.

Charity would not be allowed to set up quietly with her friends and spend her days studying plants. There would be no peace until she was safely attached to a proper man. She saw the years stretching out before her, a life of fending off eager fortune hunters and catering to her mother. Such a future made marriage seem preferable.

Something had to change.

Even as Mother lectured, Charity began to compose a letter in her head. Her father was the only one who could overrule Mother, the only one who could give her the funds and permission she needed. Fear of

Mother's wrath and her father's reply had kept Charity from asking. It was probable that Father would agree with his wife, but Charity had to ask. She couldn't live as Mother's pet any longer.

Charity wrote to her father that evening. The next night, she obediently attended the theatre with Mary and the Hunters. While the company was dull, the theater was vibrant.

Footlights illuminated the stage and the brightly-costumed actors. The elaborate ornamentation and gilt work on the walls and ceiling were harder to see but flashed occasionally in the candle light. The place was stuffy with so many bodies acting as a furnace. At times, the audience chattered over the action on the stage and at others the entire room sat spellbound, each sharing the same emotion as they laughed or gasped at the actors.

As Mother had predicted, the contrast between Mr. Hunter and Mr. Glenhaven was illuminating but it was Mr. Hunter who suffered from the comparison.

Before her time with Glenhaven, Charity had found Hunter merely tiresome, but now he was insufferable. Her cheeks hurt from trying to smile and her head ached from the effort to pay attention.

Gratefully her feigned interest in the play kept their conversation to a minimum, though it had the unwelcome effect of allowing Mr. Hunter to lean close and whisper in her ear. Her body did not shiver at his proximity. Another difference between him and Glenhaven to add to the long list she had started.

Sitting in a middle box, they had an excellent view of the stage and the audience. For many, like Mother, the audience was more interesting than the melodrama being performed. Charity was sure the carriage ride home would be full of chatter about who was sitting in which box and what they were wearing.

When the interval began, Charity hoped that Mr. Hunter would excuse himself to mingle with others, but he stayed by her side. She soon understood his motive as each young man that came to visit the box was treated to a hostile look and caustic comments. She hid her frustration behind a lifeless smile.

Mother had stayed only long enough to give Charity an approving nod. It fell to Mary and Penelope to mitigate the tension with bland, agreeable conversation. Most visitors left quickly. When the usually garrulous Mr. Simmons departed after only a brief conversation, Penelope stood.

"Mr. Hunter," she said, "Would you accompany Miss Gilbert and I across the theatre? We wanted to greet Lady Northam."

Charity wanted to hug her.

"Certainly, if Miss Radforde wishes it," Mr. Hunter replied.

"Please, don't worry about me." Charity tried to cover her eagerness.

"You must accompany us," he urged.

A few weeks ago Charity might have meekly capitulated but, thanks to Glenhaven, she was learning to speak up for herself.

"That is kind, but I will stay here." She smiled to soften the hardness of her words.

Hunter frowned at her refusal. He was not accustomed to being rebuffed but with no chaperone, he could not stay with her.

"Then it is settled," Penelope said and turned to leave.

Left with no choice, Hunter followed after.

Alone at last, Charity sighed. How would she endure the rest of the evening? And how many more such evenings would there be? How different the night might have been if Mr. Glenhaven had been beside her. She would have enjoyed his whispers. But at the moment, he was probably at the Royal Society and not thinking of her at all. It hardly seemed fair.

Her reprieve was short lived. A new complication entered the box.

Mr. Fitzroy's bow was deep and his smile charming. He paused briefly when he realized Charity was alone. He didn't enter further but neither did he depart.

"I see I have caught you in a moment of peace," he said. "So I will not impose long."

Charity wanted to tell him he should not be imposing at all. A true gentleman would make a hasty exit rather than be unchaperoned.

"You do right to frown so," he said. "But my errand shall make you smile. Might I beg the privilege of taking you for a ride in the park tomorrow?" His tone implied that all his future happiness rested on her responding in the affirmative.

"I am sorry, but I am engaged tomorrow afternoon." Charity tried to speak evenly.

"Off to another museum with Glenhaven? You certainly spend a good deal of time with my bookish friend."

Heat rushed to her cheeks. It was no business of Fitzroy's who she spent time with.

"Why Mr. Fitzroy," Mother appeared in the doorway. "What a lovely surprise."

Charity clenched her teeth together as the man greeted her mother.

"Mrs. Radforde, what a pleasure."

"The pleasure is all ours. We do not see enough of you, sir."

A ridiculous sentiment. They had met with Fitzroy on several occasions. Charity had danced with the man upwards of five times. She often enjoyed their dances but had yet to make out his character. Penelope's opinion of the man had not changed, and she continued to advise caution. A needless warning, since Charity had no interest in the man.

"I agree, ma'am. I wish to remedy the situation by taking Miss Radforde on a ride about Hyde Park tomorrow afternoon."

"I am sure she will enjoy that immensely." Mother smiled wide.

"Alas, she informs me she is not available," Fitzroy said mournfully.

Mother shot Charity a censorious look. "Charity, dear, I forgot to tell you that our appointment tomorrow was cancelled."

It was a lie. Mother knew that Charity was promised to Mr. Glenhaven for the afternoon. But to say so now would cause even more embarrassment.

"I am glad to hear that, ma'am." Fitzroy turned the full force of his smile on Charity. It had only a trace of smugness. "I shall call tomorrow."

She could only nod her agreement. He bowed over her hand and made his pretty goodbyes. Mother smirked in satisfaction, but Charity felt her stomach twisting.

Despite all her careful scheming, she was still at her mother's mercy. Father's reply could not come soon enough.

Oh, why had she not come up with an excuse or called out the lie? And what would Mr. Glenhaven think when he arrived and found her gone?

Eighteen

As Edmund sat in the Glenhaven box at Covent Garden, he regretted attending. Bringing Sophy had allowed him to pretend he wasn't there to see Miss Radforde. Certainly he hadn't come with the intention of spying on her. Yet that was precisely how he had spent the evening.

By some cruel coincidence, she was sitting in a box opposite and lower than his, affording him an excellent view. He was reasonably sure that his seat at the back of the box made him invisible to her and her companions.

Watching her sit beside Hunter had been annoying. The man was constantly whispering in her ear. But that was easy compared to witnessing the stream of eligible gentlemen coming to pay court. He knew Miss Radforde was sought after but seeing it for himself was unsettling. His hands ached from being clenched into fists for most of the night.

When he departed England, which of those men would she spend time with? Would she marry one of them? The more time he spent with Miss Radforde, the stronger his desire to keep her single had become.

He should be at her side, in Hunter's place. All those men should understand his position in her life, or rather the position he was pretending to occupy.

But with Sophy by his side, he must stay. He glanced at his little sister. Seated on his left, her eyes swept about the theatre eagerly.

Almost seventeen, Sophy was not out and Edmund was under strict orders to not socialize or leave her side. Normally, Edmund agreed with the strictures on Sophy; she was far too young to be entertaining suitors, but tonight he wished his parents were more permissive.

All he could do was watch Miss Radforde.

"Edmund?"

Sophy's hand on his arm brought him back to their box. He vaguely realized she had been speaking for some time.

"Hmm?"

"I said, who are you looking at?" Sophy brought her opera glasses to her eyes and gazed directly at Miss Radforde's box. She leaned forward in her seat.

Edmund pulled her back. "Do not stare so, they will see you."

Sophy gave him a look. "You were staring."

"I was thinking."

"About Miss Radforde?" Sophy had a particular skill of being infuriatingly correct.

Edmund did not deny her guess.

"Why would you stare at another woman while thinking about Miss Radforde?'

"I wasn't staring at another woman, but at Miss Radforde."

His sister immediately went back to looking through her glasses, though she did not lean forward, which he hoped would keep her hidden.

"Which one?"

"The one in blue."

"And the others?"

"The young lady in cream is a school friend, Miss Gilbert, and the one in grey is her companion, Mrs. Aston."

"And the handsome young man?"

"That is a Mr. Hunter. He is connected to Miss Gilbert by—do you really think him handsome?"

"Not very handsome. I am sure Miss Radforde cannot prefer him. She is very pretty and elegant, but not too elegant. Such fashionable hair and that color becomes her. Mother says she is intelligent and genteel. Oh, her friends are leaving. It is a pity that we cannot go and meet her. I would very much like to ask what she thinks of Lord Byron."

Edmund shook his head fondly. "I am sorry we cannot leave the box. Shall I ask her tomorrow?"

Sophy turned to him with hopeful eyes. "Oh, would you? If I could only know her opinion I would know if we will be friends as well as sisters."

"Sisters? Sophy, the very notion. I am not marrying Miss Radforde."

"Mama says that you will, you just haven't come to the point. Papa says it will be a good thing when she refuses you.'

"He said what?"

"Don't be cross. I am sure Papa only meant that most young women are more concerned with capturing money or a title. I am sure Miss Radforde is not like that."

How often did his family discuss Miss Radforde? Did Mama really expect him to marry her? Did Father expect her to reject him or merely wish it?

"I have no claim on Miss Radforde," Edmund said.

It was an uncomfortable truth. They had a convenient arrangement, nothing more. Miss Radforde could decide tomorrow that she no longer wanted his company, and all would be at an end. For his part, he could not imagine severing the connection. The thought of saying goodbye to Miss Radforde was the only thing dampening his excitement for his journey.

"Oh, he is very handsome." Sophy had resumed spying.

Instead of censuring her, Edmund raised his own glasses. Miss Radforde was no longer alone. Mr. Fitzroy was standing in her box, smiling and looking every inch the heir to a title.

"That is Mr. Fitzroy," Edmund muttered.

"Well, I am sure she does not like him half so much as you. And he is hardly a gentleman speaking to her without a chaperone."

Edmund clenched his jaw. Skirting the edge of propriety was

Fitzroy's way. He should never have introduced them. The man was bound to charm her. What were they saying? Knowing Fitzroy, it was all flattery and nonsense.

Mrs. Radforde arrived in the box and her welcoming smile spoke volumes. The lady had not smiled so warmly at him for a week. Did Miss Radforde also welcome Fitzroy's attention?

"Is that Mrs. Radforde?" Sophy asked.

Edmund nodded but did not take his eyes from the scene.

They watched as the three conversed and Fitzroy made his bow. That the man's visit had been short did little to alleviate Edmund's annoyance.

Sophy lowered her glasses. "I do wish we could go and speak with them." She sighed. "It is very tiresome not being out."

Edmund turned to his sister, seizing on the change of topic. "Do not be in such a hurry to grow up. You will be out and fending off suitors soon enough. Until that time, you should strive to improve your mind."

Sophy smiled, her hazel eyes brightened. "You really think I will have suitors?"

"Do you think of nothing but beaux and balls?"

"Of course I do."

"Hmmm. So next time you won't mind if we attend a lecture instead of a play?"

She made a face.

Edmund laughed. "Miss Radforde enjoys lectures."

"Oh, well, if I can meet her, I will certainly go."

Edmund thought it would be a good thing for Sophy to become friends with Miss Radforde. A sober, steady, mind combined with wit and intelligence was exactly what his sister needed.

Sophy stifled a yawn. "I am sorry that I am such an anchor and you cannot go and speak with her."

After seeing Fitzroy, Edmund did not feel equal to speaking with the Radfordes.

"You are not an anchor. I am happy to stay with you."

"You are a very good brother, but if you wish we might leave."

"You don't want to see the end of the play?"

Sophy shrugged. "I have already seen it. I only came to watch the audience and now that I have seen your Miss Radforde, I am perfectly satisfied with the evening. And if we depart now, I might get a better look at everyone in the hallways."

Edmund tried to hide his gratitude. For his sister he would have stayed but he did not wish to be tortured by watching Miss Radforde for the rest of the performance.

"Then let us depart." He stood and offered his arm.

Sophy took it with a smile. "Am I fit to promenade through the crowd?"

He looked her over in exaggerated fashion. She really was growing into a young lady. He tucked a loose piece of hair behind her ear. "Now you are."

As they turned to leave, he couldn't help taking one last look at Miss Radforde. His heart skipped when he saw she was looking directly at him. Did she see him through the gloom? He smiled and inclined his head in acknowledgment.

She frowned and looked away.

Puzzled, he turned back to Sophy, but she had not marked the interaction. Edmund was left to wonder about her frown for the entire carriage ride home.

As the carriage slowed before the large London townhouse, Edmund was surprised to see light in the drawing room window. Father was meant to be at his club and Mama had intended to retire early. What had kept her up?

The mystery was solved when they entered and the footman announced that Captain Glenhaven had returned.

"Kit!" Sophy cried and rushed off with gloves on and wrap still in hand.

Edmund paused long enough to leave his things with the footman and then strode up the stairs. When he entered, Sophy was enclosed in their brother's arms.

Kit pulled back and surveyed their sister. "You are so changed I should not have recognized you."

His warm, lyrical voice gave Edmund pause. He did not know if he had forgotten the precise timbre or if his brother's voice had grown deeper. Both could be true. They kept up a regular correspondence, but Edmund hadn't seen Kit in nearly four years.

Kit looked up from Sophy and grinned.

"Edmund!" He strode forward and they embraced.

Slightly shorter, Kit was broader in the shoulder, his muscles robust from years at sea.

"We did not expect you for another month," Edmund said.

"The Admiralty released me early," Kit replied.

"He just arrived," Mama added. "You should have written to inform us of the change. Why, if I had gone to the theatre there would have been no one here to greet you. That is hardly a proper welcome."

"I suppose that depends on what one considers a proper welcome." Kit winked. "I quite enjoyed surprising you."

"I enjoyed being surprised," Sophy said. "Now you must tell us of the Cape Colony."

They settled into chairs and Kit regaled them with stories of sailing from the tip of Africa. They talked for above an hour about his travels. Edmund couldn't help but imagine when he would be the one sharing adventures. Would his family think him changed? Kit seemed more mature than the last time they spoke.

As Kit began telling of his time in Gibraltar, Mama got up and sat at her writing desk.

"Are you wanting to write down my exploits, Mother?" Kit teased.

She waved him off. "I must write George and tell him to come to town so we can have a proper family dinner."

Kit laughed. "Whatever you wish, Mother. I am at your mercy."

"Mama, you should invite the Radfordes to the dinner," Sophy said.

"No, you shouldn't," Edmund countered.

"And who are the Radfordes?" Kit looked between them with raised eyebrows.

"Edmund is courting Miss Radforde and it will not be long before she is our sister."

"Sophy!" Mama and Edmund said together.

"What? It is only Kit."

"You do not mean Miss Charity Radforde?" Kit said slowly.

"Yes! Do you know her?" Sophy asked.

"Only by reputation. They say she is intelligent and rich. Am I to wish you joy, little brother?"

"No. I am not going to marry. Sophy has let her imagination run wild."

Kit laughed. "I think the gentleman doth protest too much."

Sophy giggled and Edmund groaned. As much as he had missed his brother, he wished to be done with this conversation.

"How long will you be on shore?" Edmund asked.

"Long enough." Kit smirked. "Now about this Miss Radforde..."

Edmund shook his head. How had he forgotten Kit's love of teasing? He moved to the sideboard for a drink. Kit followed.

"I saw her tonight, Kit," Sophy said. "Of course we did not meet, but our box was opposite hers. I should not have known her, but Edmund was staring and eventually told me why. She is very elegant. I am sure we will be friends. Though she has many friends already. She was sitting with two of them. Edmund, what were their names?"

Realizing there was no escaping the conversation, Edmund answered, "Mrs. Aston and Miss Gilbert."

The sideboard glasses clattered and everyone turned to Kit.

"Apologies, it slipped from my hands," he mumbled and quickly righted the tipped over glasses.

"You are tired," Mama said. "You should rest."

Kit waved away her concern. "But then I would miss Sophy's recounting of her night."

Sophy looked chagrined. "I do run on. That is something you will have to get used to now you have returned."

"I was only teasing. Please continue." Kit said.

But Edmund could see her embarrassment had dampened her high spirits. Sophy was much younger than Kit and had only seen him briefly over the years. It would take time for them to understand each other.

"What were you saying about Gibraltar?" Edmund asked.

Kit took up the change and continued his story.

Edmund sipped his drink, content to listen and avoid further teasing. An hour later, they dispersed to their rooms. In the quiet of his own room, his worries about Miss Radforde returned and it was a long hour before he finally slept.

The next morning, Edmund was alone in the breakfast room when Kit arrived. The long journey and late night had not dampened his high spirits. He had a bounce in his step as he entered, greeted Edmund, and filled his plate.

"It seems we are the only ones awake." Kit said as he sat next to Edmund.

"Mama and Sophy take a tray in their rooms, and I believe Father is already off on his morning ride."

Kit hummed as he began to eat.

"I am sure you might ride if you wish," Edmund said.

"Will you come with me?"

Edmund shook his head. He did not enjoy riding the way his brothers did. He would rather walk on his own legs than perch atop a horse. "I am afraid I have other engagements."

Kit raised an eyebrow. "Miss Radforde?"

Edmund didn't want to admit his brother was right and so decided to share his other appointment for the day.

"I am meeting with some members of the Linnean Society."

"Whyever for?"

"They are sponsoring my expedition."

"Are you really going, then?"

Edmund tried not to be hurt by his brother's astonishment. He had been writing for years of his plans. Had Kit thought he would never make good on his ideas? Eager to prove him wrong, Edmund explained recent events.

"I am hoping to leave in October and spend the winter in New York or Boston. I'll gather the rest of my supplies and employ reliable guides. We will depart for the interior as soon as the weather breaks."

"It seems you have it all well in hand. I always knew you would do it. I should like to have seen the look on Father's face when you told him."

"You may yet see it. I haven't told the family."

"Oh?"

"But I will, soon. There are still some details to work out."

"And is one of those details a wedding?" Kit's lips quirked and eyes danced.

"Please, I get enough of that from Sophy."

"That was not an answer."

"This is no time for me to be taking on a wife."

Kit cocked his head. "While I do not recommend a long engagement, it would be better to secure her before you leave."

"You don't understand. I have no intention of marrying Miss Radforde."

"So why do Sophy and Mama think different?"

How to make him understand? Edmund could not share the arrangement with Miss Radforde.

"They are merely being fanciful. Miss Radforde is a friend. We have common interests and I enjoy her company. That is enough for them to assume matrimony in my future."

He stopped short of saying that Miss Radforde wished to stay a spinster and had no interest in him as a husband.

Kit chewed thoughtfully. Edmund was about to give more reasons he would not be marrying Miss Radforde when his brother spoke.

"I see. If they are that quick to assume matrimony, then it seems I must be mindful where I give my attentions."

"Unless you want to be caught in the parson's noose. Mama is likely making a list of potential women as we speak."

"Perish the thought," Kit murmured.

"You should also be prepared for a house party when you take possession of your estate."

Kit chuckled. "In that I fear she will be disappointed."

"You don't intend to send George packing from Haverfield?"

"Not yet, perhaps not ever."

Edmund wanted to ask what his brother meant. Haverfield belonged to Kit through Mama's family, but it had only come into his possession four years ago. Kit, happy as a naval officer, had asked George to take possession and manage the estate. As the future Lord Glenhaven, George knew how to run an estate and by all accounts had made Haverfield prosperous.

When Kit had written about coming home, their parents had begun to talk of him taking up residence at Haverfield as a near certainty. Edmund realized he had accepted their predictions the same way Sophy accepted their predictions about his marriage. Perhaps Kit's plans were quite different.

Before Edmund could ask, Kit stood. "I think I will go for a ride."

They said their goodbyes. As Edmund watched his retreating back, he resolved to discover his brother's true plans.

Once alone, Edmund's thoughts turned to his meeting with Miss Radforde. He had planned another afternoon at the London Botanic Garden. While she drew, he could tell her of his brother's return and ask to introduce them. After Sophy's excitement last night, Edmund had realized that he wished Miss Radforde to know his siblings.

Hours later, Edmund stood outside the Radforde home. The familiar footman opened the door but instead of stepping back to allow entrance, he stood firmly in the doorway.

"Mr. Glenhaven, sir. My apologies, but the ladies are not at home."

"Not at home?" Edmund knew what the words meant but didn't understand. He had made plans with Miss Radforde; surely she had not forgotten?

"Are they unwell?" he asked.

The footman hesitated, as if unsure what he was allowed to divulge, which was its own kind of answer. To be refused on Friday when he had arranged an outing on Wednesday was both confusing and humiliating. What could she mean by it? Did she no longer wish for his company?

He recalled her frown the night before. Was she angry with him? But then surely she would just talk to him. She had never been shy about sharing her opinions.

"Perhaps." The footman looked about conspiratorially. "If you come back in a quarter-hour, the young miss will be able to receive you."

It seemed even the footman knew he had been treated abominably. Edmund gave his thanks and turned to leave with as much dignity as he could muster. The footman's information had been another blow to his pride.

It seemed Miss Radforde was not refusing to see him, but away from home. Why? She knew they had an appointment. Was it possible she had accepted an offer from one of her admirers last night? Was she with someone else?

He did not know if the boiling of his blood was from jealousy or indignation at her ill treatment. Not wanting to be caught waiting on her doorstep, Edmund sent the carriage away and turned to the green oasis of the square.

Walking would alleviate his feelings. It was merely a coincidence that he would be able to monitor the Radforde's door as he walked about the square.

Nineteen

From her perch in Mr. Fitzroy's high phaeton, Charity had a clear view of the crush of pedestrians and carriages in Hyde Park. If they had been walking, she might have found much in the surrounding plants to catch her interest. But on the road, among the carriages, all she could see were other people. Charity had no desire to categorize or study any of them.

Though she had hoped for rain, the sky was clear and the day comfortably warm. There would be no early return to Radforde House, no chance of seeing Mr. Glenhaven.

She reminded herself that she did not care to see him. She did not care to ask him why he had not come to her box last night. She did not care to learn the identity of the young woman that was on his arm, the young woman with whom he had been alone.

It was not her concern. He had made her no promises and she had no claim on him. But Charity still felt betrayed. Did he have a mistress? Would she be bold enough to ask him?

"You are quite silent, Miss Radforde," Mr. Fitzroy said as he slowed the horses to greet another carriage. "Anyone would think you were not enjoying yourself."

"I was lost in thought," she said.

"Unpleasant thoughts, it seems."

Fitzroy turned to the approaching carriage and Charity forced a smile through the short conversation. Mr. Fitzroy had proudly introduced her to many fashionable people. Like a prize horse he had bought at auction, he enumerated her pedigree and qualities.

Charity saw the envious looks of the young women and heard the whispers of the old matrons as they passed. The scrutiny reminded her of the animals at the Exchange.

Mr. Fitzroy appeared not to notice as he expertly maneuvered the horses along the crowded path. Charity supposed that being handsome and heir to a title had accustomed him to such attentions.

Other women likely swooned at his dark hair, flashing smile, and endless array of pretty words. But Charity had come to prefer lighter hair, lopsided grins, and conversations of substance. Mr. Fitzroy kept up a steady stream of chatter, but it was full of comments about the people around them. She longed to discuss something like the morphology of the plants found in the park.

"It surprises me," Mr. Fitzroy said when they were alone once more, "that you are so unknown in society. I fear Glenhaven has been keeping you all to himself."

"Or perhaps I do not care for society."

The response came too quickly for her to censure. The evidence of Glenhaven's bad influence. She had spent too many afternoons speaking her mind.

Fitzroy laughed and more heads turned their way. He leaned close to whisper his reply. His shoulder pressed firmly into hers in the confined space. She felt nothing but annoyance at the contact.

"In truth, I do not care for society either," he murmured.

"For one who does not care for society, you spend a great deal of time in it."

"What would you have me do? Run away to America?"

Charity had no reply.

Did Fitzroy know of Glenhaven's plan or was it a turn of phrase? There was no way to ask. The approach of more people delayed the continuation of the conversation. Charity kept her tongue. She smiled and talked inanely of weather and parties.

By the time they left the park, she felt like a well-beaten carpet. Mr. Fitzroy's smiles had grown tiresome and she wished he would urge his horses faster. But he seemed content with a leisurely pace as he spoke of the dinner party he would attend.

"It is a pity you will not be there, for I am guaranteed an enjoyable evening when you are in attendance."

"I am sure that is not true."

"I only speak truth. Your mere presence is a pleasure."

The empty compliment did nothing to alleviate her irritation. She had done little but nod her head and make polite noises for most of the afternoon. Was that what he found pleasurable about her? Penelope was right; he cared only about her fortune. She would not trust anything Fitzroy said, even if it flattered her vanity.

Mr. Glenhaven never used empty flattery. When he told her that orange did not suit her coloring or that she had talent, she knew he was telling the truth. His sincerity made his praise all the more valuable. In turn, she never flattered him. They were always honest and such honesty was addictive.

Charity wished she could tell Mr. Fitzroy exactly what she thought of him. But though she did not care a fig for his opinion, Mother would never forgive her for offending an almost viscount.

"I hope that you might confer the pleasure of your company more often," he said.

"I am sure we will continue to encounter one another about town."

"You are too cruel, Miss Radforde." Fitzroy smiled as if her reticence was a welcome challenge.

Did he think she was being coy? Was there nothing she could say to deter him from his pursuit? If she fully revealed her love of botany and intention not to marry, would he cease to seek her favor? Or would he see it as a challenge?

Relief filled her as they turned into Russell Square. The white stone of the house glowed in the late afternoon sun and Charity wanted nothing more than to hide in her room until dinner. But first she would need to discover what had been said to Mr. Glenhaven when he arrived. Part of her hoped that he was waiting for her in the drawing room. She turned to Mr. Fitzroy as they slowed.

"Thank you, Mr. Fitzroy, for the ride," she said. "It was very...ah... illuminating."

His smile widened. "I only wish our time together could be longer, Miss Radforde." His gaze flitted over her shoulder. She turned expecting the footman to be waiting to help her down from her perch.

But instead, Mr. Glenhaven stood looking up at her, his expression furious.

Charity tried to smile through her discomfort. Where was the footman? She wanted down and far away from the men glaring daggers at each other, but the carriage was too high to manage by herself.

"Glenhaven, what a surprise." Mr. Fitzroy did not sound the least surprised.

"I was walking about the square," Glenhaven said.

"Ah, yes, a lovely little bit of greenery, though not as enjoyable as Hyde Park. Don't you agree, Miss Radforde?"

"I think they both have their merits," Charity attempted a neutral answer.

"Come now," Glenhaven said. "You must prefer one to the other."

Charity didn't like the edge in his voice and did not want to wait and hear more. She stood up and the phaeton rocked slightly.

Only when Glenhaven reached out to assist her, did she realize her error. There was still no footman. She could not reject his offered hand without causing more trouble and she could not get down without help.

Glenhaven took her hand firmly and placed it on his shoulder. Heat crept up her cheeks as she leaned forward and his hands came to her waist. Her breath caught. She was momentarily airborne, his arms keeping her aloft briefly, then he lowered her to the street. Her heart was beating rapidly, her body alight with awareness. It never felt like this with a footman.

She looked up at him. They had not been this close since their first meeting. How different it was to be held when one knew the gentleman well. He met her eyes, smiled victoriously, and turned back to Mr. Fitzroy.

Her heart stuttered. Glenhaven was just playing the part of jealous suitor and she was a fool to think otherwise. Suddenly, she recalled the young woman at the theatre. She took a step away from him and turned to Fitzroy.

"I look forward to our next ride," she said with her best attempt at a charming smile.

Mr. Fitzroy looked amused as he tipped his hat. "I shall live in anticipation of that moment."

He urged his horses forward. Charity watched briefly before turning to the house, intent on ignoring Mr. Glenhaven.

"Miss Radforde." His icy tone froze her in place. "May I have a word?"

Charity knew she owed him an explanation for breaking their plans, but she did not feel equal to the task. Her emotions were in a riot and her patience as tenuous as a spiderweb. But she could not just walk away.

She nodded.

He glanced up at the house and Charity realized this was hardly the place, especially if Mother was watching. Without prompting, she crossed the street to the square. He followed a few steps behind.

Once through the iron gate, she waited for him. His strides were long, his hands pulled behind his back as he stopped before her.

"We need to amend our arrangement." He spoke in clipped, precise syllables.

"What?" Panic seized her. She was not ready for their time to end, not ready to hear he had found someone he wished to truly court.

"I do not enjoy being made a fool," he said.

"I have not made a fool of you."

"You promised the afternoon to me and then went on a ride with Fitzroy."

"And you took some... some...woman to the theatre."

Agitated at her audacity, she walked a few paces.

He followed. "What? She is not—well, she is, but—that was my sister!"

"Oh." Though still angry, Charity was relieved at the revelation.

"But it should not matter. I should not have to explain when you— Who I spend time with is none of your concern."

"I might as easily say the same."

He clenched his teeth, making a muscle jump in his jaw. "You may cavort with anyone you wish—"

"Cavort?"

"—but do not go riding with another man when we have agreed on an outing."

As he spoke, he moved close enough to touch. The brown of his eyes had swallowed up the flecks of green. Mixed with his anger was something else, something hurt and broken. She felt a wave of shame. He must have been humiliated when he arrived at the house.

"I did refuse Mr. Fitzroy initially."

He scoffed and stepped past her. She could breathe a little easier without him so close.

"I told him I had another engagement, but Mother wanted—"

"No doubt she is salivating at the chance to capture a title. It was clever to use me to secure an introduction."

"That is unjust! I have been nothing but honest with you. I told you I have no wish to marry. I entered into our arrangement to avoid men like Fitzroy. I can't help that my mother keeps foisting them on me."

"Refuse her! Stop being a meek miss. Tell her your plans!"

"Like you have told your family about America?"

"That is hardly the same thing and had nothing to do with—" He huffed. "We were speaking of our arrangement."

"There is nothing to speak on. We have no arrangement." Charity spun on her heel and stormed away.

Her anger carried her out the gate and across the street. Her thoughts seethed. The gall to suggest she had used him, that she had lied. From the start, she had been completely truthful with Glenhaven. He should have trusted her, not lectured her. He should have understood she was powerless to control her fate.

It wasn't until she was alone in her room that other emotions rushed in. She threw herself on her bed as tears began to blur her vision. What would she do now? What would her life be without Glenhaven?

It wasn't just the prospect of spending time with other men, it was that none of those men would be him. The stupid arrangement had ruined her hopes for her future. Even if Father agreed to help her set up her own establishment, it would not make her happy.

How could she be happy as an independent spinster when she knew the possibility of a true partnership existed? Now she knew that a man could encourage her, debate with her, and make her heart race. Now she could see what kind of marriage she wanted.

She swallowed thickly. Was it possible Mother was right? Did she love Glenhaven?

The answer was immaterial. She had ended their arrangement. She would never see him again.

Twenty

EDMUND STOOD in the path and watched Miss Radforde disappear into her home. He wanted to follow her and demand an explanation. He wanted to storm away and never think of her again. He wanted the last ten minutes to have never happened at all. His emotions were like a swarm of swallows at dusk, in constant chaotic motion.

He turned his back on the house and began to walk. The movement was necessary to ease his mind. Was all at an end with Miss Radforde? He did not want to believe that she could so easily discard him. But if she were scheming for a title, then discarding him had always been the plan. How foolish to believe her declarations about marriage. Before long she would likely be Mrs. Fitzroy.

Her flimsy defense that her mother had made her go with Fitzroy did not alleviate his frustration. Mrs. Radforde's demands were no excuse. If Miss Radforde truly wished to avoid Fitzroy, she could have said no. Edmund had seen her forcefully speak her mind on many occasions. She had easily declared their arrangement at an end.

Perhaps it was for the best. The entire ruse had been a foolish mistake, a distraction.

She did not wish to see him, so he would suppress his desire to see her. He would not go to her with hat in hand and beg forgiveness. Miss

Radforde had done him a favor by cutting their ties. Without her in his life, he could focus on his expedition.

By the time he reached home, his spirits were depressed but he was determined on his new course.

Over the next week, Edmund threw himself into his plans. He was rarely about the house as he ordered equipment, met with new expedition members, and finalized funding arrangements. Despite the frenzy of activity, his mind continually drifted to Miss Radforde.

Sometimes he wished to share his arrangements with her, sometimes he wondered how she was spending her day, sometimes he just missed her smile. He occasionally still felt angry but often the anger was directed at himself.

His words that afternoon had done him no credit. He had not behaved like a gentleman and Miss Radforde had been right to chastise him. He often reviewed the conversation and wondered what he might have said to change its outcome. If he had confessed to jealousy or tender feelings, would that have made a difference?

"Have you made a decision yet, Glenhaven?" Mr. Brown asked.

"Hmm?" Edmund blinked as he tried to remember what they had been speaking of.

Mr. Brown frowned. This was not the first time Edmund had lost track of a conversation. The coffee house around them buzzed with voices, but they were tucked into their usual quiet corner.

"Leaving next month?" Mr. Brown prompted.

"Oh, yes. I think the reasoning for an earlier departure is sound."

Mr. Brown had been advocating for Edmund to depart ahead of the rest of the expedition. At first, Edmund had rejected the plan because he had reason to linger in England. But now there was nothing to keep him in London. An early departure had become an attractive prospect.

Going early summer would allow Edmund more time to find a proper guide and the opportunity to make connections with American scientific institutions in Boston. Their information could prove invaluable.

When the rest of the expedition members arrived in autumn, all would be ready. Instead of wintering in New York, they would travel to the frontier, getting as far as the Mississippi River. Next year, the expedition could begin as soon as the snow melted, and they would have more time in the mountains.

"So should I book your passage to America?" Mr. Brown asked.

Edmund nodded. "I see no reason to delay."

He expected to feel excitement and satisfaction that his plans were coming to fruition. Instead, he wondered what Miss Radforde would think. Would she approve? Would she miss him? Would she even notice his absence?

As he left the coffee house, Edmund realized it was time to tell his family. His departure was set and he had no more excuses. Tonight was the family dinner. The evening could start by celebrating Kit's return and end celebrating Edmund's departure.

That evening, determined to share his news when they retired to the drawing room, he spent the first course trying to conceal his nerves, a task made easier by the presence of his oldest brother George.

George took after Lord Glenhaven with his broad shoulders, dark coloring, and serious temperament. Though heir to the title, he currently lived at Haverfield in Surrey with his wife and son. Kit had gone for a short visit earlier in the week and Edmund wondered if it had changed his mind about the place. Busy with all his own affairs, Edmund had not found time to discuss the matter with his brother.

George spoke at length of his son Nathaniel's accomplishments. The boy was only three but declared to be the smartest and strongest child in all of England. When George's pride was in his son, Edmund didn't find it quite so annoying.

"When Isabella is out of this confinement you all must spend a month at Haverfield," George said. "There is plenty of room for everyone and I am sure she would enjoy the company after being so long apart."

The scheme was met with smiles. Sophy looked in raptures at the prospect. Edmund remained silent. There would be no month-long family party for him. No rough housing with little Nathaniel, holding the newest Glenhaven child, or admiring George's estate management.

"Of course, Edmund," George waved a fork in his direction, "your new bride would be welcome. What's her name again?"

"Radforde," Sophy replied. "Miss Charity Radforde."

Edmund swallowed his pheasant with difficulty. "I have made no promises to Miss Radforde."

"Really?" George looked aghast. "What happened? Not as rich as we were led to believe?"

"George," Mama chided.

"How can you think Edmund only cares for money?" Sophy cried.

"Because, my dear sister, he is a third son and a country parson. He should not be courting any woman that doesn't have at least ten thousand."

"Come now, George." Kit joined the conversation. "I think Edmund could do very well on two thousand." Kit tossed a wink at Edmund, proving that he was only trying to cause mischief.

"Two thousand! You have been too long at sea if you think that sum enough."

"I don't need Miss Radforde's money," Edmund cut into the brewing argument.

"Of course, Edmund," Mama said, "No one suspects your intentions toward Miss Radforde are anything but honorable."

Her words stung. He had not been honorable when he engaged in their subterfuge or when he accused her of trickery. Half his family thought him a fortune hunter and the rest thought him sincerely attached, all of them assumed he would soon be married. The honorable thing to do was tell the truth.

"As I have repeatedly said, I do not have any intentions toward Miss Radforde. Indeed, I have no plans to marry at present."

"I told you they quarreled." Sophy declared.

Edmund hated that the family had been talking about him and that Sophy had guessed the truth. There was nothing for it now but to explain his plans.

"I will not be marrying because I will be traveling to America to conduct a scientific survey of the Rocky Mountains."

"The Rocky Mountains?"

"Are you mad?"

"A survey?"

Mama, George, and Sophy all spoke at once. Kit merely raised his glass in a mock toast. Edmund did not dare look at Father as he continued his explanation.

"I am being sponsored by the Linnean Society and will be leading the expedition. I expect to leave in a month. The work will likely occupy me for several years."

"Well." George seemed at a loss for words.

Edmund risked a glance at Father. He did not appear angry, but neither was he pleased. He ate slowly, allowing others to speak.

Unlike his brothers, Mama and Sophy were distressed, and it took several minutes answering their questions before they were satisfied that Edmund was in earnest.

"I am sure it is a great honor," Mama said. Her smile did not quite reach her eyes.

"I still don't comprehend why this expedition means you can't get married," Sophy said after the dessert had been brought out and the conversation about his plans slowed.

"Our sister has a point," Kit said. "I believe they have married people in America."

"Sophy, he may not feel he is in a position to marry," Mama said.

"But she has money, he could secure her promise. I am sure she would wait—"

Mama raised her hand. "That is enough." She glanced at Father. "We shall go to the drawing room, now."

Mama stood and Sophy followed, looking longingly at her untouched dessert. Kit reached for her plate and placed it atop his empty one. Sophy stuck out her tongue and Kit chuckled.

Edmund could not even smile at their antics. Sophy's optimistic plan had reminded him that his situation with Miss Radforde was hopeless. His anticipation for the expedition was dampened once more.

He should be pleased. The revelation had gone better than expected. Neither parent had outright objected to his plan. Though Edmund suspected Mama was unhappy with the prospect, he could not guess his father's feelings. Lord Glenhaven had not even raised an eyebrow at the news. Was he not surprised?

No sooner had the thought occurred than Lord Glenhaven turned to his youngest son.

"Tell me, Edmund." Father's tone was colder than the ice they ate for dessert. "Why did you go with your hat in hand to all the learned societies of London instead of asking me to finance the venture?"

Edmund glanced at his brothers, but they were all carefully studying their drinks.

"I did not think you would approve."

"And why should I not?"

"Because you never approve of anything I do." Edmund knew he sounded like a petulant child, but he could not help it. Since he was twelve, Father had not supported any of his choices.

Lord Glenhaven leaned forward, resting his forearms on the table. "I did not approve of you wasting your talents as a clergyman. I wanted you to show some ambition, some hint that you wanted more in life." He leaned back and spread out his hands. "This expedition to America is more than I could have hoped. I would have happily supported you. When you return, I am sure it will be to great fanfare. The right discoveries might even fetch you a knighthood."

His father's approval was more affecting than Edmund expected. His cheeks warmed and he took a drink to cover his confusion.

"It was embarrassing to have the men at my club ask for my opinion on the matter when I had never heard a whisper of it from you."

The rebuke put Edmund more at ease. "I never meant to cause you embarrassment."

"Don't feel bad, Edmund," Kit said. "It is the lot of the younger sons to embarrass their father." He raised his glass in a mock toast.

"Christopher—" Father began.

"Let us not talk about me," Kit interrupted. "I wish to know about this business with Miss Radforde."

Edmund frowned. He would much rather have Father pick apart every detail of his plan than talk further of his pretend courtship.

"I have no business with Miss Radforde."

"Oh, we know," Kit said, "You have been sulking about all week. Is Sophy right? Was there a quarrel? Or perhaps a spat? George, is a spat greater than a quarrel?"

Edmund contemplated throwing his drink at his brother. "It does not matter. I'm leaving for America."

"You told her about the expedition and she threw you over?" George guessed.

"No! It was a… misunderstanding."

"Whatever the reason," Father said. "I believe it is for the best. Now is not the time to be taking on a silly wife."

"She is not silly. She—" Edmund stopped his protest at Father's raised eyebrows. "But I agree, it is not the time for marriage."

Kit scoffed.

Father sighed. "Edmund, we will discuss your plans in depth tomorrow. But now, let us join your mother. Sophy has a piece on the harp she has been practicing all week."

Kit did not immediately stand, but stared at his empty glass. Edmund nudged his shoulder and he started from his thoughts. He put down his glass and pushed back his chair. Father and George were already in the hall.

Kit turned to him, his face serious. "Are you truly delaying marriage to Miss Radforde because of your expedition?"

"It is a bit more complicated than that," Edmund admitted.

"Complicated? Aren't affairs of the heart always complicated?"

"I suppose."

"If you love her, if any part of you wants to marry her, you should not delay. I promise there is no torture more acute than having the woman you love pledged to another."

Without waiting for a reply, Kit turned and left the room. Edmund blinked after him. Kit was so rarely serious and it seemed he was speaking from experience. Was there a woman that he loved but could not marry?

Wherever the insight had come from, Edmund knew Kit was right. The thought of Miss Radforde pledged to another was a weight on his heart. Would it always feel that way? With heavy steps, he made his way to the drawing room.

Mama was waiting for him at the door and quickly slipped her arm through his. He glanced at Sophy tuning her harp and the rest of the family settling into chairs.

"What I need to say will only take a moment," Lady Glenhaven said brusquely.

"Mama, I regret I did not tell you about America—"

"And I regret that my son gives up so easily."

"Pardon?"

"I speak of Miss Radforde. It is plain you have argued, which is only natural, given your plans, but that is no reason to end your association. One does not quit the field after a single disappointment."

Edmund opened his mouth to protest and then closed it. She was right. He had given up. After one argument he had literally walked away.

"A true partnership requires you to have the courage and humility to discuss disagreements. Speak with her."

A dozen reasons why he could not speak with Miss Radforde jumped to his mind. Reasons he had rehearsed to himself over and over in the last week, but now they seemed nonsensical. The reasons of a prideful coward. It was easier to accept their arrangement was at an end than to confess that he was jealous, that he wished for something more than a pretend courtship.

When he didn't reply, Mama patted his arm. "I don't want you to spend your life wondering what might have been."

She left him and took her seat beside Father. Edmund followed slowly, his mind working through her words.

The week apart from Miss Radforde had taught him how deeply his feelings ran, how firmly rooted she was in his heart. He could not imagine a better partner for his life. Kit was right. If he returned home and she had married another, he would always regret not being honest with her now. The truth was that he wanted to court her, wanted to see if their unlikely friendship could be more.

He sat but did not pay attention to Sophy's performance. He clapped along with the others and smiled when Kit joined her in a duet. The brightness of the melody and clear sound of their voices was secondary to his own thoughts.

With the benefit of hindsight, he could see that Miss Radforde was right to chastise him. His anger had been fueled by jealousy. He had questioned her honor and honesty. Were she a man, she could have demanded pistols at dawn. Perhaps if he had not been so unfeeling, she would not have ended the arrangement.

She was a singular woman and he was a fool if he did not try to make amends. Could she forgive him? Would she consider a real courtship? It was possible she would reject his offer. She might refuse to speak with him, she might still marry Fitzroy, but he had to try. Mama was right. He couldn't live his whole life wondering.

After the second duet, George left his seat beside Mama and came to sit by Edmund.

"Flowers," George said.

"Beg pardon?"

"Whenever I need to apologize to my wife, I find fresh cut flowers an excellent opening gambit."

Edmund half-smiled. It seemed the entire family was determined to help him with Miss Radforde.

"Thank you."

"And trust me, marriage to the right woman is worth all the torture of the courtship."

After a night of contemplation, Edmund arose early the next morning. He knew what he must do. He would apologize, he would confess his desire to properly court her. He could not leave for America without at least trying to secure her affections.

Twenty-One

Russell Square was quiet as Charity and Penelope walked along the perimeter path. It was too early for the nursery maids with their charges and the other fashionable residents were likely still abed. Charity always enjoyed the freedom of the mornings, but her visits to the square were now tainted by her memories of Mr. Glenhaven.

She could not walk past the statue of the Duke of Bedford or through the entrance gate without recalling their conversations. In the week since she had stormed away from Glenhaven, Charity had wondered several times if she had made the right decision.

In turns she felt justified, repentant, foolish, and angry. None of these emotions changed her desire to see him, only what kind of reception she would give him. But the nature of her reception hardly mattered when he had disappeared from her life.

He had not called, had not attended the garden party, or the ball to seek an audience. Without him occupying her days, she had been forced into company with other men. The time had not improved her opinion of suitors and only amplified her desire to be with Glenhaven.

It was an impossible wish, but she could not escape it.

They had come near the bronze statue of the duke. Charity stared at the spot where Glenhaven had astonished her with his offer of visiting Somerset House.

"I can continue alone," Penelope broke into her thoughts, "if you wish to do some scribbling."

Further down the path flowers in full bloom beckoned, but Charity felt no desire to examine them.

"No, I thank you."

Penelope sighed. "Charity, I wish you would tell me what happened with Mr. Glenhaven."

Penelope had made several remarks about his absence and asked several more questions. Charity had avoided saying anything of substance. How could she explain without revealing all her foolishness?

They walked in silence for a few long moments, the crunch of the gravel beneath their feet echoing in Charity's ears.

"Did he take liberties?" Penelope asked.

"What? No, he would never..."

The notion was absurd. Mr. Glenhaven did not care for her in that way. Indeed, given his disappearance, she doubted he cared for her at all. Penelope pulled Charity to a stop and took her hands.

"You can tell me if he did. I, of all people, understand such things. How strong emotions can lead you into folly. It is not your fault. It is mine for not being there. I saw you both cross the street that afternoon. I should have rushed down the stairs, I should have—"

Charity squeezed her friend's hands. "Pen, stop, you take too much upon yourself. Let me assure you that Mr. Glenhaven has not trespassed upon me."

"Truly?"

"I am sorry I made you worry."

"I don't mind worrying. Only," Penelope frowned. "What happened that day?"

Charity continued walking. This conversation would be easier if she wasn't facing her friend.

"We quarreled. He felt that I had been insincere in my actions by riding with Mr. Fitzroy."

It was the truth, or close enough.

"Of all the ridiculous." Penelope shook her head. "He was jealous of

Fitzroy taking you on one ride? He has spent countless afternoons with you. How could he doubt your affections?"

"My affections..." Charity's cheeks warmed. "Mr. Glenhaven is a friend."

"A friend? Oh, Charity, you can't possibly believe that. A friend does not act in such a manner. The man is besotted."

Her heart sped up and she hated it. She hated that she desperately wished to ask her opinion of Glenhaven's feelings. But her friend's opinion was of little value. All their outings, all the whispers and small touches were not marks of love. Penelope had observed their play acting, and they had played their parts too well.

"You must believe me. There is nothing between me and Mr. Glenhaven. In fact, I don't expect to ever see him again."

Charity wished her voice had remained steady for her declaration.

Penelope patted her arm.

"Do not pity me. My happiness is not tied to him. I do not wish to be yoked to any man."

"A feeling I know well."

Charity turned to Penelope and saw deep understanding there. Did she miss her Mr. Aston? Even after all he had done? Before Glenhaven, Charity would have declared missing such a man absurd, but now she understood that such feelings were hard to master.

"I have written to my father and asked to set up my own establishment," Charity said. "When I come of age, we might set up together with Rosamund and spend our days however we wish."

Penelope's rueful smile was not the reaction Charity expected.

"You don't believe me?"

"I think you need to reconcile with your Mr. Glenhaven."

"He is not mine."

"You have just had a misunderstanding," Penelope said. "I refuse to believe that he will forsake you so easily."

Penelope would never believe until Charity revealed the truth of her association with Glenhaven. How might she begin to explain the situation?

As they left the lime walk, the question took flight like a flushed pheasant. A familiar figure stood at the corner. Mr. Glenhaven was there, standing with his back to them.

Her heart leapt traitorously. Charity would have stopped in her tracks, but Penelope continued to pull her along.

"Ah, you see," Penelope whispered. "I will eat my bonnet if he is not here to apologize."

Was she right? It hardly seemed possible. He turned and saw them approaching. His eyebrows rose and he almost smiled. He took a step toward them and then paused as if considering. His unease gave her courage.

With each step she couldn't help but admire how fine he looked in the morning light. His slim figure was accentuated by his long coat and the black of his hat made his hair appear lighter than usual. Had he always been so handsome or had his absence increased his charms? When had he become charming?

With each step her heart beat faster, like a stream rushing downhill toward a waterfall. She gripped Penelope's arm and her friend patted her hand. They were soon close enough to greet him.

"Mrs. Aston, Miss Radforde." He gave a correct, formal bow. "I am sorry to disturb you." He spoke quickly as if afraid of being silenced. "Miss Radforde, would you do me the pleasure of accepting this."

He held out a small book. Charity looked at it and then met his pleading eyes. She took a step forward and reached for the object. It had no title. She flipped the pages, but they were empty. Why had he given her an empty book?

"Thank you?"

He glanced at Penelope. "I hoped that you might fill it with... That is, would you do me the honor of visiting Kew Gardens on Sunday?"

Though unexpected, the offer was far from unwelcome. Her emotions were in such a riot she did not know what to feel. Despite what had happened, he wished to take her to the gardens. Charity knew that she would have accepted any chance to be with Mr. Glenhaven again but the chance to see the gardens made the reply easy.

"Yes, of course, I would love to see the royal gardens."

His smile was like sunshine breaking through clouds. It warmed and stunned her at the same time.

"I thought the gardens were closed on Sunday," Penelope said.

"They are, but I have received special permission for Miss Radforde."

Some unnamable emotion swelled up; like gratitude but deeper.

"We will have to ask Mrs. Radforde," Penelope said.

His smile dimmed. "Yes, of course. If you could send word, I will make the appropriate arrangements."

"There is no need," Charity said. "I will ensure she agrees."

She was rewarded for her boldness by another sunny smile. She grinned back. They might have stood there smiling at each other for hours if Penelope had not taken her by the arm.

"It was lovely to see you, sir. Now we must return to the house."

Mr. Glenhaven let them go with a bow. "Until Sunday, then."

Charity hugged his present to her chest. Her feet did not seem to touch the ground as they crossed the street.

By that evening, the euphoria of seeing Mr. Glenhaven again had worn off and left Charity with a confused mind and doubtful heart. She examined his actions and her own feelings. He had said nothing by way of apology nor mentioned their arrangement. But there had been no opportunity with Penelope there.

What would he say when they had privacy? How would she respond? These questions plagued her over the next few days.

Charity had been prepared to battle with her mother but had met with no opposition. Mother, despite her objections to Mr. Glenhaven, had readily agreed to the outing because she wished to accompany them. Mother was fascinated by the royal family's history at Kew and would not pass up the opportunity of a private tour. Charity hoped Mr. Glenhaven had risen in her estimation.

Sunday morning dawned bright and warm. Charity fidgeted through the church service and heaved a sigh of relief when Mother didn't linger afterwards. At home, she changed quickly and made her way to the drawing room in hopes of being alone with Mr. Glenhaven when he arrived. Her reticule was heavy with both *The Picture of London* and her new notebook, but she didn't pull out either.

She could not sit, let alone stare at words on a page. She could not pretend it was the chance to examine exotic plants that made her pace about the room. All her thoughts were bent on Mr. Glenhaven and what might pass between them that afternoon.

Mother and Penelope soon joined her, all smiles and eagerness. When Mr. Glenhaven arrived, they were all there to greet him in the drawing room. Charity tried not to stare but her gaze was continually drawn to his. Each time their eyes met, her breath caught. Is this what the poet meant by absence making the heart grow fonder?

"We are so grateful to you, Mr. Glenhaven," Mother said. "I always say a private tour is the only way to visit such a place. Of course, I could not be comfortable in anything less well-sprung than my own carriage. I am sure you understand."

"I do, ma'am. But I hope that Miss Radforde will still be comfortable in the phaeton I brought."

"How gallant of you to consider her comfort. Charity, dear, you are welcome to ride in our carriage. I am sure Mr. Glenhaven would not mind."

If the man had been Fitzroy or Hunter, Charity would have eagerly agreed but with Glenhaven, she was eager for their drive alone.

"I am sure I will enjoy the phaeton," she said.

"Very well." Mother turned for the door.

Charity caught Glenhaven's eye as his grin grew wider and more lopsided. How she had missed that smile.

He offered his arm. Taking it felt as natural as breathing. Charity's anxieties began to melt in the warmth of his presence. When they exited to the street, she looked at the fine phaeton waiting in front of the Radforde landau.

"A loan from my brother," Mr. Glenhaven murmured. "When your mother wrote to say she wished to travel in her carriage, I thought we might enjoy some privacy."

That his wishes were in tune with her own was a good omen.

Mother hurried off to ensure their picnic had been packed to her satisfaction. The various bundles took up an entire bench, leaving Charity to wonder how they would ever eat so much food.

Penelope gave them a stern look before following Mother, but Charity didn't care to decipher it. All her attention was on how she would be alone with Mr. Glenhaven for the entire nine mile drive.

The birdsong seemed especially cheerful as she settled into her seat and Glenhaven sat beside her. She glanced back to see Mother and Penelope still climbing into their carriage. When she turned around, he was regarding her seriously. Before she could ask what was the matter, he spoke.

"Miss Radforde, you must allow me to apologize for my abominable behavior. It was unjust to assume you had ill intentions. You were right to sever our connection. I have always admired your honesty, so please tell me if I have a hope of regaining your favor."

Charity couldn't help but be affected by his speech, though she wished he had waited until they were away from prying ears to give it. Had he wanted others to hear? But no, Mother and Penelope were too far away and he had spoken too softly. His words were sincere, and for her alone.

"There is every hope," she replied honestly.

He released a long breath. Had he really been in doubt?

"Mr. Glenhaven, I freely forgive you if you will forgive me for my hasty words and accusations. And for not keeping my appointment. It was ill done. I should not have let Mother—"

He waved his hand. "And I should have trusted you."

"The way I trusted you after seeing you with your sister?"

His mouth twitched. "Let us both agree to trust each other in the future and be done with these self-recriminations."

"Mr. Glenhaven," the groom appeared beside them. "Mrs. Radforde is ready to leave."

With a nod and a wave, he put the horses into motion.

The stately town homes slipped by and Mr. Glenhaven kept up a running commentary of interesting facts about the plants and residents. Charity was content to just listen. She had missed his keen mind.

They went north to avoid the crowding near Hyde Park and Kensington, before turning west. When the houses grew further apart and the land scattered with fields, Charity let out a happy sigh.

"I think I will always be content as long as I have new things to see and learn."

Mr. Glenhaven chuckled beside her. "You are a unique woman, Miss Radforde."

"Am I? I feel many of my friends could make the same claim. Certainly you enjoy knowledge as I do."

"True. My desire to better understand is like a hunger. I feel I am always asking questions to feed it."

"Well, I hope your hunger has been well-satiated with our excursions."

"Our time together." He paused and then continued. "I have enjoyed it immensely. I would be very disappointed to end our acquaintance."

Charity looked up and met his eyes. There was an earnest sincerity there that warmed her more than the sun. Boldly, she laid her hand upon his arm.

"I spoke the truth before, I do not care for Fitzroy or any other," she said. "I'm sorry for my rash words in the square. I have no desire to change our arrangement."

He glanced at her hand and then up at her. He seemed troubled and, feeling foolish, she began to withdraw her hand. He caught it and gently pressed it.

"Then we are in agreement," he murmured.

He brought her hand to his lips. The contact sent a shiver up her arm. The carriage gave a jolt and he released her hand to bring the horses under control.

She swallowed and turned her attention to the road. If they had planned to convince Mother and Penelope of their attachment, such a display would have served their purpose. But though they were in an open carriage, there was no way his kiss could have been observed from behind. The gesture, like the words, was sincere.

"I am glad you accepted my invitation," he said.

"I am glad you made the invitation."

Their eyes met but she could not hold his gaze for long. "It is hard to refuse the royal gardens." She tried for a teasing tone.

"I am not above bribery. I reasoned that even if you hated me, your desire to see them might make you agree."

"A clever gamble."

"My brother recommended flowers. I thought this trip more fitting than something from the hothouse."

"How well you know me, sir."

Surreptitiously, Charity touched the back of her hand. The heat of his lips seemed to linger there. What would it be like to hold his hand? To feel his lips on hers?

She held back a sigh. She could not feel this way for a man that did not return her affections, for a man that would soon leave for America.

Twenty-Two

EDMUND HAD BEGUN the morning with the earnest intention of declaring himself to Miss Radforde, but he was finding it hard to put his intentions into action. She had forgiven him, had conversed in her lively way, but when he began to speak of his regard he could not discern if she was receptive.

True, she had touched him, but only so she could emphasize that she wanted all to remain the same between them. He did not want that. He wanted a real courtship with her, he wanted her heart. But given the choice between their ruse and nothing, he would take their ruse.

With their apologies made, they fell into their normal mode of conversation and the miles passed easily.

Though Edmund had visited Kew and its gardens before, he found his anticipation mounting as they drew near. His focus was drawn to Miss Radforde as he watched for the moment they made a turn and the Great Pagoda came into view, towering over the lush countryside. He was rewarded for his patience by her small gasp and widening eyes. Would he ever tire of giving her new things to discover?

"What does your book have to say on the gardens?" he asked, just as he did at every new place.

"Why Mr. Glenhaven, I thought you would never ask."

With a grin, she reached into her reticule, pulled out her red-bound book, and began to share the information.

"It is laid out with great taste and decorated with a variety of temples and picturesque objects by Sir William Chambers," she read aloud. "It claims the exotics are the finest collection of plants in the world."

"I wonder what the French would think of that notion."

She smiled but didn't look up from her book. "It says the new house for the African plants is 110 feet long. Why, it must be filled with exotics. And the pagoda is 163 feet high with an enchanting prospect. Do you think we might climb it?"

Edmund couldn't contain his smile as she looked up eagerly. "I think that an excellent idea, though your mother might object to all those stairs."

Miss Radforde made a face before returning to read the rest of the information.

He slowed as they approached Kew Green. Surrounded by inns, mansions, and the parish chapel, it might have been any village green except for the royal palace just beyond. They drove across it to the gate and entrance to the royal grounds. Edmund gave his name to the guard, who nodded.

"Mr. Bauer is expecting you in the Orangery," the guard said.

"Excellent, thank you," Edmund replied.

"Mr. Bauer?" Miss Radforde asked as they began to move once more.

"Yes, Mr. Franz Bauer. He is the botanic painter in residence at the gardens. He is employed to record all the plants."

"I know who the botanic painter to His Majesty is," Miss Radforde said, her voice tinged with suppressed excitement. "I just didn't know we would meet him."

"He is our guide. I arranged it all with Mr. Brown. I thought you would enjoy having Mr. Bauer share his insights."

Her quick gasp of pleasure made all his efforts worthwhile.

He pulled the horses to a stop in front of the Orangery. It was a single-story, white-bricked building, the facade dominated by large arched windows which showed an interior green with plants. They alighted from the carriage and were soon joined by Mrs. Radforde and Mrs. Aston.

Mrs. Radforde kept looking past the Orangery to the old palace beyond. A glass house could not hold her attention when a royal residence was nearby.

"Charity, dear, did you see the new palace as we approached? It is certainly an ugly pile. I never did like Gothic structures."

Mrs. Radforde spoke with more enthusiasm than Edmund had expected. She discussed the merits of the two palaces as they walked the short gravel path toward the Orangery. Mr. Bauer appeared at what looked to be a window but was actually a large glass door.

"How clever," Mrs. Aston said as Mr. Bauer pushed it open to greet them.

The man seemed younger than his sixty years. Stocky, with a wide face and beaked nose, he smiled as he approached and introductions were made.

"I am so glad Mr. Brown asked me to accompany you this morning," Mr. Bauer said, his German accent barely detectable. "I hope to show some of the wonders of the gardens." He gestured to the Orangery. "We shall start here."

They stepped inside and were hit by a wall of warm, humid air.

Mrs. Radforde gave a sound of surprise. "The air is quite oppressive."

"It's for the plants, Mother. They use furnaces and steam to make it more like their native climate."

"Well, it may be suitable for them, but it is quite intolerable for me."

"Mrs. Radforde," Mr. Bauer said congenially, "Perhaps you will like this air better when you see what wonderful things it allows us to grow in our colder climate."

He offered his arm and Mrs. Radforde took it with a smile, her discomfort seemingly forgotten.

Edmund turned to offer his arm to Miss Radforde, but she was intently examining a broad leafed plant. He watched her, enamored by the way her eyebrows came together in thought. To think he almost destroyed his chance to see that look again.

She turned from the plant and caught him watching. Her cheeks colored and she looked away.

They moved further into the building, walking down the aisle of plants that grew up toward the high, flat ceiling. Mr. Bauer explained the building's original purpose for growing oranges and how, as the royal collection of plants grew, it had become a refuge for exotic plants that could not survive an English winter. He was careful to point out plants even a layman would be familiar with, like coffee or nutmeg, as well as those more foreign, like a camphor tree from Japan.

Mrs. Radforde seemed impressed by the variety though Edmund doubted she truly understood the wonder of it all. That so many plants from all continents and climes were gathered under one roof was astounding.

It was a testament to the Crown's commitment to botany and to the work of men like Sir Joseph and all those who had collected and catalogued them. Edmund wished to be a part of such a noble cause. One day, plants he discovered in the Americas would thrive in Kew.

Unlike her mother, Miss Radforde seemed to fully grasp the achievement the plants represented. She paused to gape at everything, often lingering behind the group, furiously sketching in her notebook. Edmund wished Mrs. Radforde had not accompanied them. Miss Radforde should be allowed to tarry and examine all she wished to see.

Over halfway through the building they came to a five-foot potted palm, positioned in the full sunlight. A chair was set beside it and an easel with a half-finished botanic drawing. It seemed Mr. Bauer had been employing his time productively while he waited. Miss Radforde looked eagerly at the half-finished sketch.

"Is that some kind of fruit?" Mrs. Radforde asked as she pointed at a column of half-moon objects that seemed to drip from the trunk of the tree. Some at the top had turned yellow but the rest were as green as the large palm leaves. Edmund bounced on his heels in anticipation. He had specifically asked if it were possible to sample a banana on their tour.

"You have a good eye, madam," Mr. Bauer said. "That is a common fruit in the tropics but rare in England. Even when it can be grown it does not often bear fruit. It is a banana tree."

"I have never heard of bananas," Mrs. Aston said.

"I told you about them," Miss Radforde replied. "There was a replica at Bullock's museum." She glanced quickly at Edmund and he knew she remembered their conversation there.

"Yes, it seems it was a good likeness," Edmund said. "Tell me, Mr. Bauer, is this *musa sapientum* or *musa paradisisca*?"

"It is *sapientum*," Miss Radforde said. "Notice the purple stripes on the stalks."

Mr. Bauer smiled. "An excellent observation, Miss Radforde. The species is indeed *sapientum*."

He moved closer to the tree and pointed at the spike of bananas. "Another indication is the size and shape of the fruit. The banana is shorter and rounder than the plantain."

Miss Radforde gazed into the tree. "I understand. Is there a plantain tree in the gardens? It would be instructive to observe both species."

"Now Charity, that is quite enough," Mrs. Radforde murmured.

"Yes, Mother." Miss Radforde ducked her head and stepped back from the tree.

"I appreciate Miss Radforde's enthusiasm." Mr. Bauer smiled. "It is rare to meet a young lady with both knowledge and perception in the field of botany."

The compliment had not been directed at Edmund, but he felt a swelling of pride. Why did Mrs. Radforde not have the same pride in her daughter? Why must she think her intellect something to be hidden?

"I insist that you all sample the fruit." Mr. Bauer stepped up to the plant and plucked two yellow bananas from the bunch and handed one to Edmund. "The flavor is sweet but rich."

There was laughter as Edmund followed the instructions on peeling the strange fruit. Mr. Bauer produced a tray and a knife and soon the two bananas had been cut into pieces. The tray was passed around and they were all soon biting into the pale, white flesh.

As promised, the taste was sweet, though not as sweet as a strawberry. Edmund savored it before attempting to chew. The fruit was soft and squished about his mouth until he awkwardly swallowed. Perhaps it would be better to bite his piece in two?

"What a strange texture," Mrs. Radforde said.

Miss Radforde was grinning broadly through her own chewing,

while Mrs. Aston was reaching for a second piece. Miss Radforde did not hesitate to follow her friend, but Mrs. Radforde declined. It seemed the mother did not enjoy new experiences as much as the daughter.

As they ate, Mr. Bauer spoke at length about where the banana could be found and its many uses. Edmund found his mind wandering from Mr. Bauer's commentary as he contemplated what made the banana averse to bearing fruit in England. Was it just the temperature or the soil or perhaps the quality of the light or the air? He stopped his thoughts, reminding himself to attend to Miss Radforde instead of getting distracted.

But when he looked at his companion, she was sketching the banana tree, lost in her own observations. Perhaps she was thinking upon the same questions as himself? He couldn't wait to hear her insights on the subject.

He was seized by the idea of her sketching while he took notes and samples in the wilds of America. As they worked, they would discuss their observations. She would help him to consider different ideas, while challenging his own. They would make a good team.

Mrs. Radforde turned and noticed her daughter; a small frown pinched her features. Her thoughts were clearly not as pleasant as Edmund's. Any moment now he expected a scolding.

"Mrs. Radforde," Edmund said. "I find the heat is becoming too much. Perhaps you would like to walk out with me?"

Barely masking her surprise, the older woman agreed. Edmund caught Miss Radforde's sly, approving smile, though she made no comment and did not lift her eyes from her sketch.

"We shall not be long," Mr. Bauer said.

"No need to rush," Edmund replied.

He offered his arm to Mrs. Radforde. She took it graciously, and they moved quickly through the remaining plants and out into the fresh air. The day was warm but felt chilly compared to the heat of the Orangery.

Mrs. Radforde took a deep breath. "Ah, that is much better."

They wandered down the path, admiring the beds of flowers and stately trees. The lawn opened up before them and revealed the picturesque lake with its charming Palladian bridge. The pagoda towered in the distance, drawing the eye and exciting the imagination. Edmund wished he could be enjoying the view with Miss Radforde.

"No wonder Queen Charlotte enjoys summers here," Mrs. Radforde said. "Why, this view must be visible from every south-facing window in the palace."

The older lady turned her back on the wilderness to take in the prospect of the royal residence. The red brick was brilliant in the afternoon sun, the façade pleasingly balanced with three Dutch gables and four rows of large windows. A forest of chimneys sprouted from the roof and Mrs. Radforde began to count them.

It soon became apparent that her chief interest in coming on their excursion was to see the two palaces and imagine herself walking in the footsteps of royalty. The wealth of plants and scientific knowledge were nothing compared to the connection with the ruling family.

Mrs. Radforde had a great deal of information about the monarch and his ill health, about the queen and her elegance and taste, about the wayward Regent and his siblings. Edmund did his best to appear interested in the topic but found his mind straying.

"Do not you agree?" Mrs. Radforde looked at him expectantly.

He cursed himself. "Pardon, I have lost the thread of our conversation."

She pursed her lips and he couldn't help but notice the resemblance to her daughter when irritated. He wondered if she would also scold him.

"You are very like my daughter."

"I take that as a high compliment."

Mrs. Radforde tipped her head. "I think a unification of mind and taste important in an alliance."

"As do I."

"But a couple can be too similar in temperament." Mrs. Radforde's cool gaze seemed to bore into him.

"Surely it is better to be too similar than always at odds?" he offered.

"I believe young people are not always the best judge for what will make them happy."

Edmund could make no answer and the conversation went no

further. She turned back to the palace and soon the rest of their party emerged from the Orangery. Edmund was grateful for the reprieve as he turned to greet them.

Did Mrs. Radforde truly object to him on the basis of their similarities? Or was it merely an excuse to reject his attentions? If the mother was so set against him, how could he convince the daughter to accept his suit?

Mr. Bauer continued the tour by heading west along the path towards the botanic gardens that were generally open to the public. Mrs. Radforde took her daughter's arm and walked with their guide, leaving Edmund to offer his arm to Mrs. Aston.

In the months since their first meeting, the young chaperone had opened up more, but she still preferred to listen or stay in the background. Edmund thought she had warmed to him, at least she frowned at him less now.

"How did you find the Orangery?" he asked for want of anything else to say.

"I can't pretend to enjoy it as much as Charity, but it was all very interesting."

"That is gratifying to hear."

"It was kind of you to distract Mrs. Radforde."

"I fear it did not raise me in her estimation."

"She is a woman of set opinions."

"Is there no way for me to get into her good graces?" Edmund asked.

Mrs. Aston considered before answering. The path crunched beneath their feet, fragments of Mr. Bauer's commentary reached them, and Edmund began to despair of an answer.

"Like most mothers, Mrs. Radforde wishes for her daughter's secure and happy marriage," Mrs. Aston said. "She has very firm notions on who would be the best match, but I believe her mind would change if Charity was in receipt of an earnest proposal."

Edmund felt warmth creep up his cheeks. Miss Radforde had often spoken of Mrs. Aston as the boldest of her friends, but he had never had occasion to witness it. He liked her better when she was silently judging him. From her smile, it seemed she was enjoying his discomfort.

"I—" His voice came out too high. He discreetly cleared his throat. "I thank you, for speaking so plainly."

They fell into silence as Edmund contemplated her advice. He had wished only to earnestly court Miss Radforde. It was a little soon to speak of marriage. Of course, Mrs. Aston wouldn't understand his reticence; she thought they had been courting for weeks.

When they reached the beds of exotics, Edmund struggled to listen to Mr. Bauer's words. They approached a long glass house. It was not as impressive or well-built as the Orangery but appeared just as full of plants.

"This was purpose built for the reception of African plants," Mr. Bauer said. He gestured to the door.

"Oh, I couldn't possibly go into another hot house," Mrs. Radforde said.

"We can certainly skip the Africa house," Mr. Bauer replied as he looked to the others for their opinion.

"I can stay with Mrs. Radforde," Edmund offered. He did not wish Miss Radforde to miss anything on account of her mother.

Mrs. Radforde looked as if she might argue, but Mrs. Aston spoke first.

"Mr. Bauer, is that the aviary I see?" She gestured to the small white cupola peeking above the trees.

"It is indeed."

"I would greatly enjoy seeing it. Perhaps Mrs. Radforde and I might explore it while you are in the hot house?"

Though she had asked Mr. Bauer the question, Mrs. Aston looked to Mrs. Radforde for approval. Some mothers might object to the arrangement, thinking Mr. Bauer not a fit chaperone despite his age and position.

"Yes, I would like to see the aviary," Mrs. Radforde said.

"Of course, madam. We shall join you when we are done." He proceeded to give brief, precise directions. As the two ladies moved down the path, Mr. Bauer turned to his remaining guests. "Shall we?"

Edmund shared a smile with Miss Radforde. Now she could speak freely, ask questions, and sketch at her leisure. Now she would be the woman he knew best. They entered the warmth of the hot house and began their inspection of the plants.

"The majority of these were gathered by Mr. Masson during his three years in the Cape Colony," Mr. Bauer explained. "He sent back hundreds of new species. It is the work of a lifetime to catalogue them all properly."

"A work you are most adept at," Miss Radforde said. "I have always admired your illustrations."

"Thank you," Mr. Bauer said. "I find making them much easier here where I can examine the specimen at length and apply the paint while the subject is before me. I suspect you understand the difficulty of capturing a subject when you have only your sketches and notes to rely upon."

The two fell into a conversation about sketching, note taking, and color choices. Edmund joined the conversation when it turned to Mr. Bauer's use of microscopes. He had acquired a few microscopes for the expedition and wished to learn of his methods. As he peppered Mr. Bauer with questions, Miss Radforde wandered away with her sketchbook.

"Have you acquired a botanic illustrator for your trip?" Mr. Bauer asked.

"Mr. Brown has suggested a few, but I have yet to decide upon one. I would be happy to accept any advice."

"Have you heard of Lady Barrow?"

Edmund raised his eyebrows. The name was familiar; the Barrows were friends of his father. "You cannot mean the wife of the second secretary to the Admiralty? I do not think she will be available for the journey."

"No, I daresay she will not, but were you aware she worked with her husband to catalogue the plants and animals of the Cape Colony?"

"Really?"

"It is a fine thing to do such work with a person you love and respect. And in truth, I find women are more naturally skilled at botanic illustration. Tell me, has Miss Radforde any formal training as a botanic artist?"

"Briefly, while she was at school in Bath."

Edmund's mind was filled with the implications of Mr. Bauer's words. Did they not mirror his earlier wishes to have her by his side? It seemed he wasn't the only one who thought they would make a good team.

"Let us ask her directly." Mr. Bauer strode down the aisle of plants to where Miss Radforde stood sketching. "Might I see?" he asked when he reached her.

Miss Radforde glanced at her sketchbook nervously before handing it over. Though not an artist himself, Edmund thought her work remarkably good. She had an eye for detail and the ability to render them precisely even in quick sketches.

Mr. Bauer hummed as he looked at the drawings. "Do you create color versions at home?"

"Yes."

"And what training have you recieved?"

Miss Radforde glanced at Edmund and he smiled encouragingly.

"I have studied the illustrations in *Curtis Botanical Magazine* since I was a girl. My headmistress saw my interest and for a short period of time, a Mrs. Pope was employed as my master. But the expense was deemed unnecessary."

Edmund could guess at why the lessons had stopped. Mrs. Radforde had not thought it a worthwhile skill.

"You have a great talent, but we can all benefit from more training." Bauer closed the sketchbook and returned it to Miss Radforde.

She colored. "Thank you, sir."

"There is an excellent master in London, a Mrs. Meen. She taught the queen and the princesses here at the gardens. I could ask if she would take you on."

"You honor me, sir, but I do not think my mother... that is, I have many demands on my time at present."

Mr. Bauer cocked his head slightly but did not press. "A pity. If you ever find you have more time, I would be happy to make the introductions. Come, let me show you the most fascinating flower in our collection, the bird-of-paradise, *strelitzia reginae*, named by Sir Joseph for the queen."

They moved further into the building. Edmund lagged behind,

trying to contain his frustration. Miss Radforde was always so quick to comply to her mother's wishes, even when she hadn't inquired what they may be. Perhaps Mrs. Radforde could be prevailed upon to allow Mrs. Meen to come teach. But they would not know, because Miss Radforde would never ask.

If they married, he would employ Mrs. Meen. He would give Miss Radforde anything she wished. If she wanted, he would follow Mr. Bauer's suggestion and take her to America. With startling clarity, Edmund knew that Mrs. Aston was right. The only way forward was to declare himself.

Twenty-Three

THE SUN HAD REACHED its peak as they made their way toward the towering Great Pagoda. Charity was glad for the picnic waiting there. All the walking, talking, and sketching had left her famished. One cannot live on wonder alone but if she could, this place would provide ample nourishment.

They had left behind Mr. Bauer and the hot houses to explore the expansive park. The pleasure grounds did not hold the same appeal, but Charity was still delighted with each new folly and picturesque view. The Palladian bridge was charming, the Gothic cathedral a masterpiece, the mosque like visiting Arabia, and each small Greek temple enchanting in its design and situation.

Mother and Penelope were effusive in their praise as they came upon each new building, but their conversation seemed loud compared to Mr. Glenhaven's silences. When with Mother, he made an effort to speak, but when they walked together, Mother and Penelope taking the lead, he lapsed into thought.

She did not mind the silence. In their time together, Charity had come to value his quiet thoughtfulness and appreciated that it left her free to take her own counsel.

Her mind had been filled to the brim with all the new plants—their smells, their textures. Her sketches had not been able to capture every-thing. If she had only been with Mother and Penelope, they likely would have avoided the hothouses and hurried her past any interesting plants, but with Mr. Glenhaven's help she had explored and spoken with the royal botanic painter.

Mr. Bauer's praise and encouragement had been deeply gratifying. Charity wished Mother had heard him. How could she get her mother to agree to more lessons?

"Do you think," Mr. Glenhaven began. Then stopped and looked at her sideways. She paused beside him, glancing at Mother and Penelope well ahead of them.

"I do think, very often."

His lips quirked. "Do you think it possible you could ever go against your mother's wishes?"

She furrowed her brow. She was used to his long silences producing questions of a scientific nature. Had he been thinking all this time about her?

"I only ask because you are always so swift to dismiss your own desires. I feel you are a different person in her presence."

She frowned.

"I am not censuring you," he quickly added. "I am honored that you have allowed me to see your true self."

That honor had been bestowed unwittingly. Charity's honesty was originally due to her indifference to him. Now that she valued his good opinion, she could not retreat into her façade. He knew her too well for pretense.

"Mother has very firm notions of the kind of lady I should be. I have tried hard not to be a disappointment. Mrs. Piper's school was meant to refine me, but I only grew into a confirmed bluestocking."

"I would like to thank Mrs. Piper for her efforts. They made you a superior creature."

The compliment was said so plainly, with no attempt to charm, but it meant more than all of Mr. Fitzroy's flowery phrases.

"Thank you," she murmured.

Mr. Glenhaven's attentions had been marked all afternoon, even when they had no audience to benefit from such displays. Might his smiles and tendency to stand close be evidence of affection? She had all but declared her feelings for him in the carriage, but he had not said anything.

"My father had firm notions of what kind of man I should be. As a child, I assumed I would one day wear a uniform. It is tradition in our family for the younger sons to become officers. Kit joined the Navy, and I was for the Army. But the year the war began, Father informed me he would not pay for a commission and I would be going to Oxford. At first, I was disappointed, but it made Mama happy and I enjoyed school."

Charity tried to imagine Glenhaven in a red uniform, but it didn't quite fit. She was glad Lord Glenhaven had sent him to university instead.

"After my schooling, Father wanted me to work in the government. He had it all arranged and with his connections he was sure I could climb high. But I had no interest in that life."

"You told him you wanted to be a clergyman." Charity said.

Glenhaven nodded; his eyes unfocused as if looking back in time at that conversation.

"He was not happy. We argued. We still don't really..." He trailed off and scratched behind his ear. "The point is, I understand what it is to have an overbearing parent. I know it is hard to assert your own desires."

Charity was grateful for his story, grateful for his understanding. It must have taken a great deal of courage to stand up to his father, to choose his own path. Did Charity have that courage? Would she openly defy Mother for something important?

As Charity turned over the question, they crossed the remaining distance to the tall, octagonal tower. She had tried to assert her desire to keep seeing Mr. Glenhaven, only to be maneuvered into a ride with Mr. Fitzroy. She had agreed to today's excursion without consulting Mother, but it had been easy to secure her agreement.

Only a short while ago Charity had dismissed the idea of being introduced to Mrs. Meen. Not because she did not want to improve her skills, but because she knew what Mother would say. Her entire subterfuge with Mr. Glenhaven had been conceived to avoid confronting her mother. Her one act of defiance was writing to Papa about her own establishment. It was really quite pathetic.

She should be more like Glenhaven. Tell Mother about Mr. Bauer's offer. Urge her to consider the idea. With Mr. Glenhaven there to add weight to her argument, Mother might be persuaded.

They joined Mother and Penelope at the base of the pagoda and Charity craned her neck to look upward at the ten stories disappearing into the sky. Each level had a terrace with a white railing and a green roof, giving the impression it was multiple buildings stacked atop each other.

She wanted a closer look, she wanted to walk out on the terrace and see the view from the top. Her physical hunger was forgotten in her craving to experience more.

"Charity, you can see the pagoda just as well from here," Mother said.

She glanced at the picnic only a few yards away. The servants had done a marvelous job laying it out. Stationed between the pagoda and the bright blue Alhambra folly, it was the perfect spot to sit and enjoy a repast.

Mother was already seating herself. The climb would have to wait.

She glanced at Mr. Glenhaven and realized what she had done. If she could not climb a tower when she wanted, how would she ask for more important things? She kept her eyes on him as she spoke.

"I am going to climb to the top of the pagoda."

His lips twitched. "I will accompany you."

"Oh, dear, I am sure you are far too tired to climb all those stairs," Mother interjected. "Come and eat first and then we will decide about going up."

"No, Mother, I wish to climb them now." Charity would not concede.

Mother pursed her lips, then gave a slight shake of her head. "Very well. But do not dawdle and do not blame me if the heat and exertion are too much."

"Yes, Mother." Charity didn't hide her grin. Getting her way was exhilarating and surprisingly easy.

They walked the short distance to the entrance. Here the roof was slightly wider than those above it, supported by a series of plain white pillars. Inside, the staircase occupied almost all the interior, curling in a tight spiral as it wound up.

"Let's climb straight to the top," she said. Charity would show Mother that it would not fatigue her.

"How can I refuse one so determined?" He dipped his head and turned to the stairs.

Charity followed Mr. Glenhaven as he began to climb.

The steps wound up in dizzying succession. She paused occasionally to catch her breath but tried not to look out the windows. Still she could see the trees sinking below and the vista spreading out. The shallow stairs spiraled tighter, the floors becoming slightly smaller. Charity used the column running up the center of the staircase for support as she neared the end.

When they emerged at the top, what little breath Charity had was stolen by the view through the casement windows. It felt as if the whole of England was before them. A patchwork of fields, roads, and villages stretched as far as the eye could see. To think she might have missed seeing all this if she had heeded Mother.

"I am glad you wished to climb to the top," Mr. Glenhaven said.

"I am glad you arranged for this visit."

He dipped his head in acknowledgment and then gestured behind her. "You can see London from this direction."

Charity turned and he walked past her to the window. He opened it and cold air whipped into the small room. He stepped over the low sill before offering his hand to assist her. She looked at his hand and her heart beat faster. Was it his hand or stepping out at such a great height that filled her with anticipation?

She placed her hand on his and swallowed. His fingers closed over hers, anchoring her and quieting her fear. She leaned on his strength as she stepped onto the balcony.

The two of them squeezed between the bricks of the narrow archway, the railing immediately before them was all that separated them from the air. Her breath came quickly and he squeezed her hand. He had not released it. Did he wish to hold on as she did?

"Are you well?"

"Quite. It is…"

She glanced at him. He was not looking at the vista before them, but at her. His gaze was soft, tender.

She looked away.

He released her hand.

She gripped the railing before her for balance. What had that look meant? Her feelings had changed so much from their first meeting. Could his have undergone a similar alteration?

"There," he pointed. "There is Saint Paul's."

Charity focused on the view, the sparkling of the Thames winding like a great blue snake, the dome of Saint Paul's and Westminster's tower. They were all miles away and yet she felt closer to understanding London than before.

She had read accounts of balloonists gliding over the countryside, experiencing the world as a bird, but their words had not prepared her for the dizzying sense of insignificance. Below, the carriages were the size of a child's toy. She gripped the railing tighter, the wood biting into her palms.

The warmth of Mr. Glenhaven beside her was comforting. Without thinking, she leaned closer until their shoulders were pressed together. He was an anchor in the sea of sights and sensations.

"The world is so vast," his words echoed her thoughts.

"Even London seems small from here."

"See those?" He pointed to the Thames. "I believe those are ships."

Charity squinted at the dots of white and brown on the river. In a few short months Glenhaven would be on such a ship, leaving her behind. After a week apart she understood how much she would miss him. She would be alone, unable to take his hand, feel the heat of him beside her, or hear his voice.

"Will you miss your life in England?" she asked.

"When I began planning this journey, I did not think I would miss anything. My family are excellent correspondents. I will be kept abreast of their lives just as well as when I was in my parish."

"Hmm."

His practical answer did not answer her real question. Or perhaps it did? He would not miss her; he would be happy with only his family's correspondence.

"But I have come to realize that was a foolish notion. I will miss many things. Indeed, there are times I dread my departure."

Surprised, she turned to him.

The wind whipped up stinging her cheeks and sending an errant piece of hair across her eyes. Before she could brush it away, Mr. Glenhaven reached out and captured the escaped lock. He smiled softly as he twisted it between his gloved fingers.

Charity swallowed; she no longer felt the chill of the wind. Her stomach was a swarm of...something...she could not properly think of what. Her mind could focus only on how very close and very alone they were. Her eyes went to his lips.

"Will you miss me?" he asked, staring at the hair between his fingers.

"Yes," she said breathlessly. The single word seemed to reveal too much of her heart. She hastened to add, "Without you, I will be stuck with boring social engagements."

He lifted his eyes to meet hers. The warmth of the brown and vibrance of the green seemed to pull her closer.

"It doesn't have to be that way. If you wish to change your situation—"

What did he mean? How could she change her situation?

"You mean stand up to my mother?"

His lips quirked. "That would be one solution to your problem. But I have another proposal."

He tucked the hair behind her ear. His knuckles grazed her neck and a shudder ran through her. Her heart beat as if she had climbed ten more stories. Unable to meet his eyes, she watched his Adam's apple bob as he swallowed.

"What sort of proposal?" she murmured.

"I propose we end our arrangement and you allow me to court you properly."

His words sucked the breath from her lungs. She lifted her gaze, needing to see his eyes. The emotion she found there was unmistakable. This was no trick or jest. He truly wished to court her. All thoughts of being a spinster fled. She could make no protest, for his request answered the desire of her own heart.

He ducked his head and took a step back.

"Does your silence mean you agree or are you contemplating how to refuse me? If the latter, pray, speak swiftly and we will say no more on the subject."

Charity reached for his hand and stepped closer.

"I think it a fine idea."

His smile warmed her to her toes. He took both her hands and his eyes searched hers. She hoped he could see her feelings there.

"Truly?"

"Truly."

She didn't know if she was leaning closer or if he was pulling her, but the distance between them shrank further. She licked her lips and his eyes flicked down.

Though she had never been kissed by a lover, she felt certain he was going to kiss her. The heat of his breath made her lips prickle. She could think of nothing but him.

"Charity?" Penelope's voice was like an arctic wind. It blew them apart. As one, they looked into the pagoda. But Penelope was not standing there watching with arms crossed. The room was empty.

"Charity, do not make me climb all these steps." Her annoyed voice sounded surprisingly close.

"Coming," Charity called through the window.

Glenhaven chuckled and reached for her hand. They shared a conspiratorial smile before he helped her back inside. He kept a firm hold of her hand until they reached the stairs, where he paused and kissed it before turning to look down.

Penelope, a few stories below, looked up and saw them.

"There you are. Your mother wishes you to come down." Her voice covered the distance easily.

As they began their descent, she didn't spare a thought for the remarkable acoustics of the building. Her mind was still on the terrace and all that had been said and almost done.

What might have happened if Penelope had remained quiet? What might her friend have done if she had climbed the stairs and seen them standing so close?

Charity was proud of herself for asserting her desire to climb the tower. She had gained the view and a beautiful moment with Glenhaven. If she had stayed on the ground, would he have asked to court her? What more might she gain if she stopped always agreeing with Mother?

Twenty-Four

Edmund practically floated down the stairs.

Miss Radforde had agreed. She thought it a "fine idea." Her eyes had been full of such tenderness, her lips so close to his. If Mrs. Aston had not interrupted, he was certain she would have permitted a kiss. Mrs. Aston's severe looks and Mrs. Radforde's warnings meant nothing to him now. He would win Miss Radforde's heart, win the right to call her Charity.

Once on solid ground, they joined Mrs. Radforde in the chairs brought from London. The food was declared to be delicious, but he hardly noticed. All his senses were tuned to Charity, to the delicate smell of rose water and the brightness of her eyes. They stole glances and traded smiles until a severe look from Mrs. Aston reminded him they had an audience.

With difficulty, he tempered his behavior. When they had eaten their fill, they continued their circuit about the grounds. This time Mrs. Aston took Charity by the arm, leaving him to accompany Mrs. Radforde.

For the sake of the daughter, he threw himself into charming the mother. He complimented her at every turn and listened attentively to all her conversation. When she grew fatigued, he insisted she rest in one of the Greek temples while he fetched the carriages.

Soon they were returning to London.

He settled into the seat beside Charity and smiled nervously. They had a new understanding now and with it a new awareness. Did she expect him to speak of love? To compliment and flatter her? He was inexperienced in the art of wooing. He urged the horses forward.

They rode in silence until the Orangery came into view.

"Why do you think bananas won't bear fruit in England?" she asked.

Laughter bubbled up and burst from him. To think his father thought her a silly girl. Her curiosity matched his.

"Why is that amusing?"

He glanced from the road and saw her frowning.

"Don't misunderstand me, I am not laughing at you. It is only that I was thinking precisely the same thing earlier."

"Oh." Her forehead smoothed. "And what were your conclusions?"

The subject of bananas and the cultivation of tropical plants occupied them for much of the drive. She had just finished discussing the finer points of soil drainage for lemons when he burst out.

"You are a remarkable woman."

She colored and ducked her head. "Am I to expect such flattery now?"

"I am only speaking the truth." He removed a hand from the reins and grasped hers. "I promise I will always be truthful."

He would have kissed her hand again but released it so he might hold the reins. If only the road was less crowded or that he had more docile horses. But they were back in the busy streets around London and he could not spare his attention.

"And I am not the only one to find you remarkable," he continued. "Mr. Bauer would certainly agree with my assessment and Sir Joseph. I wish you could attend his breakfast. Miss Sarah always asks after you."

"Then I will come."

He raised his eyebrows. "Really? Your mother won't object?"

"She will certainly object, but I want to go and I have decided to start advocating for the things I want."

Hope fluttered in his chest. Did that mean she wanted him? Would she go against her mother for him?

They came to Russell Square all too soon. With a lingering look, he said his goodbyes and drove home with a light heart and full mind. His entire future plans had been thrown into question, but he did not care. He could only think of seeing Charity again.

Once home, he ventured to the drawing room and found Sophy reading. He sank into a chair opposite her.

"Are you alone tonight?" he asked.

She sighed and glanced up from her book. "There was some political dinner."

He felt lighter knowing his parents were not around. Mama would plague him with questions while Father looked disapproving. Lord Glenhaven had made no secret that he thought pursuing Miss Radforde a distraction.

"Kit and George accompanied them?" he asked.

"George joined Mama and Papa, but Kit went off on his own. Pray, was he always so moody?"

Edmund frowned. He hadn't noticed anything awry with Kit, but he had been absent and preoccupied with his own concerns.

Sophy marked her page and closed the book. "How were the royal gardens?"

A smile stole across his face. "They were memorable."

"Oh?" She giggled. "What happened? Did you ask for her hand?"

He shrugged.

Sophy gave a cry of delight.

Edmund chuckled. He did not find her exuberance annoying when it matched his own feelings.

"What is all this racket?" Kit appeared in the doorway. He was a sight, dressed in a shirt and open waistcoat, his hair in disarray. How long had he been home?

"Edmund is going to marry Miss Radforde!" Sophy said breathlessly.

"Really? How delightful." Kit's tone belied his words. He stumbled further into the room.

"Ignore him," Sophy said, "He doesn't believe in love."

"I did not say that," Kit replied. "I merely said that falling in love is no guarantee of happiness." He collapsed into the settee.

Edmund had never seen Kit indulge in alcohol to the point of actual drunkenness. But then, it had been many years since they had been together.

"To be clear," Edmund said. "I have not yet asked for Miss Radforde's hand."

Kit scoffed. "You are a fool not to secure her before she gets a better offer."

"What nonsense. Miss Radforde is not entertaining other suitors." Sophy rushed to the defense of a woman she had not met. "Is she?"

Edmund wanted his brother's claim to be baseless, but knew he wasn't the only one seeking her favor. He hoped he was the only one she truly cared for, however.

"What have you heard?" Edmund asked.

"That the heiress has other suitors and her mother favors one of them and it is not you." Kit leaned back and closed his eyes.

None of this was news to Edmund but hearing it recited so bitterly by his brother dampened his spirits.

"But, Mrs. Radforde has no right to separate you," Sophy said. "That would be too cruel."

"Life is cruel," Kit spat back. "You will learn that soon enough."

Sophy looked to Edmund with wide, shining eyes. Kit had gone too far. It was not the words so much as the callousness of the tone. He did not think a reprimand would help matters. Kit was too far gone for rational conversation.

Edmund stood. "Come Sophy, let us leave him be."

She hesitated only a second before standing. Edmund took her hand. Kit didn't even open his eyes. Once outside, Edmund instructed the footman to help Kit to his room. He would feel better after a good night's sleep.

"Do not mind him," he said as they walked down the hallway. "He doesn't really mean what he is saying. In the morning, he might not even recall speaking with us."

She nodded, but her mind still seemed to be back in the drawing room. "I think someone broke his heart."

"Perhaps. But that wouldn't excuse his behavior."

Everything was always about love with Sophy, but there were other possibilities. Kit had been away for years, fought in battles, and traveled the oceans. He might be troubled by any of those experiences.

Edmund urged Sophy to bed before proceeding to his room. He would talk to Kit in the morning and try harder to spend time with him. They should become reacquainted and if his brother was truly hurting, Edmund wanted to help.

The next morning when he arrived at the breakfast room, Kit was dressed impeccably and halfway through his breakfast.

"I thought you would still be abed," Edmund said.

"Who says I slept at all?" Kit winked.

Edmund considered his words as he filled his plate. "Kit, is something amiss?" he asked as he crossed to the table.

He waved his hand. "Nothing that you can fix. Please don't trouble yourself about me. It was a lapse in judgment, a moment of melancholy, nothing more."

Edmund wanted to believe his brother. He certainly seemed more himself this morning. He settled into the chair opposite.

"Well, you owe an apology to Sophy."

Kit heaved a deep sigh. "Yes, I know. I will speak with her."

Considering the matter closed, he tucked into his food. When Kit began to push away from the table, Edmund spoke.

"I am paying a call on the Radfordes today. You are welcome to accompany me."

"Perhaps another time."

Edmund wanted to press for details but decided against it. "Are you free tonight?"

"I might be. Why the sudden interest in my calendar?"

Edmund shrugged. "Is it so hard to believe that I want to spend time with you?"

"No, I am an excellent companion. Anyone would be lucky to be graced with my presence." Kit waved his cup grandly before sipping from it. "What shall we do together? The theatre? Tattersall's? A lecture?"

Before Edmund could answer, Mama swept into the breakfast

room. They both paused and looked expectantly. Her appearance at that hour was rare enough to spur their curiosity.

"Oh good, you are both still here." Mama smiled at them. "I am accepting an invitation to the Wyndham's ball and I require you both to attend."

"I have a prior engagement that evening," Kit said.

"Which evening?" Mama replied.

Kit waved his hand. "Whichever evening it falls on. I am going to a lecture with Edmund."

Lady Glenhaven set her sights on her youngest son. "Now, how can that be true? Miss Radforde will be at the ball."

Mama had chosen her target well. Edmund's desire to dance with Charity outweighed his desire to help his brother.

"You are confused, Kit. I am attending the ball."

Mama grinned in triumph.

"Traitor," his brother murmured.

"Come now, it won't be that bad," he said. "You might even enjoy it."

"Do you enjoy balls?" Kit asked.

As a rule Edmund did not enjoy them, but that was hardly the point. Charity would be there and, despite all the time they had spent together, they had not yet danced. A proper courtship must include dancing.

"I suppose I must attend." Kit sighed dramatically. "I shall go to the ball and dance with whomever you choose." He turned back to his breakfast.

Mama shook her head fondly. Did she have a woman in mind for Kit? Would he fare better at avoiding her matchmaking? Not that Edmund was complaining; Mama had chosen perfectly for him.

"You may not believe me," Mama said. "But I have no young lady in mind. You have only just returned, and I am in no hurry to share you."

"Then for you, I shall remain a bachelor," Kit replied. "Since Edmund can no longer be relied upon to stay single."

Mama's eyebrows reached her hairline and she moved further into the room. "Oh? Is there something you wish to tell me?"

Edmund should have been angry at his brother for shifting the conversation, but he was in too high of spirits.

"Kit has spent too much time with Sophy. My news is only that, thanks to your excellent advice, Miss Radforde and I have resolved our argument and are on good terms once more."

Mama bit back her smile, trying to conceal her pleasure. Her dancing eyes reminded him of Sophy.

"Does this mean you are postponing your trip to America?"

The question caught Edmund unawares. He had nearly forgotten he was meant to leave in less than a month. That was no time at all. What would Mr. Brown say if he changed his departure?

"I suppose I should," he said slowly.

Mama nodded. "A month is not long enough."

"It's true, Edmund." Kit pushed away his plate and stood. "That is barely enough time to read the banns. Though I suppose you could get a special license." He clapped Edmund on the shoulder and winked.

"I have not asked—That is, we have not discussed—" Edmund shook his head. How to explain the situation?

"Yes, yes, so you have said. I am sure Mama will have much to say on the subject and so I will leave you to it." Kit made his escape, leaving Edmund wondering if bringing up marriage was his revenge for having to attend the ball.

"Don't mind your brother," Mama said as she slipped into his vacated seat. "There is no need to rush through your courtship. I think delaying your expedition a wise decision."

Edmund's brow wrinkled in thought. "You do?"

He was sure that Father would not agree with her.

"Marriage can change a man, make him reconsider his choices." Mama spoke carefully, not quite meeting his eyes.

"Reconsider how?" Edmund asked.

"This trip to America might lose its appeal."

"Mama, this expedition is not some whim."

"I know that you love your work. But you do not need to go to another continent to do that work. There is much you could do here, in England."

Edmund shook his head. Did she really not understand the difference? Making new discoveries on an unexplored continent was his dream. It was all that he wanted from his life.

"I—"

"Once you marry, your priorities might change," Mama continued. "You don't expect your bride to live alone for years?"

"Of course not. I will ask her to accompany me."

Mama's eyebrows rose. "You cannot be serious."

"And why not? Other women have accompanied their husbands on such journeys. Why, Lady Barrow helped her husband catalogue the Cape Colony."

"That may be, but I do not believe one in ten thousand would agree to such a scheme. Have you asked Miss Radforde if she wishes to go?"

"No, but I have reason to believe she will be amenable."

Mama shook her head. "And if she is not? If she desires to marry you but not to decamp to America? What will you do then?"

Edmund swallowed. He didn't know what he would do. If she refused to marry him, then he would happily run across the ocean to escape. But if her answer was conditional on him remaining in England, would he stay? He wanted her to become his partner in life and work, but she might feel differently.

Mama was right. If they married, he could not leave immediately after the wedding and he could not assume she wished to accompany him. Wanting to become a botanic artist did not mean she wished to endure the hardships of such a journey.

Did he want to be her husband more than he wanted his dreams? He didn't know. He hoped it was a question he wouldn't have to answer.

CHARITY ROSE LATE on Monday morning. Thoughts of Glenhaven had kept her awake long after the house had gone quiet. When she finally slept her dreams were so sweet, she was loath to rise. Knowing she would see him soon, she dressed with care.

Though he had seen her many times, this would be the first since he announced his intention to court her. They were courting. It felt as unreal as a dream. Had he really almost embraced her atop the pagoda? Charity touched her lips at the memory. What would it feel like to be kissed by him?

The door opened. Charity dropped her hand and turned in her chair. Penelope stood in the doorway with a drawn face that made her look more like a matron than her bland clothes and lace caps.

"Your mother wishes to speak with you in the drawing room," she said.

"Thank you."

Penelope stepped back. "I take no pleasure in carrying tales. Please believe I only wish to keep you safe."

Charity frowned. Before she could ask what Penelope meant, her friend had slipped away. After a final glance in the mirror and a deep breath, Charity left her room.

She moved slowly, while her mind quickly leapt from question to question. What had Penelope said to Mother? What tale could she have possibly told and why? Would Mother renew her edict to give up Mr. Glenhaven? Charity had told him that she wanted to advocate for the things she wanted. Perhaps this was her first test.

As Charity entered the drawing room, Mother looked up from the letter in her hand. She did not smile or frown but beckoned Charity forward as she refolded the paper.

"There you are. I thought you would sleep the day away and miss our callers."

Charity resisted the urge to apologize as she moved to stand before her mother.

"Now don't look so worried. I have not called you to scold." Mother's smile did not soothe Charity's nerves.

"What did you wish to speak on?"

"Why Mr. Glenhaven, of course."

Charity swallowed thickly.

"Mrs. Aston has informed me that your relationship may have progressed."

"What did she say?" Charity cut in abruptly. Had Penelope seen them after all? Or heard them? Curse the acoustics of the tower.

Mother's eyebrows rose. "She told me that Mr. Glenhaven may have made certain advances."

"He is a gentleman."

"I did not suggest he was otherwise. But your replies prove that your companion's assessment is correct. You are more attached to him than I realized."

"I will not give up the connection." The words were out before Charity could stop them.

Mother tilted her head. "No, I see that now." She sighed. "I blame myself; I have indulged you too much. I knew you were growing partial, but I thought you were more sensible."

Why must Mother make her feel ridiculous for her feelings? Would she forbid his courtship? The thought sent Charity's heart racing. It was a greater test than she had expected but she did not hesitate.

"Preferring Mr. Glenhaven is not evidence of my lack of sense.

Indeed, it is a mark of my good judgment. He may not have a title or a grand estate, but he is far superior to every man I have ever met." Charity took a deep breath after her short speech. Glenhaven had asked her if she would go against her mother and now, she knew the answer.

Mother pursed her lips. "I am aware of the man's eligibility. And I will thank you to use a more respectful tone. I understand your feelings are strong, but that is no reason to be impolite."

"I am sorry, Mother," Charity said without a trace of contrition.

"I do not blame you," Mother replied in softer tones. "Those in love do not always act wisely. Which is precisely why I wish to speak with you. You cannot let your feelings carry you away. Many courtships do not result in marriage and virtue once lost, cannot be returned. Do you understand?"

Charity's cheeks warmed. "Yes, Mother."

"Good. When you marry, I do not wish it to be forced upon you because of impropriety."

Now Charity understood what Penelope must have said or at least implied. How dare she think they were being improper. They had not even kissed! Glenhaven was not Aston. He was not going to trespass upon her person and force her to run away with him. When would Penelope understand that?

As if summoned by her thoughts, Penelope appeared in the doorway. Charity gave her a steady look before she turned and made her way to the window. She stared out at the street and the square beyond and attempted to calm herself.

Behind her a murmured conversation began but in tones too low for her to listen. Charity was sure they were speaking of her and Glenhaven. She took a deep breath. Penelope was not just her friend, she was her chaperone, and had reminded her of that fact many times. That she meant well, did not lessen Charity's frustration and embarrassment but helped ease her anger.

With a few more breaths and further reflection, Charity was able to admit that Penelope wasn't entirely mistaken. For the first time she had an inkling of how her friend had been drawn in by Mr. Aston.

While nothing untoward had occurred with Mr. Glenhaven, she could not deny her desire. She wanted to kiss him. She had spent most of the night dreaming of being in his arms. Such powerful feelings might drag her into the same folly as her friend.

Perhaps a warning to watch her behavior was not entirely amiss.

Callers soon arrived and Charity was forced to concentrate on entertaining their guests. She was grateful that their callers included far fewer men than normal. Even when Mary arrived with the Hunters, it was without Mr. Hunter. His mother gave several assurances that her son was very sorry for his absence.

Charity was not able to get Mary alone to speak to her about Sunday or Glenhaven. Mother spent much of the time speaking of the gardens and the great honor of their private tour. Charity had heard the recitation several times already, but it still made her smile when Mother complimented Mr. Glenhaven's connections and conversation.

When Mother's recitation was over, Miss Hunter turned to Charity with shining dark eyes. "I did not think Mr. Glenhaven was well connected. Indeed, my brother said he was nothing more than a country curate. Which I thought was monstrously unfair. A handsome man should have a dashing profession. Don't you think?"

Charity sat up straighter and tried to compose an answer that did not defend Glenhaven too strongly. But Miss Hunter didn't wait for her response.

"I would much prefer an officer. Wouldn't you?" Miss Hunter turned to Mary, her dark curls bouncing with the quick movement. "I know you cannot say since you are betrothed, but I think them far superior." She turned back to Charity. "My brother says that a man with an estate is the most desirable husband."

Charity pressed her lips together. It was not Miss Hunter's fault that she had an officious, prideful brother.

"There are many qualities one wants in a husband," Charity said with as much grace as she could muster.

"Yes," Mrs. Hunter said. "But surely income is a primary concern. A country curate, for example, could never truly support a family."

"A country curate may not," Mother said. "But Mr. Glenhaven has his own quite substantial living."

"And the connections to climb further," Penelope added.

Charity gave her a look of gratitude.

"What connections?" Mrs. Hunter asked.

"Oh, he has so many. For example, on Sunday he often attends breakfast with Sir Joseph Banks in Soho Square," Charity said with a smile.

"You know, of course, that Sir Joseph is a great friend to the King," Mary added.

Despite herself, Mrs. Hunter looked impressed. "Well, it seems I underestimated him."

The clock chimed and the Hunters made their goodbyes. Charity breathed a sigh as the door shut behind them. If only seeing Mary did not involve enduring them.

"Does Mr. Glenhaven really associate with Sir Joseph?" Mother asked with a note of admiration.

"He does and with many other learned men of rank."

Mother hummed but said nothing further. Charity bit her lip. Certainly now was the time to do as she had promised Glenhaven.

"Sir Joseph also invited me to attend his breakfast on Sunday."

Mother's teacup paused halfway to her mouth. She set it down.

"You have met Sir Joseph Banks?"

"I have."

"When?"

"With Mr. Glenhaven."

"And he extended a personal invitation to his breakfast?"

"Yes."

Mother frowned. "Why did you not tell me earlier?"

"I did not think you would allow me to attend. You are always saying I must not appear to be a bluestocking."

With a smile, Mother sipped at her tea. "True, but then Mr. Glenhaven seems not to mind. And to associate with Sir Joseph certainly weighs heavier than other considerations."

"Mother, are you saying I might attend the breakfast?" It seemed too wonderful to be true.

"Certainly, with a proper chaperone, of course." She nodded towards Penelope.

"Of course."

Charity could hardly believe her fortune. She fairly bounced in her chair. A knock at the door announced their newest callers, but she could scarcely think of them.

Why had she not asked before? Would Mother have said yes weeks ago? Maybe it was only because Glenhaven had risen in her estimation. Her defense of him that morning indicated she wanted others to think well of him. But that might be part of some larger scheme.

The drawing room door opened, and Charity caught her breath. As if conjured by their conversation, there was Glenhaven.

Their eyes met and his smile hit her like Cupid's arrow. She felt dizzy, like she was once again atop the pagoda. She did not hear anything that was said by his mother or hers. Her attention was wholly on him as he moved to take the seat beside her. They did not touch but her skin prickled with awareness.

"Good afternoon," he murmured.

"I can go to the breakfast," she whispered without preamble.

His eyebrows rose. "Truly?"

She grinned and bobbed her head slightly.

"That is wonderful. I knew you might go if you set your mind to it." His hand covered hers and quickly squeezed before withdrawing.

Her entire arm tingled from the contact. It was too brief. She wanted more. She glanced about the room. Their mothers were talking amiably but she could see their darting glances. In contrast, Penelope was silent, watching them closely. Charity had the overwhelming desire to stick her tongue out at her friend.

Instead she turned back to Glenhaven and his bright hazel eyes.

"They are all watching us," she said in an undertone.

"They have always been watching us."

It was true. But before, he wasn't courting her and so their attention did not matter. Now she felt like one of her botanic specimens being minutely examined under a microscope. Could they see the flush of her cheeks? Did they note the way his body seemed to lean closer to hers?

"My mother tells me you are attending the Wyndham ball," he said.

She furrowed her brow. "Perhaps, I am not sure."

"You are not sure?"

She shrugged. "We attend so many."

"I suppose you dance with many different men at each one?" He frowned.

"You know I do. I have told you as much." Was he jealous of her partners?

"Then I hope I am not too late to request your first set."

"I was under the impression that you did not dance," she said archly.

"As a rule, I avoid balls. But I believe that a proper courtship must include dancing."

Her heart stuttered at the low promise in his voice. What would it be like to move in sync with him across a dance floor? To have their hands touch and eyes lock? When was the Wyndham ball? It could not come soon enough.

"I look forward to standing up with you," she said.

"And I look forward to showing everyone that I am in competition for your affections."

She bit her lip to stop her reply.

There was no competition. Glenhaven had won her heart. She hoped that she would soon win his.

Twenty-Six

EDMUND, Kit, and Mama entered the crowded Wyndham ballroom together. Father had abstained from attending—perhaps to show his disapproval for Edmund's continued courtship of Charity.

Candlelight reflected off the wall of tall windows, transforming them into mirrors that doubled the growing crowd. The earl had seemingly invited all of London. Conversations swarmed around them, and the noise and heat increased despite the size of the room.

Edmund searched for Miss Radforde amidst the sea of people as he absently trailed after his mother and Kit. His brother appeared in high spirits; his initial reluctance forgotten. Edmund left him to charm the young ladies Mama stopped to speak with. Edmund had already met many of them and had no interest in furthering their acquaintance.

"Now Edmund," Mama said after a young lady and her mother moved away. "You must ask at least one other lady to dance. If you only dance with Miss Radforde, people will talk."

"People always talk," Edmund said.

She sighed. "Yes, but it is not wise to invite gossip. Especially when your position is tenuous."

He frowned. "Meaning?"

"You know very well that Mrs. Radforde is not yet reconciled to your courtship. You should not give her any reasons to object. Now don't look at me like that," Mama whispered. "Surely you can understand why any mother would prefer a title and estate over a man about to leave the country?"

He nodded. Certainly Mrs. Radforde's wishes were not unknown to him, but he had started to believe she was becoming amenable. He had only spoken with her twice since their visit to Kew, but both times she had appeared welcoming. Would her opinion change when she knew of his plans for America? Would Charity's?

He had yet to broach the subject with Charity. Mrs. Aston had been unusually vigilant during his visits. Though he had tried, there had not been occasion for a private word. Perhaps tonight he might gauge her feelings on coming to America with him.

"I think, Mama, that we need not worry about Edmund's prospects," Kit said with a smile. "If Mrs. Radforde is so nice in her requirements, then we only need to make Edmund rich or better yet titled. Edmund, you must find some undiscovered plant or animal or island or some such and get yourself made a baronet. That should serve nicely."

Mama tossed him an exasperated look.

Edmund shrugged. "There is merit to the plan."

Whatever response Kit gave was lost to Edmund as he finally caught sight of Miss Radforde. She stood near the windows, looking radiant in a green gown. She was speaking with her mother and Mrs. Aston, her head tilted downward to catch their conversation. His heart leapt. It was worth attending a crowded ball just to see her.

She turned her head and their eyes met. Her smile added the brightness of a hundred more candles to the room. He indicated the crowd with raised eyebrows and a quick glance around. She gave a nod as if she fully understood his meaning. He did not think she cared for balls any more than he did. With a slight incline of his head, he tried to ask if he should come to her side. She nodded and he grinned.

"I am guessing that is your lady?" Kit said from beside him. "Or do you have regular silent conversations with young women?"

Edmund could not be annoyed with him. "Come Kit, I shall introduce you."

Kit shared a look with Mama, but no objections were made.

"Let us go quickly," Kit said. "For I mean to beg for a dance and it looks as if all of hers will soon be taken."

Edmund returned his gaze to Miss Radforde and frowned. Her party had been joined by Mr. Fitzroy.

Charity had told him that she did not care for Fitzroy and yet Edmund still felt a certain anxiety about their connection. It did not help to see Mrs. Radforde's welcoming smile. One need only have eyes to know she hoped to catch him for her daughter.

"I presume that is the title and estate," Kit said.

Edmund merely grunted in response before moving into the crowd. He wasn't sure if he wanted to arrive while Fitzroy was still there or after. He hoped her dances were full and the man would be denied any more time in her company.

As he navigated through the crowd, Edmund lost sight of Charity behind a cluster of tall gentlemen. Several steps later he encountered Fitzroy.

"Ah, Glenhaven, I should have known."

"Fitzroy." Edmund gave the briefest of nods.

"She favored me with the supper set," Fitzroy said as Edmund tried to move past.

"Then I shall encourage them to leave before supper."

Fitzroy smirked. "Even if the lady had two twisted ankles, I believe her mother would stay through the set."

"I am sure she would rather two broken legs than be forced to stand up with you."

"Her smiles say otherwise."

Edmund gave no response. He had not come to trade barbs with his old bully.

As he walked away, he told himself it did not matter if Miss Radforde smiled at Fitzroy. She did not care for the popinjay. Fitzroy did not know her thoughts on the cultivation of exotic plants or that she preferred lectures to balls. Her smiles were a meaningless façade. Edmund knew her true self. That was far more important than the supper set.

Twenty-Seven

CHARITY'S EYES roamed the crowd as she tried to catch sight of Mr. Glenhaven. She had no patience for Mother's remonstrances for her behavior to Fitzroy. Despite her claims, Charity had done nothing wrong in denying him the first set. Mother had not given up on Fitzroy but there was only one man Charity wished to encourage in his attentions.

Their interactions since the pagoda had consisted of two brief calls, with Penelope ever watchful and no mention of a walk in the square. Being close to him was thrilling but frustrating. She longed for a private word. Not because she expected him to speak of affection, but rather that they might talk easily. They could not speak on botanic painting or America with their mothers listening.

The object of her affection appeared through a break in the crowd. Mr. Glenhaven's cravat and hair were carefully styled and his green coat set off his eyes. How had she ever thought him plain? She wet her lips and tried to calm her heart.

Mother sighed but held her tongue as he approached. A few steps behind him came Lady Glenhaven on the arm of a man that could only be Captain Christopher Glenhaven. Charity had heard very little about the young officer. Though the captain was shorter, with darker hair and lighter eyes, the family resemblance was uncanny.

They greeted each other formally and Mr. Glenhaven introduced his brother to the women.

To Charity's relief, Mother was all solicitude. Captain Glenhaven executed a correct bow, but his eyes glinted with mischievous intent when he glanced at Charity.

"I am pleased to finally make your acquaintance, Miss Radforde, Mrs. Aston. I have heard so much about you."

"Really? I have heard almost nothing of you," Penelope replied.

The captain did not balk but smiled wider. "Then I must illuminate you both on the subject. Perhaps you will permit me a dance?"

"I would be delighted, Captain." Charity said.

He smiled his thanks and looked at Penelope.

"As a chaperone, I do not dance," Penelope said. She did a good job of hiding her disappointment, but Charity knew her too well to be fooled. Her friend had always loved to dance.

"Even better. I am sure to be fatigued and will happily stand beside you for a set," Captain Glenhaven said.

"Thank you." Penelope glanced at Mother. "But that is not necessary."

He pursed his lips but did not urge her further.

Why had Penelope not even agreed to his company? Was she so against men or did she merely wish not to be distracted from her duty as spy?

In the last week, Charity had struggled to be candid with her friend. She worried that any conversation might be carried back to Mother. It was annoying because Charity could use Penelope's advice for encouraging love.

The strains of the first dance began and Mr. Glenhaven offered his arm. They joined the flow of couples to the center of the room. The joy of the moment was tempered by her frustration with Penelope.

"I am sorry for how Penelope acted," she said.

"It is no matter. She takes her responsibilities seriously."

"With Mother here it seems silly she cannot enjoy herself a little. It is not as if I have anything to fear from you."

He gave her a look that reminded her of their moment on the pagoda. She glanced down to hide the rush of heat to her cheeks.

"You know what I mean."

He chuckled softly and they moved into position. The Wyndhams had chosen a lively country air to begin the set. The crush of couples and the noise of the ballroom made it impossible to carry on a conversation.

Instead they communicated with smiles, head tilts, and raised eyebrows. Their brief touches left her tingling and warm. Was her racing heart and breathlessness from the exercise or his proximity? She was like a living flame, flickering with the multitude of candles. Was this how dancing was meant to feel? Not an ordeal to suffer through, but a joyous celebration of affection?

Glenhaven matched all her steps with elegance and energy. His eyes almost never left her. When there was a pause in the dance, they did not talk of anything of substance, but she did not care. She could not have formulated any coherent thoughts. It was the most enjoyable set of her life and it ended all too quickly.

As the music faded away Charity took his arm, loath to return to her mother.

"Might I request another dance?" Mr. Glenhaven asked.

"Another?"

"Yes, if it pleases you." He sounded apprehensive.

Charity paused to look at him. "I thought you did not like to dance?"

"I do not like dancing with women I have no interest in, but with you..." His eyes brightened.

She looked away but could not help her smile. To dance a second set with him was not exactly improper, but people would talk. Would Mother be upset if they danced a second?

"Well?" He nudged her side.

"Hmm?"

"Miss Radforde, I never thought you were one to tease a man."

"I am not teasing."

"Then will you dance?"

"Oh, of course," Charity smiled. "It is a ball after all."

He shook his head and gave her a look of reproof. She laughed lightly. She understood now why Penelope had enjoyed flirting.

"I have the set after supper free, but I had thought to give that to your brother."

"He won't mind if I take his place."

"But I do not wish to be rude to such a charming man."

"Confound it. Now I know you are teasing. We will dance after supper. Until then, I shall gaze longingly at you from afar."

"While you gaze, try not to become distracted by plant classification. When you drift away in your thoughts, you have a tendency to look upset. What will people think if you are giving me an angry look?"

"Do I really look angry?"

"To those who do not know you."

He shrugged. "I do not expect to become distracted, but if I do, that will serve my purpose just as well. People will think I am jealous of your partners."

"Are you jealous?"

She did not receive an answer. Mother and Penelope appeared before them. How had they crossed the room so quickly? Her next partner waited beside them. Mr. Glenhaven took his leave and Charity resigned herself to only catching glimpses of him for the next few hours.

The times she saw him standing beside Lady Glenhaven, he was watching her, but he did not look distracted or jealous. He seemed amused.

Charity was so preoccupied with watching and thinking of Mr. Glenhaven that she forgot to modulate her conversation when dancing with Mr. Hunter. His furrowed brow when she asked his opinion on bananas soon had her returning to talk of the weather and number of couples. It was only as he was returning her to Mother that he said anything worth her notice.

"You must know, Miss Radforde, that I hold you in very high esteem and I hope that I have proven my own worth and judgment to you."

Charity made a general noise of acquiescence; unsure what Mr. Hunter was trying to say but dreading it.

"I would like to further our acquaintance. Though not titled, I have much to recommend me and I have a large, productive estate which, if I may be so bold, makes me a far sight better than certain other gentlemen who have been giving you notice."

She could not mistake his meaning and found she had no desire to be mistaken in return.

"Mr. Hunter, I don't believe it is any of your business which gentleman I bestow my attentions on." Her reply was curt and lacking in the usual deference she gave him. Mother would be furious, but Charity didn't care.

He stiffened beside her. "You speak quite plainly, though not wisely. You will regret such a hasty rejection."

"I will not."

"Then I believe we have no more to say."

"For once we are in complete agreement. I see my mother." She released his arm and bid him a curt farewell, crossing the remaining distance to Mother and Penelope as calmly as she could.

Mother raised her eyebrows but could not speak freely because she was in conversation with another lady. Charity took her place beside Penelope.

"Mr. Hunter did not seem pleased," Penelope whispered from behind her fan.

"Rejected men rarely do."

"Did he offer? Here in the ballroom?" Penelope looked askance.

"No. But he was recommending himself. As if I would even consider such an officious, shallow man."

Penelope looked as if she might speak but her eyes strayed behind Charity and she inclined her head.

"Your next suitor awaits."

Charity held in a sigh. It was time to dance with Fitzroy.

He made her an elaborate bow and barely acknowledged Penelope before leading Charity away. She comforted herself with the knowledge that the dance was a cotillion and opportunities for conversation would be limited.

Fitzroy was in fine form with his flattering remarks and clever comments. But Charity was in no mood to appreciate them, wishing every moment to be free of him. At the conclusion of the set, he escorted her to supper.

The room was filled with tired dancers and drowsy chaperones fortifying themselves for the last hours of the ball. They took seats in sight of Penelope and Mother. Charity was grateful to turn her attention to her plate. For once, Fitzroy was content to remain silent. But it did not last and at length he spoke.

"Miss Radforde, I must say you have transformed my evening with your presence. You are truly a fascinating companion."

Charity could not tell if he was being sarcastic. She knew she had been very dull, but his smile was just as charming as ever.

He smirked. Charity found her tongue loosened by the spirits and her frustration at his inscrutability. "I do wonder if you would find me quite so charming if my fortune were not so large."

Fitzroy nearly choked on his wine, spluttering ungracefully before regaining his composure.

"You do yourself a disservice and impugn my honor to imply my interests are mercenary," he said in an undertone. "What use have I for an heiress? I am not a third son in need of funding for a ridiculous expedition to the Americas."

Though Charity wished to defend Glenhaven, she did not want to give Fitzroy the satisfaction.

"What a strangely specific example," she said.

His self-satisfied smile grew, taunting her to say more. Oh, when would the next dance begin so she could be free of him? She was grateful when Penelope appeared beside them.

"Charity, your mother is feeling poorly and wishes to leave."

"But—" Charity began.

"She has already departed the ballroom," Penelope added.

"A pity you must leave," Mr. Fitzroy said as sweetly as though they had not argued. "May I escort you to the door?"

"No, thank you," Penelope said firmly.

"Then please give Mrs. Radforde my best wishes."

Fitzroy stood and Charity was left with no choice but to rise and allow herself to be ushered out.

"I must tell Mr. Glenhaven we are leaving," Charity said as they crossed to the door.

"He knows," Penelope said.

Instead of alleviating her concern, this reply elevated it. Mother wishing to depart just as she was about to dance with Glenhaven could not be a coincidence. What had happened?

Charity looked about the room for him but saw no flash of his green coat. Penelope firmly propelled her forward and all too soon they were at the entrance hall. They exchanged their shoes and collected their wraps in a rush. The footman helped them into the waiting carriage where they joined Mrs. Radforde.

Charity saw her pursed lips and lowered brows in the flickering orange light of the torches and swallowed the questions she had been about to ask. The carriage jolted into motion and Mother began to speak.

"Lady Glenhaven informed me that her son is leaving England for some ridiculous fool expedition. What's more, she seemed to think you were aware of his plans."

"I am." Charity dared say no more.

"You knew? All this time you knew the man monopolizing your time had no intention of marrying you?"

Charity did not know what answer to give. In the beginning, Glenhaven wishing not to marry had been his chief attraction, but so much had changed. He had asked to properly court her. Surely his plans had changed.

"His interest in furthering scientific knowledge does not mean he has no wish to marry," Charity said.

"Charity, dear, you cannot believe that. No sane man would take on the burden of a wife before such a long endeavor. No caring man would marry only to leave immediately. He will be gone before the banns could be read."

Charity shook her head. "No, you don't understand."

But Mother wasn't listening. "You silly girl. He has been trifling with you, a bit of fun before he abandons civilization. I daresay he will become a savage, or worse, an American. We shall never see him again. When I think of the misspent time, all the suitors who have looked elsewhere. Mr. Hunter seemed out of sorts tonight. What did you say? No matter, we can regain his favor. We could arrange a drive on Sunday."

"No, Mother, I don't wish for Mr. Hunter's good graces. I am going to Sir Joseph's breakfast on Sunday."

"No. You are not to see Mr. Glenhaven again. I forbid it."

The words rocked through Charity, jolting her like a fall from a horse. Mother was in earnest. Now that she knew of Glenhaven's plans, there would be no convincing her. Charity glanced at Penelope, but her friend's face was in shadow, her expression unreadable.

Charity had decided to advocate for what she wanted. She had decided that Glenhaven was worth defying her mother. Now she needed the courage to do it.

"I will not," Charity said quietly.

"What?"

"You can't stop me from seeing Mr. Glenhaven."

"Charity," Penelope spoke softly. "His promises mean nothing. He is leaving."

"Promises? What promises?" Mother asked.

"I am marrying Mr. Glenhaven."

The carriage fell into sudden silence.

The words were out and Charity could not recall them. She was never drinking at a ball again. The spirits kept her brain from controlling her tongue. Nervously, she spoke into the darkness trying to shore up her obvious lie.

"You see, he has not been trifling with me, his attentions have been in earnest. He asked for my hand and I accepted."

"Has he written to your father?" Mother demanded.

"I don't know." Charity swallowed.

The lies were already adding up. Mother would know soon enough that Papa had received no such letter.

The clop of the horse's hooves seemed deafening in the brief silence. Charity felt sure that in a moment Mother would renew her decree that she could not see Mr. Glenhaven.

She could not allow that to happen.

"I know you wished for a higher connection," Charity spoke quickly, "but Glenhaven's expedition is important. Great men of science are supporting him, and I am sure his discoveries will make him one of the most revered men in England. He might even receive a knighthood for his work."

Mother had sunk back in her seat, obscuring her features in shadow so Charity could not make out the impact of her words.

"My dear, it is clear you think him the best of men. Someday he may be all that you say, but now he is only a clergyman of a country parish."

Charity opened her mouth to argue but Mother raised her hand.

"Enough. We will speak no more on the matter. I will write to your father. Perhaps he will countenance a long engagement, but I would not raise your hopes."

"Yes, Mother," Charity said bitterly.

Avoiding Penelope's eyes, Charity turned to the window to watch the shadows and pools of light pass by.

What had possessed her to claim an engagement to a man who had merely professed a desire to court her? Had she truly thought the declaration would end all discussion? That Mother would just accept her choice?

And Glenhaven was her choice. There was no other man she would even consider. But did he feel the same?

She took a deep breath. The streets blurred before her eyes. What would he think when she told him? How was she to tell him? Mother would hardly keep the information to herself. No doubt, she would lecture him for daring to propose. She inwardly cringed at the thought.

When they arrived home, Mother turned to Penelope.

"Come with me, we have much to discuss," she said sternly.

Charity looked an apology at her friend, but Penelope didn't meet her eyes. She had not stopped to consider how the lie would reflect on Penelope's abilities as chaperone. She was meant to keep Charity from such foolish entanglements. Would Mother merely lecture her, or would there be other punishments?

"Mother, Penelope has done nothing deserving of censure," Charity said.

"Goodnight, Charity." Mother walked away.

Penelope patted Charity's hand. "Don't worry. I am sure she only wishes to consult my opinion."

CHAPTER TWENTY-SEVEN

Charity scoffed.

"I will come speak with you when we are done," she promised.

Charity reluctantly watched as her friend disappeared into the drawing room. For a long moment, she considered racing after and confessing everything. Every lie she had told since meeting Glenhaven wanted to spill from her like a breaking dam. But the door shut before she could move.

Trudging up the stairs, her thoughts swirled like autumn leaves on the wind. She needed to tell Penelope the truth, but how?

She paid no mind as her maid prepared her for sleep and when the girl left, she sat heavily on her bed. Wallowing in her thoughts, she did not mark the passage of time. A soft tap roused her. Penelope entered without waiting for permission.

"Oh, Charity." Penelope sat beside her and took her hand.

Overwhelmed with all the lies, her defenses reduced by the lateness of the hour and the alcohol she had consumed, Charity turned to her friend ready to unburden her heart. But Penelope spoke first.

"Your mother was not unkind. She wished to know my opinion on Mr. Glenhaven and if you had been compromised."

"Compromised? He would never—" Charity paused, remembering how close they had come to kissing.

"I informed her that I had never given him any opportunity and would remain vigilant. I know he tried to take liberties at Kew."

Charity pulled her hand away. "You were spying on us."

"I was protecting you."

"You don't understand. He was—"

"Men will say anything to convince you of their honorable intentions, but an honorable man does not hide an engagement."

"You are always ready to believe the worst in him."

"And you are blinded by your feelings."

"He is not—"

Charity stopped herself from bringing up Mr. Aston. She did not wish to argue; she was too tired, too confused, to speak carefully.

"Let us speak no more on the subject."

"Charity."

"I wish to go to bed."

She stood. After a moment, Penelope followed and left the room.

Once alone, Charity considered her predicament. Penelope thought Glenhaven had taken liberties. Mother thought they were to be wed. She would have to correct both.

But as she paced her room, Charity came to realize that the truth would never do. Mother would forbid her from seeing him and Penelope would never believe her. The only person she could be truthful with was Mr. Glenhaven.

Could she convince him to engage in another subterfuge? Or would he recoil at the notion? He might agree when she explained the circumstances. Perhaps a sham betrothal could result in a genuine one? It was not the natural order of things, but then, their courtship had been unique.

Mother and Penelope were wrong. He did not wish to take liberties, and he would not abandon her. Had her friend thought the same of Mr. Aston? Was Charity too naive, too blinded by her feelings?

She thought over their many interactions. Glenhaven was not Aston. Above all, he was a truthful man, a gentleman. There was no mistaking his look on the pagoda or his words that evening. He was not trifling with her. He was in earnest. He would not abandon her after making false promises.

She sat on her bed.

But Mother was right, he was leaving for America. Wasn't he? They hadn't spoken of his expedition in detail since their day in Kew, but it was impossible that he had cancelled.

When he left, would he ask her to wait? Is that what she wanted?

She groaned and lay in her bed. She could spend all night thinking over her conundrum. But the questions were unanswerable. She did not have enough information to form a hypothesis.

Nothing could be known until she saw him on Sunday. It was only a day away, but it was sure to be the longest day of her life.

Twenty-Eight

ON SUNDAY MORNING, Edmund approached the Radforde house with trepidation. Despite their wonderful dance, Friday evening had ended in disaster. Mama reported that Mrs. Radforde had reacted poorly to hearing of his plans for America and they had left the ball abruptly. It seemed her good will towards him had vanished.

Edmund half expected to be barred at the door, but instead he and Kit were graciously ushered in. Mrs. Aston and Charity were awaiting their arrival. Edmund did not ask after Mrs. Radforde. He was happy to avoid a meeting.

Once on the square, he felt his nerves dissipate. Charity had greeted him warmly, the day was fine, and they were attending Sir Joseph's breakfast. Whatever happened at the ball was of no consequence.

"Might we walk instead?" Miss Radforde asked as they moved toward the carriage. "The weather is so lovely."

Edmund nodded, eager for a private conversation with her.

"An excellent idea," Kit said. "I have five or six important words for Mrs. Aston that you lot shan't have the privilege of hearing."

Edmund chose not to comment on his brother's ridiculousness. He was grateful Kit would attempt to divert Mrs. Aston's attention.

After telling the driver to follow them, Edmund returned to Charity's side. She took his arm, and they began the short walk to Soho Square. Kit and Mrs. Aston trailed behind.

A slight breeze rushed by, stirring Charity's skirts and bringing her rosewater scent to his nose before continuing down the quiet street. He glanced at her, but she seemed focused on her feet. Even in silence he preferred her company to every other.

With Kit and Mrs. Aston engaged in conversation, he knew they had a rare opportunity to speak freely.

"I am sorry we missed our second dance," he said. "I understand your mother was unwell."

"Yes, that is the excuse she gave. But she is quite healthy."

"Might I inquire as to the real reason for your departure?"

"Do you recall how you invited me to Somerset House?"

"I am not likely to forget it." Edmund did not see how this line of thought related to his question.

"You told an expedient lie and wished me to help you."

"Yes, and I am glad that I did, for I do not believe we would be walking together now if I had not."

"No, perhaps not."

He glanced down at her and cursed bonnets for their ability to hide a woman's face.

"What is the meaning of this visit to the past?"

She did not reply for several long moments. He endeavored to be patient. In the quiet he heard the low murmur of Kit's voice followed by a tinkling laugh. Mrs. Aston knew how to laugh?

"It is only," she began, "that I find myself in a similar situation." Her words gathered speed like a cart racing down a hill. "At the ball, Mother heard of your expedition. She was upset and convinced that you had trifled with my affections. I tried to explain that was not the case, but she would not listen. She forbade me from seeing you and I could not let her. You must understand I did not mean to say it, but it seemed the only solution. I told her that we were betrothed," she finished breathlessly.

Edmund could make no immediate response. Betrothed? Had he heard her correctly?

"You told your mother we had an understanding?"

CHAPTER TWENTY-EIGHT

"Yes, her and Penelope."

"And they believed you?"

"It is not such a wild claim," she protested. "I daresay many expect it after your marked attentions these many weeks."

"But I haven't been courting you for weeks, not in earnest."

"And we don't need to be earnestly betrothed. It is not so different from our previous arrangement." Her matter-of-fact tone chilled him.

"How can you speak so about marriage?" he asked.

"I am not speaking of marriage, but of another arrangement."

"Arrangement?"

"If we are betrothed, Mother will not foist suitors upon me, and you can continue to call. Then when you leave for America, we may write and perhaps Father will allow me to set up my own establishment while I wait for your return."

"It seems you have given this a great deal of thought." He couldn't help the bitterness that leaked into his voice. She had told him once that she planned to stay a spinster and live with her friends. Had she always been intending to use him to gain her object? To begin with a sham courtship so they might progress to a sham betrothal?

Perhaps he would have believed such a thing earlier in their acquaintance, but he knew her now. She was not so cold and calculating. And she was not indifferent to him, he was sure of that.

Why all this talk of advantageous arrangements? Did she still not wish to marry? If he asked, would she consent to a genuine marriage instead of a counterfeit betrothal? Was he ready to ask her?

"We are nearing Soho Square," she said quietly.

Her words pulled him from his thoughts. How long had he been silent? She was always patient with his bouts of reflection, but surely she desired his answer. How could he give it on a public street? It was no place to ask a woman to be your wife.

"I wish to speak on this matter further," he said.

"I understand."

He stopped walking and turned to her. She lifted her face so the bonnet no longer obstructed his view. Her eyes were bright, her cheeks pink. She bit her lip and glanced down.

"While I see the merit of your plan, I wish to offer some amendments."

Her eyes flew to his and the joy he saw there nearly undid him. Perhaps they should speak now?

"Yes, of course."

He swallowed and leaned toward her, nearly forgetting they were in a public place and that he had not yet asked his question.

"Are we to stand out here all day?" Mrs. Aston asked.

Edmund started away from Charity and looked back at her approaching chaperone and his brother. Kit shrugged as if apologizing, but there was a glint in his eye.

"Sir Joseph's house is just there," Edmund managed to say evenly. He indicated the house on the corner and led the way.

They reached the door and were ushered into the chaos Edmund had come to expect at Sir Joseph's. In his distraction, he had forgotten to prepare Miss Radforde and Mrs. Aston. The house fairly burst with people. The conversations crowded atop each other like the tobacco smoke that swirled above them. Even in the entrance hall, people gathered and talked.

The young ladies looked about them in wonder as they handed off their bonnets and wraps. Miss Sarah appeared, her white hair neater than on previous visits but her smile just as wide.

Edmund made the introductions. Miss Sarah declared herself delighted and promptly linked arms with the young ladies.

"Come, I must bring you to my brother. He will be pleased to have two such lovely guests."

Miss Sarah tugged the young ladies into the house, leaving Edmund and Kit to follow.

Kit slung his arm about him. "I am sorry I could not keep the dragon at bay, but Mrs. Aston is quite formidable."

"I perfectly understand. She is a most contentious chaperone."

In truth, Edmund was glad for the interruption. When he spoke of his feelings and intentions to Charity, he wanted true privacy and a well thought-out speech.

They proceeded into the house. Several men inclined their heads in greeting, but Edmund did not pause to speak with them. He preferred to stay with Miss Sarah. The older lady was keeping up a running commentary while making her way to the center of the room.

"You seem quite well known here," Kit said. "I am happy to see these men recognize talent and intelligence."

Edmund smiled. Had it only been a few months since he had arrived, nervous and uncomfortable? Now he felt a part of the scientific community in London and that was almost entirely thanks to Charity. Without her, he might never have been invited to Soho Square.

Once they reached the center of the room, they came upon Sir Joseph. Though seated, he commanded the circle of men around him. A few sat but many more stood, blocking the way. Miss Sarah paused and when the men didn't acknowledge her, she spoke.

"Brother, I have brought you some new visitors."

The men parted like the Red Sea before Moses. Eyebrows rose as they realized the new guests were two young women. Was Charity nervous? He wished she was on his arm instead of Miss Sarah's.

Sir Joseph smiled broadly. "Ah, Miss Radcliff, is it?"

Miss Sarah shook her head. "Now don't be coy. You know very well this is Miss Charity Radforde. But I do not believe you know her friend, Mrs. Penelope Aston. Ladies, may I present my brother, Sir Joseph Banks?"

The pleasantries were quickly dispensed, with Miss Sarah listing off the names of the other men in rapid succession. Edmund nodded at the ones he knew.

"Now, Miss Radforde," Sir Joseph said. "When last we talked, you were convinced that a complete survey of the Americas was needed. It will please you to hear that many agree with you."

There were murmurs and nods around the circle.

"That is gratifying, sir," Charity replied. "I am sure the expedition will be a great success." She glanced back at Edmund.

Sir Joseph chuckled. "Yes, Mr. Glenhaven is to lead the expedition on behalf of the Linnean Society. They have great hopes for the venture. Though surely you are not eager for his departure."

Edmund gritted his teeth at Sir Joseph's knowing look.

"He will, of course, be missed," Charity's voice wavered slightly but her chin was lifted high.

"It is possible the lad might choose to stay, if he has found something of more interest to study here in England."

The men around them chuckled discreetly. Charity's posture stiffened.

"It is true," her clear voice cut through the laughter, "that a great many learned men choose to focus their study on our fair island. Are you saying their contribution is less important?"

Edmund grinned as the other men's smiles died out.

"Yes, remind me, brother, when did you last leave England?" Miss Sarah asked.

Everyone in the circle suddenly found the contents of their hands worthy of study.

Sir Joseph's eyebrows rose and he dipped his head in acknowledgement of the hit. He did not look the least penitent for his impertinence.

"Glenhaven!" Mr. Brown's booming voice was a welcome distraction. Most turned to him as he joined the group with his characteristic bluster. His cheeks were red and his curls in slight disarray. He did not wait to be introduced.

"Have you informed Sir Joseph that you are leaving in a fortnight? He dinna believe me."

"A fortnight?" Charity asked.

Edmund glanced at her stricken face before turning back to Brown. He had not told her of his plans because he had intended to change them. But he had not found the opportunity to speak with Mr. Brown on the subject.

"I was hoping to delay my sailing," Edmund said.

Sir Joseph chuckled, Mr. Brown frowned, and Miss Sarah tsked.

A ripple of murmurs went around the circle.

"I am still going to America," Edmund said firmly. "But I have some difficult details that I must first resolve."

He resisted looking at Charity. He hoped she knew what he meant but he did not want the entire room speculating about them.

"Details? What details?" Brown asked.

Miss Sarah shook her head. "We will leave you to your details, gentlemen. I am going to show the young women the library."

Miss Sarah swept the women away, but not before Edmund

managed to briefly meet Charity's eyes. They were full of confusion. He must talk to her. He had to explain his hopes that she would join him on his journey.

When the ladies were only a few steps away, Sir Joseph spoke.

"You see, Robert, the lad's head's been turned. He is not going anywhere."

Edmund faced the smug older man. How had he ever wished for his good opinion? "I am merely delaying my departure."

"Mark my words." Sir Joseph waved his hand for emphasis. "You will marry and forget all about America."

"Ack, you underestimate him," Brown replied. "He has botany in his blood."

"That sounds rather uncomfortable," Kit muttered. Nobody heeded him.

"I will go to America, but I will do it on my schedule and in my own way." Edmund was proud of his steady voice when his body was shaking.

Sir Joseph leaned forward, putting his hands on his knees. "I have been in your position, son. Trust me, it is better to end things before you depart. Your journey will change you. You will not be the same man when you return, and she will no longer suit. It is cruel to make her wait for you when she will be discarded."

Edmund swallowed his angry reply. He could not insult the president of the Royal Society. It did not matter that the advice was unwanted and the man completely mistaken. Glancing at their audience, Edmund forced a tight smile.

"I thank you for your advice, sir. But I will not be heeding it."

"Hear, hear," Kit said amidst the murmurs of the other men.

Sir Joseph shook his head in disappointment. "You will see. In the end you will regret not listening."

"I do not believe I will. Now, please excuse me." Edmund bowed quickly and made his escape, temporarily forgetting his brother and his manners in his need to be away.

The old man was wrong. Edmund did not need to end things. Years and distance would not change how he felt about Charity. He was suddenly sure that there was nothing that could change his heart.

But Sir Joseph was also right. A long separation would be cruel to them both. Edmund would not go to America without her. Would she consent to be his wife and his botanic artist? If she refused, would he do as Sir Joseph predicted and forget all about America? Should he ask her to be his wife first or speak of the expedition? The questions were like bees swarming his mind blocking all other thoughts.

A footman appeared before him. He abruptly stopped and the footman spun out of his way, narrowly avoiding a collision. Edmund murmured his apologies. The servant grunted and continued down the hall. After a moment, Edmund realized he was near the library. The door stood open, and he heard the murmur of feminine voices.

He took a deep breath and squared his shoulders.

There was only one way to get his answers. He would simply have to ask her.

Twenty-Nine

Sir Joseph Banks had an impressive library with high shelves filled with red leather books and plant specimens. At any other time, Charity would've been in awe as Miss Sarah detailed the collection, but she could not attend now.

Glenhaven was leaving in a fortnight. He was leaving earlier and had not told her. Even after she laid out her ridiculous betrothal scheme, he had not mentioned his impending departure. No wonder he had suggested amendments. She did not believe his protest about delays and details. Of course Mother had been upset. He was leaving in a fortnight!

It would appear to everyone that Glenhaven had been trifling with her. The damage to her reputation was nothing to the real betrayal she felt. Concealing his plans was a breach of trust. Why had he not told her? Why had he asked to court her if he was just going to leave?

How ridiculous she must have appeared to those smirking men around Sir Joseph. All of them knew more about his arrangements than her. All of them knew she was about to be discarded. Though, Sir Joseph had hinted that Glenhaven might not go to America.

Would he stay?

Was that what she wanted?

"Miss Radforde," Miss Sarah called.

Charity turned from staring blankly at a shelf of books. "I'm sorry, what did you say?"

Miss Sarah shook her head. Though older, the woman did not have a motherly air. She crossed to Charity's side.

"You really must not take anything my brother says to heart. You know these great men, their manners are always wanting."

Charity nodded, not trusting herself to give a neutral answer. Sir Joseph had done his best to humiliate her and she would not forgive him merely because of his illustrious achievements. Penelope's scowl at Miss Sarah's back told Charity that at least her friend understood.

Miss Sarah continued her defense.

"And you must understand that he meets with many ambitious young men. Far too many spend years talking of explorations that never come to fruition." Miss Sarah held up her hand to forestall Charity's protest. "I know you believe that Mr. Glenhaven is different. I feel the same. He has a very bright future. It is a pity you met him so young."

"Whatever do you mean?" Charity crossed her arms.

"He is a man unformed, on the brink of great accomplishments. The next few years will be consumed with his work. Such men cannot be husbands or lovers. They must give everything to their calling. Surely you understand that?"

"I had not considered—that is, surely where there is true affection..." Charity could not quite gather her thoughts.

"Affection makes it all the worse. Such feelings are a distraction for the man and a source of pain for the woman. Did you know Sir Joseph had an understanding with a woman when he departed on his round the world voyage? The poor girl was miserable for years while he was away. Then he returned, and they were practically strangers. All that heartache for nothing." Miss Sarah shook her head.

"Oh," Charity replied.

"I do not mean to overstep, but if I were your mother, I would advise you to give up the connection. Let him depart free of all ties. Only then can he soar to the heights he is meant for."

Charity could not immediately reply. Was she really holding Glenhaven down?

Penelope filled the silence. "We are grateful for your insight. Your experience in this matter is invaluable."

Miss Sarah brightened. "It is the rare young woman that can admit their own ignorance. Far too many rush into imprudent marriages."

"Perhaps they do not realize that being unwed has its advantages." Penelope said.

"Indeed, I have found much joy in a life with no husband." Miss Sarah smiled. "Not all have the temperament or means to be a spinster. But I suspect Miss Radforde, you would find it a rewarding existence."

Weeks ago, Charity might have eagerly told Miss Sarah of her plans to set up her own establishment, but she could not muster her former enthusiasm. Since speaking with Glenhaven atop the pagoda, her hopes for the future had begun to transform like a caterpillar in a chrysalis.

Miss Sarah's eyes slid past Charity to the door. "Mr. Glenhaven, bored of my brother already?"

Charity spun to see Glenhaven standing in the doorway. Their gazes met. He raised his eyebrows in a question she could not understand. Unable to muster a smile, she looked away.

"Miss Sarah, Mrs. Aston, I wish to speak privately with Miss Radforde." His tone was measured and firm, but she detected something else.

She returned her gaze to him. He stood ramrod straight with his hands pulled behind him, a posture she knew reflected a nervous uncertainty.

What did he wish to say? Was it amendments to her scheme or a break? Charity's stomach twisted. She was not ready for the conversation. After Miss Sarah's advice, she needed time to think.

"I'm certain you have much to say," Miss Sarah replied with an arch smile.

"But I cannot allow it," Penelope added.

At being denied, Charity did not feel relief. Somehow the thought of not speaking with him was worse.

"I am afraid I must insist," he said with quiet authority.

"You insist?" Penelope's voice rose slightly.

"Come now, Mrs. Aston," Miss Sarah intervened. "There is no harm in allowing them a few moments alone. We shall stand watch outside the door." She turned to Glenhaven. "Speak quickly. Any hint of impropriety and you will answer for it."

Glenhaven inclined his head in acknowledgement. Penelope looked to Charity. Her friend would not let the older woman dictate anything. If Charity asked, Penelope would whisk her away. Instead, she gave her a pleading look.

Penelope bit her bright red lips and turned to Glenhaven.

"Only a few moments," she said sternly.

Miss Sarah smiled and linked arms with Penelope. Mr. Glenhaven waited at the door and closed it behind them.

As her stomach erupted in flutters, Charity tried to recite the classification for butterflies. She could not recall. She knew the kingdom was *animalia* and the order was *lepidoptera* but all else was a jumble.

She swallowed. How long would he be silent? How much time did they have?

He took a step forward and paused. His Adam's apple bobbed. He took a deep breath and spoke.

"Miss Radforde, this morning you spoke of an advantageous arrangement. I understand that you thought a pretend betrothal would suit your purposes, but they will not suit mine."

Ice water dripped through her veins.

"I understand. You are leaving. Such entanglements will only hinder your work." Her vision blurred and she turned to the shelves to avoid his stare.

"You don't understand."

Footsteps echoed on the polished wooden floor, but she did not turn around.

"I understand that you have an expedition to lead and a grand future ahead."

"I want no part of a future that does not include you."

Had she had misheard him? She turned. He was only steps away. His hazel eyes glowed with affection. She caught her breath.

"Miss Radforde." He moved closer. "Charity."

Her name was like a caress. She stepped toward him, and he met her, only inches separating them.

"Please allow me to make your lie true. Be my wife?"

The butterflies were suddenly everywhere, flapping about her heart and in her head. Her thoughts scattered at their flight.

He wished to marry her? Not feign a betrothal, but truly be united as man and wife?

It could not be true.

And yet, he had never lied to her.

"But you are leaving in a fortnight."

He shook his head. "No. Sir Joseph was misinformed. I am staying here, with you." He grasped her hand in both of his and looked down at them. "That is, if you will have me?"

He was so close, his touch ignited a fire that threatened to burn away all rational thought. He was staying? He was staying and wished to marry?

"I—Mr. Glenhaven..."

"Edmund," he murmured.

She took in a shuddering breath and dropped her gaze. It fell on their hands. How would it be to hold his hand through life?

"What of your expedition? The Linnean Society? Your ambitions?" Would he really sacrifice all his dreams for her?

"I don't wish to speak of that. I only care about your answer to my very simple question."

His hands pressed hers. It was an anchor in her storm of emotions. Was it a simple question? It felt enormously complicated. But the warmth of his hand and the nearness of him made the difficulties shrink. She met his steady gaze and found herself leaning forward.

Edmund was going to kiss her, and she was going to let him. This time there would be no interruption.

"Yes, yes," she said. His lips found hers.

The riot of sensations obliterated every other thought. He released her hand only to grasp her neck and pull her closer. Warmth enveloped her as they pressed together. Her hands found his hair was softer than she expected. The moment stretched into hours but was over too soon. When their lips parted, she had no notion how long they had embraced.

Warm and languid, Charity felt as if she had fallen asleep in the summer sun. With a stuttering breath, she opened her eyes and met Edmund's bright hazel gaze. The tenderness she found there stopped any words she might have uttered. His thumb traced her cheekbone, sending a shiver of anticipation through her.

There was much to say, but she had no appetite for conversation. She hungered for his embrace, his lips on hers and her hands in his hair. As she swayed, closing the small distance between them, a knock sounded.

"Your time has expired," Miss Sarah called as she pushed the door open.

Like a startled rabbit, Charity jumped away from Edmund. As one they turned to the door. Miss Sarah's lips turned up slightly and Penelope glowered.

Charity's cheeks burned and she ducked her head. Could one tell a person has been kissed just by looking at them? She glanced at Edmund. His hair was in slight disarray, his cheeks pink, lips a little shiny, but he stood straight with a neutral expression.

"Ladies," he inclined his head. "I appreciate..."

"Not another word," Penelope said with clipped precision. "I will not be thanked for helping you ruin my charge."

"Pen! That is—"

"Really, Mrs. Ast—"

"Enough!" Miss Sarah cut Charity and Edmund off. "I will not have a melodrama in my brother's library. Sir, fix your hair and rejoin the other guests. I will stay with the ladies for an appropriate amount of time. Then you might all depart and quarrel in the carriage if you wish."

Miss Sarah's tone brooked no argument. Edmund was surreptitiously flattening his hair before she had finished her instructions. Charity wanted to help him but knew better than to try. Instead she mouthed an apology. He flashed her a lopsided smile that made her knees weak.

For the first time Charity understood why Penelope ran away with Mr. Aston. The desire to be with Edmund, to take his hand, to kiss him, it was unlike any she had ever experienced. Even with Penelope and Miss Sarah there, she longed to return to his arms.

Did he feel the same pull? She could read nothing in his perfunctory bow, he did not even meet her eyes. She followed his progress as he left the room, ignoring the other two ladies until he disappeared.

CHAPTER TWENTY-NINE

"Well, I see you did not take my advice," Miss Sarah said.

A small smile played on Charity's lips. "I confess, I did not."

"Fool," Penelope muttered.

Charity pretended she had not heard. She did not wish to fight and banish the happy glow that filled her. Edmund was to be her husband. The lie had become truth. Her future would be beside him. It was all too wonderful to comprehend.

"Mrs. Aston's anger is unwarranted, but she is not wrong in her assessment," Miss Sarah said.

"Unwarranted?" Penelope exclaimed.

"Young people must have their little larks." The older lady waved her hand dismissively. "A quick embrace does not ruin a girl, but marrying a man that will someday resent her for holding him back..."

Charity shook her head. She did not wish to listen to Miss Sarah's opinions. What did an old spinster know of affairs of the heart? What did she know of Edmund or his future feelings? Their marriage would not be poisoned by resentment. Edmund was not so petty.

Their union would be a happy one. Charity was sure of it.

A WARM BREEZE tickled Edmund's face as the open carriage rolled toward Russell Square. So much had changed since they had walked this same street only an hour before. He did not feel the bumps of the road now. It was as if he floated in a hot air balloon—weightless and free from the worries of the world.

This euphoria was directly related to Charity sitting beside him. Their shoulders brushing, their eyes meeting and then darting away all heightened his joy. She had accepted his hand. Miss Charity Radforde would be his wife. He wished to declare it to the world. He wished they were still alone in the library.

Mrs. Aston watched them with hard eyes and wrinkled nose—as if she smelled something rotten—and contributed little to the conversation. Kit was valiantly attempting to entertain them with a story about a monkey on their ship, but Edmund wasn't listening. He suspected nobody was.

The short ride from Soho Square came to an end as the carriage stopped gently in front of Radforde House. Edmund had never been so disappointed to arrive at his destination.

Mrs. Aston spoke. "It would be best if you did not call for a few days."

"What?" Edmund couldn't hide his surprise. He glanced at Charity, but she looked equally confused.

"It would be best," Mrs. Aston repeated firmly. She turned and accepted the footman's offered hand.

Kit looked between them, lifted an eyebrow and shrugged.

Charity leaned toward Edmund. "Don't worry. Once I explain, all will be well."

Edmund glanced at Kit. His brother was pointedly looking out toward the square.

"So may I call tomorrow?" he whispered as he covertly took her hand.

She bit her lip. "Perhaps a few days would be best. Mother needs more convincing."

"Convincing?"

"She is only concern—"

"Charity," Mrs. Aston interrupted.

Charity sighed and offered an apologetic smile with a squeeze of his hand. In a moment she would be gone and there was still so much to discuss between them.

"I'll miss you," she murmured.

She released his hand, twisted away, and climbed from the carriage.

He watched her as she entered her home. She snuck several glances before the door closed on her. The balloon Edmund had been riding in began a rapid descent, worries pressed upon him now that they were parted.

What did it mean that Mrs. Radforde needed convincing? Charity had said at their first dinner that she would marry higher than a third son with a dull profession. Was that Mrs. Radforde's opinion?

The carriage jolted into motion and pulled Edmund from his thoughts. Across from him, Kit cocked his head.

"I know that something of import has happened, but I cannot make out just what it might be. I would wish you joy, but I am not sure it's the right sentiment, given your frown."

Edmund shook his head to dislodge the unpleasant thoughts. Now was not the time for such musings.

"You may wish me joy. Miss Radforde has consented to be my wife."

Saying the words aloud made them real and Edmund could not stop a smile from splitting open his face.

Kit gave a whoop that caused several pedestrians to stare at their passing carriage. He reached out and slapped Edmund's shoulder.

"Congratulations. Marvelous news. Sophy will be so pleased. When is the wedding?"

"I hardly know. We were interrupted before we could discuss particulars. I have not even written to her father."

"A formality I am sure you will soon perform."

Edmund swallowed thickly. What would he write to Mr. Radforde? He hardly knew the man and Charity had not shared much about him. Edmund didn't even know where to address the letter.

"Would you like my help? One thing I learned in the Navy was how to write a good letter."

The jest brought a small smile to Edmund's face. "Perhaps."

The offer was kind, but Edmund didn't think Kit's experience extended to this style of letter. It was the type that a person only wrote once. At least Edmund hoped he would only have to write it once. Would Mr. Radforde agree with his wife or his daughter? A new type of nervousness coiled in Edmund's belly as he considered what he might say to convince the man of his worthiness.

Thus distracted, he barely marked their journey home. The stop of the carriage and Kit's gentle teasing made almost no impression. It was only when they entered the sitting room that he began to focus on the present.

"You're back!" Sophy cried. "How was the breakfast? Did Miss Radforde enjoy it? Did she speak to all the important men?" She put aside her needlework and slid forward in her chair.

"Peace, little sister." Kit held up his hands as if to physically fend off her inquiries. "Allow us to sit before you bombard us with questions."

Sophy made a face but kept silent as they greeted Mama. Kit made a big show of walking around the room and inspecting each seat while Sophy dramatically tapped her foot. Edmund settled into the chair beside their mother.

"You seem thoughtful," Mama said. "Was there some unpleasantness with Miss Radforde?"

"No, it was a lovely morning," he reassured her. Memories of just how lovely it was made Edmund smile.

"I would say it was a productive morning," Kit added as he finally settled onto the chaise.

"Productive?" Sophy wrinkled her brow. "I hope you did not neglect Miss Radforde to talk with stuffy old men."

"Of course not."

"Never fear, Sophy. Edmund was very attentive. He neglected the stuffy old men." Kit smirked as he stretched out on the chaise.

Edmund realized now was the time to announce his betrothal but was unsure how to proceed. If Mrs. Radforde needed convincing, perhaps he should wait to share the news?

"I am sure Miss Radforde appreciated your solicitude," Mama said.

"And I am sure that she won't be a miss for long." Kit quipped.

Edmund glared at his brother.

Kit smiled back.

Sophy looked between them. "What? What has happened?"

"I am sure Kit is only teasing," Mama said pointedly.

"Kit is teasing," Edmund said. "But he is correct in his statement. She will not be Miss Radforde for long."

Mama turned to him with eyes as wide as Sophy's. "You cannot mean..."

Edmund grinned. "I asked Miss Radforde if she—"

The rest of his sentence was drowned in the deluge of joyful cries. Sophy jumped from her seat, clapped her hands, raced to Edmund and threw her arms around his neck.

"It is too, too wonderful! Oh, Edmund, another sister! I just knew you would marry her."

Laughing, Edmund hugged his sister.

Mama smiled at them both. "I am delighted for you."

Sophy pulled away. "How did you ask? What exactly did she say? You simply must tell me everything!"

Edmund knew he could not possibly tell her everything about their courtship. It was hardly a good example for his sister.

"What is all this about?" Father asked from the doorway.

"Papa, have you heard? Edmund is going to marry Miss Radforde!"

Twisting in his chair, Edmund caught the frown on his father's face. He stepped into the room.

"Marry Miss Radforde?" Father asked.

"Yes! Isn't it marvelous?" Sophy clasped her hands to her chest, oblivious to their father's lack of enthusiasm.

"Is it to be a long engagement?" he asked.

"Why would it be a long engagement?" Sophy asked.

"Because Edmund is going to America," Kit answered.

Mama turned to Edmund. "But surely you aren't still going on your expedition?"

"Yes, of course I am going."

Father scoffed.

Mama frowned. "So is it to be a long engagement? Miss Radforde has agreed to wait for you?"

Edmund opened his mouth and then closed it. Charity had not agreed to wait for him. Indeed he had given her the impression that he was staying in England. In all the words and emotions, he had not mentioned his plans for them to go to America together.

"They have not had time to discuss the particulars," Kit replied for him.

"I see," Mama said.

"My hope," Edmund began carefully, "is that she will accompany me on the journey."

"Go to America?" Sophy asked incredulously.

"I do not think that likely," Father said.

"Why?" Edmund asked. "She is a curious woman, she has expressed a desire for exploration. I think she would relish the opportunity."

Mama shook her head. "You have not thought through the difficulties of such a journey. She will be all alone in a camp of men, sleeping outdoors, surrounded by wild beasts and hostile natives. Surely that is not the life you wish for your new bride?" Mama spoke soothingly but the words cut through Edmund.

His brows drew together. Mama painted a grim picture indeed. Would Charity feel the same? Did she wish for a comfortable house in England?

"If Miss Radforde will not go, what will you do?" Father asked.

"I—Well, I suppose…"

Father shook his head and Edmund could feel the disappointment radiating from him. Like Sir Joseph, he expected that Edmund would lose all his ambition once he married.

Anger and hurt washed over him. After years of misunderstanding, his father had started to look at him with pride and approbation. The return of his disapproval was an unexpected blow. Of course Father thought him a fickle and inconstant fop. He had never understood or supported Edmund's aspirations.

"Come now, no more talk of boring practicalities," Kit said. "Edmund has convinced a woman to marry him. That should be celebrated."

But Edmund did not feel like celebrating anymore. He stood.

"Excuse me, I have some business to address."

He fled from his family. Once at the stairs he paused. He should go to his room and begin the letter to Mr. Radforde, but the thought of being trapped indoors was repelling. He went down the stairs. A long walk would help him sort his thoughts.

What would he do if Charity refused to travel with him? Would he stay or go? Would they marry before he left or wait? A long separation seemed unbearable, but not going to America was equally unsupportable.

Again and again he wished he could walk to the Radfordes and speak with Charity directly. But each time he was reminded that he might not be welcome. This set his thoughts down a separate path, one where he contemplated Mr. Radforde rejecting his suit or Mrs. Radforde barring him from entry.

Edmund had assumed that once Charity accepted his proposal, all difficulties would disappear, but they had seemed to multiply.

After hours of walking, he returned home with only two resolutions. He needed to tell Mr. Brown of the change in his situation and compose a letter to Mr. Radforde. Hopefully both men would be amenable to his proposals.

He feared that he would not just disappoint Mr. Brown, but embarrass him. It was Brown that had promoted him and given his assurances to the Linnean Society. If Edmund did not fulfill his obligations, it would reflect poorly on his friend.

Edmund did not wish to cause Brown harm, but neither could he leave in a fortnight. He needed more time to decide things with Charity. She had asked for a few days, but he did not think he could wait more than one. Living in this limbo was intolerable.

He would ask Mama to accompany him on the visit. Mrs. Radforde would not turn away Lady Glenhaven. All he needed was ten minutes to frankly discuss the matter and he was sure all would be well. It just had to be.

Thirty-One

UPON ARRIVING HOME, Charity expected Penelope to immediately begin scolding her. Instead, her friend went up the stairs without a word. Confused but happy to avoid a confrontation, Charity went to her room.

The sun spilled through the window, bathing her half-finished canvas in light. It was a detailed rendering of the banana tree from the royal botanical gardens. Charity had been dissatisfied with it. She wanted instruction to properly capture the plant.

Before she had been annoyed with the canvas, but now the sight made her smile. As a married woman, she would be able to employ a teacher. Though not the chief appeal of marriage, it was one of the many advantages she would enjoy when she left her mother's house.

Grinning, Charity sat at her desk and retrieved the letter she had started writing to Elaine. Penelope refused to share in her joy, but Charity knew that her friend Elaine would relish the news.

In school, Elaine had rivaled Penelope in her preoccupation with love. But unlike Penelope, Elaine was poor and had few suitors. She left Bath unwed. Fortunately, once home, she found love with her rich and eligible neighbor.

Charity had learned of the entire courtship through Elaine's letters but had not appreciated her friend's feelings until recently. Now Charity understood and wished to share her own story. Elaine already knew of Edmund; would she be surprised to learn of the betrothal? Or had she already imagined it?

As Charity wrote, she found it hard to put into words all that she felt and spent as much time thinking as actually writing. Her task was made more difficult for not being able to fully explain her relationship with Edmund. How could she convey her surprise and joy at his offer without disclosing their strange circumstances?

What would Elaine think of a relationship that had begun with so many lies? Perhaps she would find it all terribly exciting. For many minutes Charity considered laying bare the entire chain of events but in the end, she settled on recounting the proposal and her pleasure. After she closed the letter, she added a post script.

"I must add that nothing is yet settled. So this news must be kept a secret for now. He will soon write my father. It will be an eternity waiting for the reply. I don't know what I shall do if Father refuses.

Oh, Elaine, I never imagined I would find a man like him. It is as if we were formed for one another. Is that how you feel about your Sir Phillip? It must be, and yet I am sure that my feelings are unique."

How would her friend react to such nonsense from her usually practical friend? No doubt she would rejoice that Charity was not to be a spinster after all. Elaine had always thought the idea unsuitable.

With the letter complete, Charity felt more at ease. She turned to the rest of her correspondence. A new letter from Mrs. Piper sat atop another. What would her former headmistress think of her betrothal? Her teacher had specifically charged her not to write of suitors, but surely that did not include recent events.

Charity fancied that Mrs. Piper would approve of Edmund. After the wedding they would go to Bath. With a smile, Charity picked up the letter and her eyes fell on the one beneath it. Her father's tight, efficient handwriting made her drop Mrs. Piper's letter.

For most of her life, Charity had communicated with her father primarily through letters. Even before she went to school, he was rarely at home and unlike Mother, he had not visited her in Bath. In many ways, his handwriting was more familiar than his face or voice.

This letter had to be a response to her petition for her own establishment. Although her wishes had changed, she was still eager to read his reply.

She tore open the seal.

Charity,

Your petition surprised me. Your mother had informed me that you were intent on marrying this year. I am happy she was wrong as I am currently not in a position to make marriage settlements on you. I did tell her I was determined to refuse all suitors, but I see she has not conveyed this information.

However, I can provide a small income to support your own establishment. I, of all people, understand the need to be free of her management.

Mr. Chambers will be at your disposal to accomplish the task and will be able to help with any difficulties. He cannot help with your mother, but I advise you have a conversation with her soon. I do not expect to join you in London but once you are settled, I may find an opportunity to visit.

Until then I remain,
Your Father

Reading the note sparked so many different emotions. Surprise, frustration, confusion, sadness, and annoyance burned through Charity. If Father was determined to reject all suitors, why had Mother been so insistent she find a husband? How different the past months might have been without that pressure. She would never have entered into her agreement with Edmund. Of course, then they would not be betrothed.

Should she be grateful to Mother?

The paper crinkled as her grip tightened on the letter. Anger burned hot in her breast. With her lies, Mother had manipulated Charity and the gentlemen of London. Mr. Hunter and Mr. Fitzroy would not have courted a penniless bluestocking.

Would her lack of fortune matter to Edmund? Had he been counting on the money? He had not spoken of it but then, they had not spoken about many things.

Before Edmund wrote Father she would have to explain the circumstances. Surely Father would agree if there were no immediate monetary demands. But what if he refused? What would she do if both parents opposed the match? Could she marry without their approval? How had Penelope found the courage to elope with Mr. Aston?

A knock startled Charity from her thoughts.

"Yes?"

The door opened to reveal Penelope, as if she had known the questions Charity was asking and had come to answer them.

"We need to speak about this morning," Penelope said in an even tone.

Knowing she could not avoid the lecture, Charity nodded and gestured to her bed. "Please sit."

She settled and, after a short pause and deep breath, began. "I believe you know why your behavior with Mr. Glenhaven was unacceptable and why it puts my position in jeopardy."

"I do and I am sorry. I was not thinking—"

"I know. I, of all people, know that a lover's embrace can make it difficult to think rationally. That is why I asked Mr. Glenhaven to stay away. You need time to properly consider your actions and his."

"Whatever do you mean?"

"Kissing you in the library was not the behavior of an honorable man. I doubt his intentions."

"I do not."

Charity couldn't add that the kiss had grown from the outpouring of emotion following their betrothal. As far as Penelope knew they were already betrothed.

"If his intentions are pure, then why hide the engagement? Why did everyone think he was going to America in a fortnight? Are you sure he is sincere?"

"He is staying in England. He wants a future with me."

"Admirable words, but what will that future hold?" Penelope leaned forward. "Will he take you to the country so you may be a parson's wife? Is that the life you wish for? Is it the life he truly wants? Or will you live off your fortune instead? Him, a gentleman scientist, while you keep house? Is that what you want?" Penelope kept her tone soothing, as if she were trying to calm a skittish colt.

Charity bit her lip. She had not considered much past their wedding, but she realized she had been imagining staying in London. But of course he would have to return to his parish. A quiet country life was what Edmund had run from, but without her dowry, what other option was open to them?

"These are the things I want you to consider. These are the kind of things Mrs. Piper tried to make me consider when I was enthralled by Aston. If I had listened to her, I might have saved myself great heart-break." Penelope's voice wavered.

Moved by her friend's distress, Charity wanted to take her hand but realized she still held her father's letter. Another complication to consider. What would Penelope make of it?

"I am grateful for your concern, and I promise I will think on the matter," Charity said.

Penelope sighed in relief. "Thank you. I know our situations are very different."

"Not so different." Charity offered her the letter.

With raised eyebrows, Penelope took the paper and quickly read it.

"Why, Charity, this is—"

"I know. Both my parents are determined against us."

"The lack of a dowry is unsettling, but he says you might have your own establishment in London. Is not that wonderful?"

"Oh, Pen, I don't care for my own establishment anymore."

"But don't you see this is the perfect remedy? You can be free of your mother and suitors. Few women have the chance to live as they wish. You should seize this opportunity."

"So you can seize it with me?" Charity said sarcastically.

"No." Penelope shook her head. "That is, I do wish to live with you, but my advice is not self-serving. I believe it would be for the best." She leaned forward and spoke rapidly. "I have been thinking on Miss Sarah's advice and, while I do not like the woman, I must admit she has the right of it. If Glenhaven stays here, he will always regret not going to America. He will wonder what discoveries he might have made, how his life might have been different. He will resent you. If you truly love him, then surely you would not keep him from this expedition?"

That Penelope agreed with Miss Sarah was unsettling. Charity didn't want to keep Edmund from great accomplishments, but neither did she wish for him to leave. It was selfish but she couldn't change her feelings.

She didn't have Elaine's imagination, but she could clearly see how their marriage might slowly fall apart. Without her fortune, their options would be limited, and they would return to the country. His resentment would slowly build, and her guilt would make her defensive. Their love would sour and their lives become bitter. They would become like her parents.

Seeing that Charity was considering her argument, Penelope pressed her point.

"Your love can surely survive the separation. It might even grow through the letters you exchange. When he returns, you can marry. His expedition will be a delay, not a goodbye."

Charity wanted to believe Penelope, but she also recalled what Miss Sarah said about how Edmund would change. What if he returned altered and they no longer suited? Was she willing to take that risk so Edmund could fulfill his dream?

She swallowed thickly. She loved him but did she love him enough to let him go?

"Think on it," Penelope said. With a sympathetic look, she left Charity to her introspection.

Charity stared at the banana tree drawing. Her thoughts swirled like a whirlpool as she weighed her feelings against her reason. She kept recalling the look of delight on Edmund's face when he ate the banana and the way his eyes lit up when he spoke of his plans for America. At length, she realized he was not an animal at the menagerie. She could not lock him away out of fear.

She would miss him. Every day she would ache to speak with him, to see his smile and hear his thoughts. But she had to set him free. Her heart was heavy like an elephant had sat upon it, but she was firm in her resolution.

Edmund would leave. Charity would set up her own establishment. They would both live exactly as they had planned. And someday, in the far future, they might reunite and marry.

It would not be goodbye.

EDMUND'S FOOT bounced against the floor of the carriage as he looked onto the streets of London. It was relatively quiet with mostly pedestrians taking advantage of the late spring sunshine. He was grateful for a warm, sunny day. Surely, he and Charity could walk in the square and speak frankly about their future.

"Why are you nervous?" Sophy asked Edmund.

"I am sure he is worried you will embarrass him," Kit replied.

"No, he isn't! Are you?"

"Must you tease?" Mama scolded.

Edmund shook his head. He had intended to only bring Mama on the call. But the party had quickly grown to include his siblings.

By all rights, Sophy should be the nervous one. This was her first official London outing. She had sat through a few at homes and visited family friends, but this was her first call to strangers. Mama had made an exception since Miss Radforde would soon be family. Edmund just didn't know how soon.

Mrs. Radforde still needed convincing, Mrs. Aston needed placating, and Mr. Radforde needed a letter. Edmund had written several drafts to Charity's father, but none had satisfied him. He could not lay out the plan for their future when he did not have a clear idea himself.

"I do wish Papa had come," Sophy said.

"He had other matters to attend to," Mama replied.

Edmund quietly scoffed. Lord Glenhaven was likely sitting in his study, doing nothing of great importance. He had not come because he did not approve of the match. Most fathers would be pleased their son was engaged to an heiress, but his was disappointed.

Russell Square came into view and Edmund's heart skittered. He sat up straighter. They were a little early for calls, but Edmund did not wish to drive aimlessly around London for another quarter hour.

"And there it is," Kit pointed the stately townhouse out to Sophy.

"Oh, it is quite modern."

As Mama gently reminded Sophy to be on her best behavior, Edmund reviewed what he would say to Charity.

The footman opened the door and smiled before stepping back. Edmund's heart lightened slightly. It was fanciful but he had feared being turned away again. They were directed into the drawing room with little delay and found the three women sitting at their leisure.

His eyes flew to Charity, ignoring the others. She looked lovely in the light from the window, her hair almost aglow and her blue dress brightening her complexion. Her smile was welcoming but wobbly, as if she wasn't quite sure she should be happy. She looked to Sophy as she was introduced.

Everyone declared their pleasure at the acquaintance. Edmund thought Charity's welcome the warmest and was gratified when she asked Sophy to sit beside her. Though it prevented him from taking the seat, he didn't mind. They would not sit for long.

Mama sat across from Mrs. Radforde, Sophy sat beside Charity, and Edmund took the seat next to them. Kit wandered to the window where Mrs. Aston stood.

"What fine weather we are having," Mama said.

"Yes, but I fear it will rain," Mrs. Radforde replied. "The spring weather is always so fickle."

"All the more reason to take the opportunity to enjoy this lovely morning," Kit said. "Perhaps a walk about the square?"

"That would be wonderful," Sophy said in a subdued version of her normal exuberance.

Edmund wanted to hug his siblings for their unlooked-for assistance.

"You are welcome to avail yourself of the square," Mrs. Radforde said. "But my dear Charity has already taken a walk this morning."

Holding back a frown, Edmund nodded. It seemed Mrs. Radforde did not wish for them to be alone. She still needed convincing. But what could be done? He could not become titled or gain an estate and those seemed the only things that would satisfy.

The arrival of the tea tray provided a welcome distraction and the topic of walking in the square was forgotten.

"My brother speaks very highly of you," Sophy murmured to Charity.

Charity glanced at him with the smallest of smiles. "He also speaks well of you."

"Do you often walk in the mornings?" Sophy asked.

This was not the sort of question Edmund wanted answered, but there was no way to speak in this crowded room. Even Sophy seemed subdued. How would he ever learn what he needed to know?

Unable to keep still, he stood and crossed to the window. Kit and Mrs. Aston were speaking of dancing and barely acknowledged his approach. No doubt Mrs. Aston felt it a punishment, but Edmund was happy to stare out the window, undisturbed.

Not coming would have been better than this. Being in the room, hearing her voice, but unable to communicate properly, was torture.

Mrs. Aston and Kit soon left him to his silent brooding to take their tea with the others. In passing, Kit gave him a sympathetic pat on the shoulder.

How was he to talk to Charity if Mrs. Radforde was set against him? How were they to marry if her parents did not approve? He had yet to see Charity really defy her mother. Was she regretting her acceptance? Had she been persuaded against the match?

A chill went through him. Surely she cared about him enough to withstand her mother's objections.

A shoulder brushed against his. Without looking, he knew it was Charity. There was something familiar and comforting in her scent, her warmth filling the space beside him.

"I am sorry about Mother," she murmured.

The vice that gripped his heart loosened and he managed a deep breath. He uncrossed his arms and let his hand swing to his side. Their knuckles brushed and her fingers fluttered against his.

Every part of him wanted to take her hand, but he did not need to turn around to know that they were being watched. He crossed his arms again to remove the temptation.

"I had hoped we might talk about..." He paused and shook his head.

He didn't know how to broach the subject. His thoughts were like a brook in autumn, sluggish and choked with leaves.

She filled the silence. "I wished to speak as well. We did not have the opportunity to properly discuss our future."

The word "our" made him turn slightly to see her face. She was biting her lip and wringing her hands.

"I think that—" she glanced at their audience and walked to the furthest window. He followed. It was as much privacy as they could achieve.

"I received a letter from my father. He has approved my scheme to set up my own establishment and expressed that..." she swallowed. "That he would refuse any offers of marriage."

The words were a blow to the stomach. Was she crying off the engagement?

"That has been your dearest dream," he said bitterly.

"And you might go to America and fulfill yours."

"You wish me to leave?"

"Oh, Edmund, you can't stay here. Not for me. You can't let Sir Joseph be right." Her voice was urgent and his name on her lips softened her rejection.

He stepped as close as he dared. "Our marriage wouldn't make him right. I still intend to go to America."

Her brow pinched together. "But yesterday you said you weren't leaving, that you would stay in England."

"I did not explain properly. I spoke in haste. My plans..." It seemed the conversation in the room had quieted. Edmund glanced behind him, and it felt as though everyone was straining to hear their words.

"Please, let us go to the square so that we might speak openly," he whispered.

She sighed. "Mother won't allow it."

"And you won't go against her."

"I don't wish to upset her further."

"Because she needs convincing. Because I am unsuitable. Because you can do better than a third son."

She reached out, paused, and glanced at their audience. Edmund thought she would not touch him for fear of reproof, but instead, she returned her gaze to him and took his hand.

"I can't change Mother's opinions, but I do not share them. I don't care that you are a third son, with no estate or title. You are brilliant and kind and full of ambition. And... and... I love you."

He ceased to breathe. The words were spoken so softly, so simply. He had not realized what hearing her declaration of affection would do to him. If only he could pull her into his arms and kiss her. But with their audience, he could only cling to her gloved hand.

"Charity, I—"

"And I can't keep you from going on your expedition. I won't." The last words were said fiercely, her eyes bright but determined. "I will wait for you. When you return with all your discoveries and earn the gratitude of the king, if you still wish, we will marry."

He shook his head at her description of the future.

"I do not want that. Charity, we shan't be separated. Come with me to America. You can join the expedition as the botanic illustrator." He covered her hand with both of his "We can make those discoveries together."

She blinked and looked down at their hands. "I...but how, you —no."

"No?" Edmund frowned.

"Charity, dear, come here." Mrs. Radforde's imperious voice broke over them like a massive wave, ending the conversation.

She grimaced but he knew she would not disobey. It had been foolish to have this conversation in front of their families. He was more confused than ever about their future. Edmund squeezed her hand before releasing it.

He did not follow. He needed a moment to order his thoughts. As her footsteps faded behind him, he took a deep breath and stared out at the street and the square.

The question had been asked, but he did not have an answer. Strangely, he no longer felt anxious for her reply. His heart was still pounding from her declaration and complete faith in him.

She thought he would make great discoveries, that he was brilliant. She loved him and was willing to wait while he pursued his ambitions. How could he leave a woman who loved him so completely, so selflessly?

He still wanted to go to America, he still wanted to find new plants and add to the understanding of the world. But he no longer needed it. All he needed was to be her husband.

Thirty-Three

ONE SPRING IN BATH, Miss Minerva had introduced Charity to a volume of *A Curious Herbal*. Charity had always admired plants, but the herbal helped her understand their complexity and many uses. It had opened a new world to her, right outside her window.

Walking across the drawing room, she felt that same sense of awe and wonder, as her mind shifted to accommodate all the new possibilities.

Edmund wanted her to go to America with him. It was too fantastic to be true. And yet, he had been in earnest. The offer was not made in haste, nor out of pity. He thought her capable of being the botanic illustrator. His faith in her abilities warmed her to her toes.

Even seeing her mother's frown did not dampen her spirits. Charity did not know or care what the rest of the room had witnessed. If Mother hadn't wanted a scene, she should have allowed them to go to the square.

"Yes, Mother?" Charity asked as she approached.

"Go fetch my green shawl, the one with the yellow flowers."

"Of course." Charity matched her mother's neutral tone.

She left the room with a brief nod to the rest of the Glenhavens.

Distracted, she moved slowly, her mind still in the drawing room, talking with Edmund about their future.

Should she go with him? Could she go to America and travel across the continent? She had never considered it, never thought such a thing was possible. It would take some thought.

The shawl was not where Charity expected. After searching the room, she sought out a maid, but the girl claimed Mother did not own a shawl of that description. Annoyed, she returned to the drawing room and discovered the Glenhavens had left.

Realizing she had been manipulated, Charity scowled.

Mother raised her eyebrow. "Don't look at me like that. You are the one who was being improper."

"Is it improper to take the hand of my betrothed?"

"It is improper to stand so close and whisper so furtively and disrupt the entire visit with your foolishness."

Charity closed her eyes and took a deep breath to stop herself from a hasty reply. She heard the faint clink of a teacup being lifted from a saucer.

"What were you speaking of?" Mother asked.

"He wishes me to accompany him to America."

The teacup clattered.

"He what? Why, the inconsiderate—to expect you to travel across the ocean! It is insupportable. I have been too lenient and entertained this farce long enough. Charity, I absolutely forbid you to marry that man."

She clutched the chair that stood between her and Mother like a shield. Her mouth went dry and her mind emptied. All the years of nodding and agreeing had led her to this, to Mother thinking she had control of everything. The wood of the chair bit into her hands as she tightened her grip.

"No." The word came out too quiet. She raised her voice so its volume would match the strength of her conviction. "No, Mother. I will marry Glenhaven."

Mother's eyes went wide as she took in her once meek daughter. Charity lifted her chin, her heartbeat loud in her ears. She would not relent, not on this, not ever again.

"Your father will refuse him," Mother declared. "I know he will not accept such an unworthy candidate for your hand."

"He may refuse, but not because he objects to Mr. Glenhaven. He will refuse any suitor."

Mother's color went from white to red.

Charity continued, relishing the sharing of her knowledge. "Father wrote me and said that he was determined to refuse all suitors."

"He had no right! The children are my domain and he—" Mother's chest rose and fell, too angry to finish her sentence. A knock echoed through the house, announcing more visitors.

"We will talk on this later," Mother declared. "You are in no state for company. Go to your room."

Charity did not move. Having finally defied Mother, she did not want to nod and slink away. Even if it meant sitting through more boring calls.

"Charity, go," Penelope murmured.

Her gentle plea broke the stalemate. Charity met Penelope's eyes. Instead of censure, there was understanding. With a sigh, Charity nodded. There was nothing to be gained in staying.

She avoided looking at Mother as she slipped from the room. After only a few steps down the hall, Mary appeared at the top of the stairs and stopped when she saw Charity.

"Hello, where are you going? Did you see the Hunter's carriage and decide to hide? You need not run away, it's only me."

Charity's frustrations ebbed at the sight of her friend without the Hunters. Dressed in green and smiling broadly, Mary was like an oasis of cheerfulness. Charity tipped her head toward her room and raised her eyebrows. Mary put a finger to her lips.

Silently, they moved to Charity's room.

The door was still closing when Mary spoke. "Did you think it was Mr. Hunter come to renew his advances?" Mary paced the room and glanced out the window. "Oh, someone else has arrived." She turned back to Charity. "You need not worry; the man is furious with you. I doubt he will ever visit again. Which I know will distress you greatly."

Charity shook her head. She had forgotten all about offending the man at the ball. "I was not hiding. Mother did not think me fit for company."

Mary scoffed. "What was your offense this time? Hair too plain? Dress the wrong color?"

"I told her she could not stop me from marrying Mr. Glenhaven."

Mary's mouth dropped open and her eyes grew wide. "Did you really? Oh, Charity, how wonderful. Well, obviously not wonderful that you have quarreled with your mother, but that you are to be married! And I shall be here for the wedding. There is going to be a wedding, right? I mean, he has asked you?"

Charity grinned. "Yes, and he asked me to go to America with him."

"America? He is going to America? You are going to America?" Mary sank onto the bed. "What will you do there?"

Suddenly Charity wanted to tell Mary everything. But where to begin? Did she start with the unconventional dinner conversation or why Edmund took her to Somerset House? Or perhaps with her own mad idea to avoid suitors?

She sat next to her friend.

"Mr. Glenhaven has not been courting me, or rather our courtship has been of shorter duration than you might think."

The secret came out like a tapestry unraveling, working backwards, following certain threads of explanation, trying to give the entire picture by untangling each event.

Mary listened attentively and asked only a few questions.

When Charity finally finished, she breathed a deep sigh. She was wrung out but newly washed. Confession was good for the soul.

"I am all astonishment. It is like something Elaine would dream up. I am glad it turned out right. A less honorable man might have taken advantage. You were both very convincing in your roles, but perhaps it wasn't all playacting." Mary nudged her shoulder and Charity's ears heated. Now that she knew Edmund better, she wondered if he had ever been pretending.

"Is this elaborate ruse why your mother won't let you marry him?"

"No, she objects to him for much simpler reasons. She and Pen do not know the truth. And you mustn't tell them."

"It shall be our secret," Mary said solemnly.

"Thank you." Charity impulsively hugged her.

How poor her life would be without her school friends. How unbearable it would have been if she had never gone to Bath and instead lived her life, smothered by Mother's dictates.

A brief knock was followed by Penelope entering.

"Oh, Mary, you are here?" Penelope said. Her smile did not quite erase the worry in her eyes.

Charity and Mary separated.

"Yes, I snuck in," Mary said. "I was just helping Charity plan her journey to Gretna Green."

"Mary," Charity groaned.

Penelope folded her arms. "Eloping is no laughing matter."

Mary shrugged, unapologetic about her jest. "You know Charity would never resort to such a thing, she is not…"

"Not me?" Penelope finished with raised eyebrows.

"I was telling her about going to America." Charity changed the subject.

"You aren't actually going," Penelope said.

"And why not?" Mary asked.

"Because she isn't just going to visit Boston. She will be going into the interior, where there is no civilization."

"I think it sounds like a grand adventure," Mary said.

Charity appreciated her friend's unfettered enthusiasm. Mary had lived outside of England and was not afraid of the wider world. But Penelope was right, the journey would not be easy. Charity had read enough accounts by explorers to know there would be danger and privations. Could she endure such difficulties?

Penelope turned to Charity. "Mr. Glenhaven can go on his expedition while Charity stays here. They can remain betrothed and exchange letters. I spoke with your mother, and I think she will consent to the marriage if you promise to wait."

Earlier that morning, Charity would have agreed with Penelope, would have appreciated her interference, but now the idea of waiting turned her stomach.

"I don't want to stay here," Charity said. "I want to be with Edmund."

"Too right," Mary said. "I would not wish years of letters on anyone. Waiting for word from the man you love is torture. And how will he even send her letters if he is going into the wilds?"

Charity furrowed her brow. She had never heard Mary mention that she loved Mr. Blosset. Had their love grown through their letters?

"If Mr. Glenhaven really cared for you, he would not have asked you to accompany him," Penelope said.

"Maybe he knows Charity better than you do."

Penelope huffed but did not argue the point.

Mary was right. Edmund knew Charity better than her childhood friend. He knew her ability as a botanic painter, he understood her curiosity, and he admired her mind. Most importantly, he knew her heart. He understood that being separated would never do.

Though Charity was unsure, she took comfort in Edmund's certainty. He knew what the journey would entail, and he thought she was capable of making it. In her he saw the potential to be a real botanic painter.

Could she endure the journey? Alone it would be impossible to consider, but with Edmund by her side she felt capable of anything.

EDMUND SAT at his desk and read over the newest version of his letter to Mr. Radforde. It was his fourth attempt to express himself clearly. His first letter had been too long and flowery, his second too short and formal, the third full of explanations and asides. This fourth had only the salutation and introduction. Knowing that Mr. Radforde would reject him had not helped the process.

Yesterday, Charity had said her father would refuse any offers of marriage. This revelation had been practically forgotten in the wake of the rest of their conversation. But when he sat down to write, it was all he could think about. Why had he not asked after her father's reasons?

With no guidance, Edmund had decided the letter should convey his love and commitment to taking care of Charity. He did not want Mr. Radforde to think he was a fortune hunter. But describing how he would provide for his future family was difficult when Edmund had not worked out the details.

Charity had not immediately consented to go to America and Edmund had no desire to press the issue. He wanted her with him, but agreement to such a journey should not be coerced. They would live in England, but he did not wish to return to his parish. His time in London had made the thought distasteful. He enjoyed attending lectures, visiting gardens, and discussing his interests with intelligent, like-minded individuals. He believed Charity felt the same.

It was unfortunate that the best person to help him find a position was Father. Going to Lord Glenhaven with hat in hand churned Edmund's stomach. He had considered asking Mr. Brown, but that involved telling the man he would not be going to America.

With a sigh, Edmund tossed the draft aside and rubbed at his temples. He couldn't finish it until he made a new plan for their future, and to do that he needed to talk with Mr. Brown.

The wooden chair creaked as he pushed it back. He checked the elegant clock on the mantel. At this hour, Brown should be at the coffee shop. Edmund could meet him if he took a hack.

When Edmund got to the coffee shop, his nerves had forced him into reciting the taxonomy of the coffee bean. When he saw Mr. Brown sitting in their customary corner reading a newspaper, Edmund was almost disappointed. It would not be an easy conversation. With dread, he crossed the room and took the empty seat opposite the Scotsman.

Mr. Brown glanced up and frowned when he recognized Edmund.

"Oh, lad, did we have an appointment?"

"No, but I wished to speak with you."

"Ah." Mr. Brown folded his newspaper and set it aside. "Have you come to tell me that you won't be going to America?"

"How—How did you?" Edmund spluttered.

"It's written all over you."

"Oh."

"And Miss Sarah might have mentioned something."

"She did?"

"Aye, she is a shrewd woman, but I had my own suspicions." Mr. Brown furrowed his brow. "I hate when Sir Joseph is right."

"I must apologize for wasting your time," Edmund said. "I know your reputation will suffer because of me. I assure you I never thought... That is, I never intended—"

Mr. Brown cut off his apology with a wave. "What's done is done, lad. You would hardly be human if you denied your heart. And it is not all a waste; you did help me organize the expedition. We can find someone else to lead it."

Edmund nodded. Was he that expendable to Mr. Brown and the Linnean Society?

"Now, is there anything else?" Brown asked sharply.

Faced with his mentor's disappointment, Edmund could not find the words to request his help.

"No."

Brown gave a curt nod and reached for his paper. He gave it a shake as Edmund stood to leave. As he stepped away, Brown spoke again.

"Of course, if you wished to postpone, we could accommodate. You need not go until next year."

"I—" Edmund couldn't immediately refuse the offer.

"Think on it." Mr. Brown buried his nose in the paper, ending the conversation.

Edmund left the coffee shop with no better notion of his path forward. Mr. Brown's parting offer was tempting to consider. Even if he delayed, it seemed Mr. Brown wanted him to lead the expedition. But he wouldn't go without Charity by his side, and he could not build their future on the foundation of convincing her to go.

With a great sigh, he admitted defeat. He would have to ask his father for help. Needing time and exercise to gather his thoughts, he decided to walk back home, a regrettable decision given the warm afternoon. He arrived sweating and with no coherent idea of what he would say.

The door to Lord Glenhaven's study was ajar but Edmund still knocked, the heavy wood biting his knuckles.

"What?" Father asked.

Edmund breathed deep and pushed open the door. The elegant wood desk was stacked with papers and correspondence, one wall was lined with black leather books, and two large armchairs sat near the fireplace. Edmund was surprised Father was sitting in an armchair, a book in his hand.

"Oh, Edmund," Father's eyebrows lifted into his grey-streaked hair. "Is something the matter?"

Edmund didn't know if the question stemmed from his appearance or the fact that he had never voluntarily come to his father's study.

"All is well, very well. But I did wish to speak with you."

Father closed his book and gestured to the chair opposite him. Edmund crossed the short distance and sat on the edge of the seat.

"I have decided to live in London, and I hoped that you might assist me in finding a position."

"A position?"

"Yes, a government post perhaps."

"You wish to go into government work?" Father was incredulous.

"Yes."

Edmund clenched his teeth together to stop from saying more. Was Father making this intentionally difficult as punishment? He had expected him to be enthusiastic about the request. After all these years, he was willing to be his father's political puppet.

"Pardon me, son, but I do not think such work would suit."

Edmund frowned. "Wouldn't suit? But you have always wanted me to work in the government. You practically disowned me for refusing that clerkship."

"That is true," Father sighed. "And I am sorry for it."

Edmund could not believe his ears. Was the mighty Lord Glenhaven apologizing?

"When you told me you wanted to join the clergy, I thought it a waste. I didn't understand your reasons and I tried to push you into what I thought was best. I understand now; it took me all these years, but I understand. You aren't a bureaucrat, but a man of science, a man of action. You would have hated the clerkship and you will hate any government position I might find you."

"So you are refusing to help me?" Edmund spoke slowly, still in shock at his father's admission of fault.

"I am refusing to help you make a mistake." Father leaned forward. "This engagement—"

"Is not a mistake," Edmund cut in.

Father held up his hands in surrender. "I confess that I do not understand why you wish to marry Miss Radforde. But, having mistrusted your judgment once, I am attempting to trust it now."

The fight left Edmund and he nodded.

"Good. Now what I was trying to say is that this engagement does not mean you must put aside your ambitions. There is much work to be done in England and I would like to support you in it."

It was good Edmund was sitting because the shock of his father's words was like a physical blow. He did not know quite what to say. The years of animosity between them left him ill-equipped to express gratitude.

After opening and closing his mouth twice, Edmund managed a strangled, "Thank you."

"Yes, well." Father cleared his throat. "It was long overdue." He leaned back into his chair. "This is not unconditional. You must show me a plan and we will regularly discuss the particulars of your work."

Edmund smiled faintly at the brusque tone, happy to dispense with any sentimentality. "Yes, of course." The idea of discussing his work filled him with anticipation. He had scarce hoped his father would care about, let alone support, his work.

What would Charity think when he told her? She would doubtless have many clever ideas. He couldn't wait to make plans with her. With his father's backing, a world of possibilities opened before them.

Now that he had a firm plan, Edmund could write Mr. Radforde. Once they had his approval—and Edmund was determined to get it— the banns could be read.

He could not wait for their future to begin.

Thirty-Five

CHARITY HAD NOT HEARD a word from Mother in a day and a half —since their argument over Edmund. The previous night, Mother had attended the theatre without Charity and that morning she left for calls without a word. The few times they had been in the same room, she had ignored Charity.

No doubt, Mother thought the silence and shunning a punishment, but Charity was perfectly content to stay at home and find her own entertainment, though she struggled to concentrate on anything besides Edmund and their future together.

She had made a list of things she would need for the journey and debated what supplies she might bring. She had started to reread von Humboldt's account of exploring South America and counted herself fortunate that Edmund did not wish to explore a jungle.

While busying herself with these tasks, Charity's mind would often work on her larger problem. She was not of age, she could not marry without parental permission, and both parents were against the match.

Father might be persuaded to accept the offer if he did not have to settle a large sum on her. But he was across the channel and obtaining his approval would take time. In that time, Mother would keep Charity and Edmund apart and perhaps find a way to change Father's mind. If they were to wed, Charity would need to break the silence and convince Mother.

But how?

It was no wonder Penelope had run away to Scotland with Mr. Aston. The six-day journey seemed easy compared to changing her parents' minds. What would Edmund say if Charity suggested such a measure as drastic as eloping?

As she sat in the drawing room and mulled over the possibility, Penelope joined her.

"You have a letter," she waved a small missive as she crossed the room.

Charity took the letter expecting to see the handwriting of one of her friends. But it was unfamiliar. Her heart gave a little flip. Had Edmund written to her? Was this her first love letter?

Biting her lip, she broke the seal.

Her eyes jumped over the words and raced to the bottom. She furrowed her brows at the elegant "F. Bauer" scrawled there. Why would Mr. Bauer write her?

She returned to the top to properly read it.

Miss Radforde,

Please forgive my presumption in writing, but I think you will be gratified by my information. On the advice of Mr. Glenhaven, I contacted Mrs. Meen. I detailed your talent and interest, and she expressed a desire to take you on as her student. If you are amenable, she will call on you. Please write and inform me of your desires. I will arrange everything.

Respectfully,

F. Bauer

Charity read it twice to ensure she had not misunderstood. Warmth blossomed in her chest. Edmund had asked for Mrs. Meen to instruct her? Mr. Bauer thought her talent worthy of cultivation?

"Is it from Mr. Glenhaven?" Penelope asked.

Looking up, Charity realized her friend had been closely watching her. "There is nothing wrong with exchanging letters with your betrothed."

"But you are not truly betrothed, not until your mother agrees."

"Did Mother tell you to intercept any correspondence?" Charity asked.

Penelope looked away, unable to meet her eyes. "She did."

It was monstrously unfair of Mother to assign her companion in the role of jailer. Charity was fortunate to have such a loyal friend who was not above breaking a ridiculous rule.

"Here." Charity offered the letter to Penelope. After a moment of hesitation, she took it and read.

"Ah, well." Penelope looked up from the paper. "That was very thoughtful of Mr. Glenhaven."

"It was." Charity grinned.

"I suppose you need to improve your skills for the expedition?"

From her tone, it was clear Penelope had not changed her mind about Charity crossing an ocean. She did not wish to revisit the argument. There were more important things to discuss.

She sighed. "Oh, Pen, what am I to do? How can I convince Mother to let us marry?"

Penelope raised her eyebrows.

"Besides staying in England," Charity quickly amended.

"I am not sure your mother can be convinced. She is quite stubborn and you challenging her directly hurt your cause. I think you are better off getting your father to fight the battle for you."

Penelope handed the letter back. Charity glanced down at it as she considered the suggestion. Would Father fight Mother on her behalf? His letter had indicated that he didn't wish to confront Mother and that she was responsible for convincing her about setting up an establishment. Given how often he was away, avoidance seemed to be his primary method of dealing with Mother.

"I guess there is no harm in asking for his help," Charity said.

"You will need to have me send the letter. Your mother has left instructions to the servants that anything you post must first go to her."

That Mother would take such a measure rankled. Charity should be allowed to communicate with her own father!

"Then I suppose I should write it now before Mother comes home."

Charity rose from her seat and left Penelope in the drawing room, fuming all the way up the stairs. How dare Mother try to control her correspondence, as if Charity could not be trusted. After years of being the compliant child, one act of disobedience and Mother treated her like a criminal.

Once at her desk, Charity quickly wrote out a plea to her father. She outlined her feelings for Edmund. She assured him that a small sum would suffice. She explained Mother's opposition and begged him to help her. The words flowed from her pen and she did not pause until she was done.

As she read over the letter, she realized that it would be better to send the missive with Edmund's letter. Father should receive them together. Then he could not claim he had not seen hers when he received Edmund's offer. Penelope could easily get the letter to the Glenhavens.

Charity pulled a fresh piece of paper from the drawer. She needed to tell Edmund of the change in her mother's attitude. He needed to know the difficulties before them. If Mother was monitoring the post, then she had certainly given instructions to refuse Edmund at the door.

Perhaps he would have some suggestions for changing Mother's mind.

When both letters were finished, sanded, and folded together. Charity hurried back to the drawing room. Penelope was standing at the window and Charity crossed to her side.

"Here." She pressed the paper into her friend's hands.

Penelope frowned when she read Edmund's name. "Charity."

"Pen, please. He needs to know that Mother is against us and where to send his letter to Father."

Penelope sighed. "You promise it contains no improper plans? If you eloped, it would destroy my reputation. Your mother would ensure nobody would ever take me on again."

"I promise, there are no plans for elopement."

"Good. Going to Scotland never solved anything."

Charity threw her arms around her friend. While she did not know the outcome of her predicament, it was comforting that Penelope was on her side. With Edmund, Penelope, and Father's help, Charity would find a way out, find a way to become Mrs. Glenhaven.

Thirty-Six

THAT EVENING, Edmund entered the drawing room with a light step. Even though no specific plan had been made, his conversation with Father had removed a weight on his heart. Whatever he and Charity decided about their future, they would not be alone.

Mother and Sophy were standing by the fireplace waiting for the rest of the family to arrive. They greeted him warmly as he crossed the room.

"That is a lovely dress, Sophy. Is it new?" Edmund asked.

His sister grinned as she smoothed the fabric of her skirt. "It is new. It was delivered this afternoon. You missed the arrival because you were out."

"Ah, yes. I had business with Mr. Brown."

"Oh?" Mama asked.

Edmund turned to her. "I informed him that I would not be going to America."

Lady Glenhaven was clearly pleased by the information but kept her smile mild. "I know that was a difficult conversation, but I confess I am glad you will be staying."

"But what will you do?" Sophy asked. "I mean once you marry, will you return to your parish?"

"No. My days as a country parson are over. I spoke with Father, and he is going to support my studies."

"That is fantastic!" Sophy cried. "I did not want you and Miss Radforde so far away."

Edmund looked at Mama. Though she was smiling, her eyes were bright and watery. He furrowed his brow. "Mama? Whatever is the matter?"

"I am perfectly happy. I am so glad you and your father talked." She brushed quickly at her cheeks, dashing at the tears that had spilled over.

Edmund had not realized how the rift between Father and himself had affected Mama. On impulse, he wrapped an arm around her shoulder and pulled her to his side. She rested her head briefly on his chest.

Sophy watched the interaction but made no comment. Had she known of Mama's sadness?

"We should have the Radfordes for a family dinner." Mama pulled away and Edmund dropped his arm. "Your father should become better acquainted with Miss Radforde and I believe he can help with Mrs. Radforde."

Edmund readily agreed to the idea. He wanted Father to know the real Charity, not the quiet miss with whom he had eaten dinner. And, if Mrs. Radforde was won over, all the better.

"I could invite George for a short visit." Mother tapped her chin. "Though he might not want to leave Isabella at this time."

The dinner plans were abandoned as Kit and Father entered the drawing room.

"Well, don't you all look cozy." Kit declared. "What secrets are you sharing?"

"Edmund is not going to America or returning to his parish," Sophy said quickly.

Kit's eyebrows rose. "Really? But how will you live? I know of an estate in Surrey in desperate need of a manager."

"Are you threatening to toss George out of Haverfield?" Father asked with a half-smile.

Kit pretended to be affronted. "I would never threaten my brother! At least not when he isn't here to be annoyed." He threw an arm around

Edmund. "I am merely saying that Edmund is my favorite and if he wished, I would give George his notice."

Despite knowing it was in jest, the offer brought warmth to Edmund's heart.

"I appreciate the sentiment," Edmund said. "But I could not turn George out when he is about to be a father again."

"What about after?" Kit winked.

"Christopher, leave off your nonsense," Father said, but he too was smiling.

A footman entered with a small tray containing a single letter. Since Father often received correspondence throughout the day, Edmund was surprised when the footman paused before him.

"This just arrived, sir."

Edmund shrugged off Kit's arm and reached for the letter. Having observed Charity's notes and labels on her drawings, Edmund immediately recognized her hand. A thrill went through him as he lifted it, but then he recalled his audience.

"I will read it later," he said.

"Is it from Miss Radforde?" Sophy asked.

Before Edmund could answer or tuck the folded paper into his pocket, Kit snatched it from him.

"It looks like a lady's hand." Kit pretended to examine the address closely.

"Kit," Mother scolded.

Edmund grabbed the letter back and pulled it to his chest.

"You should open it," Sophy said. "It might be important."

Looking down at the letter, Edmund wanted to obey his sister. But he did not wish to read it in front of everyone. The paper was too thick for a brief note. What information might it contain?

"We will go in to dinner," Father said firmly. "Edmund can join us when his business is concluded."

Edmund smiled his thanks. Father and Mama joined hands and left. Kit shrugged and offered his arm to Sophy with a flourish.

"Don't worry," he whispered. "I'll discover what it says."

"I can hear you," Edmund said.

Sophy giggled as she was led from the room.

Once alone, Edmund broke the seal and hastily unfolded the paper. A second sealed letter was folded into the first. Edmund turned it over and read the direction. It was a letter to Mr. Radforde. Frowning, he placed it under the single page from Charity and began to read.

Edmund,

I am sorry to report that I have not convinced Mother. Indeed, she is now determined to oppose our union. I believe our best hope is to gain my father's permission.

I told you he is determined to refuse all suitors. But I did not mention it was because he cannot provide a dowry at this time. I know you too well to think a lack of fortune would deter you from becoming my husband, but I am ashamed at not being able to bring anything to our future life.

I have enclosed a letter to my father, pleading for him to accept your suit. I told him that you did not care for money, that no man could be a better match. I wrote that if he loved me, he would give his consent.

Please enclose my letter with yours and send them to Mr. Chambers in Fleet Street. He is my father's man of business and will ensure our petitions reach him. I hope it is enough to convince him to oppose Mother.

Until we have Father's answer, I fear we will not be allowed to meet. Mother is monitoring my correspondence. If this reaches you, it will be due to Penelope's assistance.

I am sorry that our happiness must be lessened by my family. I pray that we will be together soon. Until then, remember that I love you.

Affectionately,
Charity

Edmund read the letter twice before pacing about the room and reading it again. Nothing in the letter changed his mind about marrying Charity. If anything, her mother's treatment made him more eager to take her into a new home. The utter cruelty.

What had happened since Tuesday to change Mrs. Radforde's opinion so completely? Would the woman really refuse him if he called? Edmund did not know her well, so he must rely on Charity's assessment. But every part of him wanted to rush to her side and demand answers.

He would need to write a new letter to Mr. Radforde to help him see the difficulty and the importance of his support. How long would it take to get his response? No doubt this Mr. Chambers would know.

"Edmund, your mother wishes..." Father trailed off as Edmund stopped and turned to him. Pausing in the doorway, Father frowned. "What has happened?"

Only the day before Edmund wouldn't have divulged the information to his father, but their recent reconciliation made it easy to consider sharing. Father would know what to do and Edmund would finally be able to benefit from his life experience.

"She writes..." He looked down at the letter. How to explain? After a moment's hesitation, he handed it to his father. It would be better for him to read her words.

As Father read, Edmund paced.

Each scoff and exclamation were a comfort. Father understood the unfairness of the situation.

"The audacity of the woman." Father's scowl was almost frightening. "How dare she refuse you! My son! And against her daughter's wishes! And how could there be no dowry? Absurd! I know the Radfordes have the money. We will go to this Mr. Chambers first thing tomorrow and then we will visit the Radfordes. It is time I have a plain conversation with Mrs. Radforde."

Edmund was speechless. Father handed him back the letter. He glanced at it. What would Charity think of the scheme? She had advised waiting, but he preferred Father's plan.

But what if he made things worse?

"Are you sure you can change her mind?" Edmund asked.

"Son, I have spent my whole life convincing people to my way of thinking. I can handle the likes of Mrs. Radforde. The question is, do you still want to marry Miss Radforde? Her mother and father do her no credit."

Edmund lifted his chin. "Then it is a good thing I am not marrying her mother or father."

Father smiled. "Good man."

CHAPTER THIRTY-SIX

Choked with sudden emotion, Edmund could only nod.

Having Father's support was surprisingly affecting. For years, Edmund had thought his father would never approve of him, would always be disappointed in him. He was happy to be wrong. Even if nothing could be done about Mrs. Radforde, Edmund was glad to have a tenacious and fervent parent by his side.

Thirty-Seven

As Charity sat down to a late breakfast, she found she had no appetite. Her unsettled thoughts led to an unsettled stomach. She did not know if Edmund had read her letter yet. She did not know when Father would receive her plea. She did not know what his reply would be. And she would not know the answers for weeks. For a young woman as curious as Charity Radforde, not knowing was torture.

Worse than not knowing was not being able to see Edmund, to talk with him, and plan their future. In her haste she had omitted her desire to join the expedition or her plans to employ Mrs. Meen. Could Penelope be prevailed upon to get him another letter?

Footsteps at the door pulled Charity's attention from her plate. Mother stood in the doorway, looking her over with pursed lips. Charity resisted the urge to touch her hair or smooth her skirt.

"Good morning," Charity said.

"I am so pleased you are finally awake," Mother returned.

Despite the condescending tone, Charity was glad Mother had spoken. If she was to change Mother's mind they would need to speak.

"You will join me for calls. I won't have you pouting any longer."

Charity took a deep breath. Pointing out the obvious falsehood would not help her cause.

CHAPTER THIRTY-SEVEN

"Yes, Mother."

"Oh you agree? You don't wish to appeal to your father over the issue?"

Charity clamped her teeth over the words she wished to say but Mother wasn't done.

"Far be it for me to have any say in how you conduct your life."

The unfairness of the words struck like a slap to the face.

"That is unjust," Charity burst out. "I have obeyed your every whim for months."

"Were you obeying me when you declared you would marry Mr. Glenhaven? Or when you wrote to your father for permission?"

"I didn't write him about marriage. I wrote him asking to create my own establishment."

Mother frowned, the information clearly not what she expected. She moved to the table.

"Why would you do that?"

"Because I needed freedom. I needed to spend my days as I wished not——"

"You wished to be rid of me. After all that I have done! The sacrifices I have made for you!" Mother flung herself into a chair. "The constant work and worry over your future. I see I have bestowed it all on an ungrateful creature."

Charity was a pot of boiling water bubbling over, and could not stop her words from flowing.

"You pushed me at men I had no interest in. You forced me into society when I did not wish to marry."

"And now you are insisting on marriage. Forgive me for not abiding by your sentiments but they are so changeable."

Ignoring the jab, Charity continued.

"And what was the point of all these suitors when you knew father would refuse? When you knew I was no longer an heiress?"

Mother laughed, a high-pitched, unpleasant sound. "Is that what your father told you?" She shook her head. "There is money, our marriage settlements ensured he could not touch your dowry."

"Then why did he——?"

"He lives to thwart me. I wished for you to marry and so he wanted the opposite. And it seems he is willing to lie to bring you to his side."

Charity rubbed at her temples. So she was a pawn in their feud? Did that mean Father would agree to the marriage just to oppose Mother? And would Mother counter with something else?

"Did neither of you consider what I might want?" Charity murmured.

Mother scoffed. "You don't know what you want. You are young, meek, and inconstant. My guiding hand was necessary so you would choose the right husband."

The irony that Mother despised the very qualities that she had cultivated was too great. Charity stood so fast that her chair rocked and almost tipped over. She pressed her hands on the table for support.

"I have found the right husband. Edmund is a kind man who loves me and inspires me to improve myself."

"He has no estate, no prospects, and he will take you to America where you will be scalped by a savage." Mother stood and waved her finger at Charity. "You will see, in time you will thank me for saving you from your own foolishness."

Charity shook with the desire to scream her frustration but kept her mouth firmly shut. The last time Charity had argued with her mother like this she had been a child and unable to control herself. But now she knew it would do no good. Mother would not be moved, could not be convinced of her faults. It was a mistake to even try to speak.

"If you will excuse me," Charity said.

Mother smiled as if Charity had finally done something worthy of approval. "Change into your green dress and I will send Betsy to restyle your hair."

Charity nodded, though she had no intention of complying, and fled the room.

Penelope was standing in the hall, as if she had been turned to stone on her way into breakfast. Their eyes met.

"Let us take a turn about the square," Pen said.

Gratitude and relief washed through Charity and her eyes grew blurry. Penelope took her elbow and together they escaped out the door. Charity took deep breaths, trying to calm the riot of emotions that threatened to overcome her. She began to recite the taxonomy of the English rose.

The sticky, dark feeling in her chest was precisely why she never argued with her mother. She suddenly recalled the years before Mrs. Piper's school, when she would escape to the garden to avoid Mother's criticisms. It was then that she learned to examine plants and lose herself in her thoughts to avoid her feelings.

Mother had always been this way, she would never change.

Against such a dogged opponent, Charity did not know how Father could help her. She was every bit as trapped as the tiger in the cage.

Penelope didn't ask for an explanation, just walked quietly by her side while hot tears streaked down Charity's cheeks. The deep green of the trees and grass blurred with the pale brown of the walk. The world around her was as indistinct as her future.

They had walked the entire perimeter of the square before Charity spoke.

"Tell me again why eloping is a bad idea."

A small chuckle escaped Penelope.

"I am in earnest," Charity said.

Pen sighed. "I know. But such a measure is not a real remedy."

In that moment it felt like the only answer to Charity. The walk crunched beneath their feet and Charity tried to swallow down her hopelessness.

"Is that the Glenhaven carriage?" Pen asked.

Charity turned to the road. The handsome barouche did indeed resemble Lady Glenhaven's. It was far too early for calls but perhaps after reading her letter, Edmund could not stay away. Her heart lifted and her steps lengthened as she moved to the entrance of the square.

The carriage door opened but instead of Edmund, Lord Glenhaven stepped out. The baron glanced around and saw Charity and Penelope. He frowned and turned back to the carriage. Charity's heart soared as Edmund joined his father on the street.

Their eyes met and the world seemed brighter, as if the sun had broken through a cloud. He crossed the street, his father close behind. Though she did not know what could be done, having Edmund there eased her fears.

"Charity, good heaven, what is the matter?" he asked.

Not caring how awful she must look or that she was being forward, Charity threw herself into Edmund's arms. Her newly dry eyes were wet. She didn't want to speak or think, she just wanted to stay in his embrace. His coat was rough on her cheek, his hand gentle on her back.

"You know," he whispered. "There are far better ways of catching a husband than throwing yourself at a man."

Despite herself, Charity laughed. His jest recalling her to their situation. She should not be embracing him on the street, especially in front of his father.

She stepped away from the comfortable warmth of his arms and wiped quickly at her cheeks. Turning to Lord Glenhaven she managed a tolerable greeting.

She met his eyes, they were similar to Edmund's but older and greener.

"Miss Radforde, would you walk with me?" Lord Glenhaven asked.

Charity swallowed and glanced at Edmund. But he looked as confused as she felt.

"Edmund, please wait here with Mrs. Aston. We won't be long." Lord Glenhaven offered his arm and Charity took it lightly.

They were several steps away before he spoke.

"Miss Radforde, first I must tell you that I know of your mother's opposition and I believe I can bring her around."

"Oh, sir. I do not think--"

"I am sure you believe it is not my place but since marrying you is important to my son, it is important to me. I will not lie to you. I do not see your merit but I am trying to trust his judgement. Before I speak with your mother I would like some assurances. Many a man has been ruined by a bad wife."

His honesty might have shocked Charity if she was not well-acquainted with Edmund.

"I honor your concern for your son, sir," she said. "I too have his interest near to my heart. I intend to be his partner, to support his endeavors as he has supported mine."

"You would not object then to him going to America or some other foreign land?"

Charity shook her head. "No, sir. I would like to accompany him on such journeys."

Lord Glenhaven stopped walking and turned to look her full in the face. "You would?"

"Yes, I want to be a part of his work, I want to help him with his discoveries."

He furrowed his brow much like Edmund. "My dear girl, I do not believe you understand the hardships of such a journey."

"I am well acquainted with accounts of similar journeys. I understand that we will be months from civilization, sleeping outside and at the mercy of the elements and local inhabitants. I understand there might be sickness and starvation. I understand that the days will be long but the work rewarding. Most of all I understand that I do not wish to stay at home waiting for Edmund's return. I want to live with him, not apart."

Lord Glenhaven did not make an immediate reply but the upturn of his lips spoke volumes. He glanced back, to the entrance where Edmund stood with Penelope. Then looked at Charity.

"Well, I must apologize, it seems I misjudged you. I believe you will be a good match for Edmund."

"If we can manage to get married, I believe we will be very happy." Charity said.

"I agree," Lord Glenhaven said.

He led her back to the entrance and an anxious faced Edmund. Penelope raised her eyebrows but did not speak.

"Come, it is time we settle this matter." Lord Glenhaven said. "Mrs. Aston?" He offered his arm to Penelope and they moved toward the house.

"What did he say?" Edmund asked.

Charity smiled reassuringly. "He wanted to make sure I would be a good wife to you."

Edmund frowned. "I hope you told him it was not his concern."

Taking his arm, Charity urged him to walk. "I told him that I would support your endeavors and that I was going to America with you."

Edmund paused, and turned to her. "You said what?"

"You do still wish me to accompany you?"

"Of course, but only, I have made plans to stay in London. Father offered--but I suppose that doesn't matter if--Do you truly wish to go?" He sounded awed by the idea.

"I do. Truly, Edmund, nothing would make me happier."

Their eyes met, his were so bright and excited she nearly giggled.

They reached the door. The footman opened it with wide eyes. Charity was sure he was under instructions to deny Edmund but he could not do so when Edmund was already with Charity.

Lord Glenhaven strode into the house with chin held at an aristocratic angle. Anticipation coiled in Charity's stomach. What would the baron do? What would he say? Would he demand mother give her approval?

Penelope led them to the drawing room. With each step, Charity's heart beat harder and sweat began to dampen her gloves. She held tighter to Edmund's arm. She wanted Lord Glenhaven to succeed but she had no notion how he might win.

"I shall go in with Mrs. Aston to introduce me," Lord Glenhaven said. "You two may wait here."

Charity was happy to stay outside but Edmund objected.

"Really, Father, I feel I should be there."

"Trust me son, it will go better if we do not have an audience."

After a long moment, Edmund nodded his agreement.

Lord Glenhaven patted his shoulder and then moved to the door. Charity pulled Edmund to the wall, so Mother would not see them but they would still be able to listen.

As Penelope pushed open the door, Charity held her breath.

"Look who has come to visit," Penelope said brightly.

Charity imagined the brief look of shock and outrage that must have flashed across Mother's face like lightening.

"Lord Glenhaven, what an honor," Mother said sweetly. "Charity did not inform me that you intended to visit today."

"That is my fault, ma'am. I did not tell anyone of my plan."

Charity was taken aback by Lord Glenhaven's soothing tones. She had expected him to demand what he wanted. Did he think to charm Mother instead?

She shared a look with Edmund, he shrugged.

"I came on rather urgent business," Lord Glenhaven said. "You see I am most anxious for the union of our families. A feeling I am sure you share."

"Well, I am of course very flattered by Mr. Glenhaven's offer."

"It is my family that is honored by Miss Radforde's acceptance," he countered smoothly.

"But Mr. Radforde must approve the match and he is presently not in the country." Mother spoke as if she truly regretted the circumstance.

"So I understand. But unlike others of your sex, you are competent and knowledgable. Certainly your husband trusts your judgment in these matters?"

"Of course he does," Mother said a little sharply.

"Excellent, then I think you and I might discuss the settlements. Once they are arranged we can send word to your husband. I am sure he will approve of whatever you decide."

There was a long pause.

Charity could almost hear Mother weighing her decision. If she refused she risked offending an influential aristocrat and damaging her standing in the best circles. If she agreed she would achieve a victory over her husband. For Father could not reject a reasonable settlement without angering Lord Glenhaven and dishonoring himself.

Charity marveled at the neatness of the trap. She glanced at Edmund and saw he was equally impressed.

"Very well, Lord Glenhaven, let us discuss the settlements," Mother said.

"As you wish, Mrs. Radforde."

Charity turned to Edmund in disbelief. With one clever, charming, conversation, Lord Glenhaven had solved her conundrum. It might have been more satisfying to have Mother chastised and groveling but Charity knew that would never happen. Charity did not need revenge, she only needed to be free of her cage. Her heart was ready to burst from relief and joy.

Mother and Lord Glenhaven began to discuss particulars and Edmund pulled Charity further down the hall.

"We truly are going to marry," she murmured.

"As quickly as we might," Edmund added. "I do not want you living here longer than necessary." His knuckles brushed her cheek tenderly.

She sighed and touched her forehead to his. Soon they would be husband and wife and she would be half a world away from Mother.

When she came to London, marriage was the last thing she wanted. She had done everything, including engaging in a sham courtship, to escape her fate. But now, betrothed to a man who valued her and respected her, she could think of nothing she wanted more than to be his wife.

Together they would travel and catalog the world. They would be partners, sharing difficulties and victories, long conversations and companionable silences. She would never tire of learning new things with him and about him.

Their future was an unplanted garden and she could not wait to see what they would grow together.

Epilogue

Eighteen Months Later

THE SUN WAS a ball of orange sinking into a sea of grass. Edmund smelled woodsmoke and cooking meat on the wind. The party had shot a deer that afternoon and all were eager for the coming feast. The evening was alive with the sounds of the grasslands. Crickets chirped, an owl hooted, and in the distance, there was a curious barking sound.

The barking was not from some species of canine, but a curious burrowing animal known as the prairie dog.

The prairie dog had been briefly described in the journals of Captain Lewis. Edmund had taken up the study of the animal with great interest, pausing their progress several times to jump to the ground and inspect mounds and burrows.

The French trapper that was serving as their guide found his behavior amusing. He did not see what was so fascinating about the animal or the land.

Edmund and Charity had spent several hours discussing the taxonomy of the creatures. They seemed to be something between a rabbit and a squirrel. Their days were often filled with lively debates and discussions about all they were seeing and documenting on their journey. Edmund could not imagine what the expedition would have been like without her. Their partnership was all that he could have hoped for and more.

In the end, they had determined not to go all the way to the Rocky Mountains. There was enough to explore and catalogue just beyond the Mississippi River.

Everyone they spoke to in Boston had described this part of the continent as a great desert. But once the expedition had reached the area, it was clear this was not the case. There was a unique harmony of nature at work in the land. A connection between the tall grasses, animals, and soils that both Edmund and Charity agreed must be investigated.

He glanced at his wife. She was sitting in a camp chair near the fire, her head bent over a large sketchbook as she tried to finish her drawing before it became too dark to see. He marveled at the slope of her neck, the hair that brushed her cheek. He smiled at the wrinkle in her forehead as she worked. He must be the most fortunate man alive to spend his life with her.

Her keen mind and quick observations were invaluable, not to mention her artistic skill. Mrs. Meen had been a very good teacher, refining Charity's abilities with remarkable speed and quickly declaring her a master.

Edmund couldn't believe he had contemplated making this journey alone. He was grateful every day for a managing mother and stubborn father.

Charity looked up from her paper and caught his gaze. "What?"

"Nothing."

"You were thinking about something."

"I was thinking how grateful I am that I agreed to your mad scheme."

"Which one?"

He chuckled and moved to stand behind her. He placed his hands on her shoulders and softly kneaded them. She gave a slight murmur of approval and leaned into his touch.

The rigors of the trail had been worse than anticipated. Experiencing days in the saddle was very different from reading about it. There were weeks of sore muscles and bad food.

At times, their exhaustion or frustration led to sharp words. But their habit of honesty helped them to navigate their arguments.

He glanced down at her paper and was surprised to see it filled with words instead of a drawing.

"Are you writing a letter?" he asked.

"I know it is silly since there is no way to send it, but I feel closer to them when I write."

"Do you miss them terribly?"

"I do. I miss many things, but not so much that I wish my life any different." She tilted her neck to allow him better access to the knots in her shoulder. "And they are all so busy with their own affairs that I am sure they feel the same."

"For my part, I am glad you are with me and not writing letters to me." He bent down and swiftly kissed behind her ear.

She hummed her appreciation. "That is one benefit of this journey."

"My kisses or my company?"

"Both." She smiled up at him.

He chuckled and kissed her on the lips. He meant it to be brief, but she reached up, twined her hands in his hair, and deepened the kiss. They pulled away, breathing heavy and grinning. He would never get tired of such affection.

He straightened and resumed his massage of her shoulders.

"Do you ever think what might have happened if that tiger hadn't roared and caused such a commotion?" She asked.

"I shudder to think. We would have been introduced at dinner and had a boring civil conversation about the weather."

"Are you sure you would've been civil?" She raised her eyebrows.

"No, probably not. I was determined to shake off any woman my mother threw at me."

"And I would have talked of silly things as I tried to be the perfect lady."

"To me, you are the perfect lady."

"Oh, Edmund." She patted his hand.

"I am not sure I ever thanked you properly for saving my life," he said.

"I don't think that horse would have killed you. Only knocked you senseless, maybe broken a few bones."

"Not for saving me in front of the Exchange, though I am grateful for your quick reaction."

"Then how else did I save your life?" She tipped her head to look at him with her eyebrows pinched together. He smoothed the small wrinkle there with his thumb.

"You saved my life by showing me that I did not need anyone's approval to achieve my dreams, not my father's and not Sir Joseph's. If not for you, I may never have humbled myself and looked elsewhere."

Her cheeks became a delightful pink. She ducked her head and then met his eyes again. The blue of her eyes had turned dark in the twilight.

"And you saved me from always hiding and cowering. Without you, I never would have stood up to my mother or escaped her."

They looked at each other for a long moment until the ringing of the dinner bell broke them apart.

Edmund helped her to stand and kept her hand firmly in his as they crossed to the glowing fire.

Enjoyed the Book?

YOU CAN MAKE A DIFFERENCE!

In a world full of excellent entertainment, reviews are a powerful way for readers to find my books. As a new author every review counts. And the more readers I have the more books I will be able to write!

If you enjoyed The Counterfeit Attachment I would be forever grateful if you could spend a few minutes leaving a review. It can be as short as you like and it would mean the world to me.

HATE LEAVING REVIEWS?

You can also help by sharing the book with your friends or asking your local library or book store to carry my books. Word-of-mouth is just as powerful as online reviews. Every little bit helps!

Join The Inner Circle

WANT to know what happens to Kit Glenhaven, or Penelope Aston? Join the Inner Circle newsletter and be the first to know about new releases! (Yes, Kit is in a future book.)

I also send occasional updates on my writing and fun freebies. No spam. Ever.

Sign-up at hollijomonroe.com

Author's Note

One of my favorite things about historical fiction is doing research. Grounding the story with real details is a big part of my writing process. As a result, lots of little things in this story are as accurate as I can make them.

Sir Joseph Banks really did see people on Thursdays, Exeter Exchange had an elephant named Chuny that would strut around London, Mrs. Meen taught botanical painting to the royal family, and all the items in Bullock's museum were actually there. *The Picture of London* is a real guidebook and I used it extensively in my research. To review every historical tidbit I included is not practical but I did want to note a few historical liberties.

The biggest departure from the historical record was having the characters eat a banana. The first recording of a banana tree bearing fruit in England is 1835 by Sir Joseph Paxton, gardener to William Cavendish, the Sixth Duke of Devonshire. This was notable because the hybrid Paxton developed revolutionized banana production around the world. The Cavendish banana is the variety most of us are familiar with today.

Banana trees were found in many hothouses, including those at Kew, but they did not bear fruit. Or if they did it was not noted in histories since they did not produce a consistently successful harvest. I decided that it was entirely possible that the royal gardeners managed to grow some bananas occasionally.

Another more obvious fiction is that The Linnean Society did not fund an expedition to the Rocky Mountains. However, expeditions to America, and around the world, were common and many were funded by various learned societies throughout the 18th and 19th centuries.

I also took great liberties in my depiction of real people like Sir Joseph Banks, Miss Sarah, Robert Brown, and Franz Bauer. I attempted to base their characters in reality but they are mostly creations of my imagination.

If you are interested in learning more about London in the Regency you might consider buying my non-fiction book *The Proper Guide to Regency London,* releasing later in 2023.

If you have found an error or would like to correspond about any of the historic or other aspects of the book, feel free to contact me through my website or social media.

About the Author

Holli Jo is a country girl who joined the Army and became a Captain before leaving the service to travel and pursue writing. She enjoys all genres as long as they have some romance. Holli Jo has survived live nerve agent training, deployed to Afghanistan, climbed Kilimanjaro, backpacked around the world, and SCUBA dived in Bali so she knows that sometimes staying home with a book is the best adventure of all.

For more books, updates, and to subscribe to the newsletter:

www.hollijomonroe.com

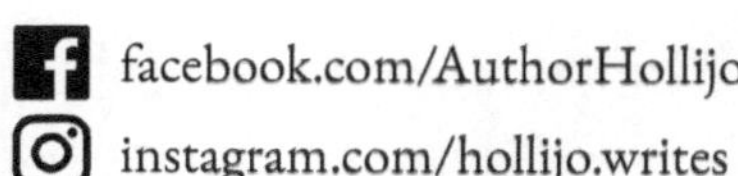

facebook.com/AuthorHollijo

instagram.com/hollijo.writes

Acknowledgments

I always worry about excluding people or hurting feelings. However, it would be unforgivable if I did not thank some important people.

My parents, who are my greatest cheerleaders and biggest supporters. Without them, I could not have finished this one. Marcee for listening to me ramble and helping me through each major revision. Whitney, Karen, and Cindy, who are so giving of their time, creativity, and knowledge. They pushed this book to greater heights.

Julia for her excellent editing. Kim for beta reading and reassuring me despite her busy schedule. Natalie for long talks and infectious enthusiasm. Heather for big smiles and championing me to others. My various family and friends who share my books and make me feel like a real writer.

I am eternally grateful.

Also by Holli Jo Monroe

The Imagined Attachment

The Proper Guide to Parlor Games